C000070664

Lottery Girl
The Complete Daily Serial

STEPHANIE BOND

Maybe money can *buy happiness...*

Copyright © 2020 Stephanie Bond
All rights reserved.
ISBN: 978-1-945002-66-3
Cover art by Andrew Brown

Introduction

Hello. I'm Mallory Green—an ironic last name once you learn my story. I grew up in the foster system, so I've had a laundry list of surnames in my relatively short life. Then I got married (a colossal mistake) and acquired yet another name I'm currently trying to rid myself of.

Green is supposed to be lucky—four-leaf clovers, the luck of the Irish… the literal color of money and prosperity. But you couldn't prove it by me. I can't remember a time when I wasn't pinching pennies and dreading opening my mailbox full of overdue bills. I'm in debt up to my unplucked eyebrows over a college education I couldn't finish, a multi-level marketing business my ex convinced me was a good idea, a lemon car that hasn't run since a month after I drove it off the lot, and vet bills for my inherited French bulldog Nessie, among other things.

As a result of my accumulated poor financial decisions, I'm working round the clock: during the week, I'm a receptionist at a soulless office building, on the weekends I waitress, and most nights I pull the late shift at the GiddyUp GoMart.

To-date I've been unlucky in life, in love, and in fortune. But that all changed the day my numbers came up—literally.

Can money buy happiness? Friend, I'm so ready to find out.

JULY

July 1, Wednesday

WHEN THE alarm sounded from my nightstand, I couldn't believe it. Hadn't I just closed my eyes? For a few seconds, I ignored it. Then next to me, a male groan sounded.

"Mallory… make it stop."

I reached over to hit the Off button. Trent was right—at least one of us could sleep in a little.

When I swung my legs to the floor and pushed to my feet, the scent of food and gasoline wafted off my hair and skin. I wrinkled my nose. I'd been too exhausted to take a shower when I'd gotten home after midnight from my cashier job.

The skitter of toenails on the floor sounded, then Trent's beloved French bulldog Nessie slid into view. She angled her head and whined, a sure sign she was on the verge of peeing on the carpet. I sighed, then pushed my feet into flip flops and walked through the dark apartment to the door. After finding the foyer light switch, I squinted in pain when the whiteness hit my gritty eyeballs. Ignoring the pile of unopened mail on the side table and the accompanying gnaw at my stomach, I picked up Nessie's leash and bent over to hook it to her collar.

"You'd better hope no one sees me like this," I muttered.

She whined again, so I quickly opened the door and stepped out into the hallway, looking both ways. There were nine other apartments on the first floor. The coast was clear, thank goodness, so I steered Nessie toward the rear entrance.

The door opened before we reached it, though, and a man dressed in running clothes appeared, obviously returning from a workout. He gave me a once-over.

My cheeks burned when I realized what a sight I must be—ratty dark hair, sleep crusties in my eyes, dressed in an Imagine Dragons T-shirt and shortie pajama pants. He, on the other hand, looked athletic and fresh despite the perspiration darkening his shirt. I'd never seen him before, but then again, I didn't have time to get to know my neighbors.

"Hi," he offered, although I suspected it was only because he felt obligated to say something.

"Hello," I managed as we sidled past each other. I was envious of his early-morning run. Once upon a time, I'd been fit and healthy. Now I felt like a hag, tired and pale.

The door led to a breezeway and a postage-stamp size square of grass between the apartment buildings that made up the complex. When I stepped outside, the Atlanta humidity clamped down on me like a moist hand. The sun hadn't yet risen and it was already steamy. In the distance traffic hummed with commuters determined to get ahead of rush-hour, which only created pre-rush-hour. While Nessie did her business, I stretched my shoulders and tried to wake up. When I walked back to the apartment, my hopes that Trent had climbed out of bed to start the coffeemaker were dashed. His snores sounded from the bedroom as I made my way to the tiny kitchen and flipped on the machine. I squashed misgivings—it wasn't Trent's fault he'd gotten laid off from his job at the architectural firm. He'd been working there only a year when the economy wobbled, and the downsizing policy was last in, first out.

A quick glance at the clock spurred me to the bathroom to shower while the coffee brewed. I was in and out in a few minutes, then rummaged in my closet and dressed in the dark so I wouldn't disturb my husband.

My empty stomach churned with anxiety. We were coming up on our fifth wedding anniversary, but lately, it felt as if we were more roommates than lovers. Between my three jobs, I was rarely home, and during the few times we were together, Trent's bitter disappointment with the way his life had turned out was palpable. I was sympathetic and supportive—it was Trent's ambition that had first attracted me to him. I was reared in the foster care system, so he'd been a rock of confidence to moor myself to. I'd been swept along by his big dreams to make his mark on the world, and I'd happily dropped out of college to work full time so he could finish his master's degree sooner. The plan was for me to return to college and finish my degree in physical therapy once he'd secured a good job.

But the good job was always just out of reach. Investing in a multi-level marketing scheme had been a costly mistake. We'd amassed what I suspected was a towering amount of debt, although Trent continued to assure me we'd be fine. Sometimes it felt as if the more I tried to help, the more Trent resented me for believing in him in the first place. But he was still pushing himself—he spent every day at a nearby Starbucks applying and interviewing for jobs online.

I downed a cup of homemade coffee while I put myself together well enough to man the reception desk of Noble Plaza, one of the most prestigious office buildings in Atlanta. I was expected to arrive thirty minutes before the first company opened, with a smile on my face. But I was still dragging when I made my way to the apartment parking garage, praying my lemon of a car would start.

When it did, I sighed in abject gratitude and gave myself my daily pep talk: This was my season of sacrifice. Hard work was its own reward. Luck would find me someday... right?

The sun was starting to peek over the horizon, so I looked heavenward for inspiration.

A dove appeared overhead, beautiful and serene as it sailed on the morning breeze. I smiled—it was a sign.

Then it swooped down and pooped on my windshield.

July 2, Thursday

"Noble Plaza, how may I direct your call?" I said into my headset. "Please hold for your party." I ended the call, then hit another lighted button on the phone console. "Noble Plaza, how may I direct your call? Please hold for your party."

The phrase was branded into my tongue's muscle recall. When I was on my deathbed and was asked for some bit of dying wisdom, I would say, "Please hold for your party."

I connected the call from memory. There were approximately thirty-five businesses and professionals who leased space in Noble Plaza, and I'd realized within hours of landing the job my life would be much improved if I didn't have to look up names and numbers. Besides answering the phone, I also directed walk-in traffic to the appropriate elevator bay, and signed for the occasional flower or food delivery. In between, I offered friendly smiles to tenants as they came and went even when my feet ached from standing or my hips ached from sitting.

If I ever finished my training to become a physical therapist, I would be my first patient.

"Hi, Mallory."

I looked up and flashed a genuine smile at the redhead who strode up to my desk. The security officer stationed nearby straightened, as did most men when Wanda Sandoval appeared.

"Hi," I returned, then nodded to the pink sheath that hugged her curves. "Pretty dress."

"Thanks," she said, striking a pose. Then she set an iced coffee drink on the counter. "For you."

My eyes widened. "Me?"

"Sure. You look like you could use a pick-me-up."

Was I sagging that badly? "That's nice of you."

She wagged a finger. "I'm not nice, please don't get that rumor started." She glanced at the security guard and made a growling sound. He looked scared... and intrigued.

Wanda was a paralegal for a ritzy firm on the fourteenth floor. Actually, it was the thirteenth floor, but this was one of those office buildings that chose to skip the thirteenth floor because of the bad luck connotation. Since I, too, was superstitious, I could appreciate the nuance.

"Do you have plans for the holiday?" I asked, then took a drink of the rich coffee.

She grinned. "My boyfriend is taking me to Aruba. You?"

I swallowed hard. "Um... nothing so exciting." The office building was closing early for the holiday, but the manager of the convenience store where I sometimes pulled the evening shift asked me to come in to help cover the rush expected for beer and fireworks. And since he'd promised to pay me time-and-a-half, I couldn't turn it down. "I'll be working."

She made a face. "Your waitressing job?"

"Actually, I have a third gig I work sometimes."

She shook her head. "You're industrious, for sure. What's your husband like?"

I smiled. "Trent is so talented—he has a master's degree in architecture. And he's really outgoing—he's more of a people person than I am."

"So he's an architect?"

My smile faltered. "He is... he was. I mean, not at the moment. He used to work for an architecture firm, but he was laid off a few months ago."

"That sucks."

"He'll find something soon," I assured her. "Until then, enjoy Aruba enough for me, too."

She grinned. "Don't worry, I will."

The sliding doors opened and a tall, handsome suited man walked in, talking on his phone. I'd seen him many times coming and going from the building—he was hard to miss.

"Mm, mm," Wanda said under her breath. "Now there's a man I wouldn't mind sharing a beach blanket with."

As if he sensed our stares, he glanced toward us and flashed a brilliant smile, then kept going.

"Do you know him?" I asked.

She fanned herself. "No, but I'd like to. His name is Ryan Livingston. He's a hotshot money manager on the floor above mine. You can bet he's rich."

He did look like money, from his trendy haircut to his impeccable suit to his saddle leather briefcase.

"It's the quickest way to get wealthy," Wanda said.

"Managing other people's money?"

"No—marrying someone who manages other people's money."

I laughed.

"In fact, I think I'll ride up with him," she said, wagging her eyebrows and pushing off from the desk.

"Thanks for the coffee."

"You're welcome," she said, then made a beeline for the man who was putting away his phone. He smiled at her in greeting, then held the elevator door while she walked on.

I stared after Wanda, admiring her moxie for going after what she wanted. I'd always been the opposite, taking whatever came my way and making the most of it. I was fortunate Trent had crossed my path and pursued me. What he'd seen in me, I wasn't sure... and I was worried whatever "it" was, I'd somehow misplaced it.

The phone console lit up. I set my shoulders and stabbed the button. "Noble Plaza, how may I direct your call?"

July 3, Friday

I WAS making toast when Trent walked into the kitchen, looking lean and handsome in cargo shorts, yellow polo shirt, and athletic sandals. He grinned. "Did you make enough for me?"

I pushed a buttered slice toward him, then squinted at the beach towel draped over his arm. "Are you going somewhere?"

His mouth flattened, then he held up a red and white For Sale sign. "The guy at the marina said we'd have a better chance of selling the boat if people see it on the water, so I'm taking a couple of friends out to ski."

My face must have registered my disappointment over being left out because he added, "It's only for a couple of hours, and it won't even be fun. You know how crowded Lake Lanier gets around the Fourth."

It was true—on summer holidays the lake attracted boats much larger than ours, and their mammoth wakes made skiing less appealing. And heaven knew we needed to sell the boat before it was repossessed; we were way behind on the payments associated with owning and storing it. Still, the thought of slogging through a day on my feet at the convenience store while Trent got a tan rankled me. "What friends?" I asked morosely.

He'd retrieved a cooler from the utility closet and proceeded to fill it with beer and soda from the fridge, then emptied the container from our ice maker into it with a crashing noise. "Dale and PJ—we're supposed to meet up with someone they think might buy the boat."

I wasn't crazy about Dale anyway—the guy went through women like changing channels and had hit on me more than once behind Trent's back. "Don't forget sunscreen."

He bit into the toast, then dropped a kiss near my ear that left crumbs on my shirt. "I'll be home long before you get off your shift. How about I make dinner?"

I smiled, instantly contrite for feeling cross. "That would be nice."

"Can you walk Nessie? I'm running late."

"Sure."

After he left, I made another piece of toast and wolfed it down while I walked Nessie, who seemed disappointed to have me on the other end of the leash instead of Trent. "Stop pouting and go already," I chided her. "He'll be back in time for your afternoon poo."

That must've cheered her up because she finally peed. I picked her up and sprinted back to the apartment. I'd have to run a red light or two to make it to the GiddyUp GoMart for my shift.

As I swung my purse to my shoulder, I spotted the red and white For Sale sign—Trent had forgotten it in his haste to leave… or perhaps he'd unconsciously left it behind because despite the fact that we could no longer afford the boat, he desperately wanted to keep it. He'd convinced me to buy the twenty-one-foot piece of precision machinery in one of his bouts of enthusiasm for all the money we'd be making when our careers expanded. We deserved it, he'd said. It was a fraction of what a vacation home would cost, and think of all the fun we'd have on the weekends.

And he was right. Until my weekends had become crowded with extra work hours, and our budget had grown too tight to maintain the boat. I hated that it had become a source of irritation between us because Trent was so attached to it. I was glad he was going to have at least one more enjoyable outing before someone took the albatross off our hands.

Which was why when I dragged myself back home eight hours later—my shirt stained with grease from the hotdog spinner and blue syrup from the fountain drinks machine—to find Trent was still out with his friends, I gave him a pass and cleaned up the mess Nessie had made by the door. She lay nearby with her paws over her eyes, embarrassed and forlorn. "He just forgot," I assured her. "He's busy taking care of things."

It was worth missing out on dinner because selling the ski boat would be a huge weight off our finances and our stress level. And I was so ready for us to get back to a happy place.

July 4, Saturday

"Anyway, Mike seemed really interested in buying the boat," Trent continued, assembling another cooler of drinks for another day's outing at the lake. "Hopefully she'll make up her mind today."

I was fastening my nametag to the blouse of my waitressing outfit. My head came up. "Dale and PJ's friend is a she?"

Trent poured ice over the drinks I'd replenished from the convenience store, the splintering sound even more grating than yesterday. "Huh? Oh, yeah... her name is Mikala, but she likes to be called Mike."

I wondered why he'd omitted that little detail before. He wasn't looking at me and his color was high... but then he'd gotten a lot of sun the day before. I was being paranoid. "Has Mikala ever owned a boat?"

"No, but she's really fit and athletic—she took to water skiing right away. And she's in sales, so having a boat would be great for schmoozing clients. Plus she makes *bank*, so she can more than afford it."

He still wasn't looking at me... and was his voice tinged with admiration? "What kind of sales?" I asked casually.

"Mike works for a liquor distributor... she specializes in bourbon."

Compared to my cobbled together career, that sounded downright exotic. "I'm sure Dale was all over her."

He frowned. "No, she's too classy for Dale. And way too smart."

I bit into my lip. "Is there room for me?"

His head came around. "Huh?"

"I was thinking I could call in sick to the restaurant—one of the other wait staff will cover for me."

His expression turned anxious. "But we really need your paycheck right now."

Pay*checks*, plural... but I didn't correct him. "It's only one day." I held up a pale arm. "And I could use some sun."

Trent closed the cooler with a *thunk*. "Sorry, Mal, but you know how small the boat can be, and there are already four of us."

"I thought you said PJ couldn't make it."

"Yeah, but Mike brought a friend yesterday who hit it off with Dale."

Someone less classy and less smart, apparently. I gave a little laugh. "Sounds like a double date."

"What?" Trent's mood darkened in a flash. "You're the one who insisted we sell the boat, and now you're giving me grief for trying to sell it?"

Remorse stabbed me. "No... I mean, I'm sorry if it seemed that way. I just thought it would be nice to spend the day together."

His shoulders sagged, then he came over to loop his arms around me. His hazel eyes were contrite. "I'm sorry about last night. But I thought selling the boat would make you more happy than my mango-lime salmon."

I smiled. "I'm sorry, too. Go have fun today and make the boat seem irresistible."

"I will." He gave me a quick kiss on the mouth. "I might be late if we get stuck watching fireworks over the water."

We'd watched the fireworks display on the water more than once, I told myself. It was spectacular... but nothing new... nothing to be jealous over. "Okay, text to let me know."

"You know cell service at the lake is spotty."

"Oh... right."

"Can you walk Nessie before you leave?"

"No problem—" But I was talking to the closed door. I looked down at Nessie, who was looking up at me, head cocked and whining.

I knew how she felt.

July 5, Sunday

"MALLORY, ORDER up!"

I hurried to the stainless counter where the order for table four sat lined up. I glanced over the plates. "The eggs with the Sunrise Platter are supposed to be scrambled."

Doug, the owner and cook, looked up from the grill and glared. "I did whatever you wrote on the ticket."

I held up the ticket. "It says scrambled."

He squinted. "It looks like 'sunnyside' to me."

"Sorry—it says scrambled."

"How am I supposed to read your hen-scratching?" he barked.

"Sorry," I murmured again.

"Take it out anyway, maybe the customer won't notice."

I pressed my lips together, but dipped my chin in consent. I piled the plates on a tray, balanced it on my shoulder, and carried it out to the dining room, maneuvering around tables and feet. My own dogs were barking after being on my feet the prior two days.

I smiled at the couple at table four and lowered the tray to the corner to begin transferring plates. The man and woman looked a little mismatched—she was tall, classically pretty, and wore the severe makeup of a 1960s pinup. He was shorter and on the chubby side and looked as if he'd just come off the golf course.

But who was I to judge compatibility? I'd once thought Trent and I would never hit a relationship snag we couldn't work through. And while on the surface we were still going through the motions, I could feel him slipping away from me. He'd gotten in late last night and announced "Mike" hadn't yet made up her mind about buying the boat. He'd been irritable and distant, a mood that had carried over to this morning because, I'd assumed, it was pouring rain with more of the same forecast all day... and had wrecked plans for another day of boating?

On the other hand, I supposed it was a good sign he was irritable—versus happy—about *not* selling the boat. Maybe he was starting to come around to my way of thinking.

"Anything else?" I asked the couple.

"It looks great," the woman said, "except I ordered my eggs scrambled. Normally I wouldn't care, but I'm pregnant and I don't want to take a chance on undercooked eggs."

"That could hurt the baby?" her companion asked, looking stricken.

"Not likely," she said. "But it's not worth the risk."

"Of course," I said quickly, picking up the plate and feeling like a heel for trying to trick her. "My deepest apologies. I'll be right back with the correct order."

There went my tip. I scurried back to return the plate to the kitchen. "The customer noticed," I said to Doug. "She's pregnant and doesn't want to risk salmonella."

He scowled. "It'll be a few minutes."

I nodded, knowing it was useless to push.

"Put Mallory's order ahead of mine," my coworker Vance said. "My table are enjoying their mimosas and won't mind waiting for food."

"That's not how I work," Doug barked.

Vance gave him a cajoling smile. "Come on… we don't want to keep a pregnant woman waiting."

Doug screwed up his mouth, but pulled out a bowl and cracked two eggs to scramble.

"Thanks," I murmured to Vance.

"Don't mention it," he said with a wave.

"He's more grouchy than usual," I observed, filling two water glasses to carry back to the dining room.

Vance lowered his voice. "Cut him a little slack—business is bad."

I frowned. "Really? How bad?"

"I overheard him on the phone saying if he didn't get an infusion of cash, he'd have to close within a few weeks."

I gasped. I really needed this job—and so did most of the people who worked at The Community Café.

"What are you two whispering about?" Our fellow coworker Kerry stopped to stick her bleach blond head between us.

"How short your skirt is," Vance chirped, nodding to her mini. "This is a classy restaurant, you know."

Kerry stuck out her tongue. "You're jealous because Mr. Longo sat in my section today."

I craned to see a well-dressed older man digging into a tall stack of pancakes.

Vance scoffed. "He tucked a twenty in my pocket and I didn't even have to bring him food." As proof, he held up the folded bill, then arranged his beautiful face into a smirk.

Kerry snatched the twenty before he could react. "This'll catch you up in the lottery pool." She ignored his protest, then looked at me. "Mal, are you in this week?"

I rummaged in my apron pocket and withdrew four dollars to hand over. I could buy tickets all day long at the GiddyUp GoMart, but participating in the restaurant pool of my twenty or so coworkers made me feel included.

And who knew—maybe someday we'd win.

But probably not.

"What's the jackpot?" Vance asked.

"Twelve million," Kerry said, then moaned. "Man, what I could do with that kind of cash."

"Me too," Vance said dreamily.

"Me three," I chimed in. Maybe money couldn't buy happiness, but it could certainly lubricate the knocks along the way.

"Mallory!" Doug screamed. "Order up!"

I flashed Vance and Kerry a watery smile, then turned to add the plate to my tray. On the way back to the dining room, I glanced at the clock.

Only seven and a half hours to go.

July 6, Monday

"NOBLE PLAZA, how may I direct your call?" I said into my headset. "Please hold for your party."

Behind the reception counter, my foot jumped nervously next to my enormous "purse" I'd camouflaged with a scarf. I checked my watch—fifteen minutes until my lunch break. I shot a worried glance toward the security officer, but luckily he'd been too busy passing out new lanyards to notice I was up to something.

The elevator doors opened and Ryan Livingston, Wanda's crush, emerged looking like an ad in a magazine. To my surprise, he headed toward me. As he walked up, a whine sounded from my purse.

"Shh," I hissed.

Nessie had a vet appointment to get her annual shots, and Trent had landed a virtual interview he needed to prepare for. Since I was eager for my husband to find gainful employment, I'd volunteered to take her during my lunch hour, which necessitated me bringing her to work with me in her carrier and stashing her at my feet, hoping no one would notice.

The man smiled wide as he stopped on the other side of the tall counter where I stood. He was even more gorgeous up close—his nose was sculpted, his jaw was wide, his teeth were perfect.

"Hi… Mallory, right?"

My heart gave an absurd little jump that he knew my name, then I realized my lanyard had tipped him off. "Right. And you're Mr. Livingston from the fifteenth floor." I rattled off his phone number, then felt like an idiot.

"Impressive," he said with a grin. "But please call me Ryan."

His eyes were like dark sapphires. "Okay… Ryan."

"I was wondering if you could keep an eye out for a delivery I'm expecting."

From my purse, a whine sounded, this one louder. I covered by making a similar sing-songy noise.

He squinted. "Was that a yes?"

I nodded, my smile frozen.

"Okay. The delivery is supposed to be here sometime this week, an envelope from Australia. Can you call me when it arrives?"

A yip sounded from my bag. "Yep," I said to cover. "Yep, yep."

Ryan angled his head. "Are you okay?"

"Um hmmmmmmm," I said in time and tune with another undulating whine. When a bark sounded, I launched into a hoarse coughing fit.

Ryan's dark eyebrows arched. "Do you have a dog back there?"

I winced, then lowered my voice. "It was kind of an emergency." The appearance of a prim woman on the other side of the lobby sent my heart to my throat. "Oh, God… here comes my boss. Please don't turn me in."

Ryan didn't have time to respond before Amelia Inez was upon us.

"Is everything okay here?" she asked.

Nessie yipped and I overdubbed with "Yep, yep," to cover.

Amelia frowned. She was a stickler for rules and time schedules. She operated on a "three strikes and you're out" policy. I had one strike already for arriving late one day last month after being caught behind a traffic accident. Her response? I should always anticipate traffic problems and leave earlier. I was pretty sure if Amelia discovered Nessie, she'd skip the second and third strike and simply eject me from the game—er, job.

"Mallory is going to keep an eye out for a delivery I'm expecting," Ryan said.

Amelia offered him a feminine smile. "Any time you need something special, don't hesitate to call me directly."

Ryan blinked. "That won't be necessary. Mallory is more than capable."

Nessie whined and I joined in with lots of nodding and humming.

Amelia narrowed her eyes at me, then kept walking.

I exhaled. "Thank you."

His mouth twitched with amusement. "Don't mention it. See you later." He gave a little salute, then turned and walked out into the parking lot, no doubt headed for lunch at some exotic place.

My face burned from the encounter. The man must think I was a rube—not to mention unprofessional. My behavior exemplified why some people worked on the fifteenth floor and received interesting international deliveries, and why some people worked the reception desk and signed for other people's interesting international deliveries.

The phone console buzzed, cutting into my musings. I punched a button. "Noble Plaza, how may I direct your call? Please hold for your party." I connected the call, then placed the switchboard on touch-tone voice assistant for the hour I'd be gone.

I scooped up Nessie's carrier and race-walked to the exit. When I reached my car, I removed her from her carrier and let her relieve her tiny bladder before bundling her back inside. As I slid behind the wheel, I glanced at the clock. With luck, I'd have just enough time to get her to the vet for her shots, then drop her at the apartment before returning to work. Who needed lunch? Fasting was all the rage.

My optimism was cut short, though, when I turned over the engine and a clicking noise sounded. "No, no, no," I groaned. "Not now!"

I lowered my forehead to the steering wheel. "Please... whatever luck I have coming to me, I need it now."

I lifted my head, crossed my fingers, then punched the starter. To my immense relief, the engine rumbled to life. I smiled, then sobered when I realized I might've just spent whatever tiny bit of karmic credit I had amassed.

July 7, Tuesday

MY LUCK ran out the following day on the way home from work in a southbound lane on Peachtree Street. The Noble Plaza building had closed early in order to test the fire alarms. I was sitting at a traffic light, happy for a couple of hours of paid time off and looking forward to making dinner with Trent, when my car simply died.

I punched the starter several times. Not only did it not respond, but the dreaded Check Engine light came on. The ten thousand drivers lined up in the lanes behind me were livid, and let me know as much by blaring their horns as they gunned around me. I turned on the hazard lights and decided I was safer sitting in the car than trying to climb out and sprint through traffic to the sidewalk. When frustration welled in my chest, I reasoned if it had to happen, at least I was on my way home versus on my way to work, and it wasn't yet rush hour.

I pulled out my phone and connected to Trent's number. At this hour he'd still be parked at Starbucks sending out resumes and taking online courses. I wasn't surprised when his phone instantly rolled to voice mail—he was probably immersed in something important.

"Hi, it's me," I said. "I'm having a little car trouble. Call me back."

The minutes ticked away. I passed the time offering apologetic waves to cars blasting by. Fifteen minutes later, I texted him. *Car trouble—can you call me?*

When another fifteen minutes had passed, I decided his phone battery must've died. I used my voice assistant to call the Starbucks where he set up his virtual office every day.

"Starbucks, this is Carla." I could hear espresso machines and milk frothers in the background.

"Hello... I'm trying to reach my husband who's a regular customer there. It's a bit of an emergency."

"What's his name?"

"Trent Green, dark hair. He uses a Mac."

"Oh, the architect, yeah, I know Trent. Your husband is a hottie."

"Er, thanks. Do you see him?"

"Uh... no. Now that I think about it, I haven't seen him for a few days."

I frowned. "Are you sure?"

"Yeah, I'd remember because—"

"He's a hottie," I finished for her.

"Yeah. Maybe he found another."

I frowned. "Another what?"

"Another Starbucks. There are, like, a million in Atlanta."

"Oh... right. Thanks anyway." I ended the call. It didn't make sense that he'd go to a location farther away from the apartment, but maybe so. Or maybe she had him confused with someone else, or he was sitting outside. Or he'd zipped home to let Nessie enjoy an early poo.

I called his number again, but it went straight to voice mail. "It's me again," I said. "I'll phone Triple A, but call me when you can."

With cars still streaming around me, I contacted Triple A only to be told my membership had been cancelled for nonpayment, but I could pay a renewal fee and they would send a tow truck. I agreed.

"Ma'am, the card was declined."

I closed my eyes. "Could you try again, please?"

"I submitted it twice. Would you like to try another card?"

"No, thank you," I mumbled, then ended the call. Then in a flash of revelation I recalled our car insurance company offered towing service, so I located the number, feeling optimistic.

"Ma'am, our records show your coverage was cancelled four months ago for lack of payment."

The stack of unopened bills sitting on the table next to the door came to mind, along with how bankrupt we'd be if someone plowed into my car and I had no insurance. I muttered thank you and ended the call. Something akin to panic blipped in my chest. Just how much financial trouble were we in? Trent was better with numbers so he'd always managed our money. When he'd said we'd be fine, I'd believed him.

So why did I have the feeling the ground was about to fall away beneath my feet?

A knock on the driver's side window startled me so badly I screamed. When I turned my head, a man stood there waving, dressed in jeans and an Atlanta United soccer T-shirt. He looked vaguely familiar, but I couldn't place him. I tried to zoom down my window, but it didn't work. I opened the door a few inches.

"I thought that was you," he said.

My confusion must've been obvious.

"I'm your neighbor, Josh... Josh English. We ran into each other in the hallway a few days ago."

The runner, I recalled. "Oh... right. I'm Mallory."

"I know." He scratched his temple. "You really don't remember me, do you?"

I shook my head.

"We were in the same physical therapy program at Georgia State."

A memory stirred. His hair had been longer. "Oh. That was a long time ago... and I didn't finish."

"Too bad," he said, then gestured to my car. "Can I help?"

I was so grateful, I could only nod.

July 8, Wednesday

"I THOUGHT you'd be happy," Trent said, his voice colored with disappointment.

"I am," I said quickly. "And you'll be great in sales. I just wish you'd told me... sooner."

He made a frustrated noise. "We went over this already. When Mike called yesterday for me to meet her boss, I had to leave immediately. I didn't have time to call and get your permission."

I blinked at the hostile tone in his voice. "I'm not saying you needed my permission. I was worried. I couldn't find you, Trent, and I was stranded."

"You figured it out, Mal—you always do."

Why didn't that feel like a compliment? I chose my next words carefully. "I think we need to figure out our finances."

He scowled. "You've been badgering me to get a job, and now I have one. I'm juggling a lot here. I'll tackle the checkbook later."

"We should at least talk about the insurance. My car can't be repaired because we don't have coverage." I wet my lips, then laid open my heart. "And why would you put me at risk like that?"

He threw up his hands. "Yeah, Mal, I did it on purpose—I *wanted* your car insurance to be cancelled. Don't forget you were the one who racked up debt on our credit cards over wild goose chases."

At the resentment in his voice, I blinked back tears. "You're right... I'm sorry." Things were finally turning around and I was spoiling them by complaining. I walked over and looped my arms around his neck. "Congratulations on your new job. We'll have two things to celebrate when we go out for our anniversary Friday."

He softened, then smiled back and nodded.

"Can you give me a ride to the office?" I asked.

"You can take my car," he said. "I'll be riding around with Mike today so she can show me the ropes."

A little finger of worry nudged my neck that my husband would be spending so much time with the classy, smart, successful Mikala who'd gotten him a job with her company. But I didn't want to sound jealous. "Maybe you can still talk her into buying the boat," I said lightly.

He frowned. "We won't have to sell it now."

"But your base salary—"

"I'll make a ton in commissions," he cut in. "Mike says I'm a natural for sales."

I needed to be supportive, I reminded myself—like Mike. "You'll be the top salesman in no time." I gave him a kiss, lingering longer than usual. "Can we have dinner this evening before I start my shift at the convenience store?"

"Don't wait for me. Mike is organizing a dinner to introduce me to some of my accounts."

I maintained my smile. "Of course."

He pulled out his keyring and removed the tiny remote for his car, then handed it over. "Be careful, we don't need two cars in the shop."

"And the insurance on your car?" I asked mildly.

"It's paid. I had to provide proof of insurance to get the sales job since I'll be using it to visit accounts."

In that context, it did make sense to pay the premium for his car ahead of mine. Things were on the upswing... no reason to belabor points that would be moot as soon as Trent's commission checks started rolling in. "Have a good day," I said, then gave him another quick kiss. "Tell Mikala I said hello."

"I told you, she likes to be called Mike."

"Right. Bye."

I leaned over to give Nessie a pat on the head, but Trent called her name and she went running, leaving me hanging. When I stepped out into the hallway, Josh English was locking his door. He was dressed in business casual clothes, carrying a leather duffel bag.

"Hi, Mallory."

"Hi," I said, suddenly feeling shy. "Thanks again for yesterday. My husband says thanks, too."

"No problem," he said easily. "I'd like to meet him sometime."

The thought flitted through my mind that the two men had nothing in common, but I nodded. "I'm sure Trent would like that. I'm driving his car today," I added with a smile.

"What will he do?"

"He's, um, sharing with a coworker."

"Ah." He fell into step with me as we walked outside to the parking area. "Yesterday you said you work at Noble Plaza—what do you do there?"

"I'm a receptionist," I said, choosing the best sounding of my three jobs.

"Nice place," he said, nodding. "And what does your husband do?"

"He's starting a new job in sales." Yesterday I'd been so frazzled and embarrassed, I hadn't thought to ask any questions about his life. "Where do you work?"

"At the Piedmont Shepherd Center."

My lips parted. The Shepherd Center was renowned for its rehabilitative programs for spinal cord and brain injuries. "I'm impressed."

"My patients are impressive, not me. Have you given any thought to finishing your physical therapy degree?"

Only a thousand times... but I shook my head. "I think that ship has sailed."

"If you change your mind, I still have all my books from the program. You're welcome to them."

"Thank you—I'll keep that in mind." I stopped next to Trent's SUV and used the key fob to unlock it.

Josh's gaze traveled the length of the vehicle. "Wow, your husband has a nice ride."

I could tell he was comparing it to my little compact we'd bought used.

He gestured to the rear tow hitch. "Do you have a boat?"

I nodded. "A ski boat."

"You probably made the right decision," he said cheerfully. "Can't afford that on a P.T.'s salary."

I managed a wobbly smile. We couldn't afford it either.

"See you around," he said with a little wave, then strode to his small, sporty hatchback.

I climbed into Trent's SUV, trying to put my finger on what was bothering me, then decided it was better to turn my mind to positive things instead of borrowing trouble. On the drive to Noble Plaza, I gave myself a new and improved pep talk: *My season of sacrifice was hopefully coming to an end. My hard work would be rewarded. Good things were just around the corner.*

I was feeling better by the time I maneuvered the SUV into a plum spot in the garage and put it into Park. The abrupt movement dislodged an item beneath the passenger seat, sending it rolling forward to stop on the spotless floor mat.

A gold-tone metal tube of lipstick that was way out of my price range.

July 9, Thursday

SHAWNA BLEW on the surface of the lottery scratch-off game card to clear the curled up debris. "Hey, I won two dollars!" She handed it across the counter to me, then squinted. "Are you wearing lipstick?"

I straightened. "Maybe."

"*Why* are you wearing lipstick?" She gestured to encompass the general tackiness of the store—bold displays for beer, meat sticks, and horny goat weed. And the lottery, of course, which behind gasoline, was the mainstay of the business. "Ain't no one who comes in here worth sprucing up for."

Foot traffic was slow tonight, so after cleaning the pizza warmer and the hotdog spinner and the cappuccino machine so we could get out of there at closing, we were killing time.

I glanced in the large hand mirror propped above the register that we used to keep an eye on shoppers, and pursed my pink mouth. "My husband likes lipstick."

When I'd handed over the expensive lipstick I'd found, Trent had dismissed it, saying "Mike" or her friend must've dropped it when they'd taken out the boat, saying something completely plausible about giving them a ride to their car. It was totally innocent. I was a jealous shrew.

"*My* husband likes Krispy Kreme donuts," Shawna offered. "Which is why he has diabetes and has blown out his damn kidneys."

I scanned the barcode of the ticket, then opened the separate register we operated for the lottery games. "Do you want cash?"

"Nah, give me another scratcher."

"Same game?"

"Sure."

I entered the transaction, then tore off another scratch-off ticket from the hanging roll and handed it back. She used her acrylic thumbnail to scratch off the waxy metallic covering to reveal the numbers beneath.

My coworker Shawna had a hard life—her little boy had asthma, and her husband was on dialysis. Next to her, my domestic dilemmas seemed like princess problems. "Bob is still on the transplant list, right?"

"Uh-huh. But the medication he has to take til then is crazy expensive." She blew on the card, then squealed. "Fifty dollars!"

I grinned. "Yay, you. Cash?"

She handed the card over the counter. "More scratchers."

I angled my head. "Are you sure?" Fifty dollars was about what her take-home pay would be for a full eight-hour shift.

"Top prize is twenty thousand, and I'm feeling lucky." She pulled out her pink rabbit-foot keychain and kissed it.

I reluctantly processed the transaction, then counted and tore off twenty-five of the two-dollar scratch-off tickets and handed over the stack.

Shawna's eyes shone with excitement. "Cross your fingers for me, Mal."

I lifted both hands to cross four sets of fingers, but accidentally bumped the mirror over the register. It fell at my feet and shattered into a thousand tiny pieces.

My coworker gasped, then leaned over to survey the damage. "Are you okay?"

I nodded, then groaned. I wasn't getting out at closing time.

She looked distraught. "That's seven years of bad luck!"

"For me, but not for you," I quickly assured her.

But she wouldn't be consoled, especially as she scratched off the tickets one by one and discarded them. "Loser... not a winner... try again." When the last of the scratchers produced nothing, Shawna looked at me as if I'd snatched good fortune out of her hands before tearfully excusing herself to the bathroom.

I turned the Closed sign and locked the door, then carefully swept up the broken glass, feeling an eerie sense of foreboding.

July 10, Friday

"YOU LOOK great," Wanda said suspiciously, surveying my flowered dress.

I couldn't hold back my smile. "Thanks. It's my anniversary. We're going out to dinner."

"That's nice. How many years?"

"Five."

She made a thoughtful noise. "What's the gift for five years?"

"Wood." I reached into my purse stowed behind the reception counter and withdrew a long narrow box, then opened it to show her the contents—an artisan wood mechanical pencil.

"It's beautiful," she said. "And perfect for an architect."

"Well... he's in sales now, but still, he loves this kind of thing. And maybe someday he'll get back to architecture."

"What kind of sales job did he get?"

"Um… for a liquor distributor."

"Oh. Well, that's a one-hundred-eighty-degree turn, but you said he has lots of different skills."

"He does," I said quickly. "Trent can do anything."

"Sounds like a keeper." She brought up her hand to whisper behind it. "Will you be getting 'wood' tonight too?" She gave me a wicked grin.

I blushed, then laughed, partly because I, too, had been hoping Trent and I would make love tonight. Between my crazy hours and his stress levels, it had been… a long time since we'd been intimate. But hopefully tonight would be a reset for us.

"How was Aruba?" I asked.

"A blast," she said. "My boyfriend proposed."

I gasped. "That's wonderful!"

"No, it's not," she said with a sigh. "Rick is a good guy, but he'll never be able to provide the lifestyle I want."

My chest pinged with awe over her self-confidence. "You told him no?"

She gave a shrug. "I had to."

"So you broke up?"

"Yes, but I waited to end it until we landed in Atlanta—I didn't want to miss out on first class."

I laughed at her irreverence. She gave a fluttery wave. "I want to hear all about your special night of wood."

When she disappeared onto the elevator, I looked back to the mechanical pencil and brimmed with pride to have found something I knew Trent would love. I'd scraped together tips from my waitressing job for weeks to be able to afford it, but it would be worth it to see the look on his face when he opened it.

The double doors slid open to admit a delivery driver carrying a bulky envelope. When I saw the package was addressed to Ryan Livingston, my vital signs jumped. I signed for it, then phoned his office to let him know it had arrived. He said he'd be right down, and I was instantly nervous to see him again after the dog-disguising incident. What must he think of me?

When he arrived, if possible, he looked even more handsome than before in a taupe-colored suit. "Hi, Mallory."

"Hello… Ryan."

He craned his neck slightly to indicate behind the counter. "Did you bring your friend to work today?"

Heat suffused my cheeks. "Not today. But is this the package you were expecting?"

He scanned the return address. "Yes, this is it. Thank you." He started to leave, then his gaze snagged on something. "What a beautiful pencil."

I glanced down to see I'd left Trent's gift sitting on the edge of the counter. "It's an anniversary gift for my husband."

"He's a lucky man," Ryan said, his eyes sparkling. "You have good taste."

I was sure my entire face was red now. "Thank you."

He lifted his package, then retreated to the elevator. I followed his movements beneath my lashes—the man moved like a sleek animal.

I gave myself a mental shake, happy to see it was quitting time. I stowed the gift in my purse, then gathered my things and made my way out to climb into Trent's SUV. Traffic was surprisingly light, so when I arrived at the apartment, I was in a good mood. It was glorious to have the night off to spend with my husband. I was looking forward to hearing more about his job and getting back to a point where he shared things with me.

Trent was standing in the living room, looking handsome in dark slacks, pale dress shirt, and a trendy colored sport coat. I registered the fact the clothes were new, which surprised me given our financial situation... but then I reasoned he deserved a new wardrobe for his new job. His skin glowed from the weekend outing on the lake—he looked virile and sexy. Longing barbed through me, making me think back to Wanda's teasing comment.

He smiled. "You look nice."

I smiled back. "So do you." I walked up to my husband feeling as if we were on the verge of something new, and it excited me. We kissed, and even his lips felt different—maybe he could feel it too.

"Happy anniversary," I said, pulling the box from behind my back.

His eyes clouded. "Oh... Mal... I didn't get you anything."

I squashed a flash of disappointment. "That's okay," I said with a dismissive wave. "Go ahead—open it."

He opened the box, then stared down at the one-of-a-kind piece.

"It's a mechanical pencil," I said.

"I know what it is," he said stiffly. "What am I supposed to do with it?"

I gave him a little smile. "I bought it before you got your new job. I know it's more of an architect thing, but surely you can still use it? And who knows—maybe you'll get back to architecture some day."

His face darkened. "You think I'll fail at this too?"

I frowned. "You didn't fail—"

He tossed the gift onto a nearby table. "I don't need a reminder of what I couldn't make happen. I want a clean slate."

I'd messed up again. "I'm sorry."

"Stop apologizing, Mal!"

"I'm—" I bit down on my tongue to stop myself, then changed tack. "Why don't we leave early and get a drink at the bar? You can tell me about your day."

He stared at me for a few seconds, then shook his head. "I don't want to do this anymore."

I frowned, then gave a little laugh. "But we have a reservation. Let's go have a nice dinner and celebrate."

He looked away and pressed his lips together, then looked back to me. "I mean I don't want to be married anymore."

I heard the words, but they didn't make sense to me. "Wh...at?"

"I want a divorce," he said, then picked up the car keys, opened the door, and walked out.

July 11, Saturday

I WANT a clean slate.

A nudge to my arm got my attention.

Vance nodded toward Doug, who was glaring at me.

"Mallory, are you deaf today? I said order up!"

I made my feet move, although my head was in a fog. When I walked past Vance with my laden tray, he touched my arm again. "You okay?"

I lifted my chin. "Everything is fine." Other than my husband had walked out and I'd gotten zero sleep last night.

"You seem a little off today."

I'd fumbled orders all morning. Conjuring up the best smile I could manage, I said, "I'm good."

He looked unconvinced, but I walked on. I couldn't stop to think about it, better to keep moving. Besides, I was sure Trent was going to call me any minute to apologize and say it had all been a big mistake, and of course he loved me.

The alternative was too much for me to absorb.

The mismatched couple was back—I was glad to see the near-brush with undercooked eggs hadn't scared them off. They were holding hands when I approached their table and the sight of it made my heart squeeze painfully.

"Here you are," I murmured, transferring plates to the table. Once again, most of the food went to her side—but then she was eating for two, after all. I accidentally nudged the salt shaker and it toppled, spilling crystals onto the table. "I'm so sorry, how clumsy of me."

Stop apologizing, Mal!

"No worries," the woman said. "I'm not superstitious."

"What's superstitious about salt?" her companion asked.

She gestured to the mess I'd made. "Turning over a salt shaker is supposed to be bad luck."

I reached forward to right the shaker, then froze, thinking about all the bad luck I'd been accumulating the past few days—maybe there was something to it.

When I realized they were both staring at me, I set the shaker upright, brushed the spilled salt into my hand, then wheeled away.

Into Kerry, who was shouldering an overflowing tray. In slow motion I watched her eyes go wide and the plates she carried slide off the tray onto the heads and laps of her customers, ending in a crescendo of bouncing, broken stoneware on the tile floor.

Followed by several seconds of utter silence.

"I'm sorry," I said in a rush.

Stop apologizing, Mal!

Doug appeared, looking murderous. After apologizing to the customers, he turned to me. "Go home, Mallory. I don't know what's wrong with you, and I don't care. Just don't be here today."

Vance gave me a pitying look as I passed him. I avoided eye contact as I gathered my things from the backroom, then exited through the kitchen. Tears hovered just beneath the surface, but I couldn't cry—I knew if I did, I might not be able to stop.

I walked to the nearest Marta bus stop and waited with a knot of other people who depended on public transportation. I'd quickly become familiar with the bus and train routes that would get me to and from each job. The trip was circuitous and long, but eventually I made it to the apartment. When I opened the door, my heart buoyed because I could hear Trent moving around in the bedroom.

He was back.

I hurried to the doorway, but my hopes were dashed by the sight of the open suitcase on the bed he was filling. He'd come back to get his clothes. Nessie lay curled up next to the suitcase, seemingly poised to crawl in if necessary.

He looked up. "Oh... hi."

"Hi," I croaked.

"I didn't think you'd be here."

My heart sagged further. "Trent... can we talk?"

He acted as if he hadn't heard me. "I thought I'd check on Nessie and get a few more clothes."

"Where are you staying?"

"With Dale."

"Trent... are you having an affair?"

He looked outraged. "What? No, I'm not having an affair."

"If there's someone else—"

"There isn't," he cut in. "Don't blame this on anyone else. We haven't been happy for a long time."

"We're going through a rough patch, that's all." I hated the pleading note in my voice, but I couldn't help it.

His hands sped up. He tossed clothes into the suitcase willy-nilly. It was clear he just wanted to leave.

"Please, Trent, talk to me. We can work through this."

He closed the lid of the suitcase, then looked up. "We can," he conceded.

My heart bounced up.

"But I don't want to," he added.

When I studied his face, it was as if I was looking at a stranger. His expression was closed and his eyes were empty, devoid of any emotion. My heart shattered.

He picked up the suitcase and walked past me to the doorway. Nessie scrambled after him, barking hopefully.

"Trent—"

"Bye, Mal."

"Wait."

His hand stopped on the doorknob. "What?" he ground out.

I was shaken by the hostility rolling off him. "What about Nessie?"

She was his dog, already entrenched in his life when we'd met. The little Frenchie and I tolerated each other, but deep down, we both wished the other would leave so we could have Trent to ourselves.

"I don't want her," he said bluntly, then left.

The word "either" hung in the air.

July 12, Sunday

"NO OFFENSE," Vance said. "But you don't look much better today."

"None taken," I said. I didn't have to look in a mirror to know I looked like someone who'd had their heart stomped and hadn't slept in... I couldn't even compute the hours.

"Are you sick?" he asked. "Because I can't afford to catch a bug."

"It's not contagious," I assured him.

I never discussed my personal life with my waitstaff coworkers, partly because I hadn't intended to be working here so long. My two extra jobs had been a stopgap measure when Trent was laid off. When I'd suggested he look for a part-time job, he'd said it would take away from his unemployment benefits. And when unemployment had run out, he'd said he needed to be free to pursue leads and keep his skills sharp. The few offers that had come his way hadn't paid well enough and he'd insisted if he took a low-paying job, it would look bad on his resume and take years longer to recover. I couldn't argue with any of it, although there were days when I wished he would rub my feet when I got home.

Kerry walked up, eyeing me warily. "You cost me a big tip yesterday."

"I'm really sorry. I'll pay you out of my tips today."

She harrumphed. "Don't worry about it. But I do need lottery ticket money from both of you."

"I'll pay you next week," Vance said.

"Nope, pay up or you're sitting out."

He frowned, then dug bills out of his pocket. "I'd share with you if *I* won," he groused.

"Me, too," I said.

"I'm not that charitable," Kerry said, wriggling her fingers.

I knew I was throwing away money I couldn't afford to spend, but I didn't want to alienate her, so I slowly counted four ones into her hand.

"What's the pot up to?" Vance asked.

"Around twenty million, I think."

He pursed his mouth. "So about a mil each if we win."

"Right. Minus taxes and whatnot."

"And what are the odds of getting all six balls?"

"About one in three hundred million," I said. They both stared at me, and I realized I'd absorbed more lottery stats than I thought from working at the GiddyUp GoMart. "I think I heard that somewhere."

"So we have a better chance of being eaten alive by a polar bear than winning the lottery," Vance mused.

We all sighed.

"Mal, Kerry, Vance," Doug shouted. "Order up!"

July 13, Monday

"So, HOW was your anniversary?" Wanda asked with a grin. "Did you get some *wood*?"

I wavered, trying to come up with the saucy retort she was looking for. But the sleeplessness and stress was catching up with me and suddenly, my vision blurred with tears.

"Oh, honey," she cooed. "What happened?"

I choked back a sob, mortified.

"Bill," she said to the security officer, "I need Mallory for a few minutes. She'll be right back." Then she was guiding me to the elevator. "We'll go to my office and get a cup of tea."

By the time we'd arrived, I'd gathered my composure a bit, but I still felt wobbly on my feet. Wanda led me to a small office and deposited me in a chair, then reappeared in a few minutes with two mugs of hot chamomile.

"Thank you," I murmured. My hands were shaking so badly, I had to use both of them to hold the mug to my mouth.

"I take it things didn't go as planned," Wanda said, sipping from her own mug.

"No, they didn't," I agreed. "He…" I couldn't seem to get the words out.

"Had a heart attack?" Wanda asked, wide-eyed. "Died?"

"He… left me."

Her face crumpled. "I'm sorry, Mallory. You didn't see it coming?"

I shook my head. "Things have been rough since he was laid off, but he'd gotten a new job and I thought things were turning around."

"Who is she?" she asked flatly.

"She?"

"The woman he left you for."

I swallowed a mouthful of scalding liquid. "He says there's no one."

She smirked. "Honey, there's always someone. Men don't up and leave a relationship until they have another place to land."

I thought back over the events of the past few weeks.

"And it's probably someone he's talked about," Wanda said. "Men are like that—they're so dumb when they're cheating they don't even realize how many times they drop her name into casual conversation."

Realization dawned. I was an idiot. He'd said her name so many times, he'd begun to sound like a Doctor Seuss rhyme.

"Mike," I said.

Her eyes flew wide. "He left you for a guy?"

"No—he met this woman named Mikala, but she goes by Mike. They hung out a few times, and she got him a job with her company." I decided not to mention the lipstick. "But that doesn't mean they're having an affair," I insisted. "I don't know what she looks like, or even if she's single."

Wanda turned to the computer on her desk. "What's her last name?"

"I don't know."

"Who does she work for?"

I told her the name of the liquor distribution company. A few keystrokes later, she said, "Mikala Morgan, twenty-six, and according to her dating profile, she's 'single and looking.' Her hobbies are traveling, working out, and hanging out with friends."

I swallowed hard. "Is there a picture?"

"Uh-huh." Wanda adjusted the screen so I could see.

My stomach sank. Mikala Morgan was a tall, toned goddess with a gorgeous face and a glorious mane of hair. Dressed in a tiny bathing suit, she was looking at the camera and laughing, as if to say, "I can have any man I want."

If she wanted *my* man, I simply couldn't compete.

July 14, Tuesday

"No LIPSTICK today?" Shawna asked.

I was cleaning the soda machine and she was pretending to dust the peach-themed souvenirs at the counter.

"No," I said, thinking mere days ago I'd been blissfully unaware my husband was planning to leave me. "How's Bob?"

She shrugged. "He has good days and bad days. We keep hoping we'll get a call about a kidney soon." Then she frowned. "But it don't seem right to hope that somebody else dies so Bob can live."

"You can't look at it like that," I murmured. "How long have you been married?"

She cackled. "I'll have to think about it... Willie is going on twelve years old, so I guess Bob and I've been married about fifteen years or so."

"How do you keep it together?"

She frowned. "What do you mean?"

"Marriage is hard, don't you think?"

She laughed again. "Yeah... but what ain't? That's life, honey. You can't just give up."

Some people can, I mused. The door opened and the owner, Ramy Asfour, came in, all smiles. "Hello, ladies, how are you?"

"Tired and ready to go home," Shawna said, cocking her hip.

"How was business today?" he asked, moving behind the counter.

"Not great," Shawna said. "You need to do some advertising, Ramy."

"I know," he said with a sigh.

"How is Aisha?" I asked.

He didn't answer, only shook his head. His wife was recovering from having a brain tumor removed. The illness had taken a toll on my boss. In his absence, the business had slipped badly. In all honesty, one of us could've handled the night traffic, but he didn't like for us to work alone.

"Mallory," he said, nodding to the lottery tickets, "would you please ring up two scratch-offs in the Big Moolah game?"

It was a policy that we not ring up our own lottery ticket sales.

"I'll take two of those," Shawna said, reaching into her pocket.

I processed the transactions, then watched as both of them went through their rituals of placing the ticket just so, then using their tool of choice to rub off the waxy coating—Ramy, a quarter, Shawna, her trusty thumbnail. He was methodical, as if taking care would produce better results. Shawna was frenzied, eager to get to the prize. He concentrated fiercely, she pushed the tip of her tongue out.

At that moment, I understood the allure of the games. More than money, more than trips and prizes, the lottery peddled... hope.

And couldn't we all use a little of that?

July 15, Wednesday

I STARTLED awake, then realized Nessie was licking my hand.

I became aware of a full-body ache, and groaned. The couch wasn't the best for sleeping, but I hadn't been able to sleep in our bed since Trent had left. His pillow, his snore strips on the nightstand—all of it was too much of a reminder he was gone, and just how many little things he'd left me to deal with.

But then, every corner of the apartment held painful reminders: framed photos, his underwear in the hamper, the coffee creamer he liked in the fridge.

Nessie whined to be walked. It was four-thirty in the morning, which was odd for her, but I conceded we'd both been thrown off kilter.

I slowly sat up and pushed my hair out of my eyes. I was still wearing the clothes I'd worn for my shift at the convenience store the night before. I'd smelled better.

But since I wasn't likely to run into anyone at this hour, I gave myself a pass and shepherded Nessie to the door, then hooked the leash to her collar. When I stepped out into the hall, I was mortified to see Josh emerging from his apartment, wearing running clothes.

"Good morning," he said cheerfully.

It was too late to escape. "It's still night time," I croaked, hoping that would somehow explain or make up for the fact that I looked as if I'd been pulled backward through a hedgerow.

He laughed, then nodded to Nessie. "Does she know that?"

"Apparently not. She's... a little off schedule." I headed toward the exit, hoping to lose him. But he moved ahead of me, holding open the door.

"Is she sick?"

"Um... no. I guess I've been neglecting her lately."

"Ah. French bulldog, right?"

"Yes. Her name is Nessie."

He leaned over and scratched her ears. "Hi, Nessie." When he straightened, he said, "They make good therapy dogs."

"They do?"

He nodded. "We have a few at Shepherd, if she ever needs some extra affection." He smiled. "Just an idea."

We'd reached the dimly lit outside area.

"Hey, did you get your car fixed?" he asked.

"Not yet," I mumbled. It was languishing in the parking lot of a repair shop demanding a deposit for the work required—rightfully so.

"Well, if you ever need a lift and your husband isn't around, knock on my door."

I made the corners of my mouth turn up. "Okay… thanks."

"See ya," he said, then jogged away.

I stared after him, bemused.

July 16, Thursday

THE NEXT day I was leaving the Noble Plaza building at the end of the day when Wanda caught up with me on the sidewalk.

"How are you holding up?"

"Fine," I said, mostly because I didn't want her to make a fuss.

"Have you called an attorney yet?"

I frowned. "No. It's… too soon for that."

She gave me a doubtful look. "Honey, don't put this off—you'll regret it."

"Mallory!" called a male voice behind me.

We both turned to see Ryan Livingston striding up. Wanda was suddenly on high alert.

His smile was like a brand new bulb. "How did your husband like his anniversary gift?"

I blinked. "He, uh… he…"

"The asshole left her," Wanda supplied.

Ryan did a double-take. "What? I'm so sorry."

"Don't be," Wanda said. "She's better off without him, aren't you, Mal?"

"I—"

"We should all go out for a drink sometime to celebrate," Wanda suggested. "How about now?"

"I have to be somewhere," I said, shaking my head. It was the bus stop, but they didn't have to know that.

Ryan made a rueful noise. "So do I. Raincheck?"

"Absolutely," Wanda said, practically on fire.

I waved goodbye and headed away from the building, two blocks down to the nearest Marta bus stop. It would be easier to go straight to the convenience store for my evening shift, but I couldn't leave Nessie alone for that long.

Two buses and a train ride later, I reached the apartment, already calculating how long it would take me to get to the GiddyUp and dreading the reverse trip home in the dark.

To my shock, the apartment door was propped open, and Trent and Dale were carrying out my couch. When they saw me, Dale stopped, but Trent said, "Keep going, man."

Anger flared in my stomach. "What are you doing?"

"Taking some furniture," Trent returned. "I have a right to half of our stuff."

"You can't take the couch," I said. Where would I sleep?

"I left you the chairs," he said, "and the bedroom furniture."

I was incredulous. "What else did you take?"

He signaled for Dale to set down his end, then heaved a sigh, as if I was the biggest witch ever. "I took the wine fridge, the armoire, the rugs, and some other things."

I glanced into the apartment to see all bare walls. "You took the artwork?"

"I left you the pictures," he retorted. "I don't want those."

"Mallory?"

I turned my head to see Josh standing in front of his own door, taking in the scene.

"Is everything okay?"

I wanted to fall through the floor.

"Hey, buddy," Trent said with a head toss, "mind your own business."

Josh slowly folded his arms. "A friend in distress *is* my business."

Trent looked back and forth between me and Josh, then leered. "Wow, Mal, I didn't think you had it in you."

"Shut your mouth," Josh said, just as calm as you please.

Alarmed, I put up my hands. "Everybody, take a breath." I turned to look at Josh with pleading eyes. "Everything's fine here."

He studied my face, then gave a curt nod and went into his apartment.

I looked back to Trent, who'd signaled Dale to pick up his end. Then my husband looked at me. "Move, Mal... you're in the way."

July 17, Friday

"THIS IS Trent. Leave a message at the tone and I'll bounce you back."

I frowned at his salesy, affected tone. Bounce you back? Who was this new person who had inhabited my husband's body?

"Trent, this is Mal… again. Please call me back. We need to talk sometime." I sighed. "Please?" I ended the call, hating how desperate I sounded, but the silent treatment was unbearable. And deep down, I still nursed the hope that if only we could have an actual conversation, we could find a way back to each other. I was open to counseling, relocating—whatever it took.

I'd scoured my mind for a cause for his sudden personality change. Could he be on drugs? Was he ill? Had the loss of his most recent job affected him more than I realized?

On the bus ride to the Noble Plaza building, I called again. "Trent, you're leaving me hanging here. Do your parents know you've moved out?" I wasn't particularly close to his parents who lived in Pennsylvania, but his mother called me occasionally and I wanted to be prepared.

On my lunch hour, I tried again. "Trent… are you ever going to talk to me? Don't you miss… Nessie?" I teared up. "She misses you." I ended the call, feeling more torn than ever.

He was rarely without his phone. I pictured him seeing my name come up on the screen and wondered if he was rolling his eyes, or yearning to answer so we could fix things. We'd once loved each other… maybe if I gave him a little time to figure things out, to let this presumed flirtation with Mikala fade, we could reconcile.

But by the end of the day, I was weak again and missing him so much, my chest ached. In desperation, I phoned Dale, the friend he was staying with. Maybe he could give me a sense of where Trent's head was.

"This is Dale."

"Hi, Dale. This is Mallory."

"Oh, yeah… hi, Mal." But his voice had changed—his guard was up.

"I'm worried about Trent and wondered if you could tell me how he's doing."

"Uh… I haven't seen him much since… you know."

"He must be working a lot."

"Yeah, I think so."

"Are you two on different schedules?"

"Hm?"

"You must see him sometimes if he's staying with you."

From the dead silence on the other end of the line, realization hit me.

"He's not staying with you, is he, Dale?"

"Uh… you should talk to Trent about this."

"I would," I ground out, "if he'd answer his phone."

"Have you left him a message?"

I closed my eyes briefly. "Yes."

"Maybe try texting him?"

"Okay, thanks anyway, Dale."

"Hey, Mal?"

His voice had gentled—maybe he was going to tell me Trent loved me and I should just give him some space. "Yes?"

"If you ever need a shoulder to cry on, call me."

I made a face. "Bye, Dale."

I disconnected the call, shot through with hurt and betrayal.

I had a good idea where Trent's head was—on Mikala Morgan's pillow.

July 18, Saturday

"SUNRISE PLATTER and huevos rancheros." I set the plates in front of the mismatched couple who had become regulars in my section on weekend mornings. "And a full roasted chicken on the side."

Not the typical order, but pregnant women had cravings.

"It's nice to see you," the woman said. "After last week, we were afraid you wouldn't be back."

I maintained my smile as best I could. "I was having an off day."

"But things are better?" she pressed.

For a few seconds, I envied the woman's best friend because she seemed like the type of person who really cared. She'd be a good mother... another sensitive topic for me since I couldn't remember mine.

"Things are... getting better," I hedged.

She dipped her chin. "I'm Hannah and this is Chance."

"I'm Mallory," I said, pointing to my nametag.

"We're married," the man supplied happily. "And we're having a baby."

"I remember," I said. "Congratulations. When are you due?"

"In the spring," Hannah said, patting her stomach. She nodded to my hand. "I see you're married. Do you have children?"

My gaze darted to my left hand where the small engagement ring and thin gold band declared that yes, I was indeed married. Technically.

I covered it with my right hand. "I don't have children, but I have a French bulldog." I showed them a picture of Nessie on my phone and they said nice things.

But the woman was studying me in a way that made me think she could see through my thin veneer of calm, and knew that just below, I was falling apart.

When I turned to go, she said, "Mallory, wait... take this."

I turned back, surprised to see her wielding the serrated steak knife I'd brought to the table. With unbelievable quickness, she dipped the knife into the roasted chicken, twisted her wrist, and came away with the wishbone. She wrapped it in a napkin, then handed it to me. "For you."

I hesitated. "What should I do with it?"

She smiled. "Hang on to it until you need a little good luck."

July 19, Sunday

"I NEED your lotto money," Kerry said, dropping a tray full of dirty dishes on the enormous pile headed for the automatic dishwasher.

Vance frowned. "For all we know, you could be cashing in tickets every week and stuffing the money under your mattress."

"Sure could be," she agreed. "So if anyone else wants to take over the lotto pool, raise your hand." Her voice and glance encompassed us, the rest of the waitstaff, and the kitchen help.

Everyone shook their heads. "No?" She gave Vance a syrupy smile. "Then shut your pie hole. I'm doing y'all a big-ass favor by taking this on. All the big pots are won by pools, you know."

Then she huffed. "But just to review, any proceeds from the tickets we buy get plowed back into the pool. And I'm happy to show anybody the tickets." She grinned and patted her generous cleavage. "I keep them in my bra."

Vance rolled his eyes. "I'll pass." He extended his four dollars. "But if you don't show up one day, we're gonna know you disappeared with our jackpot."

She snatched the cash. "I'll send you a postcard from my island."

We all laughed and gathered around Kerry. I scanned the faces of my coworkers, most of whom—like me—had more than one job and struggled to pay bills. My mind flitted back to the idea of selling hope to the masses. It was brilliant—personal *and* universal.

Because almost everyone dreamed of a different life. A few days ago, I wouldn't have said that about myself. But now I handed over my four dollars with as much hope as everyone else.

Maybe more.

July 20, Monday

WANDA STOPPED in front of the reception desk. "Did I see you getting off a bus this morning?"

I nodded. "I take the train, then the bus."

"That must take a while."

"About an hour," I confirmed. If the weather was dry—and so far, July had been unusually rainy.

She narrowed her eyes. "You don't have a car?"

"It's in the shop," I said, avoiding her pointed gaze.

"And how about that husband of yours? Is he riding the bus?"

"No. He's in sales, so he has to have a decent vehicle."

"Uh-huh. Please tell me you've contacted an attorney."

I balked. "I haven't. It's… too soon. He's only been gone a few days. He could still change his mind."

She frowned. "He's living with her, isn't he?"

"No." I looked away, then back. "Maybe."

She sighed. "Mallory, you need to start looking out for yourself. Have you at least set up a new bank account?"

I frowned. "That's not necessary."

"Have you checked your balance lately?"

I swallowed hard. "Trent wouldn't do something overt that would harm me financially."

Wanda reached forward and clasped my hand. "For your sake, I hope so." She made a thoughtful noise. "I'm here if you ever need to talk, although I'm sure you have people in your family you can turn to."

"Right," I said, nodding.

She pulled out a business card and pressed it into my hand. "This is a divorce attorney I know. She's tough, but she charges a fair rate. You could do worse."

I shook my head. "I won't need it."

"Take it anyway... just in case."

To appease her, I took the card... just in case.

July 21, Tuesday

WANDA'S COMMENT the previous day looped in my head. Not the one about contacting an attorney, but about the one about having someone in my family to talk to.

The truth of the matter was that no one in my family had met Trent, or even knew I was married. My mother had died when I was a baby, and my father had been in and out of my life until I was maybe five or six. I had no memories of him after that, and to my knowledge, both sets of my grandparents were deceased.

But there was one person in my life who'd cared more than others had. Danica Tumi had been my foster mother from age twelve to thirteen, a happy time for me that had ended when she'd had to move out of state to take care of a parent. But we'd stayed in touch, and to-date, she was the most solid good influence on my life. I hadn't talked to her in a long while, but I suddenly felt compelled to hear her voice.

"Hello?"

I smiled into the phone. "Danica? It's Mallory."

"Mallory, what a nice surprise."

"Is this a bad time?"

She laughed. "Crazy, as usual, you'll probably hear all the kids in the background."

Indeed, I could hear laughter and running feet and raised voices. "How many kids do you have at the moment?"

"Let me see—six? No, seven."

"Sounds like a handful."

"It is, but I love it. How are you?"

"I'm... fine," I said, determined not to pile my troubles onto her. "I was just calling to catch up."

"How's that handsome husband of yours?"

I squeezed the phone to fight back tears. "He's... great. He has a new job in sales and he's so happy."

"Wonderful. And are you back in school?"

"Not yet," I admitted. "But soon, maybe."

"That must mean you like your current job."

"Yes," I assured her. "It's something new every day." Between the three of them.

"Are you sure everything is okay? You don't sound well."

"It's a cold," I said, forcing lightness into my voice. "Things... couldn't be better. I was just thinking of you and... I wanted to say thank you, Danica, for... everything."

"I loved having you, Mallory. You know you're one of my special kids."

In the background, a loud thump sounded, then the howls of a crying child.

"Uh-oh, sounds like someone is bleeding," she said with a little laugh "Will you call me back soon?"

"I will."

"I love you, Mallory. Take care."

I opened my mouth to say I love you, but it came out as "you do the same."

July 22, Wednesday

"TWO SLICES of pizza, two sodas, and a candy bar," I said to the customer who appeared to be buying dinner for himself and his daughter. I was mesmerized by the way he hovered over her and the adoring looks he gave her. What I wouldn't give to have a memory of me and my father having pizza night. "Anything else?"

"I'll take a quick pick on the Mega Dollars lotto."

I rang it up and gave him the total, then waved goodbye to the little girl.

As they were leaving, another customer came in. The guy was wearing a cap. He headed to the cooler to get a bottled drink, then cruised by the condom section. Since I'd broken the mirror that helped us monitor that area prone to shoplifting, I kept an eye on him. He took his time, turning over packages to read them before making his selection. I dropped my gaze when he approached the counter so he wouldn't think I'd been watching him. When I looked up, he was practically at the counter.

My eyes widened. "Josh?"

His eyes widened. "Mallory?"

I hadn't seen him since the incident with Trent moving furniture out of the apartment. My face burned, both over the memory and him knowing this was what I did in my spare time. "This is my part-time job," I said quickly. "It's... temporary."

"I can't count the jobs I've held," he said with a laugh. "We'll have to compare notes sometime."

I nodded, then held out my hand for his purchases. With a wry smile, he handed over the two boxes of condoms and a bottle of tea.

"That's my favorite flavor," I said to cover the awkwardness. Then I caught myself. "Of tea, I mean."

He nodded, seeming amused.

The man obviously didn't want for companionship. I rang up the order, then took his money. When I gave him his change, he said, "Listen, Mallory... I don't want to intrude, but if you ever need to talk—"

"I won't," I said quickly. "Trent and I are going through a rough spot is all. We're not splitting up."

He dipped his chin. "Good. That's... really good."

I nodded. "Yes."

"Okay, then... I'll see you around."

I nodded again. "See you around."

He looked as if he wanted to say more, but changed his mind. I was glad he did.

July 23, Thursday

I WAS late, sprinting to the Noble Plaza building in mid-heel pumps, holding my mostly ineffectual umbrella close to my head, which obscured my vision. I twisted my ankle, but recovered and kept going. I couldn't lose this job.

I skidded into the lobby on a pool of water dripping from my clothes. But to my dismay, Amelia Inez stood there, tapping her foot and checking her watch.

"You're late," she admonished.

"I'm sorry. Marta was running behind."

She held up her finger. "If you're going to rely on public transportation, you need to build delays into your schedule. This is your second warning, Mallory. Don't be late again."

I thanked her and scurried behind the desk. My hair was plastered to my head, and I was pretty sure my underwear was wet.

"And for heaven's sake, lower your umbrella," she hissed. "Don't you know that's bad luck?"

She stomped off just as Wanda walked up.

"I was late," I murmured.

"I heard," she said, then surveyed my soggy appearance. "Mallory, you shouldn't have to live like this—at least make your ex pay to fix your car."

"He's not my ex," I insisted. And how could I tell her I was hoping Trent would do it on his own, as a gesture that he still cared a tiny bit about my safety and security? He still hadn't returned any of my calls. I'd lost count how many times I'd dialed his number... my pride was in shreds.

She leaned in and lowered her voice. "He's not coming for you, Mallory. You have to start thinking like a single woman."

Wanda walked off, leaving me to stew in misery in my swampy clothes. I didn't want to be single.

July 24, Friday

FOR THE first time in ages, Ramy had scheduled himself to work with Shawna at the GiddyUp, so I had Friday night free. What's a girl to do for fun?

Tackle the towering stack of unopened bills that plagued me every time I came and went from the apartment. Wanda was half-right, I'd decided—I needed to get my financial life in order, regardless of what happened with my marriage.

Talking about money hadn't been our strong suit, and I confess I leaned on Trent to take care of things. It made me feel protected. Besides, money scared me a little. I'd never had enough of it, and it had dominated every life decision I'd made. I'd been happy to let Trent deal with banking matters and credit cards and buying both our vehicles, plus the ski boat. His view on money was so different than mine—he saw it strictly as a bartering tool to get the things he wanted, untied to emotion. Our herky-jerky attitude about money had landed us in trouble more than once, but Trent was the one who could talk us out of any late fee or penalty. To be fair, in good times he was mostly efficient about opening and paying our bills. But for the past several months, neither one of us had wanted to face what was inside the bulging envelopes, even when they came with ominous messages stamped on the outside: URGENT MATTER, ACTION REQUIRED and FINAL NOTICE.

I found a bottle of white wine in the back of the refrigerator, and poured a large glass to help lubricate the task. Then with Nessie lying near my feet (paws covering her nose as if she knew what was coming), I sorted and opened all the envelopes, tossing the oldest statements that were duplicates, then reached for my calculator.

The entire bottle of wine and four hours later, I sat back, staring at the staggering amount we owed on rent, credit cards, student loans, the cars, the boat, utilities, and miscellaneous medical care. The total had seemed too large to be real, so I'd added it three times.

How was it possible that a couple in their twenties had amassed over a quarter of a million dollars in debt?

I was so scared, I couldn't even cry.

July 25, Saturday

I'D THOUGHT I'd reached every layer of numb… I had nowhere to go but "coma". Since I still couldn't sleep in the bed alone, I'd tried sleeping in various chairs, on the floor—even in the bathtub. But rest was still elusive, and now that I knew how close to the poorhouse we were, I decided I might never sleep again.

Vance floated by. "Did you see the man candy who was just seated in your section?"

"No," I said, completely disinterested.

He scoffed. "Just because you're married doesn't mean you're blind."

"He's yours if you want him."

"Alas, he looks as straight as a ruler." Vance continued on.

I poured a glass of water for the new customer, then swung by the table where Hannah and Chance were finishing their meal.

"Anything else?" I asked.

"Just the check," she said. "It was delicious, as always."

"I'll let the chef know, he'll be pleased."

"Mallory… have you used the wishbone yet?"

I shook my head, then smiled. "I'm saving it for a special occasion." In truth, I suspected I would find it in the bottom of my purse a year from now, a smelly, brittle mess, and wonder what it was. But it was harmless fun to humor her. I left the check, thanked them again, then veered to the table with the new customer. He had nice hair, I conceded… and nice clothes. And…

Crap—it was Ryan Livingston.

He looked up, then did a double-take. "Mallory?"

"In the flesh," I said cheerfully.

"Do you moonlight here?"

I nodded and smiled. "Until Amelia Inez decides to promote me."

He smiled. "You're full of surprises."

I wondered what the money manager would think if he knew I was up to my unplucked eyebrows in debt, with little to show for it? I'd texted the amount to Trent, thinking it might shock him into responding.

It hadn't.

I set the glass of ice water in front of Ryan. "Do you see anything you like?"

His gaze lingered on me, but not in a lascivious way—I wasn't pretty enough to turn the head of someone like him. He just seemed... curious? Maybe I reminded him of a sister... or a puppy.

"Give me a few minutes," he said. "I like to take my time before deciding."

His gaze dropped to my legs—my only notable feature—and I experienced a twinge of... wait, what was it? Something I couldn't put my finger on... a relic from my past.

Oh, yeah—*desire.*

But since this man wasn't my husband, I nipped it in the bud, and left him alone to peruse the menu.

July 26, Sunday

VANCE STOPPED and spoke near my shoulder. "FOR SOMEONE not interested, you sure spent a lot of time with Mr. Candy yesterday."

I tried to be nonchalant. "He works in the building where I'm a receptionist. He was just being friendly."

"You don't give yourself enough credit, Mallory." He made a figure-eight in front of me with his finger. "You're gorge under all that Everywoman thing you got going on."

I squinted. "I have no idea what you just said."

He sighed. "I'm saying if we win the lottery, we're both getting *epic* makeovers." He frowned, then looked all around. "Speaking of which, where's Kerry?"

"Doug said she called in sick."

"*Or,*" Vance said, "she won the lottery and left town."

"We should check the mail for a postcard," I agreed. Then I stopped. "Wait—has anyone taken up the lottery money?"

He shook his head. "Be my guest." He lifted a loaded tray to his shoulder, then walked away.

But I had enough problems with my own money without taking on more.

July 27, Monday

I CONNECTED to Trent's phone again. I'd lost count of the times I'd called him and the messages I'd left. I was preparing to leave yet another when his voice came on the line.

"Hello."

I blinked in surprise. "Trent?"

"Yeah," he said flatly. "I figured if I answered maybe you'd stop calling."

"All I want is to have a conversation," I said, closing my eyes and soaking up his voice. "Have you been listening to my messages?"

He sighed. "Some of them. Jesus, Mal, you're relentless."

The utter disdain in his voice was like a knife through my heart. "How's the new job?"

"Good so far."

"I left you a message about our bills… we need to figure out a schedule of how we're going to pay off everything. I set up a spreadsheet, but I'd like for you to take a look."

"It'll have to wait—my first commission check won't arrive for another four weeks or so. Until then, I can't help you."

He's not coming for you, Wanda had said.

"Where are you staying?" I asked lightly.

"I told you, with Dale."

So he was fine with telling a bold-face lie. "I talked to Dale, he said you aren't staying with him."

Silence sounded, then a sigh.

"Are you living with Mikala now? Sorry—I know she likes to be called Mike."

"Bitterness isn't becoming on you, Mal. And yes, I'm living with Mike."

I swallowed a wad of tears. "Is it… serious?"

"I've met her folks and her siblings. She has a big family, and I like all of that."

A direct hit, considering I had no family to offer him.

He sighed. "Are you there?"

"Yes," I said tightly.

"Jesus, Mal, don't cry. If you start crying, I'm going to hang up. And you have to stop calling like some kind of psycho."

"We need to communicate, Trent."

"You can communicate through my attorney."

Tears flooded my eyes. "You've been in touch with an attorney?"

Another sigh, as if I were stupid. "Mal, what part of 'I want a divorce' do you not understand? This whole situation would be easier if you'd just get over it."

I couldn't speak. *Get over it?* Like a common cold?

"I'm hanging up," he said. "Stop calling."

The call ended. I sat holding the phone until the battery died.

Then I removed my engagement ring and wedding band.

July 28, Tuesday

WANT TO drive yourself crazy? Think about your husband in bed with another woman. Worse—a beauty you could never measure up to. And even worse—imagine the two of them are laughing at you. I could picture Trent lounging with the classy, smart gorgeous Mikala, then hanging out with her Kennedy-esque family who would fold him into their brood. And I could picture him congratulating himself for getting away from me and elevating his station in life.

While I was churning, I went for broke and dug through our files until I found the report I was looking for, the one I'd tried to forget. It was a report from the private investigator I'd hired to find my father, ergo Trent's reference to the money I'd wasted on a wild goose chase. After months of searching, I'd fully expected the investigator to come back with a death certificate, saying my dad had drank himself to death in some random place.

Instead, he'd sent my father's address: The Georgia State Prison in Reidsville where he was serving a sentence for various financial crimes including fraud, tax evasion, and bribery.

Trent had joked I'd inherited my money smarts from my father. At the time it had seemed funny... now it just seemed hurtful.

July 29, Wednesday

IF I won the lottery, I thought wryly, I would buy a better umbrella. I was sprinting through puddles again, desperate to make it to the Noble Plaza building in the next thirty seconds. Because I'd narrowly missed the northbound redline train, I'd been forced to wait another twenty minutes for the next train, although I doubted Amelia Inez would find my excuse forgivable.

I felt the heel of my pump give way—it had been waterlogged one too many times. I stumbled, took off the shoes, and kept running in my bare feet. I hit the lobby on a skid, stopping near Amelia Inez, who was smiling at someone standing in my place behind the reception desk.

"Sorry I'm late—"

"You're just in time," Amelia said, then her smile dropped. "To turn in your lanyard. I've already hired your replacement." She gestured to the young woman standing behind the desk, who fought a yawn behind her hand. "I'm sorry it didn't work out, Mallory."

When she walked past me dismissively, anger and helplessness tightened my chest. I considered throwing my umbrella at her, but I needed it to fight my way through the rain back to the bus stop.

"Are you okay?"

I looked up to see Ryan Livingston standing there. He looked me up and down and I saw myself through his eyes… a plain, bedraggled, barefoot woman whose life was spiraling down.

And he didn't even know the half of it.

"I'm right as rain," I said, then stalked back outside to swim my way home to an empty apartment.

July 30, Thursday

BEING FIRED from Noble Plaza left me more time to work at the GiddyUp GoMart, but I knew I'd have to find another job soon that could provide little necessities like group health insurance and paid sick days.

When I looked in the mirror over the employee bathroom sink, I was surprised to see someone who appeared to be holding it all together, but inside everything was moving—I was on the verge of flying apart.

Until then, I was drawing on the resources that had gotten me through dozens of foster homes intact—I kept putting one foot in front of the other, trusting it would take me to a better place.

I was hoping for a busy evening to make the time pass quickly, and it seemed likely. Several of the lottery jackpots had grown, although I confess they all blurred after a while. Between the in-state and multi-state lotteries, the daily draws, the second-chance draws, and the steady release of new scratch-off games, there was something for everyone.

And we seemed to have more than our fair share of regulars. Some customers had the idea that more big jackpot tickets were sold in hole-in-the-wall convenience stores like ours, and some people were superstitious about where they bought their tickets, so we saw the same ticket buyers over and over, many with their own peculiarities.

When I emerged from the restroom, Ramy was on a tall ladder near the entrance replacing a light bulb. Shawna was pulling frozen pizza from the freezer to bake and cut into slices, so I sidled behind the counter. I glanced out in the parking lot to see one of our more colorful regulars, Mrs. Conway, hurrying toward the door. I put her in her mid-fifties. She was buxom and bouncy and garbed in "lucky" symbols—a jacket covered with four-leaf clovers, rabbits-feet hanging from her belt, and horseshoe jewelry.

She opened the door and walked in... then screamed as if her hair was on fire.

Ramy nearly fell off the ladder, and Shawna came running. "What happened?"

Mrs. Conway was pointing to Ramy. "I just walked under a ladder, that's bad luck in spades!" She was panicked, crossing herself over and over.

"Maybe if you walk back under it going the other way?" Shawna suggested.

The woman howled. "Are you trying to curse me for life?"

Ramy had climbed down and tried to calm the woman. She bought hundreds of dollars of tickets every week.

Then a memory clicked in my head. "I have something that might help."

Mrs. Conway looked suspicious. "What?"

From my purse I pulled the wishbone I'd saved. Mrs. Conway's face lit up. At the time I'd thought the Hannah woman was a little off for giving it to me, but now it seemed serendipitous. I extended the wishbone to Mrs. Conway and she grasped the other end.

"Make a wish," she said excitedly.

I wished for—what else?—a new life.

We both pulled... and I came away with the larger piece. I was worried Mrs. Conway would be upset, but instead she laughed. "You get your wish! This wishbone will negate the bad luck of the ladder, I'm sure of it."

Ramy threw me a grateful look, then carried the ladder to the storeroom. I positioned myself behind the counter next to the lotto register. I was accustomed to the long orders of people like Mrs. Conway who chose specific numbers in different combinations for each game. Ramy trusted me more than Shawna to get the orders right.

Except I was slightly off my game. When I handed over the last ticket, she shook her head. "This is wrong. You missed one number."

I apologized profusely and took the ticket back. Rather than asking Ramy to invalidate the ticket, I pulled two dollars from my purse and bought it myself. Then I reentered the numbers and completed Mrs. Conway's order.

The rest of the evening was a blur of ticket and beer sales. The time passed quickly, but my feet were killing me. On the bus and train ride home, I mused over the lore of the wishbone, and how nice it would be if wishes came true.

I was dragging by the time I arrived at the apartment. When I approached the door, I noticed a sheet of paper stuck to it. My heart and feet quickened—had Trent left me a letter?

But when I got close enough to read it, my stomach dropped. EVICTION NOTICE

I gasped. While my mind reeled, I realized someone else had walked up. I turned my head to see Josh, who was staring at the notice. When he looked at me, I couldn't bear the shame. I yanked the notice from the door, then opened the door, ducked inside, and slammed it behind me.

So much for wishes and good luck.

July 31, Friday

I WASN'T looking forward to back-to-back shifts at GiddyUp, but I conceded it sounded better than sitting in front of the TV bawling over *The Notebook* and ruminating over my looming eviction.

I was getting used to the sensation of feeling as if the top layer of my skin had been removed. I felt raw and exposed, and I couldn't stop my eyes from darting all around. I hadn't seen Trent's betrayal coming, and now I was on high-alert in case something else came out of the shadows to pounce on me.

I hated this scared, suspicious version of myself—it reminded me of my younger self when I trusted no one. When I'd married Trent I'd finally lowered my guard and relaxed. What a fool I'd been.

When I got to the GiddyUp, I was surprised to see a crowded parking lot, even for a Friday evening. I reasoned the good weather had turned everyone's thoughts toward partying for the weekend, sending them flocking for beer and condoms. But once again I welcomed a busy shift—I wouldn't have the chance to ruminate on how and when my marriage had gone south, and how long it would take to dig myself out of financial ruin.

I walked through the parking lot and past the dumpster to the rear entrance. Along the way I passed a local TV news van. My heart sank—the store had been robbed. On the heels of thinking Ramy didn't need any more grief came the horrifying realization that someone might've been injured—or worse. Why else would a news crew be here?

I jabbed the door buzzer, and after a few seconds of silence, stabbed it repeatedly, now panicked. Finally the door swung open and Shawna stood there, her eyes wide and her cheeks shiny. "You're missing out on all the excitement!"

I stumbled through the door. "Was the store robbed? Is everyone okay?"

She frowned. "What? No, the store wasn't robbed."

"Then why is the news crew here?"

"You haven't heard?"

"Obviously not," I said, tamping down my frustration. "What happened?"

"Someone won last night's Mega Dollars lottery, and they bought the ticket here!"

I grinned. "Really? That's cool. Who is it?"

"They haven't come forward yet."

My mind spooled over the batch of regular customers who came in with their lists of lucky numbers made up of happy dates of anniversaries, and loved one's birthdays and ages. I smiled when I thought of one of them claiming the prize, victorious that their elaborate system had finally worked. "I hope whoever it is deserves it."

"Me too. When I first heard the ticket was sold here, I was hoping the ticket was mine." Shawna sighed. "But I only matched one number, not even enough for a free play. Which means, I'd better get back to work."

"I'll be right there," I said. "After I stop by the restroom."

"Okey-doke."

I went into the cramped bathroom, closed the door. and hung my purse on a hook. At least it would be an interesting few days. I hoped the publicity would bring in more traffic—Ramy could use the business. And it was a shame Shawna hadn't won—the woman could certainly use the cash.

But then who couldn't?

A memory slipped into my brain—the ticket I'd had to buy the day before after messing up Mrs. Conway's numbers. On a whim, I rummaged through my purse and pulled out the rumpled square of gold-colored paper. I pulled out my phone and looked up the winning numbers for the Mega Dollars lottery: 4, 9, 28, 46, 59, and the bonus ball was 70.

I smoothed out the ticket, then looked back and forth: 4... 9... 28... 46... 59... and the bonus ball was... 70.

I went stock still as my brain tried to process what my eyes were seeing.

My ticket was a match? That wasn't possible... was it?

Unless there was some kind of glitch, and thousands of winning tickets had been printed. I held my breath while I looked back to my phone and clicked on the link that promised more details.

One winning ticket, sold in Atlanta, Georgia.

A hum of disbelief and shock began to course through my body, even more so when my eyes latched onto the amount of the winning jackpot.

Fifty-two… million… dollars.

I covered my mouth with my shaking hand.

Holy. Cow.

AUGUST

August 1, Saturday

WHAT TO Do If You Win the Lottery.

I stared at the blurry list of text, then wiped the screen of my phone. When the words still refused to come into focus, I realized my lack of sleep was catching up to me. But in the hours since I realized I was in possession of the winning Mega Dollars Lottery ticket, worth—I can barely *think* the words—fifty-two *million* dollars, sleep had been pretty much impossible.

After throwing up in the bathroom at the GiddyUp GoMart, I'd escaped by the rear door. When I'd boarded the train back to my apartment and gathered myself enough to think, I'd texted my coworker Shawna that I was feeling sick and had to leave suddenly. She'd texted back too bad, I was missing all the excitement of having a news crew there and everyone hoping the buyer of the winning ticket would show up at the place where it had been sold, but feel better.

I was so numb I'd missed my train stop and had ridden south to the airport before being jarred from my reverie. I was alternately euphoric and terrified, and I'd chewed my fingernails down to the quick. When I'd left the train I'd jogged to the apartment, feeling as if people were staring at me… following me. Was it written on my face?

I, Mallory Green, a bad-luck nobody, am an unexpected millionaire!

When I'd finally arrived at the apartment and fumbled my way inside, I'd sank to the floor in a heap. Poor Nessie, my husband's—er, make that my *estranged* husband's—French bulldog lay down near me and watched between her paws, as if she knew I was on the brink of coming undone.

Hours later, I was still lying on the floor, weak from adrenaline overload and unable to move. Nessie had succumbed, however, and lay on her side snoring. Filtered sunlight came in through a crack in the curtains.

I decided I was probably dehydrated, so I rolled over and slowly pushed to my feet. Every muscle in my body ached, as if I'd been tensed up for a long, long time...

Although hadn't I been?

Hadn't I been tense for weeks—no, *months*—even before Trent had walked out?

I made my way to the kitchen on rubbery legs, then filled a glass from the faucet. The tepid water tasted of chlorine and mineral deposits, but it was wet and what I needed. I drank it down, then another, then lowered myself to a chair to scan the article I'd pulled up on my phone.

Sign your ticket.

I backtracked to retrieve the rumpled square ticket from my purse and once again checked the printed digits against the winning numbers just in case I'd hallucinated the entire thing. But the numbers were still a match. With a shaking hand I turned over the ticket, then printed and signed my name with a blue ink pen. Then I positioned it on the kitchen counter with lots of space around it.

Find out if your state allows you to remain anonymous, and decide if you want to.

Georgia, I discovered, was not a state that allowed winners to remain anonymous, so that was a decision I wouldn't have to make.

Don't tell anyone you're a winner except trusted family and friends.

That one was easy—I had no trusted family or friends. Our social circle existed of Trent's friends and their girlfriends and wives. More than once he'd disdainfully announced I didn't trust people. I couldn't argue his point. I'd lived in more than twenty-five foster homes before the age of twelve—I couldn't afford to form attachments. But had my wariness kept people—including him—at arm's length?

I fantasized about calling Trent to tell him the remarkable news. So many of our problems had arisen from financial stress and his search for a fulfilling vocation where he could make the money he thought he deserved. If those obstacles were removed, maybe we could rediscover the love we'd shared when we were first married and the world had seemed full of possibilities. The thought of spending the money with Trent on amazing adventures seemed exponentially more fun than the thought of doing it alone.

And some part of me reveled in the notion of having something to offer him that even Magnificent Mikala Morgan couldn't.

Shot through with anticipation, I pulled up Trent's number, but at the sight of his picture stored in my contacts file, my finger halted and my heart squeezed in anguish. No... as much as I loved him, I knew it had to be his idea to come back. And there was still time for him to change his mind. Once the novelty of the affair wore off, he might realize he'd made a big mistake. Couples reconciled all the time, and were better than before. I imagined him coming back and begging for my forgiveness, then I would reveal our spectacular windfall. I couldn't help the smile that pulled my mouth wide.

Meanwhile, I recognized the urge to tell someone, and I knew if I reported for my shift at The Community Café, I'd be tempted to tell my coworkers Vance and Kerry because we'd joked about what we would do if we won the lottery. So I texted the owner Doug to say I wouldn't be able to work this weekend because of a family emergency.

Assemble a team of experts to advise you.

I bit into my lip. How could I assemble a team of experts while remaining anonymous? I skimmed the long list of recommended advisors—attorney, tax attorney, estate attorney, accountant, financial manager, therapist...

I stopped—*therapist?*

How unbelievably unnecessary. I couldn't imagine needing a psychoanalyst to help me get used to the idea of being rich.

I grinned and released a pent up squeal of elation that roused Nessie and brought her trotting into the kitchen to see what the fuss was about.

I scooped her up and hugged her tight against her protests. "I'm rich," I whispered to her, almost afraid to say it. "I'm rich," I said again, this time louder. It sounded... *good.* So I spun round and round. "I'm rich! I'm rich! I'm *rich!*"

August 2, Sunday

I SLEPT for thirteen hours in the bed I hadn't been able to sleep in since Trent had left. When I opened my eyes, it was two whole seconds before I remembered my wonderful secret. I grinned and stretched tall, then rolled over to take in the empty pillow and space on the bed next to me. I hadn't changed the sheets, so the pillow was still indented from Trent's head and still scented with the patchouli shampoo he liked. I reached over to stroke the pillowcase and my heart squeezed painfully. This was why I'd avoided sleeping in our bed—I didn't want to face the fact that my husband was sleeping elsewhere.

Before my mind could wander too far down that road I climbed out and pulled on enough clothes to be presentable if I ran in to anyone while walking Nessie.

When I walked into the kitchen, I smiled and patted the lottery ticket on the counter, then my nose wrinkled at the odor. I pulled out the trash can and held my breath against the stink as I went around the kitchen and gathered up smelly food containers and remnants of meals that pre-dated Trent moving out.

I'd really let things go.

With the bag of garbage in hand, I called to Nessie and fastened her leash to her collar. The table next to the door was accumulating more ominous looking bill notices, but I cheerfully ignored them.

My money problems were *over*.

Out in the hallway I glanced toward Josh English's closed door. I hadn't seen him since the day I'd come home to see the eviction notice on my door and to my shame, he'd seen it too.

I wondered what someone like Josh would think of my surprise windfall—probably not much, which kind of rankled me. What did I care what he thought?

I smiled when I realized that not only could I pay my back rent, but I could probably buy the entire apartment building if I wanted to.

On that thought, I practically skipped to the dumpster where I tossed the white plastic garbage bag on the heap of others awaiting collection. I hummed as Nessie sniffed the grass and did her business.

The sun was warm and fuzzy in the early morning haze. Since I wasn't going in to work at the restaurant, I had an entire day to do anything I wanted... as long as it didn't cost anything. Until I got my millions, I'd be pinching pennies. The thought blipped through my mind that it would be a fun day to be out on the lake, followed by the thought that I could now buy a yacht if I wanted—or even a house on the lake.

Or both.

I was starting to warm up to the idea of being a millionaire. I was still smiling when I walked back into the apartment. When my stomach growled, I went in search of breakfast food. I found two eggs and a container of cheese that hadn't yet begun to mold and set about making a simple meal.

Out of the corner of my eye, though, something seemed out of place. When I turned my head, I froze.

The lottery ticket was gone.

I dropped the egg I was holding, distantly registering its splatter on the tile floor.

My heart raced around in my chest as I searched the kitchen counter, patting and moving small appliances. I scanned the floor and every adjacent surface, including the refrigerator, but no luck.

Okay, that was a bad choice of words.

My mind galloped through how the ticket could've disappeared—no one had been in the apartment except me and Nessie, and the only things that had gone out were the two of us.

And the garbage.

I mentally retraced my movements gathering trash around the kitchen—I must've accidentally scooped up the ticket and tossed it out!

I sprinted out the door, down the hallway and out to the dumpster as fast as my feet would carry me. When I reached the large metal box, I realized that not only had the heap of garbage bags grown exponentially, but they all pretty much looked the same.

Fighting a groan, I reached over the wall of the chest-high metal bin and began to lift and inspect each bag of trash, most of them slick with unknown grossness. The stench was horrific. I pulled the neck of my T-shirt up to cover my mouth and nose, to little avail. My hopes of finding my bag dwindled quickly as I realized I'd lost track of which bags I'd already picked through. I started over, removing bags and reinspecting them before dropping them on the ground. Before long I had a pile of bags at my feet and could no longer reach the bags left in the dumpster. After weighing my options, I grimaced, then boosted myself up to climb over the edge of the bin and drop down inside. Instantly my tennis shoes were soaked in black smelly juice. I gagged and fought back nausea as I turned my attention to the remaining heap of bags. As I came to realize I might've already overlooked the bag and would have to go back through everything, I broke out in a flop sweat of panic.

"Mallory?"

I winced at the sound of Josh's voice, then slowly turned around to see him standing there, holding his own bag of garbage. "Hi."

He scratched his head, looking amused. "Did you lose something?"

I bit into my lip to fight back sudden tears, then nodded.

He sobered. "Hey... I'll help you. What is it?"

"It's... a piece of paper I accidentally threw away."

"Okay," he soothed as he walked to the side of the dumpster. "You can't replace it?"

I shook my head.

"Is it valuable?"

I worked my mouth back and forth. "It's... a lottery ticket."

His eyebrows climbed. "Really? It must be a winner."

I nodded again, feeling bleak.

"How much it is worth?"

"Fifty-two... dollars." I instantly felt ridiculous—he'd think I was hard up if I'd dig in the trash for fifty dollars.

Then again, he'd seen me at some of my most humiliating times... what was one more?

He pursed his mouth and nodded. "Then let's find it." He heaved himself up over the edge and into the dumpster with surprising athletic ease, and didn't flinch when his running shoes sank into the filth-juice standing at the bottom of the rancid bin. "What color is the bag?"

"Wh-white, with a red tie."

"Okay, that narrows it down a little. Do you remember if there was something in your bag that we could see through the plastic, maybe a box of cereal or something big?"

His relaxed confidence calmed me down. "A pizza box," I recalled. "From Gino's."

"That should be easy to find." He lifted a bag at his feet, then scrutinized it and patted it all over. "Ack, there's a diaper—I assume that one's not yours."

I couldn't contain the laugh. "No." Then I resumed the search.

And sure enough, within a few minutes, he held up a bag with a Gino's pizza box plainly showing through the thin plastic.

"That's it!" I cried. I tore open the bag and dug through the icky contents, humiliated all over again that he could see my trash up close and personal. When I saw the little square of gold-colored paper, I squealed in triumph and held it up. "I found it!"

Josh grinned. "Toldja."

I impulsively stepped forward and hugged him, then realized I smelled to high heaven. Actually, we both did. When I stepped back, he seemed surprised and pleased.

"Let me help you out."

Before I could object, he crouched and picked me up, cross-the-threshold style, then lifted me over the edge and set me down. By the time he heaved himself up and over, I had regained my composure, but was struck by the awkward intimacy of the moment.

"You don't have to help me put these back," I said, gesturing to the mound of bags sitting beside the dumpster.

"I'll put them all back," he said, making a shooing motion. "Go clean up your winning ticket... and I'm sure you want to take a shower."

I made a face, then nodded. "Thanks... Josh."

"No problem. I'll see you later."

He said it as a statement, not a question. I escaped, but held my breath until I'd closed the door to my apartment. I stared at the ticket, soiled but intact. Then I exhaled in abject relief.

August 3, Monday

WHEN I walked into the Noble Plaza building, my vitals signs were higher than I could attribute to the dash in the rain from the Marta bus stop. When I lowered my broken umbrella, I smiled to myself—I could definitely afford a new one now.

"What are you doing here?"

I looked up to see my former boss Amelia Inez standing near the reception desk frowning at me over the top of her glasses. "I hope you didn't come to ask for your job back."

I squashed the urge to whip out my winning lottery ticket, and smiled at the woman. I could afford to be gracious. "No. I'm here to see Ryan Livingston."

The young woman who had taken over my job appeared flustered as she consulted the company directory.

"He's on the fifteenth floor," I offered.

Amelia looked suspicious. "Is Mr. Livingston expecting you?"

"No, but I think he'll see me." I'd decided it was better to ask for his help in person than to try to explain my um, *situation*, over the phone.

The woman sniffed as if she didn't agree.

The girl who had taken my place had found the number. "What's your name?"

"Mallory Green," I supplied. "Please tell Mr. Livingston I'm here on business."

Amelia waited and watched, fully expecting, I'm sure, for Ryan to rebuff me.

My replacement relayed my message, then set down the receiver. "His assistant said you could come right up."

"Thank you." I gave Amelia a pointed look before heading to the elevator. Despite my bravado, my hand was sweaty as I punched the button for my destination. I had worn my nicest outfit and I had a ticket in my purse worth a fortune, but I still felt unworthy when I alighted into the posh lobby of Livingston Wealth Management. My shoes were a little soggy from the walk in the rain and my hair had looked better.

An attractive salt-and-pepper haired woman greeted me with a warm smile. "Ms. Green?"

"Mallory," I said.

"Mallory, I'm Janelle, Mr. Livingston's assistant. Can I get you something to drink? Coffee or tea, perhaps?"

I swallowed past my dry throat and realized I could use some lubrication. "Water would be nice, thank you."

She smiled. "Right this way."

My nerves spiked as she led me past a row of offices inhabited by suited people whom I presumed were support staff or junior partners. Following the advice I'd read online, I'd done my due diligence by looking into the firm. Ryan Livingston was a home-grown Georgia boy who had played basketball for Georgia Tech and now managed the estates of many local professional athletes.

And hopefully he'd agree to help me.

"Here we are," Janelle said, gesturing to a corner office consisting mostly of glass.

Ryan sat at his desk talking on the phone. Janelle rapped lightly on his door and he beckoned us in, then ended his phone call with a jovial sign-off to whoever was on the other end of the line.

I was bowled over anew by his good looks and impeccable grooming. The man could wear a suit. I guessed he was in his mid-thirties, and it struck me that for someone who wasn't much older than me, he had his life so much more together. Everything about the man and his contemporary office spoke of wealth, although I supposed that was the point.

"Mallory," he said, coming from around his desk. "This is a surprise."

"I'm sorry I didn't make an appointment."

"No worries at all," he said, although I could tell from his voice he was curious—or maybe skeptical—that I would need his services. He had, after all, witnessed my firing at the hand of Amelia Inez. He gestured for me to sit, so I did, clasping my cross-body purse with a death grip. After yesterday's dumpster scare, I'd put the ticket inside a plastic baggie, placed it inside the purse, and slept with it strapped to my body.

"How can I help you?" he asked.

Now that the moment was at hand, I felt light-headed. I wet my dry lips. "Have you heard that someone local won the Mega Dollars Lottery?"

He pursed his mouth, then began to nod. "I think I did hear something about that." Then he stopped and his eyes widened. "Wait—was it you?"

I swallowed hard and nodded, then fished the stained, splotchy ticket from my bag and slid it across his desk.

His mouth rounded into an O as he scrutinized the ticket. "How much was the jackpot?"

"F-Fifty-two... million."

He appeared dazed, then he laughed out loud. "No kidding?"

I smiled, feeling immense relief to finally have told someone. My tight shoulders fell. "No kidding. Will you help me?"

I watched emotions play over his face—wonder, pleasure, awe. It made me feel as if I could finally express the same sentiments. He laughed, I laughed, we both laughed.

Janelle returned with a glass of water containing lemon slices.

"Never mind that," Ryan said dismissively, then opened a cabinet behind him to reveal a refrigerator. From it he withdrew a frosty bottle and two flutes. "We're having champagne!"

August 4, Tuesday

I WON'T be able to make it in today, so sorry, I texted to my boss Ramy at the GiddyUp GoMart.

Still sick? he texted back.

I pushed down guilt for avoiding him and my coworker Shawna, and sidestepped the question. *I'll try to come in tomorrow.*

Okay, feel better.

"Hi."

I lifted my head from my phone to see Josh coming back from a run. The sun was already blistering, and his clothes were soaked through. Had his shoulders always been so wide? "Hi," I said, stowing my phone.

"You look nice," he said, nodding to my skirt and sandals.

"Thanks," I murmured, thinking anything was better than my dumpster-diving togs. "How was your run?"

"It was good." Then he grinned. "But I'm always glad when it's over."

"Are you training for an event?"

He nodded. "The Shepherd Center is having a charity 10K in a couple of months." He angled his head. "I could use a training partner if you'd like to sign up."

My cheeks warmed. "I couldn't... I haven't worked out in ages."

"Couldn't tell from looking at you," he said, surveying my figure. "But it's a good excuse to get back in the habit. Let me know if you change your mind."

I decided not to respond... I wasn't comfortable with the thought of spending so much time together.

He gestured to the turnaround where I stood on the curb. "Are you waiting for a ride?"

"Yes... a, um, coworker is picking me up."

"From Noble Plaza?"

"Um... that's right."

On cue, a black convertible Porsche pulled into the turnaround. From behind the steering wheel Ryan lifted his hand, then pulled to a stop next to me. While I stared stupefied at the car, Ryan hopped out and came around to open the passenger door for me, smiling wide. He was dressed like a billboard for a men's clothing store. "Ready for a fun day?"

I nodded dumbly, then slid into the sumptuous tan leather seat. I had barely put on my seatbelt when he was back behind the wheel and goosing the gas. As we pulled away, I glanced in the side mirror to see Josh staring after us.

"Saying today will be fun might be a bit of a stretch," Ryan admitted as he pulled into traffic. "But Aaron Hoover is the best tax attorney in the city, and he has experience with lottery payouts." Ryan grinned. "Aren't you eager to find out just how much money you'll wind up with?"

I smiled and nodded.

"I assume that wasn't your husband back there?" he asked.

I wanted to kick Wanda Sandoval for blabbing to Ryan that Trent had left me. "Oh... no, that was a neighbor... friend."

He nodded. "You and your husband... you're still living apart?"

I looked straight ahead. "Yes."

"Have you told him about the ticket?'

"No."

"Good. Don't," he said, then gunned the engine to change lanes.

Aaron Hoover was a spectacled, angular man. His office was text-book TV-lawyer with lots of mahogany and stiff furniture. He wasted no time launching into the logistics of how the money would be dispensed.

"With your prior permission, I contacted the lottery office to let them know a winner would be coming forth to claim the fifty-two-million-dollar jackpot, although I didn't mention your name. I do suggest you claim one lump sum instead of annual payouts. The lump sum is usually about sixty percent of the advertised jackpot, but if you invest the money wisely, you'll be way ahead in the long run."

Ryan gave me a bolstering smile, and I nodded. "Okay... so that's how much?"

"Just over thirty-one million," Ryan said.

Mr. Hoover leaned forward. "You'll receive one million approximately two weeks after you validate the ticket and claim your prize, then the remainder of the money will arrive between six and eight weeks later once the money is collected from the various state lotteries that participate in the Mega Dollars game."

"That sounds... wonderful," I murmured, at a loss for appropriate words.

"Now for the less wonderful part," the man said with a bland smile. "The lottery will withhold federal income tax of twenty-four percent and state income tax of six percent, but frankly, it's still not enough. This money will put you in the highest federal tax bracket. Tack the state tax on top of that, and my guess is you're looking at closer to forty-four percent in taxes."

"About fourteen million," Ryan clarified. "Which still leaves you over seventeen million to live on and to invest."

Fifty-two million down to seventeen million was a steep drop, but still enough for many lifetimes, especially considering last week I'd been fishing coins out of the furniture cushions. "Okay."

Aaron Hoover eyed me with something akin to concern. "Ms. Green... your life is about to change drastically."

"I realize that," I murmured.

"I'm not sure you do," he said, steepling his hands. "Most lottery winners don't fare as well as people might think. I hope you have a strong support system."

I smiled and kept nodding, even as I was panicking a little inside.

August 5, Wednesday

"I'M GLAD you're feeling better," Shawna said. "It's more fun to work with you than to work with Ramy."

Ramy turned his head from where he was emptying the coins from the aged video game in the corner. "I'm standing right here."

"Sorry, boss," Shawna said. "But it's the truth."

Mr. Hoover and Ryan both had stressed in order to keep a lid on the fact that I was about to be stunningly wealthy, it was best if I tried to act as if everything was normal, which included heading back to the GiddyUp, especially since everyone there was on high alert for a winner.

But I was a nervous wreck. I'd put my engagement and wedding rings back on, both to keep anyone from asking questions and as a sign to the universe that I was open to rebuilding my marriage. But I'd developed a habit of obsessively spinning them on my finger.

Shawna leaned on the counter. "Do you think the person who bought the winning ticket is gonna come forward?"

I opened my mouth. "I, uh—"

"Sure," Ramy cut in. "Take my word, whoever it is, they're biding their time."

I clamped my mouth shut.

Shawna cocked one hip. "What if they're out there and they don't even know they won? Or what if they died, and that winning ticket is sitting in a drawer somewhere?" Then she sprang up. "Or what if they lost it? Can you imagine?"

"No," I croaked.

She made a rueful noise. "Too bad you don't get a cut for selling the winning ticket, Ramy."

"Yeah, too bad," he agreed. "Still, it's been good for business."

Shawna gave me a dubious look, but said nothing. Business was not booming.

My phone buzzed, and when I saw Trent's mother's name on the screen, my pulse bumped higher. "Is it okay if I take this?" I asked Ramy, pointing to my phone.

He gave a go-ahead wave, so I scooted to the back room to take the call in private. "Hello, Alicia."

"Hi, Mallory, dear, how are you?"

I couldn't tell from her voice if she knew Trent had moved out. Alicia and I had never been particularly close, but she seemed to tolerate me well enough. The fact that Trent's parents lived six states away prevented too much togetherness, which Trent seemed to prefer, although secretly I'd hoped for a mother-daughter relationship to fill that void in my life.

"I'm fine," I hedged. "How are you?"

"Things are fine here, but I just realized I missed your and Trent's anniversary last week. I'm so sorry."

"That's okay," I said lightly. "Thank you for remembering."

"Did you two do something fun?"

"Well—"

"Of course you did," she said with a laugh. "You and Trent are such lovebirds."

So she didn't know. "He can be very romantic," I said vaguely. I didn't add "with someone else."

"How is his new sales job going?"

I gripped the phone harder. "You know Trent, he's good at everything."

"I know," she crooned. "He must be working long hours— I've left him a handful of messages and he has yet to call me back. Mallory, will you tell him to call his mother sometime?"

"Of course."

"Bye for now. I love you both."

"I—"

But she'd already hung up. I ended the call, but felt the stirrings of hope in my chest. If Trent was determined to end our marriage, why hadn't he told his parents?

Because deep down, he still loved me? Since I hadn't yet heard from his attorney as he'd threatened the last time we'd talked, it was a possibility.

I hated the way my heart kept swinging back and forth like a pendulum, but I was starting to feel very alone in my imminent wealth.

August 6, Thursday

THE NEXT morning I was still lying in my half-empty bed in a dream-fog when my phone buzzed with a text. When I saw it was from Trent, I was instantly awake.

Hi, Mal... hope you are okay. Was wondering if you could meet me this morning to talk.

My heart bounced up. He sounded affectionate, like the old Trent, the man I'd married.

I typed *Okay... how about the coffee shop on 6ᵗʰ? 8:30?* Then I backed up and typed *10:30.* I didn't want to appear too eager.

OK. See you then.

I jumped out of bed, already anticipating what to wear. I took Nessie for a walk, then nuzzled her flat mug. "Your daddy might come home... won't that be nice? Then we'll all live happily ever after."

I planned my outfit, then plugged in the iron and stepped into the shower, humming a happy song. But a few seconds into lathering up to shave my legs, the power went out. I stood in the dark for a few seconds, waiting for it to flicker on again. When it didn't, I rinsed myself and stepped out, wrapped in a towel. My mind was swirling and suddenly I remembered the past due electric bills and ominous warnings. I walked to the door and opened it enough to peek out to see if the lights were on in the hallway. They were, meaning only my apartment was affected.

Across the hall, Josh stepped out and saw me. "Hi, Mallory." Then he must've noticed my hair was wet and I was practically naked. "Everything okay?"

I jerked back and closed the door. The man had the worst timing.

I made a call to the electric company and sure enough, the service had been disconnected for lack of payment. The customer service representative offered to take a payment over the phone, but none of my credit cards could withstand the amount and when I checked our joint checking account, it was overdrawn.

How ironic that until my millions were paid out, I was utterly broke.

I ended the call and found a flashlight to get dressed by, but I wasn't able to iron my clothes or blow out my hair. It had dried by the time I left to walk to the coffee shop, but I felt plain and ungroomed when I walked in—not the way a woman wants to look after she's seen her husband's gorgeous girlfriend.

From the corner of the coffee shop, Trent lifted his hand. He looked so good to me, it took my breath away. I missed him desperately. I tried to act calm as I made my way to the table, but my nerves were jumping like live wires.

He gave me a little smile, which buoyed my hopes. Then he angled his head. "Did you change your hair?"

"Yes," I murmured. I didn't want to start the conversation by talking about financial problems.

"I was surprised you could get away from your job," he said when I sat down.

I realized he didn't know I'd been fired from my receptionist job. "I had some vacation coming to me."

"I got you coffee," he said, pushing a cup toward me.

I smiled—he was being nice. He did want to reconcile. "Thank you." I took a drink of the coffee and tried not to wince at the bitter taste. After all this time, he still didn't know I liked cream and sugar.

"How's Nessie?"

"She's fine. She… misses you."

His mouth flattened. "She'll get over it."

I realized in a flash he hadn't come with reconciliation on his mind. My gaze bounced to his left hand—he wasn't wearing his wedding ring. And since he didn't even have a tan line, I assumed he'd been taking the ski boat out a lot.

At the same time, he glanced at my hand to see I was wearing his rings.

From beneath the table he produced a set of papers with the title Civil Action, Trent Douglas Green vs. Mallory Ann Green.

My heart shattered. I spelled my middle name with an 'e' on the end. Did he really know so little about me?

"I found out we don't have to use an attorney if we both agree how our assets and debt will be split," he said happily. "The dissolution language is simple, and I came up with a spreadsheet of how our assets and debts should be allocated. This will save us a lot of money, Mal."

I looked at the paper, but the figures were blurry through my tears.

"I'll take the boat and the payments—it's already registered in my name anyway. And I'll take my car, of course."

And I would take my car… which was still sitting in a mechanic's parking lot, undrivable.

"And I'll take my student debt," he said magnanimously.

Which wasn't that much because my paychecks had funded most of his schooling.

"And you can take the rest of the debt," he said. "I think that's fair considering the medical bills were mostly yours and considering how much you spent on the private investigator, don't you?"

"Sure," I mumbled, thinking it wasn't fair at all, that he was taking debt backed with assets, and at least ten thousand of the medical bills was to pay for pricey crowns to preserve his beautiful smile… but I'd be able to afford it in a few days.

He leveled his expensive smile on me. "Good. So just sign here, and here, and I'll file the papers with the court. You don't even have to appear on the day the judge signs the decree."

I swallowed hard, then finally found my voice. "Don't these papers have to be notarized?"

He gestured to an attractive young woman sitting a couple of tables away. "Tanvi is a friend of mine and a notary public. She can notarize the papers right here."

The woman came over and offered me a small smile. She looked vaguely familiar and suddenly I realized why—she was all over the social media of Mikala "Mike" Morgan. One of her besties.

And yes, I confess I'd been trolling my husband's girlfriend's online life.

"How… efficient," I managed to get out. He'd thought of everything. I took the pen Trent offered me, then signed in both places. Tanvi whipped out her notary stamp and signed her name.

"All done," Trent said, sounding victorious.

"I'd like a copy," I whispered.

From his soft-side leather briefcase—a new acquisition—he removed a compact document scanner. He powered it up, fed in the five-page document, then hit a button. "I just emailed you a copy. And I'll send you a copy of the final decree."

He started to gather his things. "Thanks, Mal."

Thanks? Thanks for loving him and supporting him while he tried to find himself, only for him to find it with another woman and leave me with most of our five-year debt? My mouth stung with bitter words, but the knowledge of what I had waiting for me kept me calm. I was glad he was out of my life.

I pushed to my feet. "You should call your mother," I said, then turned and strode away. Near the door was a metal bin for Goodwill donations. I stopped, removed my rings, then pulled out the drawer and dropped them down the chute.

Then I walked out into the sunshine.

August 7, Friday

WHEN RYAN picked me up the following day, I tried not to feel self-conscious in my rumpled clothing and damp hair.

"Are you okay?" he asked after I'd climbed in.

I shifted against the expensive leather. "Will I be able to claim my money soon?"

"That's why we're meeting with a public relations firm, so we can get our ducks in a row."

"Okay," I murmured, fastening my seat belt.

"I can tell something's wrong," Ryan said. "Please tell me."

My cheeks flamed. "My power was cut off."

He frowned. "Why?"

I bit into my lip, mortified. "Because... I can't pay the bill." I averted my gaze from his stare. "I lost my job at Noble, if you recall, and although I have two other part-time jobs, I was already in debt. My car is in the repair shop and... I'm about to be evicted from my apartment." When I chanced a glance back to his face, I expected to see disgust or pity. Instead he seemed... impressed?

"Mallory, why didn't you say so? I'll be happy to float you whatever you need."

"I... don't want you to do that."

He gave a little laugh. "You're good for it. In fact, I'll have the bank set up a line of credit for you to draw on."

"They'll do that?"

"Of course. I'll have it taken care of by the end of the day."

It felt so nice to have someone looking out for me, I felt teary. "Thank you."

He winked. "You're welcome. And I have some good news—I talked to a family law attorney. She said the fact that your husband announced he wanted a divorce and moved out before you bought the ticket makes it unlikely he'll have a claim to the winnings. It also helps that he's already filed for divorce."

I recognized it as good news, but I was also still mourning my marriage. "Trent already filed the papers we signed yesterday?"

He nodded, looking apologetic. Then he reached across the console and squeezed my hand. "Are you okay?"

I nodded. I would be, in time. Ryan's fingers were warm and more than comforting. I missed them when he pulled away to shift gears. He pointed the car north, toward the upscale business area of Buckhead.

"I still don't understand why I need a public relations manager," I said.

"Deena works with the lottery office to help liaise with winners to make sure things go smoothly the day of the announcement."

He drove us to a swank office building and handed his car off to a valet. "I feel underdressed," I murmured, smoothing a hand over my simple navy jersey dress, looking worse for the lack of an iron.

"You look fine," he assured me. "But I have a feeling Deena will want you to use some of the line of credit for an outfit for the TV cameras the day you claim your prize."

Indeed, the woman was tall and immaculately dressed, her hair and nails and makeup so perfectly perfect, she scared me a little.

"Here's the plan I've come up with," she said, passing out a multi-page document with bullet points and timelines. "I'm thinking we'll announce a week from Monday, on the seventeenth.

The lottery office will want to do a professional photo shoot and a short press junket through all the states in the Mega Dollars Lottery."

I blinked. "Press junket?"

Deena gave a little wave. "Fun stuff, holding up a giant check, telling your story." She angled her head. "Where did you buy the ticket?"

"I... sometimes work at the GiddyUp GoMart on Piedmont. I bought a ticket there."

The woman's eyes lit up. "You're a cashier?"

My cheeks warmed. "And a waitress."

"Wonderful," Deena said, using a stylus to make notes on a digital tablet. "So you make, what—minimum wage?"

I nodded.

"Super. Do you have any other jobs?"

"I was, um, let go from my job as a receptionist the day before I bought the ticket."

"Amazing—we can use that. And where did you grow up?"

"All over Georgia."

"Good—people love it when the winner is home-grown. Are you married?"

When I hesitated, Ryan said, "Mallory is newly single."

"That won't last long," she said with a dry laugh. "And where is your family?"

I swallowed hard. "I... don't really have any family. I... grew up in the foster care system."

Deena gaped. "I couldn't have made up a story this good. People will eat it up."

While I squirmed, Ryan angled his head, as if he were seeing me in a new light. I didn't want his pity.

"So no brothers or sisters?" she asked.

"Right," I confirmed.

"And your parents are deceased?"

I wavered. I didn't want to broadcast the fact that my long-lost father was in prison. It didn't matter—even if he saw me, he wouldn't recognize me, and I'd had a string of surnames since I'd had his. "I lost them when I was very young," I said, purposely being vague.

"Fantastic," Deena said, still writing. "The media *loves* an orphan."

Ryan coughed and made wry eye contact with me. I smiled and he smiled back. The shared moment seemed almost... intimate.

August 8, Saturday

WITH A directive to maintain my normal schedule until we dropped the money bomb, I reported to my waitressing shift at The Community Café. Thank goodness my power had been restored. I'd used some of the amazing one-hundred-thousand-dollar credit line the bank had extended to pay some other bills, including my back rent, and I'd splurged on a new pair of comfy shoes for standing on my feet all day.

"There you are," my coworker Vance said when I walked in.

"We were starting to think you'd run away," Kerry accused, tying on an apron.

"No," I said lightly. "I was just feeling under the weather."

"Well, I hope you didn't have to use our horrible health insurance," Vance said.

"Hey," Doug, the owner, shouted from the kitchen. "I heard that!"

"Then do something about it, why don't you?" Kerry shouted back.

Doug's face screwed up. "You're all lucky you even have a job."

Vance looked back to us. "He actually used the word 'lucky.'"

Kerry scoffed. "If we were lucky we would've cashed that winning Mega Dollars Lottery ticket last week. Did you hear there was one winner in Atlanta, and they got fifty-two million?"

I blanched.

Vance groaned. "Do you know what I could do with money like that?"

"The winner doesn't get the whole fifty-two million," I offered. "With taxes and stuff, it's a lot less than that."

Kerry squinted at me. "So? It's a lot more than any of us are pulling down."

"Right," I agreed. "I'm just saying."

"Besides," Kerry said, frowning at both of us, "since neither one of you bought tickets the Sunday I was gone, we didn't even have a chance to win it."

"Mallory bought them," Vance said.

I shook my head. "No, I didn't."

He frowned. "You said you were going to."

"No, I didn't."

"Sure you did, else I would've taken up the money."

"You're both losers," Kerry said, then put out her hand. "Meanwhile, I covered for you last Sunday, so pay up. And pay me for this week, too."

I squirmed. "I don't have any cash on me. I'll have to pay you out of my tips."

"Then you'd better get to work!" Doug bellowed from the kitchen.

August 9, Sunday

"MALLORY, ORDER up!"

I scrambled to the counter to gather my order onto a tray. I scanned the faces of my harried boss and the sweaty kitchen workers, and I felt like a fraud. Soon I would never have to work again, while all these people would still be struggling.

"Is there a problem?" Doug asked with a frown.

"No."

"Then get moving!"

I hurried to deliver the order to the table where my favorite customers were seated. I offered smiles to Hannah and Chance, the mismatched couple who were delightfully in love. "Here we are," I said, transferring the plated food. Hannah's stomach seemed to have grown in the two weeks since I'd last seen her.

"It all looks terrific," she said, smiling up at me. Then she turned in her seat to take in all the empty tables. "This place should be packed. The food here is great."

"Thanks," I murmured. "Please tell all your friends."

"I just might do that," she said in a way that made me think she had thousands of friends and could, indeed, pack the restaurant. I studied her face—maybe she was a food reviewer?

"Let me know if I can get you anything else," I said to the couple.

"Oh, Mallory," Hannah said.

I turned back. "Yes?"

"Did you ever use that wishbone?"

I smiled. "I did, actually."

She beamed. "And did your wish come true?"

I thought back to when I'd shared the wishbone with the superstitious Mrs. Conroy at the GiddyUp GoMart just before she'd bought lottery tickets. I'd wished for a different life, then I'd gotten the bigger piece of the wishbone.

"Not yet," I said with a private little grin, "but it's about to."

August 10, Monday

"WOULD YOU like to buy a lottery ticket?" I asked the guy who'd come in to pay for ten dollars worth of gas.

"Sure," he said with a shrug. "Which game would you recommend?"

I pointed to the rainbow-colored hand-lettered sign Ramy had made that read, "The $52M winning ticket for the Mega Dollars Lottery was sold here!!!"

He nodded. "Sure—give me two quick picks on the next drawing."

I rang up the gas, then the lottery tickets, and wished him luck as he left.

"You're doing a good job of pushing the lotto," Shawna offered from where she was straightening the chips section.

"Every little bit of business helps," I said, although I knew Ramy earned mere pennies for each ticket sold.

She made a rueful noise. "Lightning don't strike twice. Whoever bought that ticket doomed the rest of us who buy our tickets here."

Guilt stabbed me. "I don't think that's true—everyone has the same chance of winning as before."

"Don't seem like it." She sighed noisily. "I can't stop thinking about someone walking in here and buying a ticket worth that much money. I wonder who it could be."

I didn't answer.

"Too bad that camera ain't working," she said, nodding to the camera near the ceiling pointing to no place in particular as a deterrent to would-be robbers. "Else we could look it up on the film."

"Yeah," I agreed. Phew. I'd forgotten all about the camera.

The door opened to admit another customer. I looked up with a smile, then balked when I saw it was Josh.

He offered me a smile. "Hi, Mallory."

"Hello," I murmured.

"How are you?"

"Fine." I flushed, wondering if he was remembering me with my dripping head stuck out into the hallway, wrapped in a towel.

"Did you get your car repaired?"

"Not yet."

He glanced at my ringless hand. "Ah... still getting rides from your coworker?"

He meant Ryan. "Um... yeah."

He nodded, then gestured outside. "Gas on pump three." Then he chose a protein bar from the rack in front of the counter. "And this."

Afraid he would connect the lottery ticket from the dumpster with the colorful announcement on the hand-lettered sign, I awkwardly maneuvered to block it, then gave him his total from a hunch-back position. He handed over cash, and I gave him change, feeling unnerved and dishonest.

"See you around?" he asked.

I managed a smile from my contorted position, and nodded.

When he left, Shawna lit up like a torch. "Who was that cutie-pie?"

"He lives in my apartment building."

"He's interested in you."

I scoffed. "He is not." Was he?

Her phone rang, saving me from her teasing. But when she answered, I knew from the look on her face something was wrong.

A few seconds later she'd ended the call, already walking toward the back room. "I have to go home."

"What happened?"

"Bob collapsed, I'm sure it's his kidneys."

"Did someone call an ambulance?"

Her face crumpled. "Do you know how much an ambulance ride costs? We can't afford it. I'm gonna drive him myself."

I gritted my teeth. "Call an ambulance. I'll pay for it."

She frowned. "I can't let you do that. You take home the same crappy paycheck I do."

"I have some money saved," I fudged. "I want to do it." I pointed to her phone. "Make the call. I promise I'll cover it."

Shawna's expression went from dubious to grateful. "You're an angel, Mal. Thank you."

"Go be with your family."

When Shawna left, I exhaled, then my chest was filled with a light, happy feeling—generosity. I'd never been able to afford to be generous, not where money was concerned. I liked it.

And one week from today I could start making more good things happen.

August 11, Tuesday

THE NEXT evening Shawna was still out looking after her husband, who was recovering in the hospital. I was working alone, a rarity, but manageable since business was moderate.

As usual, lottery sales were brisk since drawings for the Mega Dollars Lottery were Tuesdays and Thursdays, but because the jackpot had recently rolled over (from my win) and was still building slowly, demand hadn't peaked.

Still, our regulars were die-hards when it came to playing their numbers, so I wasn't surprised to see Mrs. Conway, garbed in a shamrock jacket with charms dangling all over, come in with her long list of regular numbers.

"You are my good luck," she said.

I smiled. "I am?"

"Yes. The night we split the wishbone, I won fifty thousand dollars on a ticket I bought here."

I grinned. "You did?"

"Yes. I had five numbers on the Mega Dollars Lottery."

With a start I realized that was right because the ticket I'd rung up incorrectly and bought myself was only one number off from the numbers she'd given me. "That's wonderful, Mrs. Conway."

"Yes." Then she sighed. "But I was so close to winning the big jackpot!"

I pressed my lips together, then smiled. She had no idea. "Still, fifty thousand is a lot of money."

She sighed again. "Not after taxes. And when I add up all I've spent on lottery tickets over the years, I'm still in the hole." Then she brightened. "But someday I might win big!"

"I hope you do," I said, then patiently listened as she recited the numbers from her list and dutifully punched them in.

August 12, Wednesday

IN SHAWNA'S absence, Ramy was filling in, although the man was so lifeless, he wasn't much help with the customers. I could tell his mind was heavily burdened.

"How is Aisha?" I asked.

He shook his head. "Not well. The doctor says she needs rehabilitation at the Shepherd Center, but they don't take our insurance and we can't afford it, unless…"

"Unless what?"

"Unless we get divorced. Then she will qualify for free care."

He looked so despondent, my heart broke for him.

"Aisha doesn't want to, but I'm going to do it. How can I not?" Then he groaned. "But she is so angry with me, she will not eat or sleep."

My husband had thrown away our marriage so casually, and here was a couple who couldn't bear the thought of being divorced even if it meant she stood a better chance at getting well. "I have a friend who works at Shepherd," I murmured. "He can arrange for Aisha to be treated at no cost."

Ramy's eyes lit up. "Really? How?"

"I'll work it out. Meanwhile, make Aisha an appointment."

Ramy grinned and clasped me in a bear hug. "Thank you, Mallory. Thank you. Thank you…"

August 13, Thursday

WHEN JOSH opened the door to his apartment, he seemed surprised to see me standing there. "Hi."

"Hi," I said. "I need a favor."

He crossed his arms and gave me a wry smile. "Do I have to go dumpster diving again?"

That was fair. "No. I have a friend whose wife had a brain tumor removed. Her doctor wants her to be rehabbed at Shepherd, but their insurance won't cover it."

His mouth turned down. "I wish I could help, Mallory, but I don't have that kind of pull."

"I know someone who will cover the cost, but I don't want my friend to know. Can you help me arrange it?"

"Sure, I can talk to the people in billing, but the person should know it's going to be a steep bill, north of six figures."

I nodded. "Okay."

He hesitated. "Does this have anything to do with the guy in the Porsche?"

I wanted to tell Josh the truth, but I'd promised Ryan I wouldn't tell anyone before we made the announcement Monday. "Sort of."

He nodded again. "Okay. Get me your friend's wife's name and I'll make a couple of phone calls."

From my pocket I removed a piece of paper with Aisha's name on it and folded it into his hand. "Thank you."

He held on to my hand for a few seconds. "I'm happy to help."

My fingers tingled from his touch, and I remembered the pressure of his body against mine when I'd given him an impulsive hug in the dumpster. I retrieved my hand, then fled back to my apartment.

August 14, Friday

"RYAN WILL pick you up Monday," Deena Prophet said, then held up a card. "I'll meet you at this address to have your makeup and hair done, then you'll get dressed."

"So I should bring a change of clothes?" I asked.

"I've chosen some items that will look good on camera and portray the image we're going for."

I frowned. "Image?"

She smiled. "Mallory, on Monday when you're revealed as the winner of the Mega Dollars jackpot, everyone will be watching… everyone will want to *be* you, and it's my job to make sure you look back on your special day and feel good about it. Trust me."

I lifted my gaze to Ryan's. He offered me a fortifying wink. Trent's words about me not trusting people came back to me. He was right—I kept people at arm's length, especially people who were trying to help me.

"Okay," I murmured.

"Good," she said. "After you're dressed, you'll arrive at the lottery office to officially validate and claim your prize. There will be photos, you'll receive your giant check, then the press will get a question and answer session."

"What kinds of questions?" I asked.

"Simple stuff, like how you felt when you realized you'd won, what you're going to do with the money, that kind of thing. Don't worry—we'll plant some friendly reporters and give them your fact sheet a few minutes before you go on."

I nodded, although this was starting to sound nerve-wracking.

"Have you ever been on camera before?" she asked.

I shook my head.

She walked to a cabinet, opened it, then pointed. "Ryan, can you put this camera on your shoulder and point it at Mallory? We'll do a dry run."

He seemed amused as he picked up and positioned the camera. When he looked through the eyepiece, he gave me a thumb's up. "You look great, Mallory, so photogenic."

I was sure he was lying, but I warmed under his gaze.

"Smile," he said.

I did, thinking how much I liked the fact that Ryan was looking at me. Desire flared in my stomach.

"That's the smile," Deena said. "Whatever you're thinking right now, that's what I want you to think about Monday when the cameras are on."

August 15, Saturday

"YOU WON!" Kerry shouted when I walked into the restaurant for my shift.

I blinked. "What?"

She grinned. "The lottery—you won!"

My brain was trying to figure out how she could possibly know.

"I mean *we* won," she amended, "but your part is ninety dollars." She held up the cash, then put it in my hands.

"Oh," I said. "Okay."

She frowned. "You don't seem very impressed."

I glanced around to see lots of smiling faces and high fives as employees counted their winnings. "No, it's... great. Really. Thanks. I can use it."

Kerry angled her head. "Are you okay?"

I nodded. "Never better."

Vance came sliding up. "Are we going to do it, Mallory?"

I squinted. "What?"

"Remember, we said if we ever won the lottery, we'd get a makeover."

Kerry laughed. "I believe your exact words were an *epic* makeover."

He smirked. "I don't know if ninety dollars will buy epic, but maybe an hour or two at a spa? What do you say, Mal?"

"Sure," I said, offering him a smile. "We'll do that."

Kerry shook her head. "What's that saying? A fool and their money are soon parted."

While the two of them exchanged verbal jabs, I pondered the wisdom of the adage, then happily dismissed it. It was true I'd never been particularly good with money, yet there was no conceivable way I could run through seventeen million dollars.

It simply wasn't possible.

August 16, Sunday

WHEN I arrived at the restaurant the next day for my last shift, the mood was decidedly less celebratory. I was running late, still tying my apron and rehearsing my "I quit" speech with Doug when I walked into an impromptu all-hands meeting in the kitchen.

"What's going on?" I mouthed to Vance. He shrugged, but he looked grim.

Doug asked for everyone to quiet down, then he heaved a sigh. "I really appreciate how each and every one of you contribute to the restaurant. I know I'm not the easiest boss sometimes."

A murmur of agreement and low laughs sounded.

His smile was fleeting. "The truth is, though, business isn't great and it hasn't been for a long time. Part of that's my fault because I'd rather cook than do marketing. Bottom line—unless a pot of money falls into my lap, the restaurant is closing at the end of the month."

After a few seconds of stunned silence, groans of dismay sounded. I looked around to see expressions ranging from anger to pure panic. A few of the café's employees were undocumented. Many of us worked part-time. Very few would qualify for unemployment.

"I'm sorry," Doug said, sounding like a broken man.

But it planted an idea in my head. I had to keep my mouth shut for now, but in less than twenty-four hours, I would have a pot of money.

August 17, Monday

"AS PRESIDENT of the lottery," the suited man in front of the room said, "I'd like to present this check for fifty-two *million* dollars to Mallory Green!"

Applause sounded in the room, increasing as I neared the platform wearing the surprisingly simple cotton flowered dress Deena had chosen for me. It wasn't my style, but she had assured me it was "camera-ready," ditto for the flattened hairstyle. The audience of about fifty consisted of lottery employees and reporters, all seemingly happy for me. My heart was hammering in my chest so hard, I was sure everyone else could hear it. When I climbed onto the platform, I looked for Ryan's face, but I couldn't find him in the crowd.

The president extended the giant cardboard check to me and I took it, holding it up as cameras flashed. Whatever Deena had told me to think about when I looked at the camera had completely fled my mind. She was off to the side frantically mouthing, "Smile! Smile!"

I tried to, but the lights were intense and my head was swimming. I'd been nauseous since I'd climbed out of bed and hadn't been able to eat much. My arms were shaking from holding up the check, and my knees were knocking from sheer terror. At last I was led to a pair of chairs where the spokesperson for the lottery would conduct the question and answer session.

My stomach roiled as an assistant pinned a microphone on my collar. The handsome spokesman, whom I recognized from commercials, smiled at me as he took the opposite chair.

From a few feet away, the cameraman signaled, then the host turned to me. "Welcome Mallory Green."

"Thank you," I murmured, then listened as he read the biography Deena had prepared—that I was an orphan who'd been raised in the foster care system, now a cashier and waitress making minimum wage. From the corner of my eye I caught sight of myself on a monitor and suddenly realized the woman had clothed me in something that was as near a feedsack as she could find. And my "simple" hair and makeup made me look young and rural. I was a rags-to-riches story, and we were playing it to the hilt.

The spokesman was toothy and tanned. "So, Mallory... yesterday you were being evicted from your apartment, and today you're a millionaire. How does it feel?"

My frozen smile faltered. This was supposed to be my moment to shine, my time to show the world—and Trent—how poised I could be. Instead I was being portrayed as a rube who'd spent her rent money on lottery tickets. I opened my mouth to say what Deena and I had practiced, something clever and funny that would endear me to everyone watching. Instead I leaned forward and threw up on the man's shiny shoes.

August 18, Tuesday

I HIT the replay button and watched my horrific display yet again. I couldn't get enough of it, and apparently neither could everyone on social media and the late night talk shows. Some versions of it had been photoshopped to show me throwing up cash or coins.

I lay back on my pillow and wondered if it was possible to die of humiliation.

But Nessie didn't know what I'd done—she only wanted to be walked. So at her insistence, I dragged myself up, pushed my feet into flip flops, and exited outside to walk her in the early morning air. I was still yawning when a guy I didn't know appeared and took my picture with his phone. "Hey," I said, pulling back. "What are you doing?"

"She's over here," he called. "Lottery Girl is over here!"

Around the corner came a knot of people, all holding up their phones.

"Look over here!"

"Hey, Lottery Girl, can you spare a hundred?"

"Can you help me? I'm homeless."

"I'm sick, and can't afford my pain meds."

"I want to talk to you about an investment opportunity!"

I stumbled back and scrambled to rein in Nessie. Poor thing was still peeing when I snatched her up. When I reached the door leading into the building I realized in dismay I'd forgotten my electronic key.

I cowered as the crowd converged on me.

"Mallory!"

At the sound of Josh's voice, I turned my head to see him holding open the door and waving me in. I dashed inside with a whining Nessie while he yelled at the people to leave the property or he'd call the police.

Then he stepped inside. "Are you okay?"

I nodded, trembling. "How do those people know where I live?"

"You're a celebrity now. I'm sure you weren't hard to find."

I winced. "You saw the press conference?"

He nodded, fighting a smile. "Can't blame you—that was a lot of pressure." Then he scratched his temple. "Now I see why you were so keen to fish the lottery ticket out of the dumpster. It was worth more than fifty dollars."

I nodded. "Sorry... I wasn't supposed to tell anyone."

"I understand." Then he grinned. "So... you're rich."

I gave a little laugh. "Not yet—apparently it takes a while to get the money."

"So I assume you're the person who wants to cover the cost of rehab for your friend's wife?"

I nodded. "Will you still help?"

"Absolutely. I think it's a great thing you're doing."

I smiled. "Thanks." Then I gestured to his running clothes. "I'm keeping you from your run."

"I can stay if you need protection."

"That's okay. I'll call... my team."

"Ah—Mr. Porsche."

"Ryan is a financial manager. He's been... helping me."

He gave me a little smile. "Okay. Good. See you around?"

He didn't wait for me to respond. When he turned to walk away, I realized this time it was a question, not a statement, and it made me feel... sad?

August 19, Wednesday

I WAS expecting Ryan to arrive to pick me up, so at first I was alarmed when a strange car stopped by the curb where I waited with a small suitcase and Nessie in her carrier, wearing a hat and sunglasses to disguise my face. But when the window buzzed down, I was surprised and happy to see redheaded Wanda Sandoval driving. "I'm your ride," she said. "Get in."

I put my luggage and Nessie in the back seat, then I climbed in "Did Ryan send you?"

"Yeah. He got tied up in a meeting and didn't want to leave you hanging."

"Thanks."

She gave me a pointed look. "You could've told me."

"I was sworn to secrecy."

She huffed. "Okay, the *next* time you win fifty million, promise you'll tell me."

I laughed. "I think it's a once in a lifetime thing."

"Girl, I hope it happens to me in my lifetime." She shook her head. "You must be tripping."

"I don't think it's hit me yet."

"I get that," she said, pulling away from the curb. "But you got the rest of your life to get used to being rich." She grinned. "And I'm here if you need coaching. I've practiced being rich since I was a little girl."

"Where are you taking me?"

"To the Four Seasons. Ryan reserved you a suite until you find another place to live. At least you'll be safe from stalkers."

I nodded, feeling relieved. My doorbell had rung constantly, people had shoved notes under my door, and every time I'd tried to walk Nessie, at least one person had been lying in wait to try to talk to me.

My phone buzzed with a text and I looked down. I must've made a noise or a face because Wanda said, "Who's that?"

"My husband. He's been texting nonstop, wants to meet."

"I'll bet he does," she said, her voice full of contempt. "Where does that stand?"

I told her about the dissolution agreement and property settlement I'd signed. "He already filed it with the court."

"Good. But it's not final?"

"No. Apparently, that's supposed to take a month or so."

She sighed. "Do you still love him?"

"I... don't think so." Then I shook my head. "No."

She pivoted her head. "I'm going to tell you not to meet him, but I know you will. And I can't say I blame you... it would feel good to see him grovel."

August 20, Thursday

"THANKS FOR meeting me, Mal." Trent was wearing an outfit I recognized—a shirt I'd bought him, and worn-in jeans. And he looked... contrite?

I lowered myself into a chair in the lobby of the Four Seasons hotel. "You're welcome. What did you want to talk about?" I was impressed at how aloof I sounded, and I was wearing a dress nicer than anything I'd ever owned. But inside I was quaking—he still affected me.

He was looking all around, taking in the opulence. "Are you living here now?"

"Temporarily."

"It's nice."

"I think so."

"How's Nessie?"

I conjured up a little smile. "You were right—she's getting used to you not being around."

His face reddened slightly—or perhaps he was sunburned from boating? I glanced at my watch, also new. "I don't have a lot of time." I had nothing but time, but he didn't need to know that.

"Mal, I've been thinking. That is... I've realized I may have acted too rashly in giving up on our marriage."

I was enjoying this a little. Okay—a *lot*. "Go on."

"And, well... I think maybe we should give things another go, maybe go to marriage counseling to work things out."

"Really?" I asked, crossing my arms. "And when did you come to this realization?"

He paled under his tan. "I don't want you to think this has anything to do with the lottery money, because I was already thinking this before I found out."

"You were?"

"Yeah," he said, then reached across to pick up my hand. "I miss you, Mal. I miss what we had. We were so good together, then we let bills and debt derail us. But now we wouldn't have to worry about any of that, we could just enjoy each other. I was thinking we could go somewhere amazing, like Greece or Italy, and renew our vows—what do you say?"

I felt his pull on me, familiar and powerful. He'd always been able to talk me into doing what he wanted and somehow make me feel like it was what I wanted, too.

He looked at me expectantly, his eyes brimming with hope.

I smiled and squeezed his hand. "I say no." Then I got up and calmly walked away.

And Wanda was right—it felt rather good.

August 21, Friday

"WHO PICKED this rag?" Wanda said, holding up the dress I'd worn to the press conference.

"Deena," I responded. "She said it was the right image."

"If you were Amish," Wanda said, tossing it back on the bed.

I pointed to the rolling rack sitting in my expansive suite. "These are the things she sent for me to wear to the photo shoot. I guess I'm supposed to look like someone who deserves the money."

"That's bullshit," Wanda said, then snapped her fingers. "We're going shopping."

"I shouldn't buy anything else. I don't have the money yet."

"Ryan said something about a line of credit?"

I nodded.

She grinned.

I relented.

We spent the day at Lenox Mall and Phipps Plaza, in stores I'd never before dared to walk into. Under Wanda's tutelage, I amassed a wardrobe that would make a reality star envious.

"He'll love you in that," she said when I walked out wearing a lavender lowcut Givenchy dress.

"Who?" I asked, turning in the mirror.

"Ryan."

I stopped and looked up at her. "Ryan isn't... I mean, we're not... I don't..."

She gave me a sly look. "I see the way he looks at you, and girl, he looked at you before the money happened. You need to see where this goes."

My stomach fluttered with anticipation. Ryan Livingston interested in someone like me?

Could I be so lucky?

August 22, Saturday

"THIS IS amaze-balls," Vance whispered as we settled into chaise lounges in the Four Seasons spa.

"I've lived in Atlanta all my life," Kerry said, "and didn't even know this place existed."

We were wearing white robes and sipping herbal tea awaiting our Premiere Package experience.

"This is great of you, Mal," Vance said, his eyes rolling backward in delight.

"I told you we'd have a spa day," I said. "I'm happy to treat you both."

"I can't believe you didn't tell us you won," Kerry said, sounded hurt.

I cradled my tea cup in my hands. "You understand that I couldn't, right?"

"Still," she muttered. "I thought we were friends."

I blinked. "We are." Weren't we?

"Not really," she said wryly. "Do you know my husband's name?"

I hesitated, then shook my head. To be honest, I didn't even know she was married.

"And you've never been to my apartment," Vance said. "I've invited you, lots of times."

"I... don't have much time to socialize. Until now I was working three jobs."

"Aren't we all?" Kerry said lightly.

"Two jobs after the restaurant closes," Vance said with a sigh.

"Yeah, it's too bad," Kerry said. "I complained about Doug, but honestly, the man knows how to cook. Too bad he doesn't know how to run a business." Then she looked at me. "Maybe Vance and I can come to work for you on your island."

"I second that notion," Vance said happily.

"Are you sure," Kerry said in a sing-song voice, "that you didn't take up money at the restaurant to buy tickets, and hold back the winner for yourself?"

She sounded as if she was teasing, but was she instead fishing? "I'm sure," I said, then laughed to lighten the mood. "I was ringing up a ticket for a customer at the convenience store and made a mistake. Instead of canceling it, I just bought it myself."

Vance gaped. "And that was the winning ticket?"

"Yep."

"Some people have all the luck," he said.

"And some people make their luck," Kerry added lightly.

I shifted in my chair uneasily. I could feel their resentment, and I didn't blame them. I wanted to give them some hope that their jobs were secure, but I needed to talk to Doug first.

August 23, Sunday

I SLIPPED into the restaurant in partial disguise, wearing a hat and sunglasses. I glanced over the handful of customers seated, then spotted Hannah and Chance. I made my way over, then lifted my sunglasses. "It's me, Mallory."

"Hi, there," Hannah said with a big grin.

"I saw you on TV," Chance said, then guffawed. "Your cookie-tossing was *epic*."

Hannah punched his arm. "He yelled at me from the other room to come quick, our waitress had won the lottery. Congratulations!"

"Thanks, it's still new to me. And I have to tell you, I think your wishbone had something to do with it."

Hannah gasped. "Did it?"

I nodded. "I used it just before I bought the ticket."

"Excellent," Chance said, nodding and patting his wife's hand.

"Hannah," I ventured, "do you mind if I ask you a question?"

"Not at all."

I gestured to the restaurant in general. "Do you really think this place has potential?"

She sobered. "I really do. The food is fantastic, and it's a great location." She glanced around. "It could use some sprucing up, but that won't keep us from coming back."

"It's Hannah's favorite place, and she knows food," Chance said seriously.

I thanked her, then wished them well. Then I made my way to the kitchen where I flagged down Doug.

August 24, Monday

"I THINK you're going to love this one," the real estate agent said as she unlocked the door to the mansion on Lake Lanier.

"The location alone is stunning," Ryan offered.

It was a beautiful spot, I conceded. Private docks were scarce, and this house had one. And although I'd seen a dozen gorgeous homes today, this wood and glass behemoth was the most breathtaking.

"Ten thousand square feet," she said as she started the tour. "Six bedrooms, eight bathrooms, home theater room with seating for twenty. You can buy the furnishings. Newly renovated throughout—it's a showpiece."

I lost track of the rooms, each one more beautiful than the next. The ceilings were high and the finishes were luxe.

"There's an outdoor kitchen, two huge decks, plus a private beach, and gated access to your road, so it's very secluded. Also, a state-of-the-art security system."

Ryan gave me a little nod to affirm I would probably need one.

The tour ended on the rooftop deck overlooking the sunset on the lake. In a word, it was spectacular.

"It's a great property," the agent said, "and a good value for the size."

The price tag was staggering, but Ryan and I had talked about me buying a piece of real estate that would appreciate in value. I looked up at him. "What do you think?"

"I think you deserve it," he said, squeezing my hand. "But it's your decision."

My entire life I'd wanted a home, a place to put down roots instead of moving every few months. Trent and I could never afford a down payment—renting was all I'd ever known. I was blown away by the thought I could own a place so magnificent. The fact that Ryan thought it was amazing was a bonus.

I turned to the agent. "Where do I sign?"

August 25, Tuesday

I HAD, of course, phoned Ramy to let him know I would no longer be working at the GiddyUp. He had seen the vomitous press conference and was happy for me, and hinted he had an idea who was behind the free treatments his wife was receiving at the Shepherd Clinic. This was the first time I'd been back to the convenience store, and I was walking in as a customer, through the front door.

When the door chime sounded to announce my arrival, Shawna stuck her head around the corner from the pizza oven. "I'll be right there—*Mallory!*"

I grinned and accepted her enthusiastic hug as she screamed in delight. "I can't believe you won the big one!"

I laughed. "I can't either."

"Did you know you won the day the news crews were here? Is that why you left?"

I nodded. "I was in shock... I had to leave to pull myself together. Then I couldn't tell anyone. I hope you understand."

"I do, although iffen it had been me, I would've shouted if from the mountaintops." We laughed together and she did a little dance. "I'm so darn happy for you." Then she straightened. "But on the TV clip they said you're single?"

I nodded. "My husband moved out a few days before I bought the ticket."

She threw her head back and belly-laughed. "That's the best dang part of the story!"

I hadn't felt so light and happy in a long time, and I realized I would miss Shawna's good humor. "How is Bob?"

Her smile dimmed. "He's doing okay, home from the hospital, but not well. He's in a wheelchair and it's hard to get around, but he's still on the transplant list and we're hopeful he'll get a second chance."

I touched her arm. "I want to help your family with the medical bills."

She shook her head. "You don't have to do that, Mallory, we'll get by."

"I want to," I insisted. "Someone will call you to work it all out."

She started bawling and nearly squeezed me in two. I cried with her until we laughed. This, I thought, was what money was for.

August 26, Wednesday

"DANICA? IT'S Mallory. How are you?"

"Mallory! Oh, my goodness, I can't believe it's you. Congratulations! I saw the press conference and yelled for all my kids to come in, told them you were one of mine."

I smiled into the phone. "That's so nice. I hope they didn't see the end."

"They did, but they thought it was great fun." She laughed while I groaned. "You must be so excited. Are you going to travel around the world?"

"I do plan to travel," I said. "Soon." Then I cleared my throat. "Danica, I'd like to do something for you—"

"Mallory, that's not necessary."

"I want to," I pressed. "Please allow me to pay off your mortgage."

She gasped. "That's too much, Mallory."

"No, it isn't." Her modest, crowded home would fit inside the one I'd just purchased five times over. "And I'd like to buy you a van so you can transport your children."

She was silent for so long I thought I'd lost the connection, then I realized she was weeping in gratitude.

"Thank you, Mallory. I hope you know how much I love you."

My throat clogged with emotion. "I... love you, too." And now I felt like I could finally show it.

I suddenly realized how much I was going to enjoy helping others with the money. I truly felt lucky.

August 27, Thursday

"THE BLUE cargo van to this address," I said to the salesman at the dealership, handing him Danica's address.

"Yes, ma'am," he said, nodding. He'd recognized me from my press conference, had taken a selfie to show his wife. "Is there anything else I can help you with?"

I looked around, then spotted a cute little red sports car. Delight bloomed in my chest. Why not? I pointed. "I'd like one of those." My lemon of a car could rot in the parking lot where it sat crippled.

He nodded enthusiastically. "Yes, ma'am. Would you like to drive it first?"

"That won't be necessary. I'll take a red one."

"Yes, ma'am."

"And a black one."

He arched an eyebrow. "A second one?"

"For a friend," I said, then pulled up Vance's address on my phone and showed it to him. "Delivered to this address. And a yellow one." I pulled up Kerry's address on my phone. "Delivered to this address."

"Very good, ma'am," the man said, barely able to contain his excitement over the sale.

I signed the necessary papers, then drove my new red sports car back to the Four Seasons. I felt utterly electric.

As I was handing the keys to the valet, my phone rang. When I saw Ryan's name on the screen I smiled and connected the call. "Hello, there."

"Hello, there," he said. "I see from the account activity you've been making some purchases."

"I have," I said, laughing. "Did you call to chastise me?"

"Not at all, I'm happy for you. Actually, I was wondering if you wanted to have dinner with me Saturday."

"Sure," I said. "What do we need to discuss?"

"Nothing," he said. "This, um, isn't business. I'd like to take you out on a date."

Wonder shot through me and my mouth curved into a smile. "I'd like that."

"Pick you up at seven?"

"I'll be ready."

August 28, Friday

"TOLDJA," WANDA said with a laugh. "And now you have a reason to wear that gorgeous Givenchy dress."

I looked at my reflection in the floor-length mirror and bit into my lip. "But what about the rest of me?"

She angled her head, then nodded in agreement. "I see what you're saying... and I can help."

"That's why I called."

"First stop, hairdresser. You need a new cut—and when was the last time you had your eyebrows shaped?"

"Um, never."

She rolled her eyes, then counted on her fingers. "Then to the dermatologist, masseuse, manicurist, and wax studio."

I frowned. "Does the wax studio have anything to do with art?"

"It does not. Let's go spend some of your money!"

Hours later I had been styled, shaped, cleaned, massaged, painted, and waxed.

"Much better," Wanda said, clapping her hands at my improvements. "Now, remember... just be yourself."

August 29, Saturday

"YOU ARE a vision," Ryan said.

It was worth all the trouble, I decided, just to see his eyes light up when I walked into the lobby.

"Thank you," I murmured. "You look handsome."

As always, he looked as if he'd just stepped out of a sun-drenched Ralph Lauren commercial. His grooming was impeccable, yet he was so masculine and rugged-looking, even in an expensive suit. I couldn't believe I was on his arm. More than one head turned as we made our way outside to where his Porsche sat waiting. He held open the door for me and I slid into the seat, feeling sleek and elegant. He closed the door, then circled around to climb in. He moved like the athlete he was, in total control of his body. My own body hummed in awareness as we drove through the summer night air. The bass of his stereo thrummed my senses higher. We arrived at the restaurant much too soon, but it was another sensual experience.

The chef came out to personally describe the menu and make suggestions. Every dish sounded positively exotic to me. We ordered several entrees and sampled everything. The wine was delicious and went straight to my head like a velvet bullet, making everything hazy and fun. Ryan was a good conversationalist and had a way of getting me to open up... or was it my newfound independence and power that made me feel grownup and sexy?

Regardless, it was a fierce combination of new experiences for a relative ingénue like me. When Ryan took me back to the hotel and walked me to my room, letting him kiss me seemed so natural. His lips on mine felt so different, so manly and confident. I could feel myself being swept along by the sensations he aroused in my sensitized body. But when things started to get too heated, I hesitated, and he felt my hesitation.

He lifted his head. "I should go."

My chest rose and fell, I was having trouble breathing... and thinking. I could only nod.

"Good night, Mallory. Thank you for a wonderful evening."

His eyes shone in the dim light, and kept me burning long into the night.

I was starting to feel like a completely different person.

August 30, Sunday

THE NEXT day I had to return to the apartment to get a toy of Nessie's that she constantly looked for. I was hoping to get in and out unnoticed, but as I was leaving, Josh was coming back from a run.

He smiled. "Hi, Mallory."

"Hi, Josh."

"I wondered if you were gone for good."

"I had to come back for a much-missed item."

His eyebrows climbed.

I held up Nessie's toy.

"Oh... right. How are you?"

"I'm... great." I laughed. "I'm Lottery Girl."

"Yeah, but how *are* you? This must be so hard to deal with."

I didn't like how presumptuous he was... and how right he was. "Not at all. It's wonderful being able to buy and do anything I want."

He hesitated, then smiled. "Good. I'm glad you're doing well. By the way, I met your friend Ramy and his wife Aisha. They're wonderful people."

I softened, then nodded. "Yes, they are. Thank you for helping them."

"You're the one helping them."

We locked gazes for a few seconds, then I looked away. "I need to go."

"And I need to shower."

"Bye," I said.

"See you later."

But as I walked away, I wondered—had it been a question... or a statement?

August 31, Monday

RYAN AND I were having breakfast at the hotel restaurant. I marveled at how used to his company I'd become, and how much I'd come to rely on him. The fact that his behavior had become more proprietary was an unexpected and delicious bonus.

"I double-checked that the money market accounts are set up to receive the first million of your proceeds," he said. "The wire should arrive within the next two days."

"The first million," I murmured, shaking my head. "It still seems so surreal."

Ryan smiled, then reached over to squeeze my hand, something he now did often. "It's real. And it couldn't be happening to a nicer person."

I flushed warm at his compliment and his touch, bemused and exhilarated by all the emotions swirling in my chest.

A woman walked up to our table and extended a friendly smile. "Mallory Green?"

I scanned her attire—capris, a sleeveless blouse and sandals, holding a plain purse. She wasn't dressed like a reporter. I registered she was probably a guest of the hotel who had recognized me from the media coverage.

"Yes," I said.

She reached into her bag and withdrew a thick manilla envelope, then handed it to me. "You've been served."

My mouth opened, but otherwise I was frozen in place.

Ryan frowned, then took the envelope from me.

"Maybe it's leftover from the apartment eviction," I offered weakly. "Or the divorce?"

He removed the stack of papers and scanned them. "I wish. You're being sued."

"Sued?" I parroted in a panicked voice. "Who is suing me?"

Ryan made a frustrated noise. "Who isn't?"

I blinked. "What?"

He held up three sets of documents, still reading from them, then gestured to the first. "A woman named Sandra Conway is suing you for theft, says you stole the winning ticket she purchased."

My jaw dropped. Nice, eccentric Mrs. Conway was suing me because I'd bought the ticket I'd made the mistake on?

He held up the second set of documents. "And the twenty-two employees of The Community Café claim you made a verbal contract to share the proceeds if you won the lottery."

My jaw dropped further. Through the cloud of confusion, the memory of a casual conversation came back to me with sudden clarity.

"I'd share with you if I won," Vance groused.

"Me, too," I said.

"I'm not that charitable," Kerry said.

A pained look crossed Ryan's face.

"Wh-What else?" I asked, my voice shaky.

He held up the third set of documents. "It's Trent," he gritted out. "He's claiming the lottery ticket is community property, purchased before divorce proceedings were set into motion." Ryan tossed down the papers, then pulled his hand over his mouth. "He wants half... assuming there's anything left to split."

Utter fear squeezed my heart... what about all the financial commitments I'd made?

SEPTEMBER

September 1, Tuesday

I LAY in my expensive bed at the Four Seasons as dawn delivered the day, thinking my short stint as a lottery millionaire had been good while it lasted.

I was numb from the revelation I was being sued from all sides. My twenty-plus coworkers at The Community Café were taking me to court to get the share of the jackpot they felt entitled to. The woman who purchased tickets at the convenience store where I worked claimed I'd kept the winning ticket she'd paid for. And last but not least, there was my husband who no longer wanted me, but wanted half of my winnings.

I was accustomed to the financial struggles of not having enough money, but I was unprepared for the financial struggles of having *too much* money. My tax attorney had tried to warn me, as well as the articles I'd read online about lottery winners, about the landmines ahead. But I'd been so caught up in the euphoria of being flush with cash, I'd pushed aside those concerns and spent money and made promises like a drunken sailor.

And now, it could all be taken away from me.

I was in so much trouble, I could barely breathe.

Ryan had done his best to assure me things would be okay. Even as I lay prostrate on five-thousand-thread-count sheets, he was scrambling to assemble a team to handle my cases—a litigation attorney and a divorce attorney. All of it made me feel sick. Historically, I was bad with money and I loathed confrontation, so this was shaping up to be my perfect storm of anxiety.

How had my boring little life become such a fustercluck?

From the floor I heard Nessie snuffle. I peeked over the edge of the bed to see the French bulldog push to her feet groggily. When she rolled her buggy eyes up to me, I saw the light go out of them. I'd lied to Trent about her getting over him. She missed him… and inexplicably, so did I. The satisfaction of turning down his feeble attempt at a reconciliation had been short-lived. I knew the money had been his primary motivator… but what if it hadn't been? What if he truly regretted ending our marriage and thought the money would give us a chance to start over in a different place? If he'd wanted only the money, wouldn't he have filed the lawsuit without first extending an olive branch?

As soon as the words filtered into my head, I knew my brain was playing tricks on me. I was grasping at emotional straws, fantasizing about something that would never be simply because it sounded familiar and comforting.

Which was ridiculous… I had Ryan now. What had begun as a professional relationship had morphed into the beginnings of something else. I only hoped these lawsuits hadn't stolen our momentum.

My phone dinged with a text and my heart jumped… then dropped when I saw it was from my former neighbor Josh.

Thanks for sponsoring me in the charity run. It wasn't necessary, but much appreciated.

The charity run for the Shepherd Spinal Center where he worked as a physical therapist. I'd made the donation with noble intentions—the man had, after all, helped me fish the ticket out of a trash dumpster—but now it felt vulgar, like I was showing off.

Plus my check might bounce.

Happy to give to such a good cause I texted back.

Are you and Nessie doing okay?

As per usual, his familiarity rankled me, for no discernible reason. *Of course.*

Good. Don't be a stranger.

Nessie whined, and I was grateful to have a reason to climb out of bed. I pulled on track pants and a hoodie, then yanked my hair back into a ponytail. After pushing my feet into sandals, I hooked Nessie's leash to her collar and walked out into the hushed corridor. In the low lighting, the red-carpeted hall that had seemed so regal in the daylight looked almost sinister, as if the walls of the posh hotel were telling me I didn't belong. Without the money, I would be smacked down to my previous existence of obscurity, except worse off for having gotten a glimpse of the good life.

A shiver ran down my spine—was it a foreboding?

September 2, Wednesday

THE MOUTH of my litigation attorney, Ronald Buckley, stretched into a flat line. "Just about every lottery winner gets sued over something. I remember a case where a winner was sued by her church because she didn't tithe her jackpot."

Next to me, Ryan grunted. "Who won?"

"The church, because she'd once made a comment to the minister about her commitment to tithing, and the court considered it a verbal contract."

I blinked. Wow.

"First things first," Buckley said, "what is the status of the funds?"

Ryan shifted forward. "The first million of Mallory's jackpot has already been awarded to her, the remainder of the funds will be held in escrow until the claims are settled."

I did some quick math in my head—the first million, less forty percent for taxes, less the clothes and cars I'd bought, less the money I'd pledged to pay for Ramy's wife's and for Shawna's husband's medical bills, less Danica's mortgage, less the loan I'd floated to Doug for the restaurant, and who knew what these lawsuits were going to cost me in legal fees...

I stopped doing the math.

The man glanced back and forth between the three sets of legal documents on his desk. "I'll ask a judge to prioritize the lawsuits. It makes sense to hear the Conway complaint first, since if the court rules in her favor, the other two lawsuits are moot."

My intestines cramped.

"Then the husband's complaint second." He looked up. "I understand you've retained a divorce attorney?"

"Yes," I croaked.

"Lynette Shift," Ryan offered. "Mallory will be meeting with her Friday."

"Ask her to loop me in," Buckley said, "and I'll do the same." He made a few notes on a pad of paper. "I'll ask the judge to schedule the complaint filed by your coworkers at The Community Café last."

I screwed up my courage to ask, "What do you think my chances are on each case?"

"Fifty-fifty," he said bluntly. "Every court case can go either way depending on the deposed statements, the attorneys, the judge, and about a dozen other variables."

"Is there anything we can do to protect some of the assets?" Ryan asked.

"Do you own a home, Ms. Green?"

"I made an offer on a house, but it hasn't closed yet."

"If you can close before you go to court, do it. The court tends to look on a person's primary residence as untouchable."

I glanced at Ryan and he nodded.

"Where do you live now?" Buckley asked.

"At the Four Seasons."

"For security reasons," Ryan added.

The man's mouth turned down. "Still, the optics aren't good. You don't want to go into court looking as if you're living high on the hog. A new home is one thing, but staying at the Four Seasons will only give the opposition ammunition that you have enough to share. It shouldn't matter, but it will."

"I still have my apartment. I could move back there." Maybe it would perk up Nessie, who was still out of sorts.

"Just until you close on the house," Ryan said.

"Okay, that's settled," Buckley said. "Have you made other big purchases I should know about?"

I squirmed. "A few."

His mouth twitched. "I'll need a list so there are no surprises."

I nodded.

"Now, let's go over each complaint so you know what each party is claiming, and we can establish an argument before you're deposed." He looked up. "Do you need to go to the ladies' room, or would you like a bottle of water?" He smiled a lawyerly smile. "This is going to take a while."

September 3, Thursday

WHEN I pulled my cute little red sports car into the parking lot of the apartment complex, I realized it would attract more attention than the clunker I'd been driving, and the lot wasn't exactly secure.

And considering the unbelievably sky-high insurance premium I was paying, filing a claim in the first few days would not help my bottom line.

I bit into my lip. I'd thought my money problems were over, and here I sat worried about... well, *money*.

I put the car into Park and after much fumbling, disengaged the engine. I was still getting used to operating a vehicle without a key—why did smart technology have a way of making a person feel stupid?

I turned my head to look at Nessie through the vent in her carrier. "We're back... for a while." My minuscule rear seat and pint-sized trunk were crammed full of clothes and other goodies I'd bought. But after the sobering meeting the day before with Donald Buckley about how swiftly my winnings could be appropriated, my splurges had lost a bit of their sheen.

After climbing out and unfolding myself, I circled around to remove Nessie. Behind me, a long, low whistle of appreciation sounded. When I turned I saw Josh walking toward me, but the whistle was for my car, not for me. I gave myself a mental kick for not realizing I'd parked so close to his hatchback.

"*Nice.*" He smoothed a hand over a fender and squatted down to examine the wheels. "Glad to see you got something more reliable, but... wow."

I lifted my chin. "I don't deserve a wow car?"

He stood, then back-pedaled. "Sure you do. I just didn't picture you in... this."

"Well... maybe you should."

He smiled. "I guess so. It's really nice, Mallory." He saw my bags and boxes in the backseat. "Are you moving back?"

"Just until I close on my house."

"You bought a house?"

"At Lake Lanier."

"Wow—I mean... good for you." He gestured to my things. "Let me help you."

I glanced at his chinos and button-up shirt. "You look like you're headed into work."

"I don't have an appointment for another couple of hours, I was just going in early to visit some favorite patients."

Of course he had favorite patients. The guy was a paragon of goodness—was that why he unnerved me? "I... thanks. Just grab anything."

I hoisted Nessie's carrier, then pulled a bag from the backseat with my free hand. Josh emerged with an armload. I juggled things to lock the doors, then walked rapidly into the building, wanting to get this over with. But I felt compelled to make small talk. "How is your training going?"

"For the charity run?" He grinned. "I'll never set records, but it's fun and challenging."

When I reached the door of my old apartment, I hesitated, beset with anxiety. It was silly but coming back, even temporarily, made me feel as if I was losing ground. I unlocked the door and pushed it open to be met with warm, stale air. I walked in and freed Nessie from her carrier, then went around turning on lights. "You can set that stuff on the floor," I said, gesturing to Josh.

He was taking in everything. The walls were empty and the furniture was sparse since Trent had moved out the things he wanted. I adjusted the thermostat to get the air moving, and opened the curtains in the living area.

"You have great southern light," he said. "This unit is nicer than mine."

"Do you like living here?"

He shrugged. "Sure. It's convenient to the hospital and the park, decent bars and restaurants. I'll probably be here for a while."

"You don't want a house?" I had an idea of what he probably earned at the Shepherd Center—he could afford one.

"Someday," he said agreeably. "When I have someone to share it with. For now, I like the flexibility of renting. You know what they say—when you own things, they own you."

I arched an eyebrow.

Josh blanched. "Er—sorry. I didn't mean... I think it's great you bought a house... and a car."

If only those were the only things I'd bought.

He jerked his thumb over his shoulder. "I'm going back for another load. If you want to stay here, you can just give me the key."

I held up a black fob. "There's no key."

"Cool." He took the fob, then hesitated. "I'm glad you're back, Mallory."

"Temporarily," I added.

He nodded. "Temporarily."

September 4, Friday

"THANKS FOR being here," I said.

Wanda reached over to squeeze my arm. "No problem. You're going to like Lynette."

I made a rueful noise. "I wish I'd contacted her when you first suggested I call a divorce attorney."

"Hush. The important thing is you're here now. She'll be able to help you."

I gave Wanda a grateful smile, although I had a bad feeling I might be beyond help.

She angled her head. "So... how are things with Ryan?"

My cheeks heated up. "Fine."

"I'll bet he *is* fine. Hook a girl up with some details, how about it?"

"He's... a gentleman. And he's a good... kisser."

She angled her head. "You can't be serious. Surely you've done more than kiss that beautiful man."

I gestured to the elegant waiting area where we sat. "Look where I am—my divorce isn't even final."

She harrumphed. "Too bad your asshole ex couldn't have died screaming in an accident." She leaned closer. "It's not too late. I know a guy."

I gave her a pointed look. "That's not funny."

She grinned. "Yeah it is."

I tried to hold back a smile, but couldn't. "Okay, maybe a little."

The door to Lynette Shift's office opened, and I sobered. She was older than I expected, but her eyes were sharp and shrewd.

She smiled. "Hi, Wanda."

"Good to see you, Lynette. This is Mallory Green. She has a problem ex."

The woman made a thoughtful noise as she shook my hand. "Don't we all? It's nice to meet you, Mallory. Come in to my office."

I turned to Wanda. "Thanks again."

"Call me later," she said, then turned and strutted out.

I made a mental note to learn how to strut, then followed Lynette into a modern but feminine office. It was a nice change from all the mahogany I'd been exposed to lately.

"Have a seat," Lynette said, gesturing to a set of chairs. I gingerly lowered myself into one of them. I could hear my heart pounding in my ears. Instead of taking a position behind her desk, she sat in the other chair and smiled.

"I've never met a lottery winner before. Your head must be spinning."

I nodded. "It's been... hectic."

"I understand your ex has filed a lawsuit claiming the ticket is community property, and he wants his share?"

"That's right."

"Can you start at the top? How long were you married?"

"Trent walked out eight weeks ago... on our five-year wedding anniversary."

Her mouth flattened. "You'd be surprised how often that happens. Did you have any idea he was unhappy?"

I chewed on the inside of my cheek, stalling. "I knew things weren't great between us, but I assumed it was due to his career setbacks. I thought we were just going through a rough patch, but we'd get through it."

She looked sympathetic. "That's how a marriage is supposed to work. Unfortunately, both partners have to agree. Was there another person involved?"

I nodded. "A woman he met through friends. She got him a job at her company."

"So he's working—that's good... and it demonstrates how invested he was in leaving the marriage."

My heart squeezed. So true.

"Can you remember his exact words when he said he wanted to end the marriage?"

I thought back to that horrible night. "He said he didn't want to be married anymore, that he wanted a divorce, and he left our apartment."

"Did he take anything with him?"

"No... he even left his dog Nessie. But he came back the next day to pack a suitcase... and a few days after that he came back to get furniture and art pieces he wanted."

"Did he take his dog?"

"No."

"And was there any attempt at reconciliation at the time?"

"Not on his part."

"But you were willing?"

I nodded. "I called him... several times and asked him to communicate, but he refused, even after I sent him a spreadsheet of our debt and asked how we would handle it."

"You had a lot of debt as a couple?"

My face flamed. "Almost a quarter of a million."

One delicate eyebrow arched. "Is there a home involved?"

"No, we rent—rented. That was credit cards, car loans, a boat, dental bills. Trent tried a multilevel marketing business that went bust. And I... spent money foolishly, too." On a private investigator to find my long-lost father, who wasn't lost at all, but ensconced in a state prison.

"Okay. Then what happened?"

"Then four weeks ago, Trent called and asked me to meet him."

"And did you?"

I nodded. "I was hoping he wanted us to try again. Instead he said we'd save a lot of money if we agreed how to split things and if he filed. He'd already drawn up the document, and I signed it." From my bag I removed the notarized three-page agreement.

She took it and scanned it quickly. "The asset and debt split is much more favorable to him than to you."

I nodded. "But by that time I knew I had a winning lottery ticket, so I didn't mind."

She reached for a notepad. "What was the timing of you buying the ticket and finding out you'd won as it relates to this agreement?"

I had to think. "He left on the tenth of July and I bought the ticket on the thirtieth. I found out I'd won the following day."

"So you knew about the jackpot when you signed this agreement?"

"Yes, but I didn't tell him."

She grinned. "Good girl."

"After I claimed the ticket mid-August, Trent approached me about reconciling."

She scoffed. "Of course he did."

"He suggested we go to counseling and work things out, then spend the money traveling around the world."

"And how did you respond?"

I shifted in my chair. "I confess my ego got the better of me. I wasn't... pleasant."

"That's understandable. And now he wants half."

"Right."

She took the document I'd given her and walked over to her laptop. After a few taps on the keyboard, she said, "He withdrew this filing—no surprise there since the assets are now in question." She looked up. "I understand there's another lawsuit that has priority?"

I nodded. "A customer says she paid for the winning ticket and I kept it."

"But you didn't?"

"No."

"Then I'll assume that complaint will be set aside and our complaint will be heard."

I inhaled, then exhaled. "Okay."

She scrutinized me. "How are you holding up?"

I conjured up a smile. "I'm Lottery Girl... I'm good."

She paused, then set aside her notebook. "Mallory, going through a divorce is stressful enough on its own, without this lottery business. Do you have someone to talk to?"

"Wanda's been a good friend. And my financial advisor—"

"I mean someone professional."

I shook my head. "I don't need a therapist."

She stood and opened a desk drawer, then pulled out a card and extended it to me. "If you change your mind."

To be polite, I took the card.

September 5, Saturday

"DID YOU find anything wrong with her?"

The vet tech gave Nessie's ears a scratch, then handed her furry little body to me. "No. All her vitals are fine, and we x-rayed her to make sure she hadn't swallowed something."

I frowned. "So why hasn't she been eating?"

"Did you change her food?"

"No."

The young man shrugged. "Has there been a change in her environment?"

"We moved... twice. And she's really my husband's pet, but he... left."

The guy shifted awkwardly. "Oh. Then if I had to guess, I'd say she's depressed."

I squinted. "That's a thing?"

"Absolutely. Pets rely on a routine, just like humans. They get used to people's voices and smells around their bed, and they have favorite toys. Change up something in their surroundings and it throws them off."

"What should I do?"

He hesitated. "Do you have anything of your, um, husband's that smells like him, like a T-shirt?"

My mouth flattened. "Maybe."

"That could help. Otherwise, I'd say just give her some extra attention until she adjusts."

I thanked the man, then paid a rather exorbitant fee and drove back to the apartment. When I opened the door to Nessie's carrier, she looked at me forlornly, then walked out and promptly plopped down to brood. I tried to entice her to eat, but she wasn't interested. Resigned, I went to the closet and dug out the box of clothes Trent had left that I'd been planning to take to Goodwill. I sorted through them, pressing down memories of when he or I had bought the items and how they'd looked on him. I still found it hard to believe he had so abruptly and so thoroughly removed himself from our life.

My hand closed around a thin, holey brown sweatshirt covered with paint—the work shirt he threw on when he did chores or messy projects. I brought it to my nose and inhaled. The slight scent of his faded cologne and maleness lingered there. I offered it to Nessie. She gave the shirt a sniff, then nuzzled it and groaned with joy. It brought tears to my eyes. I left it with her and returned to the kitchen to load the dishwasher, and by the time I'd finished, she'd trotted in, dragging the sweatshirt behind her, to eat from her bowl.

I watched her with wonder and replayed the vet tech's words—*pets rely on a routine, just like humans... they get used to people's voices and smells... change up something in their surroundings and it throws them off.*

I fished out the business card Lynette Shift had given me, but resistance rose in my chest. I didn't want to recount my life in foster care and my broken marriage and the complications of my unexpected windfall to a stranger, only to be told to take baths and do yoga and to, as Trent had put it, *get over it.*

I opened the trash can, and dropped the card inside.

September 6, Sunday

"THIS IS getting to be a bad habit."

At the sound of Josh's voice, I winced, then turned my head. He stood on the outside of the dumpster, holding a bag of trash. I stood inside, looking for the bag I'd discarded.

"Hi," I said feebly.

He scratched his temple, fighting a smile. "Did you lose another lottery ticket?"

"No," I said, tamping down irritation. "I tossed out a business card I didn't think I'd need."

"And now you do?"

"Something like that."

"Want some help?"

I glanced over his clothes. "You were going for a run."

"Yeah, but it can wait."

"I don't want you to mess up your nice—"

He heaved himself over and landed in the juicy gunk at the bottom of the dumpster with me.

"—shoes."

He grinned. "They'll wash. Now… what are we looking for?"

"A bag with a 26 Thai take-out box in it."

He leaned over and began to pick through the trash bags. "I love that place—the next time you do take-out from there, call me."

"They have the best mussels."

"And basil rolls," he agreed.

As he lifted bags and other debris, I noticed his well-shaped hands and strong forearms—both traits of a skilled physical therapist.

"How are things at the Shepherd Center?" I asked.

"I see miracles everyday… you should drop by sometime. Not that you need to finish your PT degree now, Miss Moneybags," he teased. "But I think you'd enjoy seeing what's happening there."

"I might do that," I said lightly, watching him under my lashes. He had that nerdy vibe going, which was kind of appealing… if I were into nerdy guys. After several more minutes of futile searching, I sighed. "I don't think we're going to find it. It's actually not that important."

"If it's important to you, it's important." Then he held up a bag and pointed to the telltale 26 Thai logo on a flattened pagoda box visible through the plastic. "Eureka!"

I grinned. "That's it."

I opened the bag and dug through it, finally locating the card Lynette Shift had given me. "Got it." I palmed the card because I wasn't keen on him seeing it. But the universe had another idea because as he helped me climb out of the dumpster, the card slipped from my hand and landed face up between Josh's feet.

He bent over to retrieve it and had plenty of time to notice it was for a Licensed Mental Health Professional. He handed the card to me and coughed lightly. "Sorry… I didn't mean to be nosy."

My face warmed. "It's okay… everyone else knows everything about me."

He wet his lips. "Ramy told me during his wife's last treatment that a customer at the convenience store is suing you for part of the winnings?"

"Along with a few other people."

"I'm sorry to hear that."

I shrugged. "My lawyers are taking care of it."

"Still… it must be stressful."

I lowered my eyes. "I don't expect anyone to feel sorry for me. Millions of people would give up an organ to be in my shoes."

A smile quirked his lips and he nodded to my stained, stinky sneakers. "Well, not *those* shoes."

I laughed, happy for a light moment in the midst of the murky mess my life had become.

"Mallory?"

I turned my head to see Ryan standing next to the building entrance, holding his phone. Even dressed in casual clothes, he looked camera-ready. I moved toward him. "Ryan? This is a nice surprise."

"Sorry to drop by—I've been calling you."

"I don't have my phone on me," I said, suddenly realizing I looked like a hobo and smelled to high heaven. "I—" I gestured to Josh. "That is, we—"

"Were looking for something I accidentally threw out," Josh supplied. "Mallory was nice enough to help me."

Ryan scrutinized Josh. "You should be more careful."

"Yes, I should," Josh agreed jovially. He turned to me. "See you later, Mallory." He broke into a jog and disappeared in the direction of the park.

Ryan looked back to me and winced. "Dumpster diving?"

"It was for a good cause," I murmured. "Sorry I missed your calls—is everything okay?"

He made a face. "I have to go to Miami to help a client."

I tried not to feel disappointed. "Okay… for how long?"

"I'll be back next Sunday. I'm so sorry I'll miss the Conway hearing on Thursday, but you're in good hands with Ron Buckley."

The depositions for Mrs. Conway's suit had been given and Buckley had scored an emergency hearing to try the case considering the other two lawsuits were dependent on the outcome. I nodded and tried to look more optimistic than I felt.

"I'm on my way to the airport. I just wanted to say goodbye, and to make sure you're okay."

His concern made me feel warm and gooey inside. "I'm okay."

"No reporters, no stalkers?"

"None that I've seen."

"Okay… I'll call you when I can." Ryan leaned in for a kiss.

I didn't want to contaminate his clothes so I stretched my neck and puckered up for a chaste goodbye that somehow seemed all the more sexy for it.

I waved until he was out of sight, already feeling his absence acutely. I was dangerously close to trusting this man with more than my money—a big step for someone who'd learned early not to believe in anyone but myself.

Then again, I *was* falling apart at the seams. The weight of the money I'd won was pulling on me. I couldn't sleep for the overwhelming feeling that things were going to get a lot worse before they got better.

I pulled the beleaguered business card from behind my back and ran my finger over the raised letters of Licensed Mental Health Professional. Maybe it would help to talk to someone.

September 7, Monday

I SETTLED onto the couch self-consciously and smiled at the woman sitting across from me. "It was nice of you to work me in on such short notice."

Imogene Ramplet was a pretty British woman with hooded, thoughtful eyes and a voice like an NPR announcer. "I sensed from your phone call this morning that you might benefit from a short session straightaway."

I wondered, though, if the phrase "lottery winner" had loosened up her schedule. Then I caught myself—if I already didn't trust my therapist, I was doomed.

"Because you have so many challenges coming at you in the next few days," she added.

"Right." I averted my gaze to look around her office. She appeared to collect flamingo what-nots and stuffed animals, which seemed rather arbitrary. When I looked back to her, she was still smiling at me. "I don't know how to do this," I said, shifting on the couch.

"Do what?"

I gestured vaguely to my chest, then to her. "This... talking thing."

"You're doing fine."

"But I don't know what to talk *about*."

She shrugged. "Whatever you want me to know."

I lifted my hands. "Until a few weeks ago, my life was normal. Boring, and normal. Then I won the lottery and all hell broke loose."

"Tell me about your life before you bought the winning ticket."

"I was working three minimum wage jobs and we were drowning in debt."

"You and your estranged husband?"

"That's right."

She paused. "Does that seem normal to you—working three jobs and drowning in debt?"

I pursed my mouth. "I guess so... but then I'm not a good judge of normal."

"And why do you say that?"

Ack, I hadn't wanted to talk about my childhood, but we were already there. I sighed and gave the Cliffs Notes version. "My mother died of cancer when I was four, my father turned me over to the foster care system. I aged out at eighteen, worked a lot of different jobs, went to college part-time when I could afford to. I met Trent and married him when I was twenty-one. We were together for five years until he walked out on me a few weeks ago."

She smiled. "That covered a lot of ground. Do you remember your mother?"

I bit into my lip. "Not her, but things about her, maybe? Sometimes I have memories of pleasant things and it makes me think it was something I did with her."

"And are you in touch with your father?"

"No. He came to see me a couple of times when I was very young, but I don't remember much about it."

"And you're an only child?"

"Yes."

"So when you married your husband, he became your family."

"I suppose."

"And you were happy?"

"I thought so... until he said he didn't want to be married anymore."

"You had no idea your marriage was in trouble?"

I crossed my arms. "I... don't want to talk about my marriage."

"Okay. Why don't you tell me how you feel about winning the lottery?"

I smiled. "At first, it was amazing. I didn't tell anyone for a few days, and it was like having the most incredible secret from the world."

"And then?"

"And then when word got out, I attracted stalkers and lost friends. I made promises to help people I might not be able to keep now that these lawsuits are happening."

"Don't you think the people you promised to help will understand that it's out of your control?"

"That's not the point." I dug my nails into my forearms. "When a person makes a promise they're supposed to keep their word."

"I can see that's important to you," she said, nodding. "Do you think things could still work out so you can keep those promises?"

"Possibly," I admitted. "But I can't stop thinking about all the worst-case scenarios."

"For someone so young, you have a lot on your mind." She leaned forward slightly. "How do you spend your days, Mallory?"

"Lately, there've been lots of meetings with lawyers, and depositions."

"And what do you do in between? I assume you're not working still."

"No, I'm not working." I puffed out my cheeks in a long exhale. "I'm kind of in limbo until these lawsuits are settled. I'll be moving into a new house later this month, but for now I'm cooped up in my half-empty apartment with a depressed dog."

Imogene smiled. "No wonder you feel lost—you went from working three jobs and living with a husband to no jobs and living alone. It sounds as if you need some structure in your life, somewhere to be. Perhaps you should pick up a hobby. Or can you find somewhere to volunteer?"

Hobbies weren't my thing, but volunteering… "Actually, one place does come to mind."

September 8, Tuesday

JOSH GRINNED. "Welcome to the Shepherd Center. You look nice, Mallory."

"Thank you." I stepped through the door he held open for me, glad I'd worn a dress. My stomach was a bundle of nerves, although I wasn't sure why a tour of the rehabilitation center had me on edge. "If you're too busy, you can hand me off to someone else."

"No, this is perfect timing. The tour will take about an hour, and we'll finish up near the time Aisha is coming in for a session if you'd like to say hello."

"That would be wonderful," I murmured. I hadn't yet received the billing for my former boss's wife's treatment, and I desperately hoped I would still be able to cover the cost. Ramy had shared the alternative was for them to divorce so she would qualify for subsidized care—a heart-breaking scenario.

"Here's your visitor lanyard," Josh said. He lifted the cording over my head and allowed the badge to fall to my chest. The movement brought us into each other's personal space. A few seconds of awkward awareness barbed between us before we both pulled back.

"We'll start in the research department," he offered, then led the way, saying hello and introducing me to acquaintances along the way.

I could tell he was well-liked, and it was interesting to see another side of him. His pride in the facility was evident as he walked me through the research labs and talked about the clinical trials, the development of new surgical techniques, pharmaceuticals, and smart prosthetics. From there he took me to the rehab areas for spinal cord and brain-injured patients, and for stroke victims. There were also special programs for pain management and sports therapy. Every piece of equipment was cutting edge, every trained professional was top-tier. "We're also planning to build a larger water training facility in the next five years."

I silently pledged if I had enough money left to donate to the project, I would. "I'm so impressed, Josh."

He beamed. "I'm glad. It's a great place to work, and to volunteer."

"Where is the greatest need for volunteers?"

"Usually behind the scenes in support roles, but there are opportunities to interact with patients, too. I'll introduce you to our volunteer liaison before you leave." He checked his watch. "Ready to meet up with Aisha?"

"As long as it's okay with her and Ramy."

"I know they'll be pleased to see you."

We circled back to the stroke rehab area where Ramy and his wife were just arriving. Ramy's eyes lit up when he saw me. He clasped me in a hug and whispered, "How can we ever thank you, Mallory?"

"By getting well," I whispered back. Aisha greeted me warmly, although she was frail. The removal of the brain tumor had taken its toll on her small frame.

Josh asked if I could observe the session and they readily agreed. I watched as Josh put Aisha through a series of physical and cognitive tests meant to strengthen the side that had been affected by the stroke. I watched him with awe. He was so patient with Aisha, so good-natured.

"A good young man, that one," Ramy remarked close to my ear.

I nodded in agreement, but a scene across the room had caught my eye.

A Golden Retriever wearing a therapy dog vest had entered the brain injury rehab area, where a young man was attempting to navigate an obstacle course. When he spotted the animal, the change in him was instantaneous. He petted and scratched the retriever's silky coat with unconsciously good mobility. And when the dog joined him on the obstacle course, the patient's improvement was nothing short of remarkable.

I recalled Josh's comment that French bulldogs made good therapy dogs.

Maybe Nessie was benefit from a little volunteering, too.

September 9, Wednesday

"SIT, NESSIE."

She looked up at me and cocked her head quizzically.

"Sit," I repeated, more firmly.

Nada.

I glanced all around the meadow of Piedmont Park where I was "training" her, to make sure no one was in earshot. Next to a tree several feet away a man in a hat was reading a book. A few yards in the other direction, a young couple were kicking around a hacky sack. I looked back to Nessie and leaned down.

"I know you can sit. Trent taught you to do all kinds of tricks."

She blinked her buggy eyes.

I frowned. "I know I'm not him, but do you see him around anywhere?" I flailed out my arm, gesturing to his absence. "It's just me and you, and I hate to see you moping around." I glanced around again self-consciously, then sighed. "And I'm tired of moping around, too. So could you just work with me here?"

She looked away.

I groaned. "In order to become a therapy dog, you have to be able to respond to basic commands, and I know you can do this."

Nessie looked back, and I took that as a good sign. I held up a treat. "Sit."

She rolled over, then looked up expectantly.

I frowned, but gave her the treat anyway. "You're a contrarian."

She gave a little bark of agreement.

"Okay, roll over." I made the turning gesture with my hand like I'd seen Trent do.

She lay down and put her paws over her eyes.

I frowned down. "I'm still here."

I sighed and reached into my backpack to withdraw Trent's sweatshirt that she loved. She perked up immediately, taking it in her teeth and tossing her head back and forth, then running in circles.

When I took it from her and held it behind my back, she barked a couple of times. How dare I?

"Sit," I commanded, then held up the sweatshirt. "Sit."

She sat, and I rewarded her with a sniff of the shirt. I shook my head. Stubborn dog… stubborn heart. To pass the therapy dog test, she would have to respond to commands without a reward.

This was going to take a while.

After an hour of training, she was fairly consistent at sitting, but only with the incentive of the shirt. I hoped by the time his scent faded from the shirt, she'd be trained to respond to my voice.

I hooked her leash to her collar and we walked back to where I'd parked along the street, but she was sluggish. At one point when I turned to urge her forward, I caught sight of someone walking behind us. The man with the hat who'd been reading nearby in the meadow. He wasn't looking at me, but it seemed too coincidental. While I stared, he stopped and removed a plastic bag from his pocket, then bent over to pick up a piece of litter on the sidewalk. He walked a few more feet, then picked up another piece.

My shoulders fell in relief. He was just a nice guy who probably lived nearby and hung out around the park. I was being paranoid.

September 10, Thursday

GOOD LUCK in the hearing. Call me after the judge's decision or anytime you want to talk and I'll try to step away from my meetings.

I smiled at Ryan's text and suddenly missed him terribly. I'd grown accustomed to his big, comforting presence nearby. But I understood he had other commitments. When he'd taken me on as a client, he probably didn't expect me to become a full-time job.

Next to me in the lobby of the courthouse, Buckley was ending a phone call. He looked stern and competent in a dark suit, carrying a weathered briefcase.

"There's been a development in the case."

"What?" I asked.

"Mrs. Conway said she'd settle for half the winnings."

I frowned. "Half the winnings for a ticket she refused to buy?"

"I know—it's robbery. But I expected this."

One part of me railed against the injustice, but another part of me reasoned I would've been satisfied with a jackpot half the size, and a bird in the hand was worth two in the bush. "What should we do?"

"It's your decision, Mallory, but I'd advise against it. It sets a precedent for the two cases that follow."

"But if I don't settle, I could walk out of here with nothing."

"Yes. And I hate to rush you, but they need an answer now."

My mind whirled with the stakes of my decision. The old Mallory would take the safe option, even if it meant going against my values. But after all I'd been through the past few weeks, I was starting to feel fearless... and I was tired of being taken advantage of.

"No," I said. "I won't settle."

Buckley nodded, then punched in a number on his phone and lifted it to his mouth. "Our answer is no. See you inside." When he ended the call, he gave a reasonable facsimile of a smile. "Are you ready?"

"I suppose," I murmured. But my fearlessness had fled, replaced by anxiety and nausea.

"Remember, be calm when you're on the stand. Make eye contact with me, with the opposing attorney, and with the judge if she addresses you." He scanned my outfit. "Good choice—you don't look rich."

"Thanks," I managed. I was wearing the gunnysack dress that Deena the public relations manager had selected for my TV debut as a lottery winner.

When we walked into the courtroom, I was instantly nervous. The dark wood of the room and the large pieces of furniture, especially the judge's desk area, were so intimidating... although I supposed that was the point.

The judge, the Honorable Evangeline Habney, was already seated, as was opposing council. Mrs. Conway was unrecognizable—gone were her garish "lucky" jackets and jangling charms and poufy hair. She wore a grandma cardigan and sensible shoes, presumably to play up the fact that I, a youngster, had stolen money from an elder who really needed it. She glared at me as we took our seats.

The pomp and circumstance of the preliminary remarks did nothing to calm my nerves—it only drove home how serious the matter was being taken. The judge explained why the hearing had been expedited and that the attorneys were in agreement the case should be ruled on as soon as possible. The attorneys gave short opening remarks. Buckley was brief and surgical—I was simply doing my job; Mrs. Conway was trying to take advantage of a minimum-wage cashier. The opposing attorney said the opposite, accusing me of keeping a ticket she had paid for.

I walked to the stand on wobbly legs to give my testimony. When I pledged to tell the truth, my raised hand was shaking.

"Ms. Green," Buckley said, "to the best of your ability, will you tell the court the events of the evening the winning ticket was sold at the GiddyUp GoMart?"

I cleared my throat. "Mrs. Conway is a regular customer of the store. She came in with lists of pre-selected numbers she wanted to play. I was more accurate at entering complicated orders, so I usually rang her up if I was working."

"And on the night in question, did Mrs. Conway come in with a list of pre-selected numbers?"

"Yes."

"Your honor, I'd like to point out that the owner of the store, Ramy Asfour, and a coworker of Ms. Green's, Shawna Dell, both submitted depositions to fact that they were present when Mrs. Conway consulted her list."

The judge nodded and indicated she had the depositions.

"Tell us about the transaction," Buckley continued.

"I punched in the numbers one set at a time because Mrs. Conway liked to have each set on a separate ticket. When I punched in one set of six numbers and handed her the ticket, she told me I'd gotten one of the numbers wrong."

"And what did you do?"

"I don't have the authority to void a transaction, so instead of asking my boss to void it and make Mrs. Conway wait, I decided to buy the ticket myself. Then I completed her order."

"And she left, satisfied?"

"To my knowledge, yes."

Buckley looked at the judge. "Your honor, as proof of my client's testimony, see exhibit A, the ticket Mrs. Conway cashed in from that date that matched all but one of the numbers of the ticket Ms. Green bought and later claimed."

"Duly noted," the judge said.

Buckley thanked me, and turned over questioning to the opposing council, a thin, precise-looking man.

"Ms. Green, is it customary for employees at the GiddyUp GoMart to buy lottery tickets?"

"Yes."

"And is it customary for them to process their own transactions?"

I swallowed hard. "No. It's not against the rules, but generally, we process each other's lottery ticket transactions."

"And why is that?"

I wet my lips.

"Isn't it to cut down on the risk of fraud?"

"Yes," I said finally.

"But in this instance, you chose to go against the rules?"

"They're not rules," I repeated. "They're guidelines. And yes, as I said, I chose to go against the guidelines because I didn't want Mrs. Conway to be inconvenienced."

"That one-time exception certainly turned out nicely for you," he said dryly.

"Objection," Buckley said.

"Withdrawn," the man said. "No more questions."

I stepped down from the witness box and took my place beside Buckley. His grimace did not give me hope, and deepened when Mrs. Conway stood and made her way to the witness stand using— I blinked—a *cane*?

When she finally took her place, she looked every inch the vulnerable senior citizen.

"Mrs. Conway, how are you today?" her attorney asked.

"Not well," she said. "I can't sleep over knowing the money that should've been mine and my family's was stolen from us by that clever cashier." She lifted her cane and pointed it at me.

"You paid cash for your tickets the night of July thirtieth?"

"Yes."

"And you distinctly remember giving the set of numbers to Ms. Green that were later drawn as the winning numbers?"

"Yes. I play the same ten or twelve numbers often, in different combinations."

"Exhibit B, your honor, is a list of numbers Mrs. Conway considers to be her lucky numbers. As you can see, the six winning numbers from the date in question are on her list, proving she gave those numbers to Ms. Green, but Ms. Green kept that ticket."

He looked triumphant when he passed questioning over to Buckley.

Buckley gave Mrs. Conway his best smile. "Mrs. Conway, do you have the receipt from your purchase the evening in question?"

"No, because I trusted Ms. Green."

"Exhibit C, your Honor, shows the register receipt from that evening. As you can see, there's a handwritten note at the bottom saying Ms. Green purchased a ticket."

Mrs. Conway shrugged. "She probably added that later."

Buckley gave her another smile. "Mrs. Conway, don't you think it's strange that of the dozens of tickets you purchased that day from the GiddyUp GoMart, that Ms. Green kept only one of the tickets?"

The woman leaned forward. "If someone steals enough tickets, sooner or later they're going to get lucky and steal a winner."

Buckley frowned. "No more questions." As he walked back to the table, I knew we'd taken a hit.

For closing statements, the attorneys reiterated their arguments. Buckley pointed out there was no evidence I had stolen the ticket, that my boss and coworker had sworn to my integrity.

But honestly, I could see the case going either way.

The judge asked for a thirty-minute recess to make her decision. While we waited, the opposing attorney came to our table and leaned down. "Last chance to settle. Split the winnings, fifty-fifty?"

Buckley shifted in his seat. "Give me a few minutes to consult with my client."

I could guarantee myself something... on the other hand, if Mrs. Conway won, the money would be gone, the subsequent lawsuits would go away, and I could disappear into the background, like before. I wavered.

"Mallory?" Buckley asked.

I swallowed hard and went against my instincts. "No. I'm not settling."

He looked at his counterpart and signaled thumbs down.

During the next few minutes, I changed my mind a dozen times, and was on the verge of telling Buckley to take the deal when the judge emerged from her chambers.

Too late.

"I realize there is a fortune at stake in this case," the judge said. "It's clear the defendant and the plaintiff have differing accounts of the transaction in question."

My chest vibrated from the pounding of my heart.

"But in the absence of evidence that a theft occurred, the law is clearly on the side of the person who possessed the winning ticket, signed the winning ticket, and claimed the winning ticket. I find in the favor of the defendant. Congratulations, Ms. Green. Enjoy your winnings."

I exhaled…. then one breath later, I tensed up again.

One lawsuit down, two to go.

September 11, Friday

ON THE heels of the ruling, I was feeling antsy and bored.

And still in limbo.

I glanced around the apartment, noticing all the blank spaces where happy pictures and shared furniture used to be. Loneliness washed over me. I longed to talk to someone, but Wanda was on a date, Ryan was still out of town, and I'd been warned not to talk to Kerry and Vance at the restaurant due to the lawsuit.

I lifted my gaze to the door and wondered if Josh was home.

Just to talk—nothing more.

I walked to the entrance, but stopped with my hand on the knob when I heard his door open. He was leaving? I looked through the peephole to see him heft a laundry basket, then walk down the hall.

Hm… I had enough dirty clothes for a load of laundry.

I hastily gathered my laundry, grabbing a couple of items from drawers to make my pile look legit, then headed to the laundry room with dollar bills stuffed in my pockets for the change machine.

When I walked in, I was met with a warm hum from the machines and the pleasant scent of fabric softener. For some reason, the combined sensory cues always made me feel cozy—I wondered if my mother had taken me to the laundromat when I was little and the good memory had embedded itself into my subconscious.

Across the room, Josh glanced up from a washing machine, then smiled in greeting. I smiled back, then carried my basket to the washer next to his.

"I figured you'd be out on a date with Mr. Porsche," he offered good-naturedly.

"Um, no. Ryan is… out of town. I decided to do some laundry."

"Ah."

I recalled the boxes of condoms Josh had purchased at the GiddyUp. "You don't have a hot date either?"

"Not unless you count the dryer," he said with a laugh. "Hey, Ramy told me the customer suing you over the lottery ticket lost her case. Congrats."

"Thanks. But that was only one of the lawsuits. My husband—my ex—wants half."

He frowned. "He walked out and he wants half of your lottery winnings?"

"He says it's community property, and since our divorce isn't final, he has a case."

"Wow… I'm sorry, Mal. That sucks."

I nodded. "Have you ever been married?"

"No." His mouth quirked into a smile. "Haven't you heard? Nice guys finish last."

I began transferring my clothes to the washer and realized I'd emptied my lingerie drawer in my haste to fill the basket.

Josh noticed the filmy garments with raised eyebrows. "You must do a lot of… lounging."

A flush traveled up my neck. "I do need to find something to do with my time. How long will I have to wait to be approved as a volunteer?"

"It should take only a few days to check your references. In fact, I got a call from the office this morning."

"And did you give me good marks?"

"Glowing," he said. "Although I warned them to keep you away from dumpsters."

I laughed.

"Hey, I was thinking about getting takeout from 26 Thai— want to join me?"

His invitation caught me off-guard, although it shouldn't have. I studied his earnest, appealing face and quiet demeanor. He was a good guy… and he would expect too much. Plus I didn't want to expose him to the drama of my life. "I, um… probably shouldn't. I'm supposed to Skype with Ryan later."

"Ah, okay."

I felt bad for following him to the laundry room. "Josh... can we just be friends?"

He looked pained. "The Friend Zone, also known as No Man's Land."

I angled my head.

Then he sighed. "Sure. That's what nice guys do." He closed the washer, then punched a button to turn it on. "Later, Mal."

"I have a few minutes to hang out," I offered.

He pulled his hand over his mouth. "I need a little time to feel sorry for myself. I'm not *that* nice."

When the door closed behind him, I didn't like the feelings he'd agitated in me.

September 12, Saturday

I WAS jarred awake pre-dawn by the trill of my phone. My mind immediately went to Ryan since he'd had to cancel our Skype call the night before. When I saw Ramy's name on my screen, my pulse leapt. It wasn't like him to call, and certainly not so early.

"Ramy, hi... is everything okay?"

"Hi, Mallory. I had to admit Aisha to the hospital last night for a fall."

"Oh, no."

"She's fine, but they want to keep her for a couple of days for observation. By the way, Bob is getting his new kidney today."

"That's great news!"

"Yes. But Shawna will be with him for several days while he recovers."

I realized the implications of both of them being unavailable. "Do you need for me to take care of the store while you're out?"

He sighed. "I know it's too much to ask."

"Not at all, I'm happy to help."

"I hired a new guy named Link and he's a good worker, but I'd feel better if someone was supervising him."

"Say no more. I'll be there as soon as I can."

I ended the call and jumped out of bed, surprised by how much I was looking forward to clocking in. It felt good to have something to do and—how had my therapist put it? Somewhere to be.

It was also nice to drive to work instead of relying on the train, although I felt self-conscious as I parked the expensive little sports car in the lot. As I climbed out, a stocky bearded guy wearing a GiddyUp GoMart nametag was climbing out of a beater Ford.

"Whew-we, that's a nice ride," he said, circling my car.

"You must be Link."

"Yep."

"I'm Mallory—I'll be working with you today."

He snapped his fingers. "Wait—you're that girl, that Lottery Girl."

I gave him a flat smile. "Mallory will do."

"No wonder you're driving such a sweet sled. How does it feel to be filthy, stinking rich?"

His words stopped me. How strange that we associated wealth with negative things like filth and stink... was that why I'd always had such a bad relationship with money?

"Let's go inside," I suggested. But the interrogation didn't stop there. Link seemed entranced by the idea I could buy almost anything I wanted—he spent most of the day thinking of outrageous expenditures.

"A trip to Mars on SpaceX... an NBA team... a movie studio..."

I laughed it off, thinking most people had no concept of how much money some things cost... it was a little humbling to realize my lottery money couldn't hold a candle to true wealth... and how much of a chasm existed between the resources of the everyday person and people at the extreme end of the spectrum.

"There's another nice ride," Link said from the counter where he rang up a gasoline sale at the pump.

I glanced out the window to see what vehicle had caught his attention, then did a double-take when I saw the black convertible Porsche. Ryan's Porsche, evidenced by the fact that the man himself stood next to his car, talking on his phone while the credit card payment processed. And from his body language, the conversation was contentious. I watched as he climbed into his car, then banged his fist on the steering wheel. He sped off with more horsepower than necessary.

Hurt and confusion suffused my chest—he wasn't supposed to return from Miami until tomorrow.

Why would he lie to me?

September 13, Sunday

I HADN'T slept well. Ryan had sent me texts as if he were still out of town. I had replied dutifully because I didn't know what else to do.

I wasn't sure what was worse—entrusting my money to someone who'd lied to me, or entrusting my heart. But I had to face that my burgeoning feelings for Ryan were one-sided... apparently his interest lay solely in my bank account. I just wasn't sure why he thought he had to woo me—I'd gone to him for his investment advice, with no expectations otherwise.

I was glad to have the shift at the GiddyUp to keep my mind occupied. Link was getting the hang of things and he was a good employee, but the man talked nonstop—mostly about my money.

"How does all that work? Do they just hand you a big suitcase of cash?"

I laughed. "No. It's all handled through bank wire transfers."

His face dropped. "That's no fun."

I didn't add that the bulk of my winnings was still being held in escrow until the suit Trent had filed could be heard. Buckley and Shift had tag-teamed to find a judge who would hold the hearing quickly. Considering Trent's lack of patience with the universe in general, I knew he'd want his money pronto, and his attorney seemed equally eager. If the stars aligned, I'd know by the end of the month whether I'd have to split the jackpot with Trent.

I was already dreading the face-off in court, which, admittedly, was uppermost on my mind because of my newfound intelligence on Ryan. When I drove back to the apartment and parked in the low light of dusk, I was feeling vulnerable and jumpy. I glanced all around the lot, but there were plenty of places for someone to hide. Unable to shake the feeling I was being watched, I locked the car doors and walked quickly through the parking lot toward the building entrance.

When I thought I heard footsteps behind me, I sped up.

But so did they.

I broke into a jog, then a sprint, to reach the entrance. I felt the person about to overtake me. When they grabbed my arm from behind, I screamed.

"Mallory—it's me."

When I realized it was Ryan, I relaxed, but only a fraction. I shook loose his hand. "What are you doing? You scared me."

He was dressed casually, which for him meant his pants didn't have a knife-pleat. "I'm sorry," he said, raking his hand through his hair. "I need to talk to you."

I pulled back. "I need to talk to you, too. You first."

He gestured to the entrance. "Can we go inside?"

I crossed my arms. "I'd rather not. Why are you here? I thought your flight didn't get in until late."

He heaved a sigh. "I lied to you about where I was. I did go to Miami, but not for business. I went to a wedding."

I closed my eyes briefly. "Oh, God... you're married, aren't you?"

"What? No!"

"Then what is going on? I saw you yesterday getting gas."

He winced. "I went to a wedding with a woman I've been seeing. It was something I committed to before I met you."

I raised my hands. "You don't have to explain."

"Yes, I do." His face softened. "I broke it off with Maria, but I should've told you."

That took the wind out of my sails. "We... don't have an understanding."

"Let's change that. I'm totally captivated by you, Mallory. You're unlike any other woman I've dated."

While I pondered his revelation, he added, "I've already talked to another financial manager in my office about taking over your accounts." He smiled. "I don't want there to be any question about where my interests lie."

I was still trying to process it all. Ryan really did have feelings for me?

He picked up my hand. "I know I've dropped a lot on you. Just think about it." He lowered a kiss to my temple, then turned and walked into the darkness.

September 14, Monday

"Do you believe him?" Imogene asked.

"I... don't know," I confessed. "I want to."

She angled her head. "Why do you want to?"

I took my time answering. I was still wary of entrapment—of saying something that would boomerang on me. "Because... Ryan is the kind of guy I've always wanted to be with."

"What kind of guy is that?"

"Someone successful... confident. Someone who has goals that are bigger than mine."

"Someone to take care of you?"

I pressed my lips together. "Is that so bad?"

"Not at all. But what about love?"

"I thought I had that with Trent," I reminded her. "So these days I'm putting less stock in love. Besides, I think that's going to be harder for me to find... now."

"Because of the money, you mean?"

I nodded. "Only someone like Ryan isn't impressed or swayed by that kind of money."

"By the way, congratulations on winning the first lawsuit."

"Thank you. And thank you for the suggestion last week to look into volunteering."

"How's that going?"

"I've been approved to volunteer at the Shepherd Center. It'll allow me to use my unfinished physical therapy degree."

She pursed her mouth. "You could still finish your PT degree, Mallory."

I smiled. "That's what Josh says."

"Josh?"

"He's a neighbor. We were actually in the same college classes, but he finished, and I didn't. Josh is the one who arranged for me to volunteer at Shepherd."

"He sounds like a good friend."

I nodded. "He's a good... friend."

September 15, Tuesday

IT WAS a busy night at the GiddyUp. The jackpot on the Mega Dollars Lottery was climbing again, and tickets were flying out the door. I ran the lottery register while Link handled everything else.

But when the door chimed and I saw Mrs. Conway walk in wearing a charm-bedecked outfit, I froze.

And so did she. "*What* are you doing here?"

Link leaned across the counter. "She's my boss. Who are you?"

"Never mind," I said to Link. "You'll need to ring up this sale." I looked back to Mrs. Conway. "That is, if you still want to buy tickets?"

She looked conflicted. I could tell she was torn between planting her morality flag and her compulsion to maintain her superstitious rituals. "Only if you promise not to steal my next winning ticket."

I frowned. "I see you forgot your cane."

Her mouth tightened, but she proceeded to the counter.

I traded places with Link and walked him through punching in the long order. His fingers were too big for the register keys, so he made lots of mistakes. But with each mistake, I took the time out to void the ticket and make him start again. It was grueling, but he eventually finished.

"Good luck," I said to her when he handed over the tickets.

The woman looked at me with a haughty expression. "One of these days, girlie, your luck is going to run out."

I knew it was a petty, hollow threat said out of spite… but why did it send chills up my spine?

September 16, Wednesday

"MS. GREEN?"

I looked up to see a mountain of a man standing in the doorway, glancing around the crowded police precinct waiting room. I pushed to my feet, holding Nessie. "That's me."

"I'm Detective Jack Terry. Right this way, ma'am."

I followed him into a large room occupied by cubicles and a grid of open desks.

He gestured to a refreshment station. "Can I get you some coffee, water?"

"No, thank you."

He proceeded to lead me to a corner office with a nice view, then closed the door behind us. He indicated a guest chair. "Have a seat."

I lowered myself to a chair, now second-guessing my reason for coming.

"Cute dog," he offered.

"Thanks," I murmured.

He sat back in his chair. "What's this about someone following you?"

I wet my lips. "I've been spending a lot of time in Piedmont Park, training my dog."

"Go on."

"And I keep noticing the same man hanging around. I think he's following me."

"You don't recognize the man?"

"No."

"Has he ever approached you?"

"No. When I try to make eye contact, he looks away or walks in the opposite direction." As soon as the words left my mouth, I realized how ridiculous they sounded.

He looked as if he planned to humor me. "Can you think of a reason why someone would be following you?"

"I, uh... won a lottery jackpot about two months ago."

His eyebrows climbed. "No kidding? That'll bring out the crazies, all right. Do you live alone?"

"Yes. I'm, um... going through a divorce."

"Hm. Could your ex be having you followed?"

I blinked. It hadn't occurred to me, but... "I guess it's possible." Although what could Trent gain by having someone tail me?

"What's your spouse's name?"

I told him, and the detective made notes on a piece of paper. "How many times have you seen this man?"

"Three or four times in the last couple of weeks. When I noticed him again today, I left and came here."

He nodded. "Better to err on the side of caution. Did you happen to take a picture of the guy?"

I shook my head. "Should I if I see him again?"

"Only if you think it's safe. Can you describe him? Age, height, weight, race?"

I tried, but everything I could remember about the man was nondescript. The best I could do was approximate his age at maybe fifty, but maybe not.

Jack Terry sat back in his chair. "Unfortunately, there's not much I can do unless the guy is caught in the act. If you can get a picture, we might be able to identify him. At least it's on the record, though. In the meantime, I suggest you buy some pepper spray. And if you see the man again, call me directly." He pushed a business card across the desk.

I took it, but even I was starting to think I was imagining things.

September 17, Thursday

"I KNOW it's not the most exciting volunteer position," the Shepherd volunteer liaison said. "But when I saw you had experience as a receptionist, I was overjoyed." She lowered her voice to a whisper. "You can't imagine how difficult it is to find a good receptionist, even salaried."

"It's fine," I said, trying to sound enthusiastic. It wouldn't put my stunted physical therapy education to good use, but it would allow me to learn the names and faces of the people who worked at the renowned spine and brain rehab center.

She positioned me behind a desk not unlike the one I'd stood behind at Noble Plaza. I gave a little laugh—that job seemed like a lifetime ago. I familiarized myself with the phone system and consulted a staff directory to start committing names and numbers to memory.

Joshua English, Doctor of Physical Therapy, Brain and Spine Injury Rehabilitation.

"Hi, friend."

At the sound of his voice, I slammed shut the directory.

"Whoa," he said. "Didn't mean to startle you. I just wanted to say hello on your first day."

I conjured up a smile. "Hi. I was just... getting oriented."

He was dressed casually, but professionally, sporting a cross-body messenger bag. "You'll be great at this." He leaned in and lowered his voice. "We've had some terrible receptionists."

"I'm glad the bar is so low."

He laughed.

I pressed my lips together. "Thanks, by the way, for making this happen."

"Are you kidding? We're lucky to have you." He smiled, then removed a small box from his bag. "A welcome gift."

I gasped. "That's not necessary."

He winked. "Oh, but it is. Have a good day."

I waited a full ten seconds after he walked away before opening the box. Then I smirked.

A friendship bracelet.

I removed the delicate woven band in a geometric design containing every color in the rainbow and fastened it around my wrist with the tiny tassels at each end.

It was the nicest thing anyone had ever given me.

September 18, Friday

"SIGN HERE... and here... and here... and here," the banker said, removing colored flags as I went through the forms to close on the Lake Lanier house. I remembered reading somewhere that when a person bought a home, it felt as if you were signing your life away. Now I understood why.

The difference was there would be no mortgage. Ryan had agreed it was best to sink as much cash as possible into the home to hopefully shelter it from the impending lawsuits. But it was a scary prospect because it brought the balance in my accounts alarmingly low—and I still hadn't paid for Aisha's treatment, Bob's transplant surgery, and so on.

The banker smiled. "Congratulations, Ms. Green, on your new home."

The real estate agent handed me a ring of keys and added her thanks. I told myself that my misgivings were merely a mild case of buyer's remorse. Everyone had qualms when transacting such a large purchase. Next to me Ryan clasped my hand under the table. It made me feel as if I was doing the right thing... and having him there almost made it feel as if it was *our* home.

When we left the meeting I looked up at him. "Where do you live?"

He smiled. "I have a condo in Buckhead."

"Why haven't you invited me?"

He raised an eyebrow. "Does that mean you've been thinking about our... understanding?"

"I have."

"And?"

"And why don't we have dinner this evening at my house, and next time at your house?"

He grinned. "That's a deal." He raised my hand for a kiss, then frowned. "That's new."

He was looking at the colorful bracelet Josh had given me. "It's a friendship bracelet... from a friend."

"Still... we can do better than that—you should be wearing gold and diamonds."

With some effort, I matched his smile. Ryan wanted only the best for me... he thought I deserved it... and what was wrong with that?

September 19, Saturday

I WAS standing in my state-of-the-art kitchen eating a grilled cheese sandwich and watching the sun set over the lake in pink and orange hues. It was so gorgeous, I wanted to cry. And it was so quiet, I could hear myself chew. From a distant room in the my new cavernous house, I heard Nessie bark, then start to howl.

She was lost again.

"Nessie," I called, "follow the sound of my voice."

I kept calling for her until I heard the scratch of her nails on the wood floor. She looked forlorn, and was dragging Trent's sweatshirt behind her.

"Are you hungry?" I asked, pinching off a piece of my sandwich.

She was unimpressed.

"Sit," I commanded. "Nessie, *sit*."

She turned and walked a few yards away, then lay down with her beloved sweatshirt. I was hurt and betrayed over what Trent had done to me, but what he'd done to Nessie was unforgivable.

"What would you like to do tonight?" I asked her. "Play hide and seek? Watch *Lady and the Tramp* in the theater? Drink water out of all eight commodes?"

She covered her eyes with her paws, shutting me out.

I hadn't counted on the house feeling so huge and making me feel so... small. And isolated. My mind wandered to the setting for nearly every horror movie made: *A young woman holes up alone in a mansion, unaware she's being watched...*

When the panel of the security system dinged, I screamed and dropped my sandwich. I walked over the screen, my heart pounding in my ears.

Car arriving.

I swallowed hard—I wasn't expecting any visitors. In fact, I was on the verge of hightailing it back to my apartment. Ryan had a business dinner to attend, and...

Apparently, I had no friends.

While I chewed on that revelation, I realized I'd left the can of pepper spray I'd bought in another purse at the apartment—some Girl Scout I would make. When the car pulled past the camera, my pulse shot to double-time because I didn't recognize it. I'd programmed Detective Jack Terry's number into my phone, so with my phone in one hand, I went around the room searching for a weapon. I settled for the cast iron skillet I'd used to grill my sandwich, and decided it would have to do. Then I watched the security screen to see who would emerge from the vehicle. The man who'd been following me? A reporter? A random stalker who haunted property tax records?

Or just your run-of-the-mill serial killer?

The door opened and out climbed... Wanda? She grinned at the camera and held up a bottle of champagne.

I rushed to the front door and flung it open. "Hi!"

"Hi, yourself." She frowned at the pan I held. "What's going on?"

"You scared me to death—why didn't you call? And where's your SUV?"

"It died, this is a rental. And I did call, like twelve times—is your ringer turned off?"

I checked my phone. "Oh… sorry."

She laughed as she walked past me into the house. "Were you going to fry me to death?"

I closed the door and turned the deadbolt. "It was all I could get my hands on."

"Girl, you need a gun."

I balked. "I so do *not* need a gun."

"If you're going to live out here in the middle of nowhere by your skinny-ass self and that scaredy-cat dog, you need a gun."

I sighed. She was right. I needed a gun.

September 20, Sunday

AGAINST MY counsel's advice, I slipped into The Community Café and took a seat at a small corner table.

Doug must have seen me walk in because he appeared, eyes wide. "Mallory, should you be here with the lawsuit and all?"

"I come in peace," I said. "Do the employees know about me buying the restaurant?"

"No, I'm on the down-low like we agreed."

I squinted. "I think you might want to check the meaning of that word."

"I told everyone the bank gave me an extension."

"Good. Hopefully, this will all be settled soon."

Behind him, Kerry appeared, hauling a tray full of food. When she spotted me, she couldn't unload the plates fast enough. She signaled Vance, then barreled toward my table. He followed, looking less bloodthirsty.

"Go," I hissed to Doug.

He vamoosed, giving Kerry a wide berth.

"You have a lot of nerve coming in here," Kerry said as she marched up.

I sighed. "I was hoping we could talk."

"Not unless you're here to talk about how we're going to split up that lottery money."

"That's not fair," I said calmly. "I bought that ticket with my own money, separate from this place. Besides, I bought you a car!"

"Thanks, by the way," Vance said, leaning in. "*Love* it."

Kerry swatted at him. "She's trying to buy us off." Then she glared. "Our attorney said we're not supposed to talk to you."

I nodded. "My attorney said the same. I just really miss you guys."

She gave a harsh laugh. "Yeah... we were so close."

I raised my hands. "Okay, I'm leaving."

"We'll see you in court," Kerry said.

As I made my way toward the door, the conversation at the spa came back to me, of Kerry and Vance accusing me of being aloof, of rejecting their overtures of friendship. Would things have progressed to this point if I'd only been more open?

For some reason, a flood of feelings seemed to converge and when I reached my car in the parking lot, I was glad I didn't have to insert a key into the door because I was blinking back tears of frustration and loneliness.

"Mallory?"

I turned at the sound of an unfamiliar man's voice, and tried to blink my vision clear. I could see the outline of him approaching, and my mind immediately went to the man who'd been following me. My throat convulsed around a scream, but before I could get it out, he came into focus.

Chance... and Hannah. Two of my favorite customers. I exhaled.

"Hi," Hannah said with a wide grin. She looked much more pregnant than when I'd last seen her.

"Hello," I said, chastising myself for being so jumpy. "How are you?"

"We're well," Hannah said, fairly glowing with good health and happiness.

"Nice ride," Chance offered.

"Thanks."

"I see you're enjoying some of your winnings," Hannah said. "Good for you."

I decided not to mention the pleasure had been fleeting—and was now turning into something less fun. We exchanged more small talk, then said goodbye. When I swung into the car, I immediately locked the doors.

Then I thought of the wishbone Hannah had given me... and was struck by the notion that I wished I'd saved it for another occasion.

September 21, Monday

IMOGENE NODDED thoughtfully. "And have you seen this mysterious man recently?"

"No," I admitted. "But I still feel as if I'm being watched."

"But don't you think that has something to do with the fact that you've been in the news, that so many people know your face and your name? And that you're about to go up against your husband in court in a few days?"

I nodded. Every time I thought about facing down Trent in a courtroom, I practically retched.

"You're Lottery Girl—it's natural to feel as if you're being watched all the time."

"I suppose you're right."

She started to say something, then looked as if she'd changed her mind.

"What?" I prodded.

She smiled, then angled her head. "Mallory... is it possible you've manifested this man you think is following you to justify not trusting people?"

I chewed on my lower lip for several long seconds.

"Okay," Imogene said, accepting my silence. "Is there any truth in what your coworkers accused you of, that you rejected their offers of friendship?"

"Probably."

"Why do you think that is?"

I squirmed. "Because every time I've gotten close to someone, they leave."

She nodded. "And because of that, is it possible that when you start to feel too much, you shut down?"

"Maybe," I said. "I've always had trouble making friends... to be honest, I don't know if I know how to be a friend."

She pointed to the bracelet on my wrist. "Someone obviously disagrees."

September 22, Tuesday

I WAS working one more shift at the GiddyUp as a favor to Ramy. But to my surprise, when I arrived, Shawna was working instead of Link.

"Mallory!" She caught me up in a dancing embrace.

I'd missed her smiling face. "How is Bob?"

"The doctors say he's doing great. He's up and around and walking every day. I'm so grateful, Mallory, for everything you've done."

I maintained my smile. Ryan was paying the hospital installments out of the line of credit the bank had extended to me.

"I heard that nasty Mrs. Conway lost her case, good enough for her. I hope it cost her a bundle."

"She came in the other day to buy tickets."

"She did not."

"I think she put a hex on me."

Shawna harrumphed. "I'm going to talk to Ramy about banning her from the store."

"She would make a stink, and he needs the business. I'm expecting her to show again tonight since the jackpot is still climbing."

My coworker snapped her fingers. "I'll take care of it."

While I waited on customers, Shawna disappeared into the backroom, only to appear a few minutes later with a tall stepladder. She positioned it so that anyone who walked in had to walk under it. I shook my head, but she gave me a thumbs up.

Sure enough, when Mrs. Conway came in and realized she'd walked under another ladder, she ran from the store screeching she'd been cursed and vowed not to come back.

We were still laughing when another customer walked in, a young man wearing a ball cap. From the corner of my eye, I noticed he made a beeline for the condoms section and grabbed an armful—another guy hoping to get lucky in a way that had nothing to do with the lottery. A few minutes later he approached the counter and tossed down the boxes.

I smiled in surprise. "Josh?"

He pushed back the bill of his cap and balked. "Mallory? Do you still work here?"

"I'm just filling in as a favor to my former boss."

"Ah." He glanced at the pile of condoms and a red flush crept up his neck. "They're, um, for a friend."

I rang them up and bagged them without comment, even though once before he'd purchased enough condoms for ten people. This was the same guy who did laundry on Friday night? It appeared Josh was keeping secrets.

He seemed to be in a hurry to leave. After he hastily paid for the items, he grabbed the bag and headed for the door.

"See you later," I called after him.

September 23, Wednesday

"So HAVE you seen it yet?" Wanda asked.

We were sipping wine on the rooftop deck of the lake house, enjoying a late summer breeze.

"Seen what?" I asked.

"Ryan's penis, that's what."

I choked on my wine. "We're taking things really slow. He just got out of a relationship and so did I."

She scoffed. "All of my best relationships evolved out of first-date sex. It's all about chemistry."

"Are you dating someone new?"

A frown marred her pretty face. "No. But I ran into Rick the other day, and can you believe he's already seeing someone else?"

"You turned down his marriage proposal," I reminded her. "You said he'd never be able to provide you the lifestyle you wanted."

"That's true," she said. "But dammit, he didn't have to get over me so quickly."

I laughed. "I think you care more about him than you pretend."

She made a face. "Change of subject—are you ready to face Trent in court tomorrow?"

I took a large drink from my glass. "No."

She picked up the wine bottle. "Then let's go pick out something lethal for you to wear."

September 24, Thursday

I WAS relatively sure my gorgeous yellow shirtdress was compromised by my quaking arms and legs. I had to stop in the ladies' room to throw up before going into the courtroom. When I emerged from the stall, Mikala Morgan was standing at the mirror stroking red color onto her sensuous lips.

She cut her gaze to me and recognition dawned in her doe eyes. "Oh... hello."

"Hello," I murmured, then moved to the farthest sink to wash my hands.

"Nice dress," she offered.

"Don't," I said. "Just... don't."

She screwed up her red mouth, then gave me a once-over. "What did he see in you?"

I dried my hands on a paper towel. "I honestly don't know."

Deflated by my candor, she stalked out of the bathroom. I wanted to throw up again, but found a mint in my bag and willed my stomach to settle. Hopefully, the hearing wouldn't be as bad as I expected.

Except it was *so* much worse.

Trent testified first, painting me as a cold, jealous wife who complained, no matter how hard he tried to support us financially. He'd offered to work on the marriage, he said, but I wasn't amenable. He'd had no choice but to leave for his own mental wellbeing. He'd met with me to discuss the community property in good faith, and had given me ample time to reveal the fact that I was sitting on a jackpot. He was handsome and convincing, conjuring up teary eyes on command. I felt as if I was watching a stranger—I didn't even know this person.

"Obviously," he finished, "Mallory drove me away so she could keep the money all to herself."

My attorney pointed out if I'd wanted to leave the marriage, I would've filed for divorce, but instead he had. And he was the one who'd moved out and moved on with another partner. I was only trying to protect something I'd acquired after he'd left the marriage. But Trent put on a great performance.

When it was time for my testimony, I tripped on the way to the stand, and it went downhill from there. I had to admit under oath that I knew I had the winning ticket when I'd met with him to discuss the property division, yet I'd said nothing. And his attorney had tracked down a list of everything I'd purchased with the money.

"A suite at the Four Seasons, a mansion on Lake Lanier, a top-of-the-line van, *three* fancy sports cars, a gold watch, thousands of dollars worth of clothes... the list goes on and on," he said dramatically. "Ms. Green isn't the frugal blue-collar cashier she'd have you to believe. She's a greedy, greedy woman who willfully and purposefully schemed to hide community assets acquired while they were still married from her husband. Assets that could have a huge emotional impact on this man who's just trying to get back on his feet."

After the attorney was finished dissecting my character, even I hated me.

At the end of the closing arguments, the judge seemed torn. "I'll review everything and render my decision tomorrow at noon."

September 25, Friday

LYNETTE SHIFT gave me a bolstering smile as we took our places at the defendant's table, but I could tell she was as worried as I was. I hadn't eaten since yesterday and hadn't slept since the day before. Ryan had called but I wouldn't see him... I was wound up like a giant spring.

Trent, on the other hand, looked handsome and relaxed as we waited for the judge to emerge and render her verdict. He turned and blew a kiss to Mikala, who sat in the gallery like a supportive partner. The gesture of affection shook me to the core—never in our five-year marriage had he blown me a kiss. I would've remembered... because I would've cherished it.

When the door opened and the judge appeared, my attorney had to help me to my feet. Since the judge didn't make eye contact with me, I had a bad, bad feeling about the outcome.

I was right.

"While the defendant made a strong argument for not revealing the existence of a lottery ticket worth approximately fifty-two million dollars, the fact remains that the couple was still married when the wife acquired the ticket with money that was a shared resource of the marriage. Georgia community property law is clear in these circumstances, so in the matter before me I find for the plaintiff. The proceeds of the winning ticket will be split, fifty-fifty." She banged the gavel. "Case adjourned."

Trent's side of the courtroom exploded in a frenzy. Just like that, my net proceeds from the jackpot went from seventeen million to about eight million, give or take.

And still one more lawsuit to go.

September 26, Saturday

I UNLOCKED the door to my apartment and walked inside. After yesterday, the bittersweet memories of my marriage were just plain bitter. I wanted to get rid of anything that reminded me of it so I wouldn't have to keep thinking how wrong I'd been about Trent.

A Goodwill truck was set to arrive soon. I went from room to room emptying drawers and cabinets, filling boxes and bags, and stacking small pieces furniture. Into another bag went photos and personal files, all bound for the shredder.

When a knock sounded, I checked the peephole, expecting to see a driver. Instead it was Josh, apparently returning from a run.

I opened the door and registered he was getting buff from all the miles he'd logged—or maybe I hadn't looked close enough before. "Hi."

"Hi. I saw your car in the parking lot. Everything okay?"

I nodded. "Just rounding up everything for Goodwill."

"You're clearing out?"

"Yeah."

"So you're letting go of the apartment?"

"It's paid until the end of the month, I think, but yeah. I moved into my house."

He nodded. "Cool." Then he wiped his hand over his mouth. "Listen... about the other day at the convenience store—"

I held up my hands. "You don't have to explain your purchases to me."

"I know, but I want to. I assume you noticed the, um, *quantity* of the items I bought?"

I smiled. "You mean the many, many boxes of condoms? Yeah, I noticed."

"I, um... buy them for patients."

I squinted. "What?"

He sighed. "For the young guys in wheelchairs. Even if they're paraplegic, not everything below the waist is immobile."

I smiled. "I do remember that much from my training."

"Many of these guys live with their parents, or their caretaker is a family member who does their shopping for them, and some of them are too embarrassed to ask for condoms."

I laughed. "So you're their supplier?"

He flushed beet red. "I guess you could say that."

"That's really nice of you."

"What can I say? I'm a nice guy."

"So you keep telling me."

The door at the end of the hall opened, and a guy with a clipboard appeared. "Green?"

"That's here," I said. I looked at Josh. "See you around?"

He nodded, then disappeared into his apartment.

I stared after him, fingering the bracelet around my wrist.

September 27, Sunday

I WAS getting ready for bed when my security system sounded. After two false alarms from wild animals strolling into my yard, I wasn't immediately worried—until I looked at the camera.

It was the man who'd been following me, standing near the dock, obviously unaware he was being caught on film. My heart vaulted to the back of my throat. The doors and windows were secure, but all it would take was a large rock to breech them. The alarms, as Wanda had pointed out, were only there to warn me, and to give me enough time to call the police.

Who would probably take forever to get to my remote location.

I fumbled for my phone and pulled up Detective Jack Terry's number, then dialed, praying he'd answer.

"This is Terry."

"Detective," I said, choking in my relief. "This is Mallory Green. I talked to you the other day about a man following me. He's here, in front of my house."

"What's your address?"

I gave it to him.

"That's the east side of Lake Lanier."

"Yes, my house is on the water. It's rather large, lots of windows."

"You bought the mansion in Clay Cove?"

"Um… yes. You know it?"

"Yeah. I'm on my way. I'm assuming you have an alarm system?"

"Yes."

"Stay away from the windows. If he approaches the house, set off an external alarm."

"Okay."

I hung up, but the blood was rushing through my ears. I called for Nessie and stayed near a monitor, avoiding the windows. For a while, the man stood staring at the house. Then he took a few steps forward. I hit the button for the external alarm, and the air was filled with decibels that had me covering my ears and Nessie scrambling for cover. The man bolted and went off-screen. A few minutes later I heard the sound of a powerboat. I looked out to see the lights of a runabout approaching my dock at a breakneck speed. The driver expertly slowed to pull alongside the dock. Jack Terry himself jumped from the boat and hastily secured the lines. My phone rang and it was him.

"Hello, Detective."

"Are you okay?"

"Yes. The man ran away when I set off the alarm."

"Okay, kill the alarm. I'm going to check the perimeter, then I'll come to the front door."

He ended the call and from the monitor I watched him scan the area all around the house, his hand on his weapon throughout. A few minutes later the doorbell sounded and I let him in. His big body was a comforting sight.

"I didn't find anyone," he said. "Are you alright?"

"Just shaken."

"Do you have him on film?"

I nodded.

"I'll get that footage from your security company first thing tomorrow. Will you be okay tonight? Is anyone else here?"

"I'll call someone to come and stay."

"That's probably best. Okay, goodnight, Ms. Green."

"Detective?"

"Yeah?"

I gestured to the boat. "How did you get here so fast?"

"I live on a houseboat on the lake. I keep a runabout for fishing, and sometimes it comes in handy."

"Well... thank you."

"Sure thing."

When I closed the door, I called Ryan.

"Mallory? Is everything okay?"

"No," I said. "How would you feel about spending the night?"

He paused for two seconds. "I'm on my way."

September 28, Monday

"AND IS Ryan moving in?" Imogene asked.

"No. He's only staying until I... feel safe."

"Has this caused the two of you to grow closer?"

"Yes, I think so, although we still haven't slept together."

"So you trust Ryan?"

"Yes." I smiled in revelation. It felt good to trust someone.

"Did the police identify the man who was stalking your house?"

"Not yet."

"It's going to be difficult for you to truly feel safe until they get to the bottom of it."

I nodded. But I was smart enough not to tell her—or Ryan—that I was buying a gun. I'd arranged to meet Wanda at a sporting goods store later in the day, and I confess I was nervous as we walked in and made our way to the rear counter under the giant GUNS sign.

"Howdy, ladies," the man behind the counter said. "How can I help you?"

My throat tightened. I felt out of place in the hyper-masculine setting, surrounded by racks of camouflage clothing and pallets of beef jerky.

Wanda, however, felt no such compunction. She cocked a hip. "We need a *gun*."

The man's smile was indulgent—we were, after all, standing in front of a glass counter displaying a veritable smorgasbord of weapons. "Did you have anything special in mind?"

Wanda nodded. "Something that will fit in a purse, but could do some damage."

"So for self-protection?"

"That's right. For her," she said, pointing. "She has a stalker."

He held up his hand. "I don't need details, no offense. I'm just here to help you find the right weapon in case you find yourself in the position of having to defend yourself." His eyes swung to me. "The gun will be registered in your name?"

"Yes," I said, then stepped forward.

"I'll need to see some I.D."

I pulled out my driver's license and handed it over.

He glanced to my face to confirm my identity, then gave it back. "Fill out this form and I'll submit the background check while you decide what you want to buy." He positioned a form on the top of the counter, then handed me a pen. "Let me know if you have any questions, flag me down when you're done."

After he walked away, Wanda clasped her hands together. "This is so exciting! I wish I had a stalker."

I rolled my eyes her way and she looked contrite.

"Sorry... I know it's scary. This is the right thing to do."

I believed her. I'd thought buying a house in a remote location would be safer. Instead, I was starting to realize what a sitting duck I would be for any crazy person who wanted to get to me. An alarm was simply a deterrent, and next time, Detective Terry might not be as available. Still, my hand was shaking when I lowered the pen to fill out the form.

I reviewed the questions, then frowned. "Am I addicted to a controlled substance? Am I a fugitive from the law? Who would answer yes to those questions?"

"An insane person," Wanda said pointedly.

Still, it was a low bar as far as vetting was concerned. I checked no in all the appropriate places, then signed the form and flagged down the salesman.

After scanning the form, he handed it off to someone else who disappeared, presumably, to submit it. I wondered vaguely if my background check would flag me as a lottery jackpot winner.

"Do you have any experience with handguns?" the man asked.

"N-No."

"For your size and your, um, situation, I'd recommend going with something like a Glock 42 or a thirty-eight special." He reached under the counter and removed an array of handguns, setting each of them on the counter. "Go ahead and try them," he urged.

I reached for the black one—the Glock?—and hefted it in my hand. It felt surreal. I set it back down.

"No automatics," Wanda said, reading from her phone. "Do you have a snub-nose .357 revolver?"

"Sure," the guy said, replacing the guns and moving down the counter.

I looked at Wanda in puzzlement.

"I texted Rick," she said.

"Your old boyfriend?"

"Yeah—he knows a thing or two about guns." She read from her phone screen. "He says automatics jam too often. You need a .357 revolver with thirty-eight caliber shells. Basically, a heavier gun with light ammo so it won't kick."

I pursed my mouth. "Okay."

The salesman had removed two revolvers from the case. "Here you go, one's a Ruger and one's a Smith and Wesson."

My pulse jumped when I picked up the first one. The revolvers looked so much more... gunny. The metal felt cold in my hand... and powerful. "This will, um, do some damage?"

"Yep," he said with a flat smile, then pointed at a paper target behind him on the wall. "It's not loaded, of course. But hold it up with both hands, lace your fingers, line up the sight."

I did, shakily at first, then growing more steady as I sighted the bullseye.

"That's it," he said. "Now, shift your weight forward. Lean into it."

I leaned in and a surge of confidence flooded my chest.

"How does it feel?" he asked.

It felt... trustworthy. "I'll take it."

September 29, Tuesday

"SORRY I'M going to be late," Ryan said.

"No worries," I murmured into the phone. "Nessie and I will be okay."

I was feeling better since Wanda had helped me purchase a .357 revolver and given me a bare bones demonstration on loading one shell and setting the safety. It would do until I could sign up for lessons at a shooting range.

"Is the alarm set?"

"Yes."

"Good. How was volunteering?"

"It was great," I said cheerfully. I hated working the reception desk at the Shepherd Center—I wanted to do something more hands-on.

"Okay, gotta run. See you in a couple of hours... I hope."

I ended the call, then sighed and set down my phone. I turned back to Nessie, who was standing a few feet away. "Okay, I'm counting on you to get me off the reception desk at Shepherd." I held up a treat. "Sit."

She was distracted, looking behind me as if I was hiding Trent's sweatshirt from her, like before, to offer as a reward. But after the court verdict, I'd burned it, determined we both would be rid of him.

"You don't need it, Nessie." I snapped my fingers to get her attention. "Sit, Nessie. Sit."

She stopped, then heaved a sigh. Then she rolled her eyes up at me... and sat.

"Good girl!" I cheered, then gave her the treat. "You might be a therapy dog after all."

Nessie endured my praise. She didn't look happy, but maybe a little less sad.

September 30, Wednesday

"I'LL HOLD the board while you climb on," Ryan said. We were floating in the water next to my dock between two paddleboards. Larger boats rarely ventured to this cove, so the water was calm and the sun was high. He was coaxing me to try to mount a board, but I was distracted by the sight of his muscular shoulders dappled with droplets of water. Ryan had made no secret of the fact that he wanted to sleep with me, and I'd decided tonight was the night.

Before you lose all your money, my mind whispered.

"I've never done this before." How many times had I said those words in the past few weeks? "You'll have to teach me."

With Trent's laughter over my inept waterskiing skills reverberating in my head, I heaved myself up over the edge and half-fell, half-rolled onto the board. So much for grace. When I glanced at Ryan, he was staring at my bikini bottoms, which, considering how invasive they'd become, were offering him a show.

His jaw hardened. "You're killing me."

Feminine satisfaction filled my chest. "Maybe we can remedy that... later?"

His eyes went dark with desire. "Absolutely." With renewed enthusiasm, he expertly pushed himself onto his board and demonstrated how to fasten the tether to my ankle. I moved gingerly, but managed not to capsize. Still, I was glad Ryan insisted I wear a bulky life jacket.

"Now stand on your knees with the paddle in front of you," he said, showing me. "And paddle around to get the feel of it."

I did, and after a few wobbles, I got the hang of it. My confidence raised a notch.

"Now put the paddle on the board in front of you and one at a time, put your feet where your knees were." He stood in one fluid motion, tall and lean with his back to the sun.

I concentrated, and used everything I remembered about physiology to tense and control my muscles. I teetered, but countered, and after long precarious seconds, managed to stand.

"That's good," he shouted. "Plant your feet wide and keep looking ahead while you paddle. It's easier to keep your balance."

I followed his instructions and like a child, I was shot through with pleasure. "I'm doing it!"

"Of course you are. You look like a pro!"

It was a magical day, with the wind in my hair and the sun on my face. For a while, I allowed myself to forget about lawsuits and stalkers and obligations. At the moment, I was having fun with a wonderful man who seemed to enjoy my company.

In the distance I heard a rumbling noise that escalated to a roar. Suddenly a large cruiser appeared.

"What's a boat that size doing back here?" Ryan asked.

"Maybe they're looking for someplace to anchor."

"Let's head toward that rock," Ryan said, nodding to a large flat outcropping. But before we could make headway, the boat veered toward us.

"What the hell?" Ryan shouted.

The boat circled us, banking and leaving us in the vortex of a wide wake. A handful of people were on board, all of them whooping. My stomach dropped when I recognized Trent standing at the helm. Apparently he'd traded in the ski boat for something larger—this boat looked seaworthy. But why not? He had millions now—my millions. On the back of boat the name "Money for Nothing" was written in large script. After the victory lap, the boat veered off and sped away.

"Watch out!" Ryan shouted as the waves undulated closer, growing larger and larger. "Drop to your stomach."

I tried, but we were rocked from all sides. I was thrown from the board and went under. My ears clogged with the rumble of churning water. I couldn't see anything with all the foam. A tug of my ankle tether from the board above me jerked my body around. Even with the life jacket, I was scared. I could hear Ryan shouting my name. I fought to reach the surface, and just when I thought my lungs would burst, my head broke through. I gulped, taking in water with oxygen, sputtering, but alive.

Ryan was next to me in a flash. "Are you okay?"

I nodded, still coughing. He helped me onto my board, then climbed onto his. The waves were still tossing us around.

"That was my ex," I said, "showing off his new purchase."

Ryan cursed. "I'm going to report him. He could've killed us."

The thought left me shaken and humiliated. It wasn't enough that Trent had dragged me into court and taken half my winnings—he wanted to gloat at the risk of harming me? I was sure Ryan was wondering how I could've married someone who treated me with such disdain, because I was asking myself the same question. Small indignities came back to me in a flood—sly digs to my confidence, physical aloofness, casual indifference. It was akin to bleeding to death from a thousand paper cuts. Why hadn't I seen it?

"Can we go back to the house?" I asked.

"Of course. After that jackass move, it'll be a while before the waves settle down." Ryan's expression gentled. "Are you sure you're okay?"

"Yes," I assured him, then gave a little water-logged laugh. "I just hope no one else shows up wanting their share of the jackpot."

We paddled back toward the dock, both of us on our knees to better maneuver in the choppy water. By the time my house came into view, I was fighting nausea.

"Who's that?" Ryan asked.

I followed his line of sight to the dock where a young slender woman stood silhouetted in the sun. She wore a filmy dress and platform sandals, and one hand held the handle of... a suitcase?

She waved, then cupped her hands around her mouth. "Mallory?" The words echoed off the water and throughout the cove. *"Mallory Green?"*

I shielded my eyes with my hand... I didn't recognize the woman, but something about her seemed familiar. Ryan and I paddled within a few feet of the dock.

"Yes," I said warily, hoping she wasn't another process server. "Who are you?"

She grinned. "I'm Delilah—your sister!"

OCTOBER

October 1, Thursday

"ARE YOU sure it's okay for me to leave?" Ryan asked.

We were standing in the kitchen of my humongous lake house. He was dressed for his commute to his financial management firm in midtown Atlanta, I was still in my full-coverage pajamas. Our planned sensual escapade for the previous evening had been interrupted by the appearance of a Florida woman named Delilah Miracle who claimed she was my half-sister—same father, different mother.

I lowered my coffee cup and nodded. "Delilah seems harmless... she hasn't asked for anything."

"Yet," Ryan added dryly. "I don't mean to sound judgmental, but she seems a little... rough. I wish you hadn't offered her a place to stay."

"It seemed silly—and stingy—to send her away with all these empty bedrooms."

"Mallory, you don't owe her anything even if she is your sister—and she probably isn't."

"She goes by my family name."

Although granted, I hadn't used "Miracle" in a long, long while. When I'd lived with foster families, it had been simpler to temporarily adopt their surnames... and it was safe to say back then I'd stopped believing in miracles. The names had merged into a blur until I'd gone to live with Danica Tumi. I'd happily taken on her last name and years later after I'd left her home, I'd legally changed my surname to Tumi to acquire a driver's license. When I'd met and married Trent, taking on his name—Green—had been an easy choice. I'd finally felt as if I belonged to a name.

And now it seemed I'd have to change it again. Back to Tumi?

Unbidden, another name came back to me... *Buggy*... my mother's nickname for me. I hadn't thought about it in years. She'd written it on the back of the one picture I had of the two of us. *Me and Buggy, at the park.* I assumed my father had taken the photo.

"Anyone can lie about their name," Ryan offered. "I understand you must be lonely with both of your parents gone, but you can't afford to take this woman at face value... this is what con artists do."

I allowed my own lie about both my parents being deceased to slide by. "Do you think there's a resemblance?" I recognized the question as desperation on my part. Delilah was a little younger and a *lot* prettier.

He squinted. "Maybe around the eyes?"

I was crestfallen.

"Regardless, as soon as I get to the office I'll have my guy run a background check based on the scant information she supplied last night. Until you hear from me, keep your guard up."

I dipped my chin in concession—better safe than sorry. "At least I won't be alone in case that man shows up again."

He made a face. "If he does, promise you'll call the police first, then me."

I was pleased that he cared. "I will."

Ryan lowered a kiss to my mouth and made a noise of frustrated longing. "We keep getting waylaid."

My bare toes curled. "I'm sorry my life is so chaotic at the moment."

He smiled. "Yeah... what happened to the quiet receptionist I met?"

I opened my mouth to say I could barely remember that woman, but apparently his question had been hypothetical because he was already halfway to the door that led to the garage, talking into his phone. When the door closed behind him, I took another sip of my coffee, but it had grown cold.

I called for Nessie. When she didn't appear, I assumed she'd gotten lost in the house again and would howl for me when she was ready to be found.

I'd put my coffee mug in the hi-tech microwave and was trying to figure out how to turn it on when Delilah appeared, looking as fresh as her name in a bikini top and booty shorts that showed off a handful of flowery tattoos sprinkled over tanned skin. Her light brown wavy hair was piled on top of her head in a haphazard knot. She was an earthy, sexy vision of vitality and youth.

Next to her I felt like a haggard, harried husk.

"Hi, Sis!" she shouted, then threw her arms around me and rocked me side to side.

My arms were pinned, so I had to endure her bear hug. "Good morning."

She pulled back, then stretched tall, flexing her curvy bod. "For real, that is some room you put me in—I could have a party in there. And the mattress is amaze-balls. I slept like the freaking *dead*."

"Um… good."

She picked up my purse sitting on the counter. "Oh my freaking God, is this an Edie Parker?"

I shifted foot to foot—it was one of my over-the-top splurges before I realized my winnings were at risk. "Yes."

She stroked it as if it were a pet. "Wow, Zoe Milana posted a selfie yesterday with one *just* like this."

I turned back to the microwave and pushed a start button. "There's coffee if you want some."

"I'm more of a Diet Coke girl—you got any?"

"I think there are some sodas in the fridge."

She opened both doors to the giant refrigerator and whistled low. "I've lived in apartments smaller than this. Ah, there's a regular Coke—that'll do." She pulled out the tiny can then popped the top and took a fizzy swig. "But, dang, I could drink ten this size."

I pulled my steaming mug from the microwave and blew on the liquid. "How about some breakfast?"

"You got donuts?"

"I have eggs. And toast."

She screwed up her pretty face. "Pass. But thanks." She took another slurp of the soda, then looked around. "Where's your hot boyfriend?"

"Um, *Ryan* went into the office."

"You two serious?"

"Our relationship is still… new."

"Aw. That explains why you sleep in separate bedrooms."

I blinked. "Er… yes. I'm going through a divorce."

"Because of the lottery money?"

Warning flags went up in my mind that she was getting too personal... but I'd offered the information unsolicited. "No, my husband and I split before I won the money."

"I read somewhere that he sued you for half of the jackpot?"

That was public knowledge, I realized. "Yes... and he won."

"Holy shit, really?" She looked worried. "So now you're only half as rich?"

"Um... right." I gestured to the breakfast bar. "Why don't we sit and talk?"

After falling onto a stool, she emptied the can of Coke and crushed it in her hand. "What do you want to talk about, Sis?"

I took in her winning smile—authentic, or counterfeit? "I was a little too stunned last night to absorb all the details about our... connection. Do you mind going over it again?" In truth, I wanted to make sure she told the same story.

"Sure. Where do I start?"

"Tell me again what you know about our father?"

She shrugged. "Just his name, really—Gordon Miracle. My mom had a few pictures of him holding me when I was maybe five or six."

That last part was new. So when he'd visited his other daughter, I would've been seven or eight and already in the Georgia state foster system. That stung. "And what was your mother's name?"

"Honey Jakes. She died two years ago, emphysema. She was a heavy smoker."

All that information was the same as before—was it rehearsed? "Again, I'm sorry. I lost my mother when I was very young." Too late, I realized I'd revealed yet more details about my life.

"Life sucks, don't it? Honey never married Gordon, but I always went by Miracle anyway."

"Do you have any siblings?"

"No, it was just me and Honey." She angled her head. "Does our dad live around here?"

Did she want information, or was she fishing for details to bolster her story? "I haven't heard from him in over twenty years." Not a lie. "You haven't kept up with him?"

"Nope. I thought he might show up at Honey's funeral, but he didn't. I remember seeing an address in Georgia on the envelopes the checks came in, but those stopped when I turned eighteen."

I frowned. "Checks?"

"He sent money to Honey, you know, for clothes and stuff for me."

I suppose I should've been glad he'd supported at least one of his daughters, but I was shot through with jealousy. "So... how did you know about me?"

She looked to the ceiling—was she trying to recall her memories, or trying to recall her script?

"After Honey died I found a letter Gordon had written to her saying he had another daughter named Mallory Green, that you were married and living in Atlanta, and that I should know I had a sister."

Shock reverberated through my body. He'd known details about my life?

"I tried to find you on social media," she said, "but came up empty."

"I don't have any accounts," I murmured. Trent, who had aspired to be a social media influencer, had pronounced me hopelessly uncool.

"And then one day last week," she continued, "I was scrolling through funny videos, and there you were, puking your guts out after winning the lotto." She grinned. "It was meant for me to find you!"

I manufactured a smile. "That's quite a coincidence, all right. Do you still have your mom's letter?"

She winced. "I lost it."

Hm. "Why do you think your mom didn't show you the letter?"

"I think she was afraid I'd leave her to go look for you."

"Why would you do that?"

"Because I always wanted a sister."

I inhaled sharply against the sudden sensation in my chest. It must've been pain because my eyes watered. Thankfully the ringing of my phone pulled me out of the moment. When I saw Ryan's name come up on the screen, I excused myself and left to walk into the hallway.

"Hi, Ryan."

"Are you alone?"

I peeked around the corner to see Delilah taking a selfie with my purse. Unease niggled at the base of my neck—I didn't have much cash inside, but I had a wallet full of credit cards. "Not really, but she can't hear me."

"Okay, well, I just got the background report."

"And?" I held my breath.

Delilah glanced over her shoulder, then fingered the catch on the purse. After the space of two heartbeats, she bit into her lip and set it down.

"And... she checks out," he said. "Gordon Miracle is listed on her birth certificate as her father. Looks like you have a sister."

I tried to exhale, but a myriad of sensations crowded my chest. "I have a sister."

October 2, Friday

"I'M SO sorry the judge didn't see things our way." My divorce attorney Lynette Shift steepled her hands on her desk and looked apologetic. "I know it wasn't the outcome you were hoping for."

I didn't feel the need to respond. I wasn't sure what hurt the most—hearing how Trent had portrayed me to the court as being unsupportive and greedy, or seeing how enamored he was with his new girlfriend who'd been there to cheer him on. "So Trent already has his half of the money?"

"Oh, no. It will likely take several weeks to process the paperwork and distribute the funds out of escrow."

"But I saw him the day before yesterday. He did a drive-by of my lake house in his new boat, and it looked expensive."

"With the court's judgment, any bank will give him a line of credit." Then she frowned. "Was he harassing you?"

I replayed in my mind the episode where he had circled me and Ryan on paddleboards in his big obnoxious boat. "More like showing off."

"If you feel threatened, we can take out a restraining order."

"That's not necessary," I murmured. "I'm sure it was just an impulsive stunt. He has what he wants now, so I probably won't hear from him again." Wow, that hurt more than it should've.

"The settlement will delay your divorce being finalized, so if he bothers you again, let me know."

I nodded. Trent had obviously fallen out of love with me some time ago... but when had he begun to hate me?

Probably the moment he found out I'd won a multimillion-dollar lottery jackpot.

Lynette sighed. "I understand you're also being sued by your former coworkers?"

I nodded. "At the restaurant where I used to work. We had a pool for the lottery. And even though I bought my ticket separately with my own money, they want a share."

She sat back in her chair. "So winning the lottery hasn't been all you thought it would be?"

"Not exactly." I offered up a little smile. "But hopefully I'll be able to do some good things I couldn't have done otherwise... if I have any money left once the lawsuits are over." I pushed to my feet. "Regardless of the outcome, thank you for your help."

She stood and came around the front of her desk to shake my hand. "I'll be in touch as the paperwork for the settlement and the divorce works its way through the system."

Lynette followed me to the door, then nodded to Delilah who was sitting in the waiting area, scrolling on her phone.

"Is she a friend of yours?"

"My sister, actually."

She frowned. "I thought you were an only child, and an orphan."

Again, I ignored the bit about me being an orphan. "She's a half-sister, actually. I didn't know about her until a couple of days ago."

The woman's eyebrows climbed. "She just showed up?"

I nodded.

Her mouth tightened. "Be careful, Mallory."

I conjured up a smile. "I'm doing my best."

October 3, Saturday

"S*IT*," I said to Nessie.

She looked up at me and cocked her head.

"Your dog isn't very obedient," Delilah offered from where she was lying in the grass nearby.

Part of me marveled over the fact that she was comfortable sprawling in the meadow of Piedmont Park and part of me was annoyed—because it was something I'd never do? Apparently, she'd inherited all the bohemian genes, and I'd gotten the ones marked GG (Good Girl). Of course we were probably each more like our mothers than our shared father. One thing was certain—I wasn't used to the constant companionship and conversation. Her presence was starting to wear on me.

"She's not really my dog."

Delilah laughed. "Did she come with the gi-normous house?"

"No. She belonged to my husband."

"He didn't want her?"

"So it seems."

"Douchebag."

I felt a sudden rush of affection for her, and a laugh bubbled to the back of my throat.

"So why did you marry a douchebag?"

I swallowed the laugh. "He wasn't… like that when I married him. He changed."

"And you didn't?"

Her question stopped me. I'd been quick to blame Trent for growing away from me while I stood strong and consistent, but that wasn't exactly true. Hadn't I become increasingly more resentful of his choices even as I'd pretended to go along with them?

I opened my mouth to defend myself, but a movement next to the tree where I'd first spotted the man who'd followed me caught my eye. A man was standing there, alright, and he was looking at me.

He grinned and lifted his hand. "Hi, Mallory."

I inadvertently smiled and waved. "Hi, Josh."

He came loping over, dressed in running clothes. His hair and T-shirt were wet with perspiration. I attributed my happiness to see him on the fact that it was nice to have a break from my prattling sister.

"Out for a run?" I asked.

"Yeah. Still training."

"Training for what?" Delilah asked.

We both turned our heads and watched her unfold her lithe body from the grass like some wood nymph. Her hair hung loose and wavy to her waist. She wiped both hands over her butt to dislodge bits of debris. Josh was riveted.

"For a 10K I'm running soon."

"Cool," she said with a smile, then stuck out her hand. "I'm Delilah."

"I'm, uh…"

"This is Josh," I said to rescue him. "He's a friend of mine." Borne out by the woven bracelet he'd given me and I was wearing. "Josh, this is my, um, *sister* Delilah."

He beamed. "I can see the resemblance."

What a liar.

"Nice to meet you," she said, oozing pheromones. "What do you do, Josh?"

Since he once again seemed dumbstruck, I answered. "Josh is a doctor of physical therapy."

Her eyes lit up. "A doctor, huh? Wow."

He blushed to his ears. "Thanks."

I pushed my tongue into my cheek.

"What are you two doing?" he asked.

I gestured to Nessie, who was rolling in the grass. "I'm trying to get Nessie ready for the therapy dog exam, but she's not as excited about it as I am."

"Good," he said with a wink. "None of us at the clinic want to lose our receptionist."

"You're a receptionist?" Delilah asked me.

"I volunteer at the Shepherd Spinal Center, where Josh works."

"I need a job," she said to Josh. "Do you have something there for me?"

His Adam's apple bobbed. "I can ask."

She grinned, rendering herself even more beautiful. "Super." She reached forward, grabbed his arm and produced a bright pink lipstick. "Here's my number in case you need to reach me."

I watched in awe while she wrote her phone number on the underside of his forearm in large pink numbers. "There," she said, ending with a flourish. "Don't sweat it off."

He stared at his arm. "I won't."

"We won't keep you from your run," I said.

"Oh, right... okay, see you later?"

Except he wasn't looking at me when he took off.

"Count on it!" Delilah shouted.

October 4, Sunday

"HOLY FAMILY tree," Wanda said. "You knew nothing about this sister?"

She had agreed to meet me at the handgun shooting range. We were waiting in line behind a knot of people to sign in. I was surprised to see a cross-section of gun enthusiasts—in addition to the expected burly guys sporting beards and ball caps were young women in athleisure wear and a trio of women in their fifties who looked as if they'd come straight from church.

"I had no idea she existed," I admitted.

"She just showed up on your doorstep?"

"Pretty much."

"What's she like?"

"Me, only younger, taller, and prettier."

"Ouch. Is she staying at the house with you?"

"For now."

"I'll bet that's putting a crimp in your love life."

"Ryan's been working a lot," I hedged. "And there's no need for him to stay with me now that Delilah is there."

"Does Sis have a job?"

"She's out looking for one, actually." I was hoping she'd find something to get her out of the house during daylight hours. I wanted to get back to volunteering, but I wasn't quite ready to leave Delilah to her own devices.

When the three church ladies walked up to the counter, they each removed unloaded handguns from their proper handbags and presented their permits to carry a concealed weapon.

"That's what you should apply for a-s-a-p," Wanda said.

"I need to wait until I decide if I'm going to change my name when the divorce is final. Else a permit will be one more thing I'll have to change my name on."

"Of course you're going to change your name," Wanda said with a snort. "Aren't you?"

"Probably."

"What's your maiden name?"

"I have several," I said vaguely.

The door behind us opened, admitting a tall, slender man with a neat beard. I noticed because my head was constantly on a pivot in case my stalker returned. To my surprise, Wanda waved. He smiled and headed toward us.

"I hope you don't mind," she whispered. "I called Rick to meet us here and show you the ropes."

"That explains why you're dressed up," I offered dryly, scanning her jumpsuit and jewelry.

She scoffed. "I am not."

"It's okay if you miss him."

"I don't. I'm looking for someone rich, remember?" She grinned. "Will *you* marry me?"

"I'm not rich yet," I reminded her. I glanced down at the zippered case that held my spanking new revolver. Which only made it more ridiculous that I felt it necessary to go to such extremes to protect myself from the people vying for my money.

October 5, Monday

"A YOUNGER sister you never knew about?"

My "mental health professional" Imogene Ramplet was making furious notes. I imagined this was the kind of revelation most therapists lived for.

"That's right," I confirmed. "Delilah knew about me but didn't know how to find me."

Imogene looked up. "Until you won the lottery?"

I nodded.

She pressed her lips together. "And you've confirmed she's your sister?"

"We haven't had a DNA test, but my, um, boyfriend ran a background check on her and it appears she's who she says she is."

"And how do you feel about having a sister?"

"I don't know how I'm supposed to feel," I admitted. "I had lots of brothers and sisters in foster care, but this should feel different, right?"

She gave me a little smile. "No one can tell you how you're supposed to feel, Mallory. You get to decide. Besides, you only just met her. Don't you want to get to know her first?"

"I'm trying. She's living in my house, and we spend a lot of time together."

"I'm sensing a 'but'?"

"But we don't have a lot in common, and—" I stopped and bit into my lip.

"And?"

"And... she's kind of annoying."

Imogene laughed. "Sounds like a sister, alright."

My mood buoyed a bit. She was right—Delilah and I barely knew each other. In time perhaps I'd feel closer to her.

"Is your boyfriend Ryan still staying at your house, too?"

"No. He's giving us space to get to know each other."

"Ah. So the arrival of your sister has impacted your romantic relationship, too."

"Some," I conceded. "But Ryan and I are taking things slow anyway."

"That's probably for the best considering all the upheaval in your life at the moment." She looked back to her notes. "And how are you feeling about having to split your winnings with your estranged husband?"

I crossed my arms. "Not great. He already took a lot from me... and now this, too."

"You mean emotionally he took a lot from you?"

I nodded. "It's not fair."

She leaned forward. "No, it doesn't seem fair. But I should point out that while he can take your money, he can't take from you emotionally unless you let him."

"I know that," I mumbled. "I'm trying to let it go."

"Are you taking care of yourself?"

"What do you mean?"

"Are you sleeping well?"

"I'm still getting used to the new house," I countered.

And when I did sleep, I had nightmares about being stalked. Then I would lie awake, wondering if I could trust Delilah who lay in bed down the hall. I thought cash was missing from my wallet, although I couldn't be sure. I was going to have to keep better track. She still hadn't found a job, so she was probably running short of funds.

"You look like you've lost weight," Imogene remarked.

I shrugged. "Maybe."

She set aside her notebook. "Mallory, you've had to deal with several life-changing events back to back. You need to be good to yourself, and spend time with people who care about you."

I nodded, then realized she was staring at my arm. Fondling the friendship bracelet had become a nervous habit, simply because it was there.

I dropped my hand.

October 6, Tuesday

"SHEPHERD SPINAL Center, how may I direct your call?" I smiled into the headset microphone because I knew it affected the way my voice sounded. "I'll connect you. Have a good day."

I transferred the call, then gave a friendly nod to two female doctors walking by. The sight of their white lab coats stoked envy in my stomach, then I smirked to myself—if they knew I'd cashed in a lottery ticket worth fifty-two million, *they'd* probably feel envious of *me*.

"It is a private joke?" Josh asked.

I turned back to see him standing next to the reception desk. "Yes."

"Okay," he said cheerfully. "Hey, it was nice to meet Delilah. You've never mentioned a sister."

"I didn't know about her until a few days ago."

He pursed his mouth. "Oh."

I batted my eyelashes. "Did you find something for her to do around here?"

"Not yet. Does she have experience in the medical field?"

I nodded to his arm, covered with the long sleeve of a dress shirt. "Maybe you should call and ask her, or did you sweat off her number?"

He looked mildly irritated. "I wrote it down, but I thought I'd ask you first."

I hesitated. "She doesn't have a college degree." Of course, neither did I.

"That limits the possibilities, but not every job requires one. What kinds of jobs has she held?"

"Mostly waitressing." Which dominated most of my work history, too. Hm—maybe we had more in common than I realized.

"I have a friend in PR, I'll see what's available... if it's okay with you."

I frowned. "Why wouldn't it be?"

"Just asking. The number she gave me is a Florida area code."

"That's where she was living before."

"But she's going to be in Atlanta for a while?"

"It looks that way," I hedged.

"Got it." Then he grinned. "How is Nessie coming along with her training?"

I made a face. "She's stubborn, but she's smart. It has more to do with me, I think. She doesn't see me as her master."

"Be persistent, she'll come around." Then he winked. "At least that's my philosophy." His glance bounced to the friendship bracelet, then he walked on.

October 7, Wednesday

"I GOT a job!" Delilah crowed.

I looked up from filling Nessie's food bowl to see my sister dancing barefoot in celebration. "Did Josh call you?"

She stopped, then made a face. "Yeah, but the only job available was for a receptionist, and that sounds pretty sucky."

I managed a flat smile.

"But then I got another call from a place where I applied, and I start Friday!"

"Great—doing what?"

"Working at a restaurant called Plaid."

I squinted. "I've heard of it—it's in Buckhead."

"It looked ritzy," she said. "I'll bet the tips will be terrific."

"Probably, if you're a good waitress."

"Actually, the job is bartender."

"You know how to bartend?"

"No." Then she grinned. "But how hard could it be? I'd rather fib a little to get my foot in the door, then figure it out once I'm in."

A finger of misgiving prodded me. Was she doing the same to me?

She angled her head. "Buy me lunch to celebrate?"

I surveyed her sunny face and smiling eyes. She was hard to resist, for sure. "Okay."

"Yay! And I know just the place. It's so cool." She looked me up and down. "Do you have anything to wear that's... cute?"

I glanced down at my shorts and T-shirt. "This is cute... isn't it?"

"If you're a boy."

I frowned. "I'll change."

I went to my bedroom and found a casual skirt and blouse I hoped would suffice. When I emerged and walked over to get my purse from the counter, I hesitated—it had been moved. I glanced to Delilah, who was holding up a compact mirror and blotting her perfect face with a sponge.

I opened my purse and surreptitiously peeked inside my wallet to see a twenty was missing from the three I'd had. Delilah was still primping, seemingly oblivious. I pressed my lips together— what was twenty dollars? If she'd asked me, I would've given her that and more. Maybe she was too proud to ask... plus she had a job now and would be making her own money. I closed my purse. "Ready?"

She turned her head and grinned. "Yeah. Can we take your car, please? I hate mine."

She drove a battered car with one missing hubcap versus my little red convertible. "Sure."

"With the top down?"

I glanced out the window to see a sunny fall sky. "Sure."

She bit into her plump lip. "Can I drive? I'll be really careful, I promise."

I sighed. "Sure."

She squealed. "We're going to have so much fun!"

Despite my reservations, it was impossible not to feel lighter around her. And truly, it was more fun watching her drive the convertible than driving it myself. I envied her zest and fearlessness, even if it was a little reckless.

It sort of reminded me of being with Trent.

She drove to Little Five Points, an eclectic part of town I rarely visited, and parked near a Moroccan restaurant she'd found through social media. We sat on the floor at a low table and ate with our hands. She told me about growing up in Florida, hanging out on the beach with her friends and her mother. Compared to my childhood, it sounded idyllic.

After lunch, we strolled through the quirky collection of shops with colorful signs and storefronts.

Suddenly Delilah gasped. "A palm reader! Let's do it."

I shook my head. "I don't know..."

"Come on, it's only ten dollars—I'll pay for it."

At least she was being generous with my money. Her enthusiasm wore me down, and I relented with a laugh. She dragged me inside where a heavily made up woman took our money and pulled Delilah into a curtained booth. I wandered around the shop, scrutinizing an array of crystals, incense, and charms. One bauble in the shape of a rabbit was marked "for luck and money."

I smirked. *Be careful what you wish for.*

From the intermittent squeals inside the booth, I presumed the woman was telling Delilah her future was full of wonderful things. At least she was passing out positivity in return for her fee. Indeed, Delilah came out flushed and bouncing. "That was amaze-balls! She said I'm going to find everything I've ever dreamed of in Atlanta. I can't wait to hear what she tells you, Sis."

I entered the booth with skepticism and pulled the curtain closed behind me. Low lights lit the woman's face and set the mood for a mystical experience. She smiled at me and reached for my palm. I surrendered it and tried to relax. Maybe she would tell me my life was about to right itself and I would enjoy a prosperous, happy future.

Instead, her face instantly puckered and she made a rueful noise.

After a long, uncomfortable silence, I felt compelled to ask. "What do you see?"

The woman glanced up, then blanched. "I'm very sorry to tell you this."

My pulse ratcheted higher. "Tell me what?"

"You... or someone close to you... is going to die."

October 8, Thursday

"HI, THERE." Ryan stepped back and opened the door. "Welcome to my place."

I walked through the threshold of his condo and was instantly nervous. I'd known from his address, the stately building, the valet parking, and the rigorous security that it was a nice place. But I wasn't fully prepared for the grandeur. His penthouse condo featured two walls of glass that offered a panoramic view of Buckhead, the ritziest part of Atlanta. His furniture was minimalist and luxe, the color palette various shades of ivory and the palest gray. It looked like a gleaming showroom, with nary a personal knickknack or photo in sight. His living space was like his wardrobe—impeccable.

What did he see in me? I asked myself for the hundredth time.

"It's spectacular," I said on an exhale.

His grin rendered him even more handsome. "I'm glad you approve."

"How could I not?" I asked, circling in place.

"Let me give you the full tour." He led me from room to room, pointing out items he was proud of—his state-of-the-art theater and speaker system, his wine collection, his closet with an automated shelving system. It confirmed for me that someone like Ryan could show me how to enjoy my money, assuming I had any left when the last lawsuit was over.

"How do you like my bedroom?" he asked in a silky voice.

I surveyed the California King bed sitting low to the floor, fitted with perfectly tucked pale sheets. I could picture Ryan reclining there, half clothed and so-sexy, like a cologne commercial. "It's... wonderful. Very... masculine."

A little frown marred his forehead. "Not too masculine, I hope." He pulled me into his arms. "After dinner, I was hoping maybe you could spend the night?"

My throat convulsed—I wasn't quite ready for intimate sleepovers. "I... didn't bring a change of clothes... or toiletries."

He grinned. "You won't need a lot of clothes... and I'm sure I can round up some toiletries."

Items his previous girlfriend Maria had left behind?

"I... shouldn't. I don't want to leave Delilah alone in the house."

He looked concerned. "Has she done something to make you suspicious of her?"

She had, but I felt oddly compelled to protect her—maybe this was part of being a sister? "It's not that. She doesn't know how to operate the security system... and I don't want to ask her to take care of Nessie."

"Ah. Has she asked you for anything?"

"No. And she starts a new job tomorrow, bartending at a place not far from here—it's called Plaid?"

He nodded. "I've been there a few times. It's nice." Then he squinted. "Are you sure she got a job there?"

My hackles raised a little—was he insinuating she wasn't classy enough to work there? He'd made the comment before that Delilah was a little rough. Admittedly, I'd had some of the same thoughts, but it sounded worse coming from someone else. "I don't think she'd lie... about that."

He was instantly alert. "You've caught her in other lies?"

I shook my head. "No. That came out wrong. It just doesn't seem like something anyone would lie about."

He made a thoughtful noise. "Still... you probably should drop in sometime, just to be sure. Con artists have a knack for making people believe they're earnest and trustworthy." Then he pulled me close. "I'm just looking out for you."

I nodded and lifted my mouth for a nice kiss. I could get used to being looked out for.

October 9, Friday

RYAN'S ADVICE had stuck with me all day. I owed it to myself to know if my sister was being truthful about her whereabouts. So after Delilah had left wearing a long coat of mine in deference to the cooling temperatures (she hadn't needed a coat in Florida), I waited an hour or so, then drove to Buckhead and handed my keys over to a parking valet. Plaid was part restaurant, part night club and business was booming.

As I walked up to the entrance, I felt woefully underdressed in my casual clothes, but decided for a quick in and out, it didn't matter. I just wanted to see Delilah working behind the bar, then I'd leave.

The hostess's quick glance over my outfit reinforced my suspicion I was out of place. I scanned the busy area, looking for the bar, but I didn't want my sister to spot me. "Can you direct me to the restroom?" I asked. It would give me a reason to roam.

The woman's mouth turned down. "The lavatories are for paying customers."

It was the only time I'd been tempted to tell someone I was a millionaire, so there. Instead I smiled and said, "I promise to buy a drink."

She gestured. "The restrooms are that way, past the bar."

I threaded my way through well-clad bodies that vibrated in time with music throbbing overhead. I marveled that everyone in Atlanta seemed to know about this place except me. Then I reminded myself that my three jobs had limited my time on the social scene.

At the entrance to the bar, I held back, craning over heads for a glimpse of Delilah. Then I spotted her. She was hard to miss since she was standing on the bar, gyrating to the music *Coyote Ugly*-style in a bright yellow dress—*my* dress, I realized, which the last time I looked, still had the tags hanging on it.

She held a bottle of vodka in one hand and as I watched, she knelt and poured shots into the waiting glasses of a crowd of men and women who were enjoying the show. She somehow made it look fun instead of trashy. Then she stood and danced again, her loose hair swinging side to side, before jumping down behind the bar to rowdy applause. People were literally throwing money at her.

I was fascinated. She'd probably make more money this evening than I'd made in a week at the convenience store.

One of the cheering men turned in my direction, and I blinked in surprise—Josh?

He waved in recognition. "Mallory!"

I froze, then realized I couldn't leave now. I slunk through the crowd and offered a smile. "Hi."

He grinned. "You came to support Delilah on her first night?"

I nodded. "She invited you?"

"Yeah, and I brought friends," he said, gesturing to the people around him. "Let me introduce you."

"I can't stay," I said, feeling like an outsider. "I just came to say hi to Delilah."

We both looked up to where she'd ascended the bar again and was swaying to the music. She looked like a movie star.

"She's really something," Josh said.

"She sure is," I yelled over the noise, then gestured to the door. "I have to go... will you tell her I was here?"

"Absolutely," he said, without looking at me. "Later."

"Later," I murmured, then made my way back through the horde of bodies all pressing forward to watch my sister perform.

As I steered my car north toward the lake house, I marinated in irony. Delilah had arrived in *my* town, was living in *my* house, wearing *my* clothes, and now was taking *my*... friends.

My sister was enjoying *my* life more than I was.

October 10, Saturday

"JOSH SAID you were at the bar last night," Delilah remarked.

She was sitting cross-legged on the grass at Piedmont Park, blowing dried dandelion shoots into the air. The white starburst buds danced on the breeze, tumbling and lifting higher, distracting Nessie, who turned away from my commands and pulled at the end of her leash.

I sighed. "I just stopped by to say hello. You were busy, so I didn't bother you."

She winced. "Are you mad about the dress?"

"No. But I wish you'd asked."

She looked contrite and childlike. "I'm sorry. I didn't think you'd mind since you loaned me your coat. You have such nice things."

"Delilah, you should know that despite the lake house and the car and what you might see in my closet, I don't have a fortune at my disposal."

"I know you have to wait until the lawsuit with your former coworkers is settled. But even if they get some of the lottery money, you'll still be rich, won't you?"

"I've made a lot of financial commitments. I hope I'll have enough left to honor them, and some extra besides." A nest egg would be nice, but I wasn't counting on it.

"So what's the story with Josh?"

I turned my head. "What do you mean?"

"Is he up for grabs?"

I looked back to Nessie and shook her leash to regain her attention. "You'll have to ask Josh."

"Did the two of you used to date?"

"No. Why do you ask?"

She shrugged. "I thought I sensed something between you two." Then she grinned. "But you have Ryan."

"Right," I agreed, then snapped my fingers at Nessie. "Nessie, come. Nessie.... *come.*"

Nessie sat, I groaned.

"What are you trying to teach her?"

"She has to get an obedience certificate before I submit an application for her to be a therapy dog. She has to know how to sit, stand, come, heel, and lay down on command, with no treat."

Delilah pushed to her feet. "Let me try."

"Be my guest." I handed her the leash.

She knelt down and unclipped the leash, then stood and said, "Nessie... sit."

Nessie sat.

Then she said, "Nessie... stand."

Nessie stood.

"Roll over," Delilah commanded.

Nessie rolled over.

I gaped. "How did you do that?"

"It's all in the way you present yourself," she said. "You have to act as if you're in charge. People listen to you when you act like you know what you're doing." She laughed. "I guess it works with dogs, too."

Delilah leaned over to give Nessie a scratch, and Nessie nuzzled her hand, much like the group of people last night who'd tossed tips her way.

Once again, warning flags rose in my mind. My sister was a good actress, it seemed.

October 11, Sunday

WHEN I pulled up to the lake house, I was surprised to see Ryan's Porsche parked on the driveway. I looked up to see him and Delilah on the rooftop deck, lounging in chairs. By the time I climbed out of my car, they had come to the railing and waved. When I looked at the two of them outlined in the sun, I was struck by what a beautiful couple they made. Then I gave myself a mental shake. I was letting my envy get the better of me.

At best, it was unflattering... at worst, it was pathological.

"Hi," Ryan called down. "I hope it's okay that I stopped by."

"Sure," I said with a smile. "I'll be right up."

I walked inside to drop my purse, then I put my gun case in a drawer. I'd been to the shooting range with Wanda, and I was getting more comfortable with the revolver... but I wasn't yet comfortable sharing that information with Ryan or my sister.

On the way up the stairs to the deck, I passed Delilah coming down. "I'm going to take Nessie for a walk," she said.

"Okay... thanks for keeping Ryan company."

"No problem."

But at her solemn tone I wondered if Ryan had made her uncomfortable with questions. I sensed he still didn't trust her, so I wouldn't be surprised if he'd let her know he was watching out for my best interests.

When I reached the deck, I took a moment to appreciate the view. The trees around the lake were starting to turn color, although it would be a few weeks until the foliage was in peak array. Still, it was beautiful and peaceful in the glassy cove, with fewer and fewer boats coming by as the temperatures cooled.

"Hello," Ryan said. He was standing at the railing, looking sexily wind-blown.

I joined him and accepted a warm kiss. "Hi, yourself. Did you and Delilah have a nice chat?"

"She's... interesting," he said. "What would you think if I asked my guy to run a more thorough background check?"

I hesitated because I feared a deeper dive into her background might reveal the fact that our father was in prison. "I don't believe that's necessary."

"Have you thought about asking her to take a DNA test?"

"I think she might be offended."

He scoffed. "Not if she's really your sister."

"I'll think about it," I promised, then smiled. "Did you get caught up on work?"

"I have to get back to write a proposal," he said wryly. "Gotta keep the lights on. I just drove up to give you this." He reached into his pocket and withdrew a long, thin black velvet box.

Pleasure sparkled in my chest. "What's this?"

"Open it."

I lifted the lid of the small box and gasped. Inside was a gold and diamond tennis bracelet. "It's gorgeous. And it's too much, Ryan."

"Nonsense," he said, withdrawing the bracelet. "You deserve better than this little piece of fabric jewelry." He fastened the gift over the friendship bracelet Josh had given me. They looked incongruous next to each other and inexplicably, a knot formed in my stomach.

But I smiled up at him. "I love it."

He smiled back. "Good." He kissed me again, thoroughly and with enough intensity that our bodies began to react. With a groan, he pulled back. "I wish I didn't have to go."

"So do I." I did want to spend more time with him, even if I wasn't ready to jump into bed.

"I have a busy week, but I'll try to get away for the deposition on Thursday."

I nodded. "Okay, see you then."

He kissed me again. I stood and watched him descend to his car. He waved and climbed inside, then drove away.

I held out my wrist and studied the dazzling bauble. Then I bit into my lip—it was the second nicest gift anyone had ever given me.

October 12, Monday

"AND WHAT do you think the gift means?" Imogene asked, admiring my bracelet.

"Ryan says I deserve nice things."

"And don't you?"

I hesitated. "Yes... absolutely. I'm just not accustomed to having them. The house, the car... this bracelet... it all feels strange."

"But good?"

I nodded. "Who wouldn't want these things?" Delilah openly coveted the diamond bracelet, telling me how lucky I was to have money *and* Ryan.

Lucky, lucky, lucky.

"So... how are you and your sister getting along?"

I sat back and stroked my bracelet—the less expensive one. "Fine, I guess. I'm considering asking her to take a DNA test."

Imogene leaned forward. "Are you having doubts about whether she's actually your sister?"

"I just think it's better to be sure, don't you? I don't want to get—" I broke off.

"Go on," she urged.

I tried again. "I don't want to get invested in her if she's a fraud."

"That's reasonable."

"On the other hand... I'm not sure if I want to know."

"Why?"

I gave a little shrug. "I'm not sure I can put it into words. I guess I don't want her to leave." Even though she did things to annoy me, life was more interesting when she was around.

"And as long as you don't know if she's truly your sister, you have a reason to keep her at arm's length."

The woman had a point. This push-pull relationship I'd developed with Delilah was decidedly dysfunctional.

But wasn't that the basis for most family relationships?

October 13, Tuesday

"WHERE ARE you headed?"

I turned to see Josh walking behind me in the hallway of the Shepherd center, and offered a smile. "I'm using my lunch hour to attend the therapy dog orientation. It's for potential handlers, to find out more about the program."

"Cool. Can I come, too?"

I squinted. "Why?"

He shrugged. "I use therapy dogs with many of my patients. I know what's required on my end, but it would be good to know the other side of it too."

"Fine with me," I murmured. I stepped forward to punch the elevator button. When I stepped back, he loosely clasped my arm. "Wow, nice bracelet."

I glanced down at my wrist, which suddenly seemed overloaded with jewelry, then looked up to the elevator lights, wishing the car would come sooner. "Thanks."

Josh positioned himself next to me and looked up to the lights, too. "Mr. Porsche?"

"His name is Ryan. And yes, he gave it to me."

"Ouch, his gift outshines mine by a mile." He sighed. "This is why nice guys finish last, I suppose."

I turned to look at him. "Are you up for grabs?"

He pivoted his head. "Excuse me?"

"Are you… available? My, um, sister wants to know."

"Ah." He shifted foot to foot, then pursed his mouth and looked back to the elevator lights. "Yeah, I guess I am."

I looked back to the lights. "Good. I'll tell her."

"Good."

October 14, Wednesday

THE DOOR chimed when I walked into the GiddyUp GoMart.
"Be right with ya," Shawna Dell yelled around the corner where she worked the hotdog cooker.

"I can wait," I said.

She stuck her head out, and her face erupted into a huge grin. "Mallory!" Hotdogs forgotten, she came around the counter and embraced me. She smelled like grease and smoke, a scent Trent had loathed when I came home from my shift reeking of it, but which felt oddly comforting to me at the moment.

I pulled back. "How are you?"

"I'm good. Still fat and sassy, as you see."

I laughed. "How's Bob? And your boy?"

She hesitated, then gave a dismissive wave. "Let's don't talk about that. Tell me what you're up to. Are you doing lots of fun things? Traveling? Enjoying the good life?"

"Life is... different," I said. "Has Mrs. Conroy been back?"

"Not since the ladder incident when she ran out of here. Good riddance, I say."

I winced. "But how is business?"

"Better, actually, since the new exit from the interstate opened. This place might make it after all."

"Good." I glanced around. "Is Ramy here?"

"He took a deposit to the bank, he'll be sorry he missed you."

"I'll catch up with him later, I just came by to say hello."

"It sure is good to see you," she said, then her eyes welled with tears.

I was immediately concerned. "Is something wrong? Is Bob okay?"

She gulped back tears. "He needs another surgery."

"Is it his donated kidney?"

"The kidney is fine, but he has an infection the doctors are worried about. They're gonna open him back up again."

"It'll be okay," I soothed. "And don't worry about the medical bills." I had promised her previously I would take care of them. Since my money was still in escrow, the bills were being paid through the line of credit the bank had extended to me—at a hefty interest rate.

She embraced me again. "Thank you, Mallory... thank you... thank you."

I let her cry and over her shoulder I saw the sign displaying the fact that the $52M Mega Dollars Lottery Winning Ticket Was Sold Here!!!

I sighed. At the rate my jackpot was being siphoned away, I'd be back here working the evening shift soon, soaking up grease and smoke.

October 15, Thursday

"MS. KLINE, you worked at The Community Cafe with Mallory Green?"

The door to the meeting room opened and I looked up, hoping it was Ryan, but it was yet another attorney for the opposing side. The deposition had been underway for an hour, but interviews were only starting. I was sitting with my attorneys on one side of a long table; Vance and Kerry and their attorneys sat on the opposite side. Vance was more low-key and avoided eye contact with me. Kerry, however, seemed to relish her role as lead witness.

She leaned forward to speak into the microphone. "Yes. We were both waitresses. I still work there, but Mallory quit after she cashed in the lottery ticket worth fifty-two million dollars." She gave me a look of near-loathing.

Her lead attorney made a rueful sound that sounded as if he were judging me. "When you and Ms. Green were both employees, did you manage the pool for buying lottery tickets for employees?"

"I did."

"And did Ms. Green participate in the pool?"

"Every week. And when she didn't have the cash, I spotted her."

"And did you spot for other employees as well?"

"Yes, because it was understood that we were all in it together, and if one person won, we all won."

"That's the way lottery pools generally work," her attorney agreed. "And do you remember having a discussion with Ms. Green about what would happen if any of you won the lottery?"

"Yes. The three of us were talking—me, Vance Decker, and Mallory. Vance said if he won the lottery, he'd share it with us. That's when Mallory said so would she."

"And you believed her?" the attorney pressed.

"Absolutely," Kerry said. "We were friends, after all."

I pushed my tongue into my cheek. She really should make up her mind.

"And how did you find out Ms. Green had won fifty-two million dollars?"

"When it was announced in a press conference."

"So she kept the information from you and the rest of your approximately twenty coworkers?"

"Yep. She called in sick for a couple of days, then showed up as usual, didn't say a peep about winning a jackpot. After she claimed the ticket, she invited me and Vance to the Four Seasons hotel where she was living in a suite to be her guest at the spa."

"And did she pay for everything?"

"Yep. And a few days after that, Vance and I both received brand new convertibles."

"You didn't ask for them?"

"No. It was clear to both of us that Mallory felt guilty and was trying to buy us off." She made a sound of contempt. "If that was the aim, I could've used the cash. Unlike Mallory, I have bills to pay. And now I owe taxes on an expensive car I don't even need."

I leaned over and whispered to Ron Buckley, my attorney, and he asked for the floor.

"Ms. Kline, in the conversation you mentioned earlier between you, Ms. Green, and Mr. Decker, do you recall your comment about sharing the winnings?"

She squirmed. "No."

"Are you sure, because my client remembers and I can ask Mr. Decker to corroborate."

I glanced over at Vance and his face reddened—he remembered.

Kerry made a huffing sound. "Okay, okay. I said if I won, I wouldn't be as generous as the two of them."

"Meaning if *you* won the lottery with a ticket you'd bought on your own, you wouldn't share?"

Her mouth tightened. "That's right."

"Thank you," Buckley said. "I just wanted to get that relevant information on the record."

After a few more questions, the microphone was passed to Vance, who answered the same questions Kerry had been asked in similar fashion, then added, "The week Mallory won the lottery, Kerry was absent and Mallory said she'd take up the lottery pool money."

"And did she?"

"Maybe she did... maybe that's the money she bought the winning ticket with." Then Vance repeated Kerry's version of our conversation. "I said if I won the lottery, I'd share the winnings, then Mallory said if she won, she'd share the winnings, too."

"And you believed Ms. Green? The comment wasn't made in jest?"

Vance looked across the table to me, then averted his gaze. "Yes, I believed Mallory. I thought we were friends."

When it was my turn to speak, I insisted I hadn't offered to take up the pool money in Kerry's absence. "I didn't collect any money, and I didn't buy any tickets on behalf of the employees."

"The winning ticket you bought was while you were at your other job and with your own money?" Buckley asked.

"That's right."

An attorney for the other side took over the questioning. "So you want people to believe the week Ms. Kline was out sick and you were supposed to take up money for the lottery pool, that you didn't take anyone's money and that just happened to be the week you won a fifty-two million dollar jackpot?"

I swallowed hard. "Yes."

He gave a harsh laugh. "That's quite a coincidence. But let's say hypothetically you did buy the lottery ticket with your own money. Did you forget about the verbal agreement you'd made with your coworkers that you'd share your winnings?"

"To be honest, it didn't cross my mind because it was said in passing, in a casual conversation. Besides, I did share my winnings with Kerry and Vance—I gifted them cars."

The attorney grimaced. "You obviously didn't learn how to share when you were a child."

His comment landed like an arrow—had having nothing when I was a child made me a greedy adult?

My attorney objected and asked for the comment to be stricken from the deposition, but it was a glimpse of how things could unfold in the courtroom.

And once again, I was suffused with mixed feelings about the ramifications of the money I'd "lucked" into.

October 16, Friday

WHEN I entered Plaid, I was dressed for it this time. The hostess scanned my body-con red dress and strappy high heels and offered me a "you're one of us" smile. I made my way to the bar and shimmied through the undulating crowd to reach Delilah's section. She had attracted a devoted set of groupies, I noticed.

Including Josh.

I sidled in next to him, satisfied when he looked over and did a double-take. "Mallory?" He looked me up and down. "Is that you?"

"It's me." I waved to Delilah, who was preparing a pitcher of an apricot-colored concoction while her audience looked on. She waved back with a grin. Her eyes were dilated and her cheeks were pink. She was in her element, and I had the eerie sensation she could morph into whatever identity was required for attention.

"What brought you out tonight?" Josh asked over the music.

"I just wanted to be with friends."

He smirked, then nodded in concession. But I noticed he did glance at my wrist to see if I was still wearing both bracelets.

I was.

And I was teasing him—Wanda had said she would try to join me. I turned to look for her. Even amongst the colorful crowd, her head of blazing red hair would be hard to miss.

I didn't see her, but in the rear of the bar, someone else caught my eye—or rather, his hat did. It looked like the hat the man who'd been following me had worn, but in the low lighting, I couldn't be sure.

I grabbed Josh's arm. His head came around. "Is something wrong?"

I turned back to point out the man I'd seen, but he'd disappeared. Or had I seen him at all?

"Mallory, are you okay?"

I released Josh's arm. "Yeah. Sorry about that." I was projecting my unease over Delilah onto people in general.

He smiled. "Anytime."

October 17, Saturday

"ARE YOU expecting someone?" Delilah asked. She stood in the middle of the park meadow, giving Nessie commands.

I sat nearby on a quilt we'd brought to spread out on the fading grass. "No. Why?"

"You keep looking around."

I was scanning for the man I thought was following me, but I didn't want to say anything—I didn't want to scare her, and I didn't want to sound paranoid. "I'm just taking in the scenery."

She scoffed. "Are you sure you aren't looking for Josh?"

I glanced up sharply. "Josh? No."

"Really? Because the two of you looked pretty cozy at the bar last night."

"Josh and I are just friends."

"So you keep saying."

"Besides, I have Ryan."

"So you keep saying," she repeated, then gave me a pointed look. "Having two boyfriends at once never works—trust me."

I rolled my eyes. "I don't have two boyfriends, and I'm not looking for Josh."

"What then? You've been jumpy all morning."

I sighed. "Remember I told you about the man who came to the house?"

"The stalker you had to call the police on? Yeah."

"I thought I saw him last night at the bar."

Her eyes blinked wide. "No kidding?"

"I don't think it was him," I said. "But it spooked me. And this is where I was when I first noticed him."

Delilah looked all around. "Those two guys with the frisbee are looking over here."

"They're looking at you," I said dryly. "Just promise me you'll be careful when you're at the house alone."

"I will be." She smiled. "And thanks."

I frowned. "For what?"

"For being sisterly."

Her words made my chest tighten with affection... and with doubt.

October 18, Sunday

I WAVED goodbye to Delilah as Ryan and I drove away from the house. He was taking me to dinner to make up for the fact that he'd missed the deposition. But it was impossible to be angry—his business was booming, and I admired his ambition.

"Delilah seems to be settling in," he said mildly. "Is she staying for good?"

"I haven't asked," I admitted.

"Have you thought any more about asking her to take a DNA test?"

"I haven't ruled it out."

He shifted in his seat. "Maybe you won't have to."

"What do you mean?"

He grimaced. "I took the liberty of running a more extensive background check on Delilah."

I held my breath. "And?"

He exhaled. "She still looks legit on paper. No criminal history, no arrests."

Considering our father's current predicament, that was a relief.

"I'm sorry if I overstepped," he said, reaching for my hand.

"You didn't," I said with a smile. "I know you're only looking out for me."

He lifted my hand for a kiss, then frowned at my wrist. "You're still wearing the bracelet made of thread?"

The two bracelets were in sharp contrast to each other, one demure, one dazzling. "Considering how the deposition went, I think it's important I don't give the impression that I'm only interested in material things."

"Smart. Okay, I'll try not to feel slighted," he teased. "Does Buckley have any idea when the judge will hear the complaint?"

"He says it could be next month, but hopefully before the end of the year." I sighed. "I just want it to be over. I've been thinking about offering a settlement."

Ryan gave me a sharp glance. "Absolutely not. People will take advantage of how good and kind you are by making you feel as if you owe them something, but you don't. The more you give, the more people will want—including family."

His support warmed me inside... but I didn't like the thought that even if the lawsuit went my way, I would always be a target for people who were more attracted to my money than to me.

October 19, Monday

"SO YOU'RE not going to ask Delilah to take a DNA test?" Imogene asked.

"Right," I said. "I want to trust her without..."

"Proof?"

I nodded. "I've been told I have a problem trusting people."

She shifted in her chair. "Can I offer a piece of advice?"

"Of course."

"Sometimes the people who say that are the people you shouldn't trust."

That made sense—hadn't Trent told me countless times that my need to "protect myself" had pushed him away? In hindsight, I hadn't protected myself nearly enough.

"So you and your sister are bonding?"

"I think so. We're very different, but I find myself wishing I were more like her."

"How so?"

"She seems so free... and happy."

"You aren't happy?"

"I—" I stopped. "I'm not *un*happy." Was there something in between?

"Why do you think your sister is more happy than you?"

I shrugged. "Because she grew up with more security."

"You mean she had a mother and you didn't?"

I nodded. "And our father was more involved in her life, at least financially."

"You don't talk much about your father. When did he die?"

I pulled at the tassels on my bracelet. "He didn't, actually."

Her eyebrows went up and she consulted her notes. "I thought you said you were an orphan, that you were raised in foster care."

"That's true. After my mother died, my father made me a ward of the state and disappeared from my life. But he didn't die... he's in prison."

I could tell she was trying not to react to my bombshell. "And you know this how?"

"A couple of years ago, I hired a private investigator to find him."

"Ah. And does your sister know he's in prison?"

"I don't think so."

"Why haven't you told her?"

I shrugged again. "I don't know. She has some good memories of him... I guess I don't want to take that away."

"So you're starting to care about Delilah?"

I nodded.

"Don't you think that's a good thing?"

I thought about what she would want me to say, what she would write down in her notes. "Yes. I think I'm making progress, that I'm starting to trust."

But I couldn't shake the feeling that my track record for gauging people's motives wasn't the best. What if I was putting my trust in the wrong person... again?

October 20, Tuesday

"GOOD MORNING," Josh said when he walked up to the counter where I stood, receptioning.

I frowned at his sneakered foot. "Are you limping?"

"I see you haven't forgotten everything from PT school."

I smirked. "What happened?"

"Sprained it, which is cutting into my training, darn it."

"So that's why we didn't see you in the park Saturday."

He lifted an eyebrow. "You were looking for me?"

My neck warmed and I suspected it was getting splotchy. "Not me—Delilah."

"Ah." He smiled. "I really like your sister."

I worked up a smile. "She likes you, too. You should call her sometime for a real date."

"I might do that."

"Good." I shuffled papers at my elbow. "How is Ramy's wife Aisha?"

"Improving. She has an appointment later today if you want to say hello."

"I'd like that."

"I'll call you when she gets here."

"Okay."

He cleared his throat. "I, um, don't have your number."

I gave him a wry smile. "I don't have a pink lipstick."

He fished an ink pen out of his pocket. "Will this do?"

I hesitated, then took the pen and turned over his hand to write my cell number. "Only because I might not be at the desk when Ramy and Aisha arrive."

"Right," he said, holding up his inked hand. "So... later?"

I gave him a curt nod. "Later."

October 21, Wednesday

"DETECTIVE TERRY."

I smiled into the phone. "Hello, Detective. This is Mallory Green. You were kind enough to come to my house at Lake Lanier when I had a trespasser. You left a message to call you?"

"Hello, Ms. Green. I'm just following up. The company that services your security system sent me a still of the man who was on your property, but so far, we haven't had a hit on our facial recognition search. At least you know he's not a violent felon."

I sighed. "That's good... I suppose."

"And for good measure I contacted your husband's divorce attorney. He swears they didn't hire anyone to tail you."

"I didn't think so, but thank you for checking."

"Have you seen the man again?"

"I—" I thought of the maybe-glimpses and almost-there's and realized I had nothing concrete to add. "No."

"Okay, well, let's hope he was just some random guy who wanted to talk to Lottery Girl, and now that he's been spooked, you won't see him again."

"Yes. Thank you, Detective."

"Take care."

When I hung up, I imagined the big man closing the folder on my case and filing it away. I realized I should probably do the same.

October 22, Thursday

"THANK YOU for arranging this," I said to Ryan.

"Of course," he said. "I told you I'd find another manager in my office to handle your finances so there's no conflict of interest. You'll like Anna. She's new and she'll do a great job overseeing everything."

I followed him to Anna's office, where he made introductions. Anna was young and pretty and it was clear she was enamored with her new boss. Ryan left to get back to his own client roster, leaving us bereft of his presence to stare at one another.

"You must like working for Ryan," I offered.

"I do," she said breathily. Then she must've remembered why the boss had handed me off to her because she straightened. "Have a seat, Ms. Green." She indicated a chair next to a table where financial papers were spread out—my papers, I realized.

"Please, call me Mallory." I took the chair and she pulled one close to me.

"You are so lucky," she oozed.

When I didn't respond right away, she added, "I've never worked with a lottery winner before."

"Oh." I smiled. "I'm sure Ryan has made you aware of all the, um, issues involved."

"Yes. I understand that most of the money is in escrow awaiting distribution by the court to your husband, and pending a decision by a subsequent lawsuit by former coworkers."

I made a rueful noise. "That's the gist of it."

"And you have debt accruing against those funds."

"Right—medical bills I've offered to pay for two friends. And I'd like to pay off a mortgage for a woman I owe a great deal to."

"And you loaned money to a restaurant owner?"

"Yes, with the thought of buying it if I can. Also, there are lots of legal fees, which are still piling up."

She gave a curt nod. "And I see you've been taking out quite a bit of cash from your line of credit?"

I frowned. "No."

She frowned back. "No?" She pulled a set of statements closer. "The records show cash withdrawals of approximately fifteen hundred dollars each of the last four weeks."

I shook my head. "Not by me."

"Have you given anyone else access to your accounts?"

I opened my mouth to say no, then realized one person had had access to my wallet and therefore the debit card against the line of credit.

I managed a smile. "Why don't I work directly with my bank on this matter?"

She smiled. "Excellent. Let me know if I need to step in. Now about these medical bills…"

October 23, Friday

AFTER DELILAH left for her bartending job—outfitted in clothes from my closet—I slipped into her bedroom and gasped at the mess. The unmade bed was a jumble of wrinkled sheets and squashed pillows. Dirty clothes and containers of half-eaten food covered every horizontal surface. The carpet was stained from unknown spills. I opened a window to let the cool fall breeze help to dispel the pungent odor.

Then I set about opening every drawer and potential hiding place, carefully moving the contents inside and replacing them. I didn't want Delilah to know I'd searched her room, especially since I didn't know what I was looking for, although cash seemed likely. Most of the drawers were empty, so I was able to move through the bureau quickly.

From there I went to the walk-in closet where she'd stored her clothes that were clean—there weren't many, although I noticed she'd "borrowed" several items from my closet. I was going to have to start locking my bedroom door. I checked the pockets of the clothes, plus the drawers in the built-in storage units and all the little cubby holes, but came up empty.

In the bathroom, the vanity was strewn with makeup containers and used cotton pads stained with lipstick and nail polish, crumpled tissues, and dirty hand towels. My sister, it seemed, was a slob.

I opened the vanity drawers and moved items around gingerly. The makeup and toiletries were of higher quality than I would've attributed to her, but I didn't find anything else that raised my suspicions. I conceded it was likely she'd simply put the cash in her own purse, or deposited it into an account of her own. I stood and looked all around the bathroom.

My gaze landed on the commode—specifically the tank. It was a favorite hiding place in movies, after all. I moved a tissue holder from the top of the tank, then lifted the lid and peered inside.

Nothing.

I decided she wasn't hiding anything and started to replace the heavy lid. Then on a hunch, I flipped over the lid.

Taped to the inside were lots of little baggies.

Full of lots of little pills.

October 24, Saturday

IT WAS a gorgeous autumn day in Piedmont Park. Hardwoods were erupting in shades of yellow and pale orange, and pick-up soccer games had yielded to touch football. In the far corner of the meadow, a pumpkin-painting contest was underway for pink-cheeked children. I was sitting on a quilt spread over a little patch of thinning grass, watching Delilah put a spell on Nessie. My sister's luxurious hair was plaited into piles of complicated braids that made her look angelic.

She had insisted on plaiting my hair as well, but mine looked more like the ragged pigtails of Pippi Longstocking.

I hadn't said anything about the pills, had simply returned them to their hiding place except for one small bag. I thought back to all the times Delilah had seemed happy and animated—had she instead been high?

"Nessie, sit," Delilah commanded above her.

Nessie sat.

"Nessie, come."

She walked over to calmly stand next to my sister.

"Nessie, down."

She laid down.

"Nessie, up."

She stood up.

"Nessie, heel."

Delilah walked and Nessie trotted next to her on the left, maintaining the same pace. My sister looked back to me and grinned. "She did it!"

I lifted my hands to clap. "Very good."

"Do you think she's ready to take the obedience test?"

"I think so. I'll try to get it scheduled for next week."

Delilah beamed, then picked up Nessie for a nuzzle. I was a little envious of how much the dog had taken to her.

Of how much everyone had taken to her.

"Delilah, speaking of tests...."

She turned to look at me with raised eyebrows. "Yeah?"

"I'd like for you to take a DNA test."

A frown furrowed her pretty brow. "DNA? Why?"

"The same reason most people take a DNA test. I'll take one too."

Realization dawned. "Oh. You mean you want to see if we're really sisters?"

I nodded.

She looked hurt for a few seconds, then gave a shrug. "Sure, whatever."

"Okay, I'll buy them on the way home and we'll do them together." If we weren't sisters, turning her out wouldn't be an issue. She could go and take her drugs with her.

The palm reader's dire warning came back to me—was Delilah the one who was destined to self-destruct?

October 25, Sunday

RYAN AND I were making dinner when Delilah wandered into the room. She looked sullen and moody—she'd barely spoken to me since the previous day. But now I wondered how much of her ill mood had to do with the fact that I was no longer leaving my purse out in the open.

"Hi," I offered.

"Hi. Hi, Ryan."

"Hello, Delilah." He gave me a curious look, then asked, "Do you want to eat with us?"

She gave a little shrug. "If my *sister* is okay with it."

Ryan might not've heard or understood the snarky inflection on the word, but I did. "Absolutely, join us. Ryan is making linguini with clam sauce."

She made a face. "Will I like it?"

I bit down on the inside of my cheek.

"Sure you will," Ryan said good-naturedly.

I hadn't told him about the cash withdrawals, the pills, or the fact that I'd asked Delilah to take a DNA test. I was getting hip to the fact that families kept secrets from outsiders. Lies had a way of bonding people. It was as if she and I were locked in a game of Chicken.

"Put out another place setting," I said to her, gesturing to the cabinet that held the linens. I avoided Ryan's questioning look and took another drink of wine.

"What the *heck* is this?"

I turned, then froze. Delilah was holding my revolver.

"That's my gun," I said, holding up my hand. "Be careful— it's loaded."

"You have a gun?" Ryan asked.

"It's loaded?" Delilah screeched. She yanked back her hand and dropped it.

I watched the revolver fall in slow motion, barrel over grip. My breath rushed out in terror as I imagined it landing on the tile and discharging, killing one or all of us.

It clattered to the ground and we all flinched.

But thank heaven, it didn't go off.

"Oh, my God," Delilah said, waving her hands. "Oh, my God!"

"Don't touch it," I said. "I'll get it."

I walked over and knelt, making sure the safety was still engaged. Then I picked it up by the grip and returned it to the case. "There. Everyone, relax."

"Relax?" Ryan exploded. "What the hell, Mallory? Someone could've been killed."

"Why do you have a gun?" Delilah demanded.

"I know that," I said to Ryan, then turned to Delilah. "I bought it because I was being stalked. This is *my* house, remember, and I can have a gun if I want."

Ryan coughed lightly. "I think I should go."

I didn't stop him. He gathered up his things and left after lowering a quick kiss to my cheek. But I could feel the tension between us.

After he left, Delilah gave a little laugh. "That was dramatic."

"It's not funny," I snapped. "He's right, someone could've been killed." The palm reader's prediction mocked me.

Delilah's mouth tightened, but she only looked away. "Sorry."

"I'm going to my room," I said, seething. "And from now on, keep your hands off my things."

October 26, Monday

"DO YOU believe in psychics?" I asked.

Imogene smiled. "Psychics? You mean, like people who talk to the dead?"

"Or predict the future?"

She sat back in her chair. "I know enough about the mind to know we don't know everything about it. Do I think some people have sensitivities for picking up on things around us that other people can't? Yes. But that's a far cry from predicting the future." She angled her head. "Why do you ask?"

I wet my lips. "My sister and I had our palms read a couple of weeks ago, and the palm reader told me that I or someone close to me was going to die."

Her eyes clouded. "Mallory, you can't put any stock into that. It's something a person made up to scare you into coming back and paying more money. She might've known you were Lottery Girl and saw an opportunity to make a lot of money."

I nodded. It was possible Delilah had mentioned my winnings to the woman.

Imogene made a thoughtful noise. "But it obviously scared you."

"Lately I've been thinking about how precarious life is."

She smiled. "Family has a way of making you think like that, about living and dying. And in some respect, the fortune-teller was right—we're all going to die someday, and chances are someone close to you will die sometime in the future."

I understood what she was saying and recognized the foolishness of believing the ramblings of a stranger with a spooky voice ... so why couldn't I shake this sense of foreboding?

October 27, Tuesday

"HI, THERE," I said to Josh as he limped up to the reception desk. "How's your ankle?"

He winced. "Healing. And I really hate to ask you this, but do you think you could rewrap it for me?"

I blinked. "Uh..."

"I hate to bother the doctors with something like this, and it feels a little awkward to ask my intern to do it."

"Okay, sure," I said. "But I have to warn you—I'm a little rusty."

He grinned. "I can talk you through it."

I glanced at my watch. "Is now a good time? I was about to take my lunch hour."

"Yeah, follow me."

I picked up my bag and followed him self-consciously through the halls of the clinic to his office. The plaque on his door read "Joshua English, Doctor of Physical Therapy." In front of his door sat a giftbox of chocolate-covered strawberries, with a card.

"Is it your birthday?" I asked.

"No." He retrieved the card and opened it. "It's from the parents of a patient. That was unnecessary, but really sweet." He bent to lift the box and carried it inside where he flipped on lights, revealing a tidy work space. On his desk sat a framed photo of a smiling couple I presumed were his parents.

My envy was acute.

He gestured to the treats. "Want one?'

My stomach growled, so I took one, pondering the man in front of me who bought condoms for his paraplegic male patients and inspired thank you gifts from parents.

He popped a strawberry into his mouth and groaned. "That's good."

I nodded in agreement, and made a mental note that if the final lawsuit went my way, I would subscribe to weekly deliveries of chocolate-covered strawberries.

Josh pulled an elastic bandage from one of his supply cabinets, a package of cloth wipes, and a bottle of antiseptic. Then he limped over to the exam table and lifted himself onto it. "I have to admit this is the first time I've been on my own exam table." He slipped off his untied shoe, then began to unwrap the thick bandage around his ankle.

I gestured to a chair. "May I?"

"I'm in your hands."

I pressed my lips together, then moved the chair close enough to sit down and prop his foot on my knee, telling myself this was a clinical procedure, nothing more. I examined the yellow and purple skin. "This was a bad sprain. Are you sure you don't have a fracture?"

"I had it x-rayed—no broken bones, but it hurt like hell."

"Were you Dumpster diving?" I grinned.

He laughed. "No, nothing so heroic. I wasn't paying attention, tripped over a curb."

"I don't think you want to run this race," I teased.

"I'm not a natural runner, that's for sure."

"Then why do it?"

He shrugged. "Sometimes it's good to get out of your comfort zone."

I wiped down the bruised skin with the antiseptic, conscious of both of my bracelets moving up and down my wrist, one silky and light, one prickly and heavy.

"That feels good," he said in a hoarse voice.

Suddenly the room was fraught with awkwardness. I didn't look up, just carefully unwrapped the new bandage and drew on my muscle memory from the physical therapy classes I'd taken to recall how to properly bind the joint.

"That's perfect," he said. "See, it's like riding a bicycle."

I kept my head down until the bandage was secured with a metal clip, then busied myself tossing the trash while Josh put his sock and shoe back on. When he finished, he stood and tested it.

"Feels good. Thanks, Mallory. Really."

I made brief eye contact. "What are friends for?" Then I gave a little wave. "Later."

I didn't wait for him to respond—I got the heck out of there.

But out in the hall, I smiled to myself. It had felt good to do something useful. That had to explain why my feet felt so light.

October 28, Wednesday

IN THE pallor of the mood in my house and with tension lingering between me and Ryan over the found-gun episode, I was feeling lonely.

After Delilah left for work with a slam of the door, Nessie retreated to her bed. I roamed around the big empty house thinking how many times I'd wished for a room of my own growing up, when I'd been stacked head to foot with other kids in the system, sometimes in group homes, sometimes in foster care.

Memories assailed me and on impulse, I reached for my phone. I pulled up Danica Tumi's number and connected the call, already feeling guilty for pulling her away from her many foster wards.

"Hello?"

"Danica, hi, it's Mallory. Did I call at a bad time?"

Her musical laugh floated over the line. "It's never a bad time to talk to you. I can't tell you how much the kids and I are enjoying the van. It's been a godsend, Mallory."

"I'm glad," I murmured, hoping I'd still be able to pay off her mortgage when the dust and lawsuits settled. "Danica... do you know anything about my family, specifically my father or any siblings I might've had?"

"I never met your father," she said carefully. "But..."

My pulse quickened. "But?"

"He called several times to ask about you."

I frowned. "He did? I didn't know."

"He asked me not to tell you. He just wanted to know if you were well."

"And did he continue to call after I left your house?"

Silence sounded, then, "Yes. When he realized you and I stayed in touch, he called once a year or so to see if you were okay."

"So you told him I was married, and where I lived?"

"Just the city where you lived, no details." She sighed. "Did I do the right thing? I haven't heard from him in a few years now."

Because he was holed up in prison. "It's okay, Danica. I'm not angry. But did he ever mention any other children?"

"No... never."

"Okay, thanks."

We talked a little longer, until the raucous clatter in the background could no longer be ignored. It made me recall when I was one of the kids vying for her special attention. I promised to call again soon, then said goodbye.

I pondered the fact that my father had kept tabs on me all those years and if it made a difference in how I felt about him giving me up as a ward of the state.

I decided no.

October 29, Thursday

WHEN NESSIE'S name was called to put her through the tests for her obedience certificate, I was ridiculously nervous. How many times had she balked at my commands? Why hadn't I brought Delilah along? Nessie seemed to respond to her much better.

But since I would be her handler during the therapy sessions, she had to demonstrate obedience to me.

I stepped into the training area and unhooked her leash, then put it in my pocket. She would be required to respond to a series of voice commands with no urging and no reward. She had to want this.

"You may begin," the instructor said.

I stared down at the little French Bulldog I'd been saddled with when her beloved master had dumped the both of us. I'm sure she'd felt equally saddled with me. I brought her bug-eyed face to mine. "Come, on, Nessie. Let's show him. Let's show *everybody*."

I stood, then looked down and, as Delilah had suggested, used my most commanding voice. "Nessie, *sit*."

When she cocked her head—her general declaration of stubbornness—my heart sank.

Then she sat her fuzzy little rump on the floor.

I wanted to cheer, but had to contain myself, per the guidelines. "Good. Nessie, stand."

She lumbered to her feet in a way that was far from graceful, but she stood.

As she proceeded through the test, my confidence grew and so did hers. At the end of the test, the instructor gave me the thumbs up and at last I could pick her up for a squeeze and a cuddle. "You did it," I whispered. "*We* did it."

And I conceded we couldn't have done it without Delilah.

I felt the familiar push-pull on my heart when it came to my maybe-sister. Unbeknownst to her, I hadn't yet sent off the DNA tests. Didn't the fact that she'd agreed to take one indicate she was telling the truth?

Unless she'd done it to call my bluff, hoping I wouldn't send them in?

October 30, Friday

STILL FEELING torn over Delilah, I decided to go back to Plaid, telling myself I might learn something while watching her that would give me more insight into what I should do.

Or I might see my stalker and be able to corner him until the police arrived.

It certainly wasn't to see Josh, although he was there, as usual, parked at the bar with assorted friends, favoring his gimp ankle.

"Hi," he said cheerfully over the music and the noise. He looked as if he'd already had a couple of beers. "Can I buy you a drink?"

"Sure," I said. "A glass of white wine."

He flagged down Delilah, who glanced my way with a stony face. She poured the white wine, then pushed it toward Josh.

Then she grabbed him by the shirt collar and pulled him across the bar for a long, wet kiss.

The crowd went crazy. My stomach did a little flip, but I decided it was embarrassment for the both of them.

When Delilah released Josh, he looked dazed—but pleased. He blushed to his ears and grinned like a buffoon. When he stepped back, instantly other men were vying for a kiss, holding up bills. But Delilah shook her head, gave me a haughty look, and went back to pouring drinks.

Josh handed me the glass of wine, still grinning, oblivious to the smear of bright pink lipstick all around his mouth.

"Thanks," I said, wickedly electing not to tell him. "That was entertaining."

But he was looking past my shoulder. "Hey, there's a guy over there staring at you."

I turned around so quickly, I nearly spilled my wine. I expected to see my stalker, but when I saw a hand go up, my shoulders fell. It was PJ, Trent's other buddy. As he made his way toward me, Josh started to turn away, but I grabbed his arm. "Stay," I pleaded from the side of my mouth.

He stayed.

PJ finally got close enough to speak. He was so wasted, he could barely stand. "Hiya, Mal—you look *hot*."

I managed a smile. "Hi, PJ. How are you?"

"Great," he slurred. "Trent's been treating his friends right with all his money." Then he gave a little laugh. "I mean, with all *your* money."

I swallowed my anger. "That's nice."

"Wanna dance?" he asked, leering.

"Sorry, bud," Josh said. He put his arm around my waist and pulled me against him. "She's taken."

I stiffened, but endured his wandering hand. I'd asked for this.

"Oh, yeah, bro, no problem. Mal's a great girl, I always told Trent he was lucky to have her." Then he snickered. "He said he's lucky, alright. Now he has your money without having to be married to you."

My head went back to absorb that blow.

"Time for you to go," Josh said. He turned PJ and shoved him in the direction of the door. The man was too drunk to object.

Josh turned back to me. "Forget it—he didn't know what he was saying."

I nodded, but my face burned with humiliation.

"Come on, drink up," Josh said, nodding to my wine.

I felt a grateful rush of... friendship. "Thanks for that. Also, you have my sister's pink lipstick all over your face."

October 31, Saturday

I DIDN'T expect Trick or Treaters at my house for Halloween, but I'd bought candy anyway, knowing Delilah would eat it for breakfast if I didn't give it out.

For the occasion I'd dressed Nessie in a superhero costume, complete with cape and eye-mask, and I'd bought an eye-mask for myself. I turned on all the outside lights, turned off the security system, and set the colorful decorations Delilah had brought home outside the entryway.

"I'll be working," she'd groused, "but I love Halloween."

We still weren't talking, really, although I suspected the kiss she'd planted on Josh had made her feel somewhat better.

I was pleasantly surprised when the doorbell rang and the first knot of costumed children arrived, accompanied by parents who were driving them around. When the kids kept coming, I surmised word had gotten out virally that I was giving out king-sized candy bars. I recalled the few times I'd gone Trick or Treating as a child—we'd always targeted the larger homes because they gave the most lavish candy bars or toys. Nessie was a big hit with the kids and seemed to enjoy the attention. The fact that she was so amiable in a crowd gave me added hope she'd make a good therapy dog.

I was starting to worry I'd run out of candy, but the visitors trickled off when dusk fell. I assumed most parents wanted their children home early. When the doorbell rang again, I opened the door with a ready smile.

And dropped my bag of candy.

The man who'd been stalking me stood on the other side of the doorway.

I opened my mouth to scream, but my voice failed me. All I could do was stumble backward and try to close the door, but the bag was wedged between the door and the facing and kept it from closing. It sprang open as I retreated into the house. Panic seized me. I distantly registered Nessie barking hysterically. The man appeared in the open door and advanced toward me, his hand out menacingly.

I scrambled to the other side of the breakfast bar to put a barrier between us. "I've seen you," I managed to get out. "Leave now. The police are on their way."

I hoped the lie would scare him off. I measured the distance between me and the switch for the external alarm, but I'd dismantled the security system. My mind whirled, and landed on the fact that my gun was in its case on the counter in front of me, in preparation for going to the range the following day.

"I'll give you money," I said, reaching for the case.

"I didn't come here for money," he said, his voice low. "I came here for you."

Oh, God, he was going to kidnap me? I opened the case and pulled out the revolver, turning off the safety as I lifted it, like I'd practiced at the shooting range. There was a shell in the chamber. "Leave now," I said. My hand shook violently and my mask had fallen askew, obscuring my vision.

"Buggy—"

I heard the sound of the shot before I realized I'd pulled the trigger.

The man fell to the floor and instantly I was overcome with what I'd done. "Oh, my God, oh, my God." I dropped the revolver and ran toward his body, expecting to see guts spilling out and a river of blood.

Instead he rolled over, unscathed. "You took ten years off my life."

I'd missed.

I sprang back from him. "Get out of my house, now!" Then I stopped as a word he'd said landed in my mind, stirring a long-distant memory. "What did you call me?"

He sat up gingerly and smiled. "Buggy… it's me… Dad."

NOVEMBER

November 1, Sunday

"YOU SAID you were an orphan," Ryan said, his voice slightly accusing.

We were standing at the rail of the rooftop deck of my house on Lake Lanier, staring down at my long-lost father Gordon Miracle, who was skipping rocks off the dock in a way that made me think he'd missed it terribly while he'd been incarcerated. Morning fog rose from the still water in the cove as cooler air temperatures collided with the warm surface. Nessie sat near him on her haunches, occasionally barking encouragement. She was happy to have a man around again.

I pressed my lips together. "I am an orphan... technically. After my mother died my father turned me over to the state."

"You had no idea what happened to him?"

I considered lying again, but look where that had gotten me. "Um... not exactly." I shifted foot to foot, then opened my mouth to let the truth fall out. "A couple of years ago I hired a private investigator to look for him."

"And?" Ryan prompted.

"And... the investigator found him—in prison."

Ryan's eyes bounced wide. "Prison?"

"Only state prison," I said, as if that made it better. "He committed tax fraud, not murder."

Ryan pursed his mouth. "So you're the only one in the family with a loaded gun?"

My neck grew moist every time I thought about how close I'd come to shooting my father. The prediction of the palm-reader Delilah and I had visited came back to me.

You... or someone close to you... is going to die.

"It would've been self-defense," I mumbled.

Ryan pulled his beautiful hand down his handsome face. I knew he was thinking this relationship was turning out to be less fun and more trouble than he'd imagined. A mere three months ago I'd been a newly single lottery jackpot winner of unimaginable wealth. Now half my money had been siphoned off to my soon-to-be ex-husband, another lawsuit still hung over my head, and relatives were popping out of the woodwork.

"I'm... sorry?" I murmured, unsure of what else to say.

He considered me with his dark sapphire-colored eyes, then sighed. "I suppose you're going to let him stay here, too?"

"He has nowhere else to go. The halfway house where he's been staying turned him out two days ago. And I have all this room."

Ryan glanced down to where my father was scratching Nessie's head. "He seems like a nice enough guy, but I don't like this."

I swallowed hard. "There are a couple of other things you're not going to like."

He folded his arms. "What?"

"Anna at your office alerted me someone has been making cash withdrawals on the line of credit."

His expression darkened. "How much?"

"About six thousand dollars over the past month."

"Let me guess—Delilah?"

"I assume, although I haven't confronted her yet."

He scoffed. "You don't actually believe she'll cop to it, do you?"

"I want to give her a chance to defend herself. Besides, it's not a lot of money in the scheme of things, and I already obtained a new card and PIN."

He looked as if he wanted to say more, but instead he grunted. "What's the other thing?"

I squirmed, surprised by how protective of her I'd become. Why did I feel compelled to keep the secret of the pills I'd found in her room? "I... have to bail on our plans for today," I said, chickening out. "I should be here when Delilah gets up. It was late when she got in last night, and Gordon was already asleep."

"What was her reaction to the news?"

I hesitated. "It was hard to tell. She was surprised, and angry I hadn't told her he was in prison."

"So it wasn't just me you hid the truth from?" Ryan asked dryly.

My chin went up. "Like you didn't tell me about having a girlfriend?"

He had the grace to blush. "Maria and I had been over for a long time, but you're right—I should've told you." He reached over to lift my hand. He kissed the inside of my wrist, near the diamond tennis bracelet he'd given me, igniting little firestorms all over my body. His gaze flickered briefly over the fiber friendship bracelet Josh had given me, but he didn't comment. "Maybe when the lawsuit is over, you and I should take a trip... alone."

"That would be nice... if I can afford it."

He gave a little laugh. "Don't worry about that. When the judge hears the gratuitous claims your former coworkers have made, he or she will rule in your favor."

"You don't know that."

"I choose to be optimistic."

I gave him a grateful smile. "Then I will be, too."

"I'll leave you alone to be with your... family."

I walked down to the ground level with him, feeling fortunate to have someone looking out for me, and someone patient enough not to push me to have a physical relationship while my life was in pieces. When he climbed into his Porsche, he leaned his head out. "Do me a favor?"

"What?" I asked.

"Get rid of that gun."

I didn't respond, just stepped back and waved as he turned the car around and pulled away. I turned and watched my father from a distance, still marveling over the fact that he was here, in the flesh. When he'd pushed to his feet after I'd almost shot him in the kitchen, I'd recognized in his face the sharp features I remembered, now softened and lined with age. From the abbreviated conversations we'd had last night and this morning, I hadn't been able to ascertain much about him other than he was congenial and seemed eager for a fresh start. He acted as if he'd been gone from my life for a couple of months rather than a couple of decades.

All night I'd lain awake, my emotions vacillating between elation and rage. This morning they had settled somewhere closer to hope.

Nessie spotted me and barked. My father turned from his rock-skipping and smiled in greeting. My heart bounced high—how many times had I yearned to see that smile when I was growing up, feeling unwanted?

I hugged myself and walked toward him, wishing I knew what to do, what to say... how to behave. I hadn't been anyone's daughter in a long while.

He wore dark jeans and a checkered shirt, inexpensive clothes I assumed he'd been given at the halfway house. He was of average height and weight with graying brown hair, unremarkable in looks, but an accomplished conversationalist, which left me feeling tongue-tied and... young.

"Hi, Buggy," he said, easily reverting to the nickname he'd called me when I was little.

"I prefer Mallory," I said.

His smile dropped a fraction. "Okay... Mallory. That's only right since you're all grown up now. Was that fellow Ryan your boyfriend?"

I nodded.

"I thought you were married."

I managed a little smile. "I was... for five years. He, um... changed his mind."

He made a mournful noise. "What man would be crazy enough to leave you?"

I let those words hang in the air, wondering if he'd realize *he* was the first man who'd left me. Then his eyes clouded—he realized.

Behind me, the door opened and Delilah stepped out, eyeing Gordon warily. All I could think is never could I ever look that good just rolling out of bed. Her long tousled hair hung free and she wore an oversized yellow T-shirt of mine. It made me look chubby, it made her look ethereal.

He beamed. "Delilah... my lovely girl, it's so good to see you again." He held open his arms.

She ran toward him, presumably to give him a bear hug. But when she reached him, she put her hands on his chest and gave him a shove. He careened backward and fell into the water with a splash that startled Nessie.

I gasped. "Delilah!" I ran toward the edge of the dock, looking for something to throw to him. I was still untying a buoy when his head popped up.

"What was that for?" he sputtered, treading water.

She frowned down. "For not coming to Honey's funeral."

He coughed, then nodded. "Fair enough." Then he swam to the edge of the dock. When he reached it, he gave us a boyish grin. "Give your old man a hand?"

Delilah stood there stubbornly, arms crossed.

With a sigh, I reached down to pull him out.

November 2, Monday

IMOGENE RAMPLET'S eyebrows shot up. "I think the question here is why you felt the need to lie to people about being an orphan."

I lifted my shoulders. "In my mind, it wasn't a lie. I was abandoned by both my parents."

"Your mother didn't leave by choice," she said carefully.

"But my father did. And chose to support his other daughter instead of me."

"Do you think that could've had something to do with his own grief over losing your mother?"

"You'd have to ask him."

She angled her head. "That should probably come from you. Have you had that conversation?"

I shook my head.

"Why not?"

I pressed my lips together. I had no answer.

"Don't you want to know?"

I didn't respond.

She checked her notes again.

"Mallory, your half-sister shows up and takes money from you and stores what might be illegal drugs in your home, yet you ask no questions. Now your father has shown up and once again you choose to remain silent about decisions he made that affected your life. I can talk to you about your family members, but unless you can convince them to join you in group therapy, you're going to have to have some candid conversations with them on your own."

"I... have issues with confrontation."

"Don't you think you deserve answers?"

I nodded. "I asked Delilah to take a DNA test."

Imogene looked surprised—and pleased. "And did she agree?"

"Yes. We both took them." I bit down on my lip.

"And?"

"And... I haven't sent them off."

"Did you change your mind when your father showed up?"

"That's part of it, I suppose. Obviously he believes Delilah is his daughter—he supported her financially until she was eighteen."

"So that's enough proof for you?"

I didn't respond.

Imogene shifted forward. "Mallory, what's the worst thing that could happen if you confront your sister and your father with questions?"

"I don't know."

"Are you afraid they'll tell you things you don't want to hear?"

"Maybe."

"Are you afraid they'll leave?"

"They won't leave," I blurted. "As long as I have the money."

She gave a little nod. "So you think the money is the only reason they want to be around you?"

I shrugged. "Why else?"

She smiled. "Maybe because you're a smart, funny, kind person."

"With money."

She clicked her ink pen. "Let's get back to your fear of confrontation. Would it help if we role-played?"

I frowned. "How does that work?"

Imogene scooted to the front of her chair. "Pretend I'm Delilah. Ask me the hard questions you want answered."

When I hesitated, she rolled her hand. "Go on... ask me."

I felt silly, but I dragged myself to the front of my chair, and pictured my sister's smirking face staring back at me. "Delilah," I stammered, "I need to talk to you about a couple of things..."

November 3, Tuesday

"WHAT DO you want to talk about?" Delilah responded in a bored voice.

Despite my "rehearsal" with my therapist, my armpits were moist. "Um… someone has been making cash withdrawals on one of my accounts."

Delilah frowned. "That sucks."

I bit down on my tongue. "Yes, it does… especially since it's money I don't yet have. Was it you?"

Her expression changed to something akin to hurt. "No, it wasn't me. I can't believe you'd think I'd steal from you."

She'd stolen twenties from my wallet plenty of times, but it seemed petty to say so. Warning flags sprang up in my mind and I realized why her behavior seemed familiar to me—it reminded me of the way Trent responded to me any time I questioned his behavior. He had a way of making me feel as if *I* was the bad person for bringing it up—even if I had plenty of justification. I took a deep breath, then reached into my pocket and withdrew a small packet of pills I'd removed from her hiding place under the lid of the commode tank. "What are these?"

Her face paled. "Where did you get those?"

"Where do you think?"

"You searched my room?"

I tamped down the urge to apologize. "Technically, it's *my* room."

She reached out to grab the baggy, but I pulled it back. "*What* are these?"

Her mouth tightened, then her eyes suddenly went all moist. "They're generic Adderall… I've been taking them since I was a kid. I can't afford the prescription anymore, so I sell them to pay for my own."

Even as I softened toward her, I remained suspicious. "How do I know you're telling the truth?"

She shrugged. "Take one. Within a few minutes you'll start to feel like you can do almost anything. Not that you need it— your life is already perfect."

I wanted to laugh, but I was so taken back by her sincerity, I could only stare. In her mind, I guess my life did seem perfect. I might've thought the same if I'd met a lottery jackpot winner, before I knew the kind of grief the money could bring.

"My life isn't perfect," I murmured.

"It isn't?" She gestured to the half-dozen beautifully furnished rooms visible from where we stood. "Perfect house." She pointed to my diamond bracelet. "Perfect boyfriend." She pulled on the collar of the designer dress of mine she wore. "Perfect clothes." Then she angled her head. "And now that dear old dad is back, you have the perfect family—well, except for me, of course, because you think I'm a thief and a drug dealer. Oh, and you don't believe I'm your sister anyway."

My throat convulsed. "I... didn't say that."

She tossed her hair. "I sell uppers to college kids who need to get good grades. But I didn't make any cash withdrawals from your bank account."

"Okay," I said, wanting to believe her. "Where do you get the pills?"

"I have a supplier."

"You mean a dealer?"

She tossed her head. "Yeah, I guess. He sends me pills, I send him money."

"How?"

She hesitated. "Are you going to turn me in?"

I frowned. "No... not yet."

"He has a network in Atlanta. I pick up the pills and leave the cash at a storage locker in Buckhead."

"Sounds dangerous."

She scoffed. "It's not cocaine... it's not even weed."

She had a point—was I being naïve? Trent was always telling me I was too uptight. I stowed the baggy in my pocket and decided to drop the subject—for now.

"Did you get those DNA tests back yet?"

Delilah's voice was light, but she wasn't looking at me. Instead she was buttering a piece of toast with fierce concentration... feigning nonchalance? The warning flags in my mind waved wildly. "Not yet."

She lifted her gaze, blinked prettily, and gave me an irresistible smile. "Then I guess you're stuck with me for a while." She took a bite out of the toast and chewed happily.

I had whiplash from her mood change, but then my feelings were all over the place, too. "I guess I am."

November 4, Wednesday

RAISED my hand but hesitated before rapping on the frame of the open office door.

Josh had been poring over a diagram in a thick textbook, but lifted his head and smiled. "Hey, Mallory."

"Hi," I murmured. The last time I'd seen him he'd come to my rescue at the bar where Delilah worked when Trent's drunk friend PJ had cornered me to paradoxically hit on me and insult me at the same time. "Are you busy?"

"Just brushing up on some techniques I haven't used in a while, nothing that can't wait. Come in." He stood and cleared a guest chair of trade periodicals to make room for me, then gestured to them. "The offer of my old textbooks and reference material stands if you ever decide to finish your physical therapy degree."

"Thanks," I murmured, but at the moment, I couldn't foresee a time when my life would ever feel regular again. "I see you're getting around better on your ankle."

He grinned. "Yeah, I'm back to my training runs. The dancing last weekend must have loosened it up."

"Things must've gotten more interesting Friday night after I left."

"I wouldn't say that, but the music definitely improved—and I did have a couple of beers too many."

I pictured him on the bar, dancing with Delilah. He could pull it off, I realized.

"Are you volunteering at the reception desk today?"

I nodded. "I'm on my lunch hour. I, um... need a favor." Then I winced. "Another one."

He seemed unfazed. "Okay."

I reached into my pocket and withdrew the little bag of Delilah's pills I'd kept. "Can you tell me what these are?"

He reached for the bag and held it up. "Yeah, looks like uppers—some kind of amphetamine."

"Generic Adderall?"

"Could be," he said, nodding. "Or maybe diet pills."

"How can you tell?"

"The code stamped on the pill," he said, then handed them back. "Sixty milligrams is pretty strong. Where did you get them?"

I worked my mouth from side to side.

"Oh," he said in realization. "Delilah?"

I nodded. "She said it was a form of Adderall, that she's been taking it for years, but I wanted to double-check. I guess she was telling the truth." I pushed to my feet to leave. "Thanks."

"I thought you normally volunteered on Tuesdays," he offered.

"I do, but this week things are a little hectic at the house."

"Everything okay?"

I lifted my shoulders in a shrug. "My long-lost father showed up."

His eyebrows climbed. "No kidding?" Then he squinted. "I thought you were an orphan?"

"So did I," I said lightly to defer more questions. "And now I have a sister *and* a father."

"Wow… lucky you." But I could tell he was thinking about the coincidence of my far flung relatives appearing just after my lottery win.

"Lucky me," I agreed. "Sorry for the interruption—thanks again." I turned to leave.

"Mallory?"

I turned back.

Josh pulled his hand over his mouth. "It's none of my business, but Delilah really should try to wean herself off that stuff if she can."

I frowned. "Is it dangerous?"

"Not in the way some drugs are, but it does have some nasty side effects, and if she's getting these off the street, who knows what's really in them."

"Right," I said. "I'll talk to her… although you seem to have more sway over her than I do."

He blinked. "Me?"

"Yeah, you." I gave him a dry smile. "The next time you're kissing her, you should try to work that in."

He blushed. "*She* kissed *me*."

"Semantics," I said with a dismissive wave. "She likes you."

He frowned. "Why are you telling me this?"

I manufactured a smile, then held up the wrist that bore his bracelet. "That's what friends are for."

He opened his mouth to say something.

"Gotta get back to reception," I said, then turned and strode away.

November 5, Thursday

DELILAH STARED out the passenger window, then heaved a sigh. "Ugh, this traffic! I need to get back to the house."

I surveyed her jittery hands, her jumping knee. "What's wrong?"

"I forgot to take my meds. My mind is all over the place." She gave me a sad smile. "It's why I was never good in school, and was always getting into trouble."

I nodded toward my purse sitting in the console between us. "I still have the bag I took from your room."

Her eyes lit up as she reached for the purse. "You do? All of them?"

"Yes, all of them."

"I thought you'd take a couple just to have fun."

"That's not my idea of fun."

She pulled out the baggy and practically tore it open, then swallowed a pill dry. She looked like a junkie, I realized with no small amount of concern.

"What is?" she asked, stuffing the remaining pills into her own purse.

"Hm?"

"What *is* your idea of fun?"

I shrugged. "I enjoy taking the paddleboard out most days, although it's getting too cold for it now."

"Sis, you have millions of dollars—when are you going to start enjoying it?"

"I don't have millions of dollars *yet*," I reminded her. "If I lose the lawsuit, I could wind up with less than a million, and that doesn't count my legal fees and other debts."

"That's still a lot of money," she muttered. "More money than I'll make in my lifetime."

"Don't sell yourself short," I admonished. "You can do anything you want to do."

"Yeah," she said with a little laugh, "as long as I take my pills."

I wet my lips. "Have you considered weaning yourself off?"

"Why?"

"How about so you don't go to jail for selling uppers?"

She scoffed. "No one goes to jail for selling candy." Then she shifted in her seat. "Besides... I can't."

I turned my head. "You can't what?"

The longer she took to answer me, the more concerned I became.

"I can't... stop selling them."

"Why not?"

Again the long, concerning silence.

"Because I owe my dealer a lot of money."

My heart sank. "How much?"

She hesitated. "Ten grand."

I gasped. "For your own pills?"

"And for... other things," she said vaguely. "A loan here and there when I was between jobs. My piece-of-shit car is always breaking down. I'm making decent money at the bar when I work, but they won't give me more than two nights a week."

I wet my lips. "I'll give you the money to pay off your dealer."

She squealed. "You will?"

"*If* you agree to start tapering down your dosage. And see a medical doctor for a prescription."

"I will," she said, bouncing up and down in the seat.

I saw a sign up ahead and smiled, then put on my turn signal. "I'm going to stop and get gas."

"This place looks like a dump," Delilah said when I pulled into the parking lot. "What kind of name is the GiddyUp GoMart?"

I pulled the sportscar next to a gas tank. "I used to work here."

She laughed. "No way."

"Yes way. Will you pump the gas? I'd like to go in and say hello to a friend."

"Sure."

I hopped out of the car, then jogged across the parking lot to the entrance. When I opened the door, the bell chimed, bringing back lots of mostly good memories. Inside, Shawna Dell was berating the new employee Link about something he hadn't done to her liking. When she spotted me, though, she stopped fussing and came around to give me a hug. I clasped her hard, then asked for an update on her husband and son.

"This woman, Link," she gushed, "is a pure angel. She's spending some of her lottery money on my family's medical bills."

Link perked up—when he and I had worked together, he'd prattled on endlessly about things I should buy and how he'd spend a jackpot. He pointed to the hand-lettered sign above the counter proclaiming the winner of a $52 million dollar prize had purchased the ticket HERE! "I keep playing with every spare dollar I got, hoping to hit it big like you did, Mallory."

I smiled, but couldn't help noticing the sign was looking creased and worn about the edges, much like the way I felt.

Link looked out the window and did a double-take. "Who's that hottie standing next to your car?"

"That's my sister," I offered wryly.

"Looks like she's having trouble with the nozzle. I'll go out and help her." He hurried from behind the counter and sprinted outside to the car, where he chivalrously took over the task of pumping gas into my car and struck up a conversation with Delilah. She preened under his attention.

Shawna made a soft, whistling noise. "That's your sister?"

"Half-sister, yes."

"She looks like trouble," Shawna muttered, then went to ring up a customer.

Indeed, Delilah and Link were talking and laughing like old friends. He leaned into her, she touched his arm. Then she looked all around and removed something from her purse—the baggy of pills, I realized. She angled her head as if she were asking him a question. He nodded, then pretended to take his time with the gas nozzle while removing cash from his pocket. The exchange was so smooth, I might not have noticed it if I hadn't been staring.

They continued to chat while I paid Shawna for the gas. I said goodbye, then nodded to a flushed, happy Link as I passed him in the parking lot. When I climbed back into the car, Delilah was already belted in.

I started the engine. "You and Link seemed to hit it off."

She laughed. "Tell people what they want to hear, and they fall in love with you."

I tried to laugh with her... but I couldn't get over the feeling that she'd done the same thing where I was concerned.

November 6, Friday

"EXCUSE ME."

The bank branch manager looked up from her desk. Her harried expression morphed into a smile. "Hello. How can I help you?"

"The teller told me you could assist me. Someone unauthorized withdrew cash from one of my accounts at your ATM. Can I see the footage from your camera?"

She looked concerned. "I'm sorry that happened. What's your name?"

"Mallory Green."

Her smile froze. "You're Lottery Girl?"

"Um... yes."

Her smile thawed, then widened. "I knew you banked with us, I mean we were all told, of course." She reached out to pump my hand. "It's a pleasure to meet you."

"Thank you." I glanced at her nametag—her name was also Mallory.

She laughed. "It's why I remembered your name. I thought it was ironic that someone named Mallory won the lottery. You know, considering the origin of our name."

I squinted. "Pardon me?"

"You don't know? Mallory means bad luck."

I was stupefied. "No... I didn't know."

"Well, obviously it doesn't apply to *you*," she said, then her expression took on a pinched look, as if she were reflecting on the state of her own life.

"The camera footage?" I prompted.

"Oh... right. We're happy to help, but we need a police report in order to pull the footage." She leaned over and opened a desk drawer, then walked her fingers through hanging folders. "Here's the form to provide to the police. Once you get it filled out, you can drop it off to me and I'll handle the request personally." She stood and extended the form.

I thanked her, then left mulling her revelation that my parents had saddled me with a name that doomed me to unluckiness. The banker believed I'd thwarted the seemingly guaranteed misfortune... but had I?

Time would tell.

I drove to the police precinct in Midtown to file the report. A woman named Brooklyn who manned the window like an efficient bulldog found an officer to help me. When it was finished, I asked if Detective Terry was available, and she led me back to his office. The man had come to my rescue via speedboat when the guy who'd been following me had shown up at my house.

I stood at the door of his corner office and surveyed him for a few seconds before knocking. The Detective was standing near a window, seemingly mired in his own thoughts. His square jaw was hardened as if he were gritting his teeth. I couldn't imagine what someone with his job had to wrestle with mentally.

But when I knocked, he turned and his face morphed into a semblance of a smile.

"Ms. Green... have you had any unwanted visitors lately?"

I smirked. "You might say that. I wanted to let you know the man following me was my father."

His dark eyebrows climbed high. "Your father? You didn't recognize him?"

"It's a long story," I said with a wave.

"With a happy ending?"

I hesitated. "Time will tell. Goodbye, Detective."

"Take care, Ms. Green."

November 7, Saturday

GORDON AND I sat on the dock in folding chairs, fishing with rods he'd found among the sports gear the previous owner had left. He'd made himself at home in my home, doing little chores here and there and making suggestions where the landscaping and upkeep were concerned. I vacillated between liking it and resenting it. Call it pessimism, but I felt some kind of confrontation brewing. Imogene's voice sounded in my head, pushing me to ask questions.

"So how does your parole work?" I asked.

His head turned. "Hm? Oh... it's no big deal."

When I realized he wasn't going to elaborate, I pushed. "I'd like to understand."

He shrugged. "I check in with my parole officer once every two weeks. He just wants to know where I am and what I'm doing. It's not very interesting."

"How did you wind up in prison?"

He shifted in his chair. "I started a business and I was sloppy with my bookkeeping. The IRS came calling, and I didn't have enough money to fight them."

He made it all sound very innocent. "What kind of business?"

"An import/export business—I bought and sold all kinds of things from souvenirs to canned food to exotic animals."

"Exotic animals?"

"You'd be surprised how much money people will pay for a fancy parrot."

I smiled, then cleared my throat. "Is that, um, something you're looking to get into again?" It was my way of asking if he intended to get a job anytime soon.

"Maybe," he said vaguely. "For now, I'm just enjoying getting to know my girls. It warms my heart to see you and Delilah together... although she didn't get in until dawn this morning."

He sounded almost... fatherly. "I noticed." I wondered if she'd been with Josh.

Probably.

"She's a handful, isn't she?" Gordon remarked.

I decided not to comment. "It would've been nice to know I had a sister."

He reeled in his line slowly, then cast again. "I didn't know where you were."

A lie. I mulled letting him get away with it, then said, "Danica Tumi told me different."

He was quiet for a long while, then sighed. "Okay, so I did know where you were... but I wasn't in a position to be a father to you. I drank a lot after your mother died, and until I was locked up. The silver lining of being incarcerated was it forced me to get sober." He finally turned his head to look at me, then gave me a charming smile. "It looks like I did the right thing. You turned out great, Buggy."

I was struck dumb by his casual assessment, how he'd managed to avail himself of responsibility, yet somehow take credit for my independence. And drop back into my life at a time when it most benefitted him.

"You got a bite!" he said, pointing to my line, that was being pulled under. "Reel it in!"

I yanked up on the rod, cranking the reel against the resistance. A few seconds later, the line loosened and sprang up. The hook jumped out of the water, empty.

"Ah, you let it get away," Gordon said, disappointed. "When you get a good one on the line, you have to set the hook so they don't get away." He laughed. "Like people, you know?"

I tried to smile, but while he rebaited my line with a fat, curly worm, it occurred to me that he and Delilah spoke the same language.

November 8, Sunday

"THOSE TWO seem to be getting along," Ryan observed wryly.

The weather was turning crisp and the foliage around the lake offered stunning color variation. We stood at the rail of the rooftop deck, watching my father and sister fish from the dock. Occasionally their laughter would ride on the wind up to me, inciting a pang of envy. "Yes," I murmured. "They're very much alike, I think."

We were drinking coffees he'd brought on his impromptu visit. We still managed to have lunch once or twice during the week, and he continued to be attentive despite every reason for him to run in the opposite direction. Even though he'd turned my account over to a junior financial manager in his office, it felt good to know Ryan was looking out for me. He'd never hidden his distrust of Delilah even as he endeavored to be friendly, and I sensed he felt the same about Gordon.

"Has he asked you for money?"

"No," I said, then drank from my cup. "And he says he's looking for a job."

Ryan made a noise I couldn't decipher, but I guessed he was trying to be neutral. "I could have my guy run a background check on him."

I gave a little laugh. "He's been in prison and he had another family—that's about as bad as it gets, don't you think?"

He smiled. "You have a point." Then he sobered. "Did you ask Delilah about the money withdrawn from your account?"

"Yes. But she said it wasn't her."

"Do you believe her?"

"I want to." I didn't mention I'd filled out a police report to get the camera footage because deep down, I feared it *was* her.

"Has she done anything else I should know about?"

Maybe it was just my mood, but something about the way he said that made me uneasy—as if he was my overseer. On the other hand, I was the one who'd asked him—*paid* him, indirectly—to look out for my best interests.

Plus he was supposed to be my boyfriend, I reminded myself. Of course he cared. Still, there was no reason to reveal the situation with the pills because we were handling it between ourselves, sister to sister, and she'd agreed to go legit with her own usage.

"No," I said.

Ryan was staring down at her. I turned to look and was struck anew by how beautiful she was, dressed in loose jeans and a big sweater, her golden hair piled on top of her head in a loose knot.

"Is she dating anyone?" he asked, not taking his eyes off her.

"Not really," I offered. "She seems to like Josh."

He turned his head and squinted. "Josh?"

"My former neighbor... my um, friend."

"Oh... right." Then he made a face. "What does she see in *him*?"

I balked. "Josh is a nice guy."

"He seems kind of boring... for her."

I was confused—if Ryan didn't like Delilah, why did he care who she dated? "Josh is funny, and he has a good job," I said, feeling inexplicably defensive. "Maybe she's attracted to the... stability."

"You're probably right," he said with a little laugh. "He seems predictable enough."

Why did his assessment rankle me?

Then Ryan turned toward me. "I was thinking... how about next Sunday you come to my place? You could spend the night."

My pulse kicked up a few notches. My life had become so alien and chaotic, it would be nice to have an intimate evening to look forward to. "I'd like that."

He pulled me close, then lowered kisses to my neck. But I decided his distrust of Delilah ran deep because I had the feeling he was looking over my shoulder the entire time, watching her.

November 9, Monday

"I'M GLAD to hear you're having frank conversations with your father and sister," Imogene said.

"Only a couple," I murmured. "I still don't feel as if I know them."

She set down her pen and leaned forward. "Mallory... families who live together for years don't always know how to talk to each other and share. The three of you have known each other for less than a month. You can't expect it to be a seamless transition to a close, loving family."

"Delilah and my father seem to be growing closer every day. I feel like the odd person out."

She nodded. "Sometimes two people just have communication styles that are in synch. Maybe it's because your sister is younger, or maybe your father doesn't feel as guilty about parenting her since he supported her financially."

I wet my lips. "I don't think he feels guilty about not parenting me. Maybe... he just doesn't like me."

She made a thoughtful noise. "I'm sure that's not the case. Perhaps you remind him of your mother."

"Maybe he didn't like her, either."

She pursed her mouth. "That's possible. You were too young to know what their relationship was like." She smiled. "That's why you need to keep asking questions."

But I could feel a wall of resistance rising in my chest just thinking about it. I pushed to my feet and paced to the window and back. "You're supposed to be counseling me on how to cope with being a lottery winner, not all this personal stuff."

Imogene smiled. "It's all wrapped up together, though, isn't it? I've found that people who have good relationships with other people tend to have a good relationship with money."

I stopped pacing. "And the opposite it true?"

She hesitated, then nodded. "Yes. In my experience, people who have failed relationships with other people typically have a similarly bad relationship with money."

I thought back over my broken childhood, failed marriage, passed over friendships, and relative poverty. If Imogene was right, I needed to fix one in order to fix the other. Else I was doomed to a life of loneliness and indebtedness.

November 10, Tuesday

"HI, THERE," Josh said, walking up to the reception desk where I kept an eye on the phones.

"Hello," I offered, giving in to the rise in my mood to see him. Josh was perhaps the only person—other than Wanda—who didn't trigger an avalanche of mixed feelings in me.

He was... how had Ryan described him? *Predictable.*

Josh leaned on the counter. "We missed you at the bar Friday night."

I laughed. "I doubt it. Speaking of, did you manage to work in a lecture about Adderall to Delilah in between... everything else?"

He smirked. "No, it didn't, um, come up."

"You don't have to feel awkward," I teased. "I know the two of you watched the sun rise."

He frowned. "Me and Delilah? No. When I left around one on the morning, she was dancing on the bar. She must've found someone else to spend the night with."

I tucked away that little nugget of info, wondering why it gave me a lift even as I worried about what kind of person Delilah had gotten herself involved with. I'd thought her recent manic moods were a symptom of her weaning herself from the amphetamine as she'd promised, but perhaps this new man in her life was the cause of her hyper highs and lowly lows.

Meanwhile, Josh didn't seem excessively distraught over the news.

"Hey, how's Nessie's therapy dog training progressing?" he asked.

I smiled. "She earned her certificate of obedience, a small miracle. The next step is a live evaluation with a real patient." I leaned forward. "Is it too much to ask if I request it to be with one of your patients?"

"Not at all. I have several patients in the program. Set it up and let me know if I can help on my end."

"Thanks," I said, and meant it.

He pushed off the desk with a wave. "That's what friends are for."

November 11, Wednesday

I WAS attempting to balance my checkbook at the kitchen counter—a depressing activity involving lots of negative amounts—when the security system chimed. I glanced at the display screen to see a United States mail truck pulling up the driveway. I yelled for Gordon because he was expecting a package—containing what, I wasn't sure, but he'd mentioned it often enough for me to be aware... and suspicious.

He came hurrying through the kitchen to exit the front door and met the postal worker at the mailbox. Curious, I watched as the carrier handed Gordon what appeared to be a bin. My father carried the container to the door and walked in.

"Did you get your package?" I asked.

"No," he said, nodding to the load he carried. "All this mail is addressed to you."

I frowned. "Me?"

"The mail carrier said it was forwarded from a previous address?"

I padded over to investigate the container full of envelopes of all shapes and sizes, each bearing a bright yellow "forwarding" label. "I filled out a change of address card when I moved from my apartment."

He scratched his head. "Looks like it all caught up to you. What is this stuff?"

"I have no idea." I picked up a blue envelope with a Texas return address, opened the flap, and removed a card. A note had been written inside.

Dear Lottery Girl,

I'm writing to ask if you can send me some money to help make my rent. My husband was laid off from his job and I barely make enough cleaning houses to feed us and our three kids. Since you have so much, I was hoping you could spare some, and maybe someday we can pay you back. Two hundred dollars would help a lot. God Bless and thank you.

Sincerely,
Karen D.

"She wants you to send money?" Gordon asked.

"Yes," I murmured, moved over the woman's simple request.

He picked out another envelope and opened it, then scanned the letter. "This lady needs a wheelchair for her mother."

I opened another envelope. "This minister needs hymnals for his church."

Gordon gaped at the mountain of mail. "All these people are asking for money?"

"Looks like it." I exhaled. "How will I get through these?"

"I'll help," he offered, surprising me. He shrugged. "Got nothing else to do."

That was so true. "Okay… thanks."

A knock sounded at the door. When I opened it, the postal carrier stood there holding a second bin of letters. I gasped. "These are mine, too?"

The woman nodded. "And two more in the truck."

November 12, Thursday

"HERE'S SOMEONE else who needs surgery," Gordon said.

I made a mournful noise. Two days of reading about everyone's financial needs was starting to wear on me. "So much sickness."

"I think we can pass on this one," my father said dryly. "She wants butt implants to feel better about herself."

We both laughed, glad for the break in the tension. I was enjoying the time with him, and was secretly ramping up my courage to ask about my mother, their marriage, and why he'd abandoned me—you know, the small stuff.

We'd turned the enormous dining room table into a work table, sorting cards and letters by the reason for their request— medical, housing, education, miscellaneous—and by the amount of money they'd requested. Some asked for as little as a dollar. The highest requested amount was from a town in Missouri that was going bankrupt, but was offering itself for sale for a mere twenty-five million dollars.

"You'd get your own water treatment plant, five cemeteries, and a World War II-era cannon," Gordon cajoled.

"Tempting," I said, "but I don't even have that much money."

My father looked back to the letter, then coughed lightly. "Um… how much do you have, Buggy?"

A little finger of unease ran up my neck, raising goosebumps. But I reasoned it was a fair question. "It's hard to say. Before Trent's lawsuit, after taxes, I had about seventeen million."

He looked up and whistled low.

"But," I rushed to add, "Trent basically got half. And now my half is being contested by a group of former coworkers I was in a lottery pool with."

He looked panicked. "Can they win?"

"It's possible." My attorney had told me many times any given civil case had a fifty-fifty chance of succeeding. "If the judge rules in their favor, my eight million or so could be split up."

He set the letter aside and picked up another one. "Where is the money now?"

I hesitated. "It's in escrow until the lawsuit is settled."

"When will that be?"

"My attorneys are pushing for a date this month, but it's hard to say."

He gestured to the expansive room we sat in. "Is this house paid for?"

I nodded, still uncomfortable with the line of questioning. "And my living expenses are covered by a line of credit."

"You're saying you might be left with—"

"Nothing," I cut in. "Or very little."

He looked incredulous, then gestured to the pile of letters we'd gone through. "So you don't know if you'll even have money to help these people."

"That's right."

He pushed back from the table and stood. "Then I have better things to do."

I frowned at this sudden change in demeanor. "Like what?"

"Like fishing."

He turned and strode away from the table, his body language jerky. When he walked through the kitchen, I saw him stop and stare at a bottle of beer Delilah had left sitting on the counter. I held my breath and counted to three, then to ten...

He pulled his hand over his mouth, then kept walking.

I exhaled, then reached for another envelope.

November 13, Friday

"SIGN HERE," my financial manager Anna said, pointing to a line on the form. "And here."

"Remind me what this is for," I said.

My head was spinning after another session going over my personal accounts. Everything coming in seemed to be in limbo, while everything going out seemed to be in high gear. The medical bills for my former boss Ramy's wife Aisha were arriving with regularity, as were the invoices for Shawna's husband Bob's multiple surgeries. The legal fees were especially alarming, and they were still flooding in.

"It's an extension of the line of credit," Anna said. "Ryan was able to negotiate a better interest rate this time around." Her voice bounced when she said his name.

"That's... great," I said, glancing through the glass wall of her office to his office on the far side of the department. He looked breathtakingly handsome in a pale-colored suit that was a perfect foil for his dark complexion.

"Yes, he's great," she gushed.

While I signed the paperwork, she organized everything into neat file folders. Managing my money was taking up a surprising amount of resources.

"Anna, I've received hundreds of letters from people all over the world asking for money. If I have the funds when the lawsuit is over, how would I handle making charitable contributions?"

She straightened. "I recommend that you donate only to 501C charitable organizations. That way you can at least get a tax break." She frowned. "You'll always get letters from people with sob stories, Mallory, but you can't help everyone. Besides, there are lots of con artists out there just waiting to pounce on people like you."

I realized her words probably weren't as insensitive as they sounded—she was supposed to be looking out for my money, after all. "Thanks," I said, then pushed to my feet.

"By the way," Anna said, "did you find out from your bank who made the cash withdrawals from the account?"

"Not officially," I said. "But I have a good idea who it was, and I'm handling it."

November 14, Saturday

"NESSIE, SIT," I commanded, standing above her in the park. She lifted her poppy eyes to me and considered me for a few seconds, then lay down. "No!" I said with a moan. "If you don't obey me, you're not going to pass the evaluation."

My father sat on a nearby bench reading a book. "She always does what Delilah tells her."

"Everyone does," I muttered.

"What was that?"

"Nothing," I said, louder, then joined him on the bench. Since learning I might not be rich after all, he'd been distant and spent more time away from the house. I nodded to a tree. "That's where I first noticed you following me."

He looked up from the book, then smiled. "Yeah, I thought you were onto me."

"Why didn't you just come up and talk to me?"

"Would you have listened?"

"Probably not," I agreed, "but at least I wouldn't have shot at you."

His laugh rumbled out. "That was close, but I've dodged bullets before."

I looked over to see if he was being serious. "You mean in prison?"

He nodded. "Not everyone was in for an overdue tax bill. I had to make deals to protect myself."

I frowned. "What kind of deals?"

He didn't look up. "You don't want to know, Buggy."

"Mallory! Hey!"

I lifted my head to see Josh jogging toward us. I waved and stood, relieved for a diversion from the unpleasant topic of conversation.

"Hi," I said, surveying his ankle. "You're back in top form."

"As top as it gets," he said good-naturedly. He glanced toward Gordon and I managed a flat smile.

"This is Gordon Miracle... he's my father. D-dad," I said, stumbling over the word, "this is Josh English, he's a... um..."

"Friend of Mallory's," Josh finished, extending his hand. "It's a pleasure to meet you, sir."

"Nice to meet you, too," my father said, acting his part.

"Josh also knows Delilah," I couldn't resist adding. "They're even better friends." Once again, Delilah hadn't made it home this morning.

My father's eyebrows rose. "Ah. She's a beauty, that one."

I kept smiling.

"Both your daughters are lovely," Josh said, the liar. "Mallory... can I have a word?" He gestured for us to step away out of my father's earshot, and I obliged.

"What's up?"

A flush was working its way up his neck. "I want you to know that Delilah stayed at my place last night."

For all my teasing, the news felt like a blow. "Oh." It felt as if Delilah was borrowing my things again.

"On my couch," he added. "She wasn't in any shape to drive home."

"Okay," I said cheerfully.

"Mallory—"

"You should get back to your run," I cut in, backing away. "Thanks for looking out for my sister."

He looked pensive. "You're welcome." Then he jogged away.

November 15, Sunday

I'D BE lying if I didn't admit that knowing Josh and Delilah were, um, sleeping on each other's couches, made me more eager to spend the evening with Ryan at his place. Delilah had been extra inquisitive when I said I might be "late." I tactfully chose not to gloat over spending the night with my perfect boyfriend, but I didn't hide the fact that I was taking an overnight bag.

I'd been to Ryan's condo in Buckhead a handful of times, and none of the visits had resulted in carnal knowledge of one another. But since both of us had been anticipating the time together, the air felt electrified the minute I passed the threshold of his magnificent living space. We made a good show of opening a bottle of French Bordeaux and chatting about his latest professional sports client. Ryan enjoyed the trappings of his success, and while I wasn't yet comfortable in his world of designer furniture and exotic travel, I was warming up to the fact that Ryan wanted to sleep with me... and it had been a long time since I'd felt wanted.

Halfway into the bottle of wine and after some heavy petting, Ryan pulled back and asked, "How about I run us a bubble bath?"

I happily agreed, feeling languid from the wine. He led me into his palatial bathroom lined with huge slabs of marble, poured a full bottle of almond-scented bubble bath into a giant tub, then turned on a series of faucets to whip up a froth. He gave me a deep, wet kiss, then asked me to undress while he watched.

Thank goodness for the alcohol. I stepped out of my heels, then removed my dress as sexily as I could, bolstered by the gleam in his eye while he sat in a chair nearby and nursed his glass of wine. I knew better than to try to dance my way out of my clothes, but the steam in the room and sound of the water made my limbs more fluid than usual. I managed to remove my bra and step out of my panties without falling, and I was gratified by his murmurs of approval when I was fully nude.

"Get in," he urged.

For a half second, I hesitated, recognizing what a vulnerable position I'd put myself in. Ryan could do whatever he wanted to me, good... or bad. I was flattered by his attention, and I wanted this... but did I really know him? In the low lighting, his eyes were hooded and his expression was almost... predatory. It sent a tingle up my spine, and gooseflesh over my shoulders. The moment felt a little dangerous.

I dismissed the feelings, chalking them up to my own insecurities and lack of experience. Ryan had never been anything other than a gentleman, and so patient.

I stepped into the tub and lowered myself into the silky water, instantly immersed in the piles of white foam. With the warm water lapping at sensitive areas and Ryan's gaze on my skin, I felt alive. He walked over and leaned down to kiss me... it was a good, sexy kiss, full of promises of what we would share.

A clanging noise broke into the humidity of the room. It took me a few seconds to recognize it as a ringing phone.

Ryan groaned. "Sorry. Let me turn this off." He pulled away and glanced at the screen, then cursed. "I have to get this."

I nodded, but he'd already answered. I understood, though, that he had to be on call for his high-profile clients who lived in different time zones. It was one price of success.

But from the tone of his voice, I sensed it wasn't business.

"What do you want?" he asked, his voice low. "No... I can't... I *can't*. Don't—" He held the phone out—the screen was black. He cursed, then wheeled back to me. "I'm so sorry, Mallory—I have to go."

I balked. "Is something wrong?"

"A friend is in trouble," he said, sounding anguished and angry.

"Then you should go," I said, trying to hide my disappointment. I half-rose from the water, feeling exposed and unnecessary. "I'll leave."

"No. Take your time," he said, punching buttons on his phone. "Your Uber won't arrive for another thirty minutes."

"Oh. Okay." I awkwardly settled back into the water, deciding to wait until he left before getting dressed.

"I'll call you," he said, then blew me a kiss.

When Ryan left the room, I felt like a cord that had been yanked from a socket and left to lie on the floor. In the water.

Ryan might want to sleep with me—he might even have feelings for me—but he had commitments elsewhere. Because the voice on the other end of the line had very plainly been female.

November 16, Monday

"So you didn't sleep with him?" Imogene asked, her voice clinical.

"I didn't get the chance," I said dryly, then sighed. "Then again, I think it's a sign from the universe that I should wait until my divorce is final."

"That means something to you, doesn't it?"

I nodded. "I was faithful during my marriage, and even though Trent moved on a long time ago, this is something I want to do for myself. I took my vows seriously. I can wait until the papers are signed."

"When will that be?"

"I have an appointment with my divorce attorney in a couple of days to get an update. Wish me luck."

Imogene opened her mouth, but I cut in.

"Scratch that. I don't want to hear the word 'luck' ever again."

November 17, Tuesday

"HI, MALLORY." Josh loped up to the reception counter at the Shepherd Spinal Center, looking boyish and fit.

I'd been practicing my most friendly-friend smile, determined not to think about the fact that he was most likely sleeping with my sister. "Hi, yourself."

He squinted. "Are you okay? You look like you're in pain."

I tried to relax my stupid face. "I'm fine. How are you?"

"Great," he said cheerfully, then sobered and pulled an overnight envelope from his bag. "This was leaning against the door of your old apartment. I thought it might be important."

I glanced at the return address of my divorce attorney's firm and my intestines crimped. "Thanks."

"Hey, I wanted to invite you to the charity run on Saturday, since you were good enough to sponsor me."

"Right," I said, nodding. I'd made that generous pledge back when I thought I'd always have money. "Nessie and I will be there, cheering you on."

"Terrific," he said with a big smile. "Delilah's coming, too. Invite your dad if you want, and make it a family affair."

"I will," I said through gritted teeth. "Absolutely."

Because we were nothing if not one big, happy family.

"How's that going?" he asked.

"What do you mean?"

He averted his gaze, then looked back. "When I met your dad, I couldn't help but notice... I mean, I recognized some signs..." He trailed off, then sighed. "My father drank, too."

I bristled. "Gordon is sober."

He nodded. "Good. Is he in a twelve-step program?"

"I... don't know." He'd been spending more time away from the house—was it possible he was attending meetings? I'd assumed the worst—that he was out doing something he shouldn't be doing, like brokering ostriches on the black market.

"I didn't mean to pry," Josh said.

Irritation blipped in my chest. "Don't you think you should be talking about this to Delilah instead of me?"

His expression closed down, and for a split second I regretted my outburst. But I didn't like how familiar he'd become with my family dysfunction. He probably thought he could fix it.

"Right," he said. "Sorry. Have a good day, Mallory."

"I will," I said, pretty sure I wouldn't.

"Good," he said, backing away with a nod.

"Good."

November 18, Wednesday

THE PAPERS delivered to my old apartment, many of them so chock full of legalese I could barely understand them, were spread over the desk of my divorce attorney, Lynette Shift.

"How much longer?" I asked.

Lynette gave me a stoic look. "I wish I could tell you for sure, but my guess is at least another two weeks, if not more. When this much money is in play, the paperwork has to pass through so many hands."

I sighed. "I just want this to be over."

She gave me a little smile. "I know you do. For people like us, it's hard to move on emotionally until we can close the book."

She'd mentioned she, too, had suffered through a messy split. To my horror, her words of solidarity made me tear up. She made a sympathetic noise, then reached forward to pat my hand. "I'm sorry you're having to go through this, Mallory, but you'll be happy again someday."

"Promise?" I blurted, feeling like a complete fool. I couldn't express my breakdown was related not just to my divorce, but the general brokenness I felt inside at the state of my life.

"Yes," she said, squeezing my fingers.

I gave myself a mental shake—if I were going to fall apart, I should save it for my therapist—her hourly charge was a third of Lynette's. I sniffed. "Sorry... I'm fine... really."

"Okay," she said warmly. "Meanwhile, have you decided whether you want to change your name? You can always do it later, but it's easier if we attach it to the divorce decree."

It almost felt easier to keep Green than to choose another wrong surname to attach myself to. "Do I still have time to let you know?"

She nodded. "Yes. You still have time."

November 19, Thursday

WHEN I knocked on the office door, sadsack Mallory at the bank looked up and smiled. "Hi, Mallory."

Gratified she hadn't called me Lottery Girl, I smiled back. "You left a message about the ATM footage?"

She swept her arm toward a guest chair. "Have a seat."

While I settled myself, she clicked on various files on her computer screen. "We pulled the security camera footage for the times of the four withdrawals. I have stills from the videos."

My pulse ratcheted higher as the photos loaded. When I had proof Delilah had made the withdrawals, what would I do with the information? Confront her? Ask her to leave?

Send off the DNA tests?

"It's a woman," Banker Mallory confirmed, adjusting her monitor so I could see. "The same one each time."

The photo finished loading and I stared at the face of the woman who was definitely not Delilah. She was harshly pretty, with a dark pageboy and severely short bangs.

"Do you know her?" the banker asked.

I shook my head. "Can I get a copy of one of the photos?"

"Sure."

As the printer whirred and chugged to spit out the black and white photo, I wondered who the woman was… and how was she connected to my money?

November 20, Friday

"LONG TIME, no see," Wanda shouted, swinging into the seat I'd saved for her in the bar at Plaid.

"Hi," I said, outrageously buoyed by the appearance of the bubbly redhead. "Thanks for coming."

She leaned in and peered at me. "You don't look so good."

"Thanks," I said dryly.

Then she nodded to the other side of the room where Delilah was undulating across the bar, pouring shots for her adoring fans as she went. "Your sister, on the other hand, looks smoking hot."

"Thanks again," I said, lifting my grapefruit martini for a drink.

Wanda snagged a passing waiter and ordered a martini for herself, then grinned. "So... catch me up, and by catch me up, I mean, tell me how good Ryan is in bed."

I gave her a flat smile. "I can't."

"Sure you can."

"No, I mean, I *can't*."

Her face fell. "Still no wiggle?"

"Nope." I held up my wrist. "But he gave me a bracelet."

She squinted. "Ryan gave you a bracelet made of thread?"

I looked up to see only the friendship bracelet Josh had given me was visible. "Not that one." I pulled back my sleeve to reveal the diamond tennis bracelet. "That one."

Her eyes sparkled. "Now you're talking. That's *gorge*."

I nodded agreement, then asked. "How's Rick?"

She made a face. "He's around. Still dating that bone-rack of a woman who cuts hair—ugh."

I sensed even though Wanda had turned down Rick's marriage proposal due to his lack of funds, she truly cared about him and regretted her decision. "I hope it's not too much to ask you to talk to him about how to get rid of my gun?"

Her eyes flew wide. "You want to get rid of your gun?"

"Yes," I said, electing not to go into detail about Delilah dropping it on the floor, narrowly escaping shooting me and/or Ryan and/or herself, and me nearly murdering my own father.

She shrugged. "I guess I could text him."

Her voice was indifferent, but she yanked up her phone and used her thumbs to type in a message before I could blink. I hid my smile behind my drink. "How's work?"

She sighed. "Bor-ing. I wish you were still there."

I gave a little laugh. "If I don't win my lawsuit, I might have to crawl back and beg Amelia Inez for my old job."

"Pshaw—you're gonna win." Her phone lit up and she pounced on it. "Rick texted back—funny because you'd think he'd be on a hot date with his hair honey."

"What did he say about the gun?"

She read from the screen. "He said you could sell it, but it's kind of a hassle. If you give it away and someone does something stupid with it, it could come back to haunt you." She looked up. "Does that help?"

"Yeah, thanks." For now, I'd keep it, locked in a drawer. I picked up my glass for another drink, then stopped when someone across the room caught my eye.

Pageboy haircut, severe bangs. It was the woman from the ATM photos. I gasped.

"What is it?" Wanda asked.

I pointed to the woman and told Wanda what she'd done.

She squinted. "Hm… she looks familiar."

"You know her?"

She shook her head. "No, I don't think so." Then she stood. "But let's go confront her."

Before I could protest, the woman looked up and made eye contact with me… then turned and bolted. Although I didn't know her, she obviously recognized me.

"Let's go after her!" Wanda said.

But I put my hand on her arm. "It's okay. I have what I need."

"Are you sure?"

I nodded, then glanced toward my sister, who was still performing for her fans. I now knew how the woman was connected to my accounts—through Delilah.

November 21, Saturday

"DELILAH SAID she'd meet us at the 10K," I said, hitting the fob to unlock my car.

"She didn't come home last night," Gordon said.

"She was with Josh." At least I thought she was.

"So is your sister serious about this guy Josh?"

"You'll have to ask her."

"I thought you were friends with him. He hasn't said anything to you about his intentions?"

"Intentions?" I asked with a little laugh. "No."

"Well, she met him through you, didn't she?"

"Yes."

"So you must have given them your blessing."

"They're adults, they don't need my blessing. Can we talk about something else?"

He surveyed my shiny little red sportscar sitting next to the faded compact he drove. "She's really something. I bet she's fun to drive."

Subtle. I stopped next to the driver's side door and looked over. "Do you even have a driver's license?"

He grinned. "Brand spanking new."

I frowned. "That's not comforting." Then I sighed. "Okay, you can drive—if you don't speed."

He ran around the car excitedly and took the key fob. "I wouldn't dream of it."

I circled around to the passenger door and slid in. "I need to make a stop on the way."

"No problem. Where?"

"The post office," I said. Inside my purse were the DNA tests.

Delilah had given me so many reasons not to trust her, I told myself. It had nothing to do with her seeing Josh.

Nothing at all.

November 22, Sunday

"CAN I say again how sorry I am?" Ryan asked as we were seated at a table inside the restaurant at Plaid.

I smiled. "You've apologized a dozen times. It's okay, really." Frankly, I was relieved the interruption had saved me from violating my personal principles. Most people would think I was soft in the head for wanting to honor my wedding vows until the divorce was final, but it gave me a satisfying sense of closure.

Trent would say I was being self-righteous, but I didn't have to care what he thought anymore.

"It's not okay," Ryan insisted. "I can't believe you're still talking to me."

"Buy me brunch and I'll forgive you," I teased, enjoying having some leverage. When the waitress took our drink orders—mimosas—I glanced at him over the menu. "How's your friend?"

He looked up. "Hm?"

"Your friend you had to talk off a ledge—what was his name?"

He winced. "Let's don't talk about it, it'll only put me in a bad mood. What looks good to you?"

"I'm not—"

"How about the crab cakes benedict for two?"

I smiled. "Sure, that sounds lovely." I took a drink of my water, trying to recall if I was allergic to shellfish.

Decision made, he set aside the menu. "How are things with your sister and your father?"

"Strange," I admitted. "It's like we're all moving around each other, like a Rubik's Cube."

"Have you thought about asking them to move out?"

I gave a little laugh. "I'm starting to think it might be easier if *I* move out."

His eyes widened. "I confess I didn't think we were there yet, but if you want to move in—"

"No," I cut in more vehemently than I meant to. "I mean… no, I wasn't hinting and I agree we're not there yet."

He seemed to relax.

"I'll probably let them live in the house for a little while longer, maybe until the lawsuit is settled and I know more about my future. I know I've defended Delilah to you, but I've come to realize that you were right to be suspicious of her."

"What did she do?"

"Remember the cash withdrawals that were made from my account?"

He nodded.

"I got a picture of the woman at the ATM."

"It was Delilah?"

I shook my head and brought up the picture of the girl with the pageboy haircut on my phone. "It was this woman. I don't know her, but she was at the bar Friday night, which leads me to believe she knows Delilah. It looks like Delilah put this woman up to it so she wouldn't be on camera."

He looked concerned. "Have you confronted your sister?"

"Not yet. I'm waiting."

"Waiting for what?"

"For the right time," I said lightly, happy when the arrival of our mimosas diverted his attention. I'd have the results of the DNA tests within a couple of weeks. Then I'd confront Delilah—sister or not.

November 23, Monday

"THOSE ARE some pretty serious accusations," Imogene said.

I splayed my hands. "What else am I supposed to think of Delilah? And it's not so much about the money—I offered to pay off her drug dealer for more than what she stole from me. But it's the lying I can't bear. Not again."

"Who are you referring to? The people who lied to you?"

"My husband," I admitted. "And my father. He said he didn't know where I was when I was in the foster care system, but he did."

Imogene made a few notes on her paper. "Mallory, don't you believe that people make mistakes?"

"Of course."

She hesitated, clicking the end of her pen. "Is it possible that people see you as someone who doesn't forgive, so when they make a mistake, they lie about it?"

I balked. "You're saying it's my fault that people lie to me?"

"No. You're not responsible for the actions of others. I'm merely asking if you think it's possible that people lie to you not because they're trying to take advantage, but because they're desperate for you to think well of them?"

"I... hadn't thought about it like that."

Imogene sat forward. "Do you want to try to heal your family?"

"I... yes." Assuming Delilah *was* family.

"Then may I suggest something?"

"Of course."

"Why don't you invite your father and your sister to our next session? This would be a safe place for you to ask them questions and sort things out."

"I doubt they will agree to that."

"But you'll ask?"

I bit deep into my lip, then nodded. "I'll ask."

November 24, Tuesday

"ARE YOU going to wear your medal to work every day?" I asked Josh.

He smiled down at the colorful 10K medal hanging around his neck over his dress shirt. "Maybe. I'll probably never run another one. And I know why you're being snarky."

I sat straighter, ready to deflect his next words. "Why am I being snarky?"

"Because you're nervous," he said, then reached forward to pet Nessie's head. "But relax—you'll both do great."

He was right—I was nervous about the pet therapy evaluation session. Nessie would have to prove she could focus even with lots of distractions, allow many people to pet and hug her, and basically keep her cool if everything around her fell to pieces. I, too, was expected to be on model handler behavior.

"Ready?" Josh asked.

I nodded and followed him toward the physical therapy area. The observer from the pet-therapy program was waiting, clipboard in hand. I greeted him, but he didn't look happy to be there. And I saw the way his nose wrinkled when his gaze passed over Nessie.

My ire flared—maybe she wasn't the cutest dog, but she was sweet. And loyal.

A trait Trent hadn't appreciated, but I valued dearly.

"You can do this," I whispered to Nessie. But beneath my hands, she was trembling from all the new sensory inputs.

"Meet Wayne and Raj and Luke," Josh said, nodding to three young wheelchair-bound patients who sat in a semi-circle.

We exchanged greetings, then they began to move their chairs through an obstacle course Josh had set up. Before long, the young men were racing and whooping like children. In the midst of the activity, the observer called for time-out and inserted Nessie into the fray. I had no idea how she'd react to the strangers and the frenetic, noisy movement, but I stood by to give her commands when necessary.

She was a champ, eager for the attention, and generous with her licks when the patients needed a boost. She was happy to ride in their laps or to run alongside the wheelchairs as if she were heeling alongside me in the park. After the patients had left, the program observer smiled at last and handed me the pass certification, then congratulated us both.

"Toldja," Josh said. He pulled me into a hug that lasted a few seconds longer than it should've. When we pulled apart, I recalled the first impulsive hug I'd given him in the dumpster when he'd unknowingly found my unclaimed jackpot lottery ticket.

That hug seemed like a lifetime ago.

"Let's call Delilah and tell her," he suggested, pulling out his phone.

I nodded. "Go ahead." Then I nuzzled Nessie and listened to Josh talk excitedly with my sister.

When my own phone buzzed, I pulled it out with one hand, frowning to see my attorney Ronald Buckley's name on the screen. I connected the call.

"Hello?"

"Mallory, Ron Buckley here. I know this is last minute, but we just got word the judge will hear the Community Café complaint tomorrow."

"Tomorrow?"

"He wants it off the docket before the Thanksgiving holiday. I assume you can be there."

I swallowed hard. "I'll be there."

November 25, Wednesday

I SAT with Buckley in the courtroom behind the table, waiting for the judge to emerge to render his verdict. I could smell my attorney's sweat—not a good sign. Ryan sat behind us in the gallery, my sole supporter.

A few feet away sat Kerry Kline and Vance Decker with their attorney. In the gallery behind them sat a smattering of other former coworkers, most of whom I recognized. I understood why they'd all jumped on board the lawsuit—they had nothing to lose and everything to gain.

My energy was fading after long hours of testimony and cross-examining, and synching responses with previous depositions. When the door to the judge's chambers opened, my legs had gone to sleep.

"All rise," the bailiff said.

I pushed to my feet shakily.

"Be seated," the judge said.

I fell back into my seat.

"I've reviewed the transcripts of the depositions," the judge said. "And I've listened to the testimony about the conversation at the center of this case. I'm sympathetic to both sides—sometimes we say things as utterances of whimsy and fantasy. For this case, however, I considered the conversation in the context of the situation." The judge's intense gaze swung to me. "Since the conversation about what they would do if they won the lottery took place among coworkers who were participating in a lottery pool, I find the utterance of Ms. Green that she would share the lottery if she won to be a legal, binding contract."

The bottom of my stomach fell out. Buckley groaned. The other side cheered.

"Silence!" the judge shouted, rapping his gavel. "I'm not finished. Continuing, Ms. Green didn't say *how* she would share her winnings, so it was left up to me to decide what's fair. I find for the twenty-two plaintiffs to receive from the lottery ticket jackpot winnings, the amount of two hundred fifty thousand dollars each." He rapped the gavel again. "Case adjourned."

"We'll appeal," Buckley said to me over the melee that erupted on the other side.

"No," I said. "No appeal."

"But they just took five and a half million dollars of your money."

"I want this to be over."

He sighed, then conceded with a nod. I turned around to see Ryan holding his head in his hands.

Let the fallout begin.

November 26, Thursday

CONSIDERING THE verdict, I was sure Ryan would renege on my invitation to Thanksgiving dinner. To my surprise, however, he showed up with flowers for the table centerpiece, and two bottles of pricey wine. Other than giving me a sad wink when my father brought up the lawsuit, he seemed just as attentive as before.

And thankfully he and Delilah seemed to have buried the hatchet because I saw him extend his wine glass to her in a little toast, and her clink her glass to his.

Gordon had put the turkey in the oven early, so the house was full of good smells as the strays arrived. I'd invited Wanda, and Wanda had invited Rick, who hit it off with Gordon. Delilah had invited Josh, and the two of them did most of the cooking of the sides. I watched him over my glass of wine and wondered if this was the first of many holidays Josh would be at our family gatherings.

Football played in the background, and impromptu card games erupted. For a few hours I was able to forget about the fallout of the lost lawsuit, and get glimpses of how a holiday gathering was supposed to be. I put aside my weird feelings about Delilah and Josh, and didn't object when Ryan's hand clasped mine during the brief blessing that Wanda said over the food. When he squeezed my fingers, I conceded maybe I'd been wrong—maybe he did have feelings for me that weren't wrapped up in my winnings.

Then again, it wasn't as if I was completely broke. I'd get a complete accounting in a few days, but I felt sure I'd walk away with a few hundred thousand. Considering I'd once worked three jobs to make ends meet, that still felt like a win to me.

When I looked around the table at the motley group of family and friends—flawed as they were—I felt lucky.

November 27, Friday

"YESTERDAY WAS nice," Delilah said. "It was almost like a real family."

I looked up from a plate of leftovers. "Yeah." Remembering my promise to Imogene, I said, "Speaking of—"

"Look, Sis," Delilah interrupted, "I don't mean to be pushy, but with the lawsuit not going your way, I know everyone's going to be standing in line to get what you promised them."

I squinted. "Where is this going?"

She crossed her arms. "You said you'd give me enough money to pay off my dealer—ten grand."

"I haven't forgotten."

"Well... I need it now."

I frowned. "Today?"

"Yeah, today."

I gave a little laugh. "Delilah, the banks are closed until Monday."

She grimaced, then smacked her hand on the counter. "But you'll get it Monday?"

I started to say yes, then back-pedaled. "If you'll do something with me on Monday."

She looked suspicious. "What?"

"Go with me to my therapist for a family session. I'm going to ask Gordon, too."

She looked confused. "Why?"

"I'd like for us to... get some things out in the open."

"In front of a stranger?"

"Think of her as a... referee."

"Sounds dumb."

"But you'll do it?"

"And afterward we'll go to the bank?"

"Yes."

She sighed. "Okay, I'll do it."

November 28, Saturday

"SO YOU'LL join us?" I asked Gordon.

He was tinkering with the security system panel. "Hm?'
"You'll join me and Delilah at my therapist's office Monday morning?"
He scratched his head. "Why?"
"Because I'd like for the three of us to talk."
"We talk all the time."
"Not about the important things," I murmured.
He turned back to the security system screen. "How do I disarm this thing?"
"Why would you want to?"
"I'm just trying to learn how to use it." He pointed to a black button. "Is this the motion detector alarm?"
"Yes, but I usually don't turn it on because of all the wildlife up here."
He grunted, then pointed to a yellow button. "What's this?"
I squinted. "I don't know—maybe the silent alarm?"
"Why do you have a security system you don't know how to use?"
His voice seemed overly strident. When I looked at him, his face was flushed. "Dad... relax."
"We're all sitting ducks up here, you know."
I frowned. "What do you mean?"
"Look at all that mail you received," he sputtered. "And you keep making the news. People will try to get to you."
"You're the only stalker I've had," I reminded him, although I appreciated him posturing over safety like a real dad. "Will you come?"
"Hm?"
"To the therapist's office Monday morning?"
He heaved an exasperated sigh. "Under duress."
"Good enough."

November 29, Sunday

"WHO WANTS hot chocolate?" Gordon asked, pushing to his feet.
Ryan had dropped by for his regular Sunday visit. The four of us were sitting around the firepit on the rooftop deck. It was a Norman Rockwell moment I tried to brand into my brain. Because

as lovely as the moment was, it felt precarious. I attributed my feeling of foreboding to my general pessimism when it came to family and personal relationships, and the fact that most good things simply didn't last.

Take the lottery jackpot, for example.

"Me," Delilah said, raising her hand.

"I'll take a cup," Ryan said.

I stood. "I'll help you, Dad." I was getting more used to calling him dad and I was starting to visualize how our family might start to gel once we worked through some issues, hopefully with Imogene's help.

When we got to the kitchen, he put the chocolate in a pan to melt while I pulled mugs from the cabinet.

"Now why are those lights flashing?" Gordon asked, pointing to the security panel.

I peered closer. "The garage door is open. I'll make sure Ryan closes it when he leaves."

"This is too complicated," he said, shaking his head. "In my day, people didn't have to lock their doors."

"Marshmallows?" I asked, holding up the bag.

"Absolutely, Buggy. I'll take two."

I pressed my lips together to keep from chiding him over the nickname—I was warming up to it. I opened the bag and dropped marshmallows into each cup, then he poured the milky chocolate up to the rim.

"I'll carry these up," I said. "Will you bring napkins?"

"Be right there," he said.

I smiled to myself, reveling in the normalcy of the situation. I even allowed myself to think my life might work out after all.

When I neared the top of the steps leading to the deck, I heard Ryan and Delilah's voices. I couldn't tell what they were saying, but they were in a heated discussion. When I topped the stairs, they looked up and separated.

"Everything okay up here?" I asked.

"Fine," Ryan said with a smile. "Here, let me help you with that."

I glanced to Delilah for confirmation, and she, too, gave me a forced smile.

I looked back and forth between them, wondering if Ryan had confronted her about the woman who'd withdrawn money from my account? Or did he know something about Delilah that I didn't?

When I walked him to his car later, I accepted a nice goodnight kiss, but noted he still seemed distracted.

"Did you and Delilah have words earlier?" I asked.

He made a rueful noise. "It was silly. She made a comment about the bracelet I bought you."

"Why kind of comment?"

He picked up my wrist and lifted my sleeve to reveal the sparkling ring of diamonds, then higher to reveal the inexpensive friendship bracelet Josh had given me. "That you like one as much as the other."

I swallowed hard. "That *is* silly. They're... different, is all."

He smiled. "That's what I said." He lowered another kiss to my mouth. "Can we have lunch after you meet with Anna this week?"

I nodded, then stepped back and waved as he pulled away. This week I'd find out how much—if any—money I had left.

And after that, how many—if any—loved ones I had left.

November 30, Monday

I CHECKED my watch, then shot Imogene a little smile. "Delilah is always late, and Gordon indulges her."

"We have time," Imogene said, her voice patient even though we'd been waiting for fifteen minutes. "But while we're waiting, let's talk about that statement—Gordon indulges her."

"He does," I asserted, irritated.

"But he doesn't indulge you?"

"I... don't expect him to."

"But Delilah does expect it?"

"Yes. She expects everyone to indulge her—you'll see."

"So you're upset that Delilah gets what she expects out of life?"

I saw where this was going. "You're saying instead of being envious of Delilah, *I* should expect more out of life?"

She gave me a little smile. "That's for you to decide, Mallory."

I glanced toward the closed door, then heaved an exasperated sigh. "Maybe you're right. Maybe the judge would've ruled in my favor if I expected more out of life. It sure seems as if people who try to play by the rules don't get anywhere."

"Nice guys finish last," she quipped.

I flashed back to when Josh had expressed a similar sentiment.

"What was that?" she asked.

I blinked. "What was what?"

"Something caused you to react."

"No, it didn't," I protested, then glanced at my watch again. "Do you mind if I call to see what's delaying them?"

"Not at all." She sat back in her chair and wrote in her notebook. Someday I'd like to see what she'd written about me. Poor little messed up Lottery Girl.

I retrieved my phone, then pulled up Gordon's number and connected the call.

He answered on the first ring. "Hi, Buggy. I was just about to call you."

I frowned at the pet name, but brushed it off. "Is something wrong?"

"Is Delilah with you?"

"No, I'm with my therapist… waiting for both of you to join us."

"I can't find your sister."

I squinted. "What do you mean, you can't find her?"

"Her car is here, and her purse, and her clothes, but she's not in the house. It took a while, but I've checked every corner of every room."

"Did you call her phone?"

"It's here, next to her purse." He made an anguished noise. "You don't think she went swimming, do you?"

"Not in this weather, the water temperature is too cold." My mind swirled… a slow drip of panic set up in my stomach. Could she have been high or tipsy and fallen off the dock? Or worse— could she have harmed herself? Her behavior lately had seemed a little manic. I was suddenly overcome with regret for all the cross words we'd exchanged.

"I'm coming home," I said, then strode to the door and left. Imogene's voice floated after me, but I didn't stop to explain.

When I reached my car, I exited the parking garage and raced toward the interstate, glad for the extra horsepower the little sportscar had to offer. Something was wrong, I could feel it. I was ashamed for thinking losing most of the jackpot money was the worst thing that could happen. Losing my sister was the worst thing. And if I was somehow responsible, I'd never forgive myself. The words of the palm-reader came slamming back to me.

You... or someone close to you... is going to die.

I was still a few miles away from the house and breaking all kinds of traffic laws when my phone rang. I didn't recognize the number that flashed up on my dash panel, but under the circumstances, I thought it prudent to answer in case someone was trying to reach me concerning Delilah.

I connected the call with the touch of a button. "Hello?"

"Hello," said a mechanical male voice. "Do not hang up..."

Convinced it was a telemarketing call, I reached for the end button.

"We have your sister."

I froze. *What?*

"Do not go to the police," the voice intoned. "Get five... hundred... thousand... dollars and wait for instructions to deliver the ransom. Repeat—do not go to the police... if you want to see... your sister alive."

DECEMBER

December 1, Tuesday

"YOU DID the right thing by contacting me," Detective Jack Terry said. His face was grim as he stood wide-legged in my kitchen at the lake house. He glanced over notes he'd written about my sister Delilah as I'd dictated the scant details of her disappearance. "I just wish you'd done it yesterday as soon as you received the phone call."

"The kidnapper told her not to," my father ground out.

Gordon had been a mess since the day before when I'd arrived home after getting the call telling me Delilah had been taken and to gather five hundred thousand dollars for a ransom. He was angry I'd called the detective, insisted I was further endangering her life.

I was equally afraid, and a nervous freaking wreck.

Jack Terry's eyes snapped to Gordon. "I was talking to Ms. Green."

Gordon looked defiant, but held his tongue.

"I was too scared," I said. "But it's been twenty-four hours and I haven't heard back from the kidnappers, so... I didn't know what else to do."

"Do you have any idea who could be responsible for this?"

"It must be the guy Delilah's been selling pills for," Gordon said.

"She's a drug dealer?" Jack asked, looking concerned.

"She sells generic Adderall," I supplied. "She said she did it to afford her own prescription. I found a stash of pills in her room."

"Are they still there?"

"No. Last Friday she asked me for money to pay off her dealer—she said she owed him ten grand."

Jack frowned. "Did you give it to her?"

"The banks were closed, but I told her I'd give it to her Monday—yesterday."

He was writing furiously. "Did she tell you her dealer's name?"

"No. Delilah said she dropped off the money and picked up pills at a storage locker in Buckhead."

The detective gestured to my state-of-the-art security system. "The cameras must have captured a picture of whoever took her, or maybe their car?"

"The system wasn't turned on," I murmured. "I must not have reset it when I left."

"I told you that thing was too complicated," Gordon grumbled.

Jack's mouth twitched downward as he glanced around the room, encompassing Delilah's purse and phone on the breakfast bar. "The crime scene has been compromised. Any fingerprints the kidnappers might have left when they took her are probably gone." Then he nodded toward the window where rain slanted against the pane. "Ditto for footprints or tire tracks. Have you gone through her phone?"

"It's password protected... I tried a few combinations, but no luck."

"I'll contact the service provider," Jack said. "But it could take a while to access her phone."

My own phone rang, startling me. I reached for it, but the detective's hand stopped me.

"If it's about your sister, put the call on speaker and keep the caller on the line as long as possible."

But when I glanced at the screen and saw it was sadsack Mallory calling from my bank, I held it up for him to see. "It's my bank. I should answer."

I connected the call and after verifying my identity and account number, was told my cash would be available for pickup at the midtown location tomorrow at noon, with the recommendation that I bring a secure container. When I ended the call, I glanced to the detective. "The cash will be ready tomorrow at noon."

"Ms. Green, we have prop money for situations like this—you don't have to supply actual cash if you don't want to."

Gordon made an exasperated noise. "Are you trying to get Delilah killed?"

"It's standard operating procedure for the GBI," Jack said, removing his own phone from an inside jacket pocket. "I'm calling them now to let them know about the kidnapping."

Gordon straightened. "Absolutely not—no more police."

The big man eyed my father for a few seconds, then swung his gaze back to me. "Ms. Green, could we speak in private?"

My father's face reddened, but I lowered my chin. "Right this way." I led him into the cavernous dining room and closed the French doors behind us. My hands were shaking. I hadn't eaten or slept since the phone call. It all felt so surreal.

Like the whole of my life since I'd won fifty-two million dollars in a lottery jackpot at the end of July.

When I turned, Detective Terry seemed to be weighing his words.

"Ms. Green, do you trust your father?"

My mouth opened. "You don't think *he* had something to do with this?"

"You came to me because you had a stalker, who turned out to be your long-lost father. How much do you really know about him?"

I swallowed. "I know he... just got out of prison."

The detective's eyes bounced wide. "Seriously?"

"For tax evasion," I added. "Besides, he'd never endanger Delilah."

He pulled his hand across his mouth. "You win the lottery, then a sister you didn't know you had shows up, then your long-lost father. Could they be in on this together?"

I opened my mouth to deny it, but couldn't. Last week more of my lottery money had been sloughed off from a lawsuit filed by former coworkers. I'd made the comment to Delilah that worst-case scenario, I'd have a few hundred thousand left... and now I was being shaken down for that amount.

"Has your father been acting strangely?"

My thoughts went back to Gordon's recent fixation on the security system—had he disarmed it purposely? Had he and Delilah cooked up this plot to con me out of what was left of my money? The idea left me feeling completely empty. Only a few days ago we'd been sharing a happy Thanksgiving feast and drinking hot chocolate around the firepit. Had I been so desperate for a family that I'd underestimated their capacity for deceit?

At my waist, my phone rang again, slicing through my dark thoughts. When I saw Ryan's name on the screen I relaxed only a fraction—I didn't need the distraction. "It's my boyfriend calling."

"Answer if you need to."

I hesitated. "I probably should only because he's called three times. Otherwise he might drive up here."

"Does he know your sister?"

I nodded, but didn't add that Ryan didn't trust Delilah.

"Answer," the detective urged. "Maybe he's heard something."

I connected the call. "Hi... Ryan."

"Mallory," Ryan's voice sounded strained. "I've been worried. You missed your appointment with Anna and you and I were supposed to have lunch today."

I winced. "Sorry... I forgot. I'm swamped right now... dealing with other... paperwork."

"Okay, we can reschedule," he said easily. "Anything I can help you with?"

"No," I said, more forcefully than I'd planned. "But thanks. I'll call you later." I disconnected the call, hoping Ryan would understand that I hadn't wanted to get him involved in this predicament. "He doesn't know anything," I said to the detective.

"Does your sister have a boyfriend?"

Josh's face rose in my mind. "Not really... there's one guy."

"Could he be involved?"

I scoffed. "Absolutely not. Josh English is the most trustworthy, decent, sweet, handsome guy you'd ever want to meet."

Jack squinted. "Handsome?"

I balked—where had that come from? "I meant 'honest'— he's the most trustworthy, decent, *honest* guy you'd ever want to meet."

One side of Jack's mouth lifted. "Don't forget 'sweet.'"

I smirked. "Plus Josh is a doctor, so he doesn't need to kidnap anyone for cash."

"Ah. Still, maybe he's heard from her?"

That was a thought. I pulled his number up on my phone and connected the call. Thinking he might be with a physical therapy patient, I expected to get his voice mail; instead, he answered.

"Hi, Mallory. This is a surprise."

His voice felt like a warm, comforting blanket. "Um, hi. I'm sorry to bother you at work, but I was wondering if you've talked to Delilah lately."

"Hm... not since early Saturday morning."

So she'd spent the night at his place Friday after getting off work at the bar. Josh insisted she'd been surfing on his couch occasionally, but I suspected he was trying to be discreet.

He gave a little laugh. "Is Delilah missing?"

I swallowed hard. "Missing? No, Delilah's not *missing...*" My gaze bounced to the detective. "She just didn't come home last night."

"I wouldn't worry about her," Josh said. "She's probably with the guy who keeps calling her."

I squinted. "What guy?"

"I don't know his name, but she made the comment that if you knew how deep she was with him, you'd be angry."

When the implication of his words sank in, my breath caught in my chest—surely Delilah wasn't referring to... *Ryan?*

In a flash, disparate memories flooded back to me. Ryan had presumably run a background check on Delilah and told me she was legit... and after I'd told him I was thinking of asking her to take a DNA test, he'd allegedly run a more "extensive" background check and told me a DNA test wasn't necessary. And then there were the barbed exchanges and heated discussions between the two of them—I'd assumed Ryan was distrustful of Delilah for my sake... but was he instead in cahoots with her from the beginning?

Was Delilah even my sister, or had Ryan found her to play a part?

Even as my mind protested his involvement, something he'd once said rose in my mind. *Con artists have a knack for making people believe they're earnest and trustworthy.*

Was it possible that he, Gordon, and Delilah were all in this together in an attempt to get the last of my money?

"Mallory," Josh said, cutting into my thoughts. "Are you there?"

I blinked to clear my head. "I'm here."

"If I hear from Delilah, I'll tell her to call you."

"Thanks, Josh. Bye." I disconnected the call, then slowly lifted my gaze to Jack Terry.

He looked concerned. "What?"

"I don't know who to trust anymore."

His jaw hardened. "You can trust me, Ms. Green. What are you thinking?"

With broken words, I explained some of the troubling connections I'd made. The detective wrote down Ryan's name. Then he sighed. "There are no shortages of suspects—her drug dealer, your ex-con father, and your financial guru boyfriend. Is there anyone else who's shown more than a passing interest in your winnings, anyone who unnerved you?

I started to shake my head, then another person came to mind. "There was a guy I worked with at a convenience store—Link. He was fixated on my money, asked a lot of questions that made me uncomfortable."

"Did he know your sister?"

I nodded. "They met once that I know of... and I know he bought some uppers from her."

Jack scowled as he made more notes. "And the list keeps growing. Anyone else?"

I searched my mind again. "A woman stole six thousand dollars from my account." I pulled up her photo on my phone. "I don't know who she is, but I saw her one night at the bar where Delilah works, so I assumed Delilah put her up to it."

"You didn't ask your sister about the woman?"

"I... hadn't gotten around to it."

He studied me for a few seconds, then nodded. "Okay. Anything else?"

"Not that I can think of."

He turned and gestured to the piles of letters on the long dining room table. "What's all this?"

"People who've written asking for help."

His dark eyebrows climbed high. "Asking for money?"

I nodded.

He whistled low. "With you being such a public figure, I need to let the GBI know what's going on."

"Won't that only complicate things further?"

"I'll retain lead on the case—this is just in case we need their resources."

I noticed the way his face tightened. "In case things go sideways, you mean?"

He pressed his lips together. "Even if your sister is in on this, she could still get hurt."

From the way my heart pinched, I realized my sister's wellness meant more to me than anything else. While the detective made the requisite phone call, I stood churning over the turn of events.

Back when I was working three minimum wage jobs and wishing my life was more exciting, I should've been more specific.

When Jack Terry and I emerged from the dining room, my father was agitated and pacing the kitchen floor. Nessie had found a corner and was observing us through her paws, picking up on the anxious vibe in the room.

"Any news?" my father asked.

I shook my head and studied him warily. If Gordon was in on the kidnapping, he was a good actor because he seemed genuinely concerned... although he could be genuinely concerned that the APD and the GBI were involved.

My phone rang again and everyone froze. When I glanced at the screen, the word 'Unknown' was displayed. When Jack saw the message, he said, "Remember, keep the caller on the line as long as possible, ask to speak to Delilah."

With heart pounding, I put the phone on speaker and connected the call. "Hello?"

After a pause, the mechanical voice sounded. "Do you have the money?"

I gripped the phone harder. "Not yet."

"Do you want to see your sister again?"

The elevated electronic monotone sounded more sinister than a human voice. "Yes! The bank needed time... I'll have the money tomorrow at noon."

"All of it?"

"Yes—five hundred thousand, like you said."

"Cash—no monopoly money. You won't get your sister until we count every dollar."

I glanced at Detective Terry. "Okay. Let me speak to my sister."

"No. Wait for another call tomorrow. And if you're working with the police, you're going to be sorry."

I gave Jack a panicked look. He rolled his hand to remind me to keep talking.

"Please… let me talk to Delilah."

The call disconnected with a loud click, then silence filled the room.

December 2, Wednesday

WHEN I walked out of the bank branch pulling a black rolling suitcase, my blouse was stuck to my back from the sheen of sweat encasing my body. Gordon had ridden with me, with Detective Terry and two other police officers following at some distance, although I hadn't seen them. A trace had been placed on my phone so if and when the kidnappers called, the police could track it if I kept the caller on the line long enough. So far, though, the only person who'd called was Ryan—twice. And twice I'd let it roll to voicemail. I was numb from worrying if he or Gordon or even Delilah herself were involved.

My suspicions vacillated from guilty to not guilty and back again. At times I found myself hoping they *were* in on it—at least Delilah would be okay. The same might not be true if her drug dealer—or a complete stranger—was behind the crime.

The detective had been able to eliminate Link after an interview—I just hoped the man wasn't blabbing to every customer at the GiddyUp GoMart that Lottery Girl's sister had been kidnapped. Jack had decided not to question Ryan, but he'd put him under surveillance. The detective himself had spent the night at my house with the excuse of being nearby in case the kidnappers called again. But I sensed he thought Gordon had something to do with the kidnapping and was worried about leaving me alone with him.

I, too, was leaning toward Gordon's involvement because my father appeared to be falling apart at the seams. He hadn't slept or eaten, and I'd smelled alcohol on his breath more than once. He'd hotly denied kidnapping his own daughter for the sake of a ransom. But the more he protested, the more I wondered.

My head was on a pivot until I reached my car. Gordon jumped out to help me put the heavy bag into the trunk. There were a few seconds when both our hands were on it and I thought how easy it would be for him to simply take the money and run. The funny thing is, I think he was thinking the same thing. After a brief stare-down, I released the suitcase... and waited.

One Mississippi... two Mississippi... three Mississippi...

He lifted the bag into the trunk and closed it, then locked gazes with me again. "Now what?"

"Now we go back to the house and wait for the phone call."

I walked to the driver's side door and watched my father. He was pale and drawn, and he kept pulling his hand across his mouth, as if he wanted to say something... or do something. When he climbed into the car, he moved unsteadily. He could be worried sick about Delilah... or worried sick about going back to prison if he'd done something to violate parole.

Or both?

Before I could open my door, my phone rang. My pulse spiked until I saw Detective Terry's name on the screen. I connected the call.

"Hello, Detective."

"Is the money secure?"

"It's in the trunk, yes."

"How are you doing, Ms. Green?"

I wanted to laugh, but the sound came out sounding strangled. "I want this to be over."

"So do I. We just got the court order to unlock your sister's phone so soon we'll be able to see her calls and if she used her GPS to drive to her dealer's drop-off location in Buckhead."

"How soon?"

"Hopefully within a couple of hours."

"What if the kidnappers call before then?"

"We'll keep working both angles," he promised. "Has anyone else reached out to you?"

"Ryan called twice. Both times he left messages to call him back... and he doesn't sound like himself."

"Call him back. See if he reveals something to you. Don't forget to use the app on your phone to record the call. An officer has been tailing him all morning, but he went straight from his condo to his office."

"Okay," I murmured, feeling sick.

"I'll meet you back at your house," Jack said.

I disconnected the call, then activated the app and phoned Ryan. It was cold standing outside the car, but I didn't want to talk in front of Gordon.

Ryan answered on the first ring. "Mallory?"

"Hi," I said, trying to sound normal. "I'm returning your calls. What's up?"

"I need to talk to you. Can you meet me for lunch?"

"Sorry, no, I can't. I'm... committed to... something else."

He made a frustrated noise. "I really need to talk to you, Mallory. I... have something to tell you—something I'm not proud of—and I'd rather it be in person."

Hairs stood up on the back of my neck. "Does this have anything to do with Delilah?"

"Indirectly, yes."

I gripped the phone harder. "Do you know where she is?"

"No... should I?"

I closed my eyes briefly. "Ryan, if you had something to do with her kidnapping, you need to tell me now."

Silence vibrated over the line, then, "*Kidnapping?* Delilah's been kidnapped?" His voice escalated to a screech. "And you think *I* had something to do with it? That's insane!"

He sounded completely dumbfounded. If he was involved, he was a good actor. My phone beeped with another call coming in— from an unknown number.

"Ryan, I have to go. I'll call you later." I connected the new call. "Hello?"

The line buzzed with the sound of the mechanical voice. "Did you get the money?"

"Y-Yes," I said. My teeth were chattering.

"Listen carefully. Drive to the Doraville Marta station to catch the 1:00 p.m. southbound train. Ride to the Little Five Points station. Take the escalator to the top level. Find the vending machines. Leave the money there."

"I want to talk to my sister."

"After we get the money, you get your sister." The call ended with a beep.

Shivering, I opened the door and swung into the driver's seat. "They called again."

Gordon's face flushed cherry red. "What did they say?"

"I have to call Detective Terry."

He grabbed my hand to stop me. "Mallory—what did the caller say?"

His movement hitched up his sweater to reveal a gun stuck down in his belt.

My gun.

My heart jumped to my throat. "D-Dad," I said carefully. "You know more than you're letting on. It's time to come clean before someone gets hurt."

His jaw hardened, then a sob escaped him. "I think it's a guy I knew in prison called Snooze. I owed him for protecting me, and couldn't pay up. When he found out my daughter won the lottery, he said he was going to get what was coming to him, one way or another. I've been worried sick he'd come to the house to rob you... but I didn't know he was capable of this."

I swallowed hard—an ex-con had Delilah? The palm-reader's prediction came back to me. *You, or someone close to you, is going to die.* "Dad, you have to tell Detective Terry."

He was shaking his head. "If the police are involved, Snooze might hurt Delilah." Gordon patted the gun. "I'm the father, I should take care of this."

"No," I said through gritted teeth. "You're carrying a concealed weapon without a permit. That alone is enough to send you back to prison."

His eyes teared up. "What do you care?"

I searched his face—the face of a man who'd made many mistakes. But he was the only dad I had. "I care," I said softly. "Now... put the gun in the glove compartment. Then I'm going to call Detective Terry, and you're going to tell him everything while I drive to the Marta station."

Gordon looked distraught.

"Dad," I said, more firmly, "it's the best chance we have to get Delilah back safely."

After a few seconds, his head dropped, then he nodded. "You're right." He pulled the revolver out of his waist, then placed it inside the glove compartment. I exhaled, then phoned Detective Terry and played the kidnapper's recorded message for him. He told me to follow the instructions, the police would go to the Little Five Points station and set up surveillance.

"My father has something to tell you," I said, then handed the phone to Gordon. He haltingly told his story while I sped toward the Doraville Marta station. Thanks to my stint without a car, I was familiar with the train schedules and most stations on the north and south lines.

When I reached the Doraville parking lot, Gordon was just ending his call. He looked relieved, if beleaguered. "I'm riding with you," he announced. "No way should you be on the train with a suitcase full of money."

I conceded—the plan was for us to be back on the train and long gone before the kidnappers showed up. As instructed, we caught the 1:00 p.m. southbound line. When we boarded the train, I looked all around, wondering if we were being watched, but I didn't see anyone suspicious. The ride to Little Five Points would take us about thirty minutes. I was tense, especially now that I knew Delilah was in real danger. A few minutes into the ride, Gordon reached over to clasp my hand and give me a reassuring smile.

"We'll get through this," he said.

I nodded, wanting desperately to believe him.

Little Five Points was the intersection of the north, south, east, and west train lines, and the largest station in the system. It was no accident the kidnappers had chosen it as the drop point, I realized, because the station was always crowded with bodies hurrying to catch trains. No one would notice someone leaving a suitcase, or someone collecting one. Plus there were numerous trains and exits for a getaway.

With Gordon flanking me, I rolled the suitcase to the up escalator to climb to the second level. My heart was pounding in my chest—I was hoping to see Delilah waiting for us. But when we located the vending machines, the only people standing still were a couple of kids trying to get a soda from one of the machines. Glancing all around, I rolled the suitcase to a corner next to the last machine, then parked it.

"Let's go," I said to Gordon, who was still standing, still looking around.

"I want to see if Snooze has the balls to show up."

"Let the police handle it." I tugged on his arm. "Let's go."

We had made it back to the down escalator when Gordon's eyes went wide. "There he is!"

Before I could stop him, Gordon was barreling back to where we'd left the suitcase. A stocky guy wearing all black was casually walking away with it. When he saw Gordon running toward him, he took off running, too.

"Freeze, Atlanta PD!" Jack Terry shouted, joining the chase. The stocky guy picked up the suitcase and ran with one arm in front of him, plowing through pedestrians, heading for a tall set of stairs going down. Screams sounded and people jumped out of the way. Gordon fell behind, but Jack Terry kept pace and overtook Snooze with a tackle. The man went down hard. The suitcase bounced on the floor, then over a half wall.

I watched, mesmerized, as it fell, tumbling in mid-air, headed for the tracks below. Then a horn blared and a train T-boned the suitcase with a loud report. The piece of luggage blew apart, sending bills mushrooming into the sky, then raining back down over the train, the tracks, and the thousands of pedestrians who abandoned running for their trains in favor of running for hundred dollar bills.

December 3, Thursday

"BUGGY, YOU need to get some sleep," Gordon said.

It was true. I was a shaky, strung-out mess. The ex-con Snooze had been arrested, but had yet to give up any accomplices or the whereabouts of Delilah. I'd tried to lie down and rest, but nothing felt right except pacing and working off the energy my body kept generating. In solidarity, Nessie was trotting along with me, "heeling" without being prompted.

"I'll sleep when Delilah is home," I said.

He slumped in his chair. "I'm sorry... for all of this."

"I know, Dad... you don't have to keep apologizing."

He jammed his fingers through his hair. "But it's true. This is all my fault."

It was some of his fault, but I was too tired to keep forgiving him. "Why don't *you* go get some sleep?" He hesitated, but his eyelids were sagging. On top of everything else, I suspected he was alternately drinking again, and going through withdrawal. "Seriously," I added in a gentle tone. "One of us needs to be thinking straight."

Gordon dipped his chin, then pushed to his feet. "Wake me if you hear... anything."

"I will."

He headed down the hallway toward his bedroom, his shoulders bent, his feet dragging. I could only imagine how he must be feeling... because I was feeling the same—that it was my fault Delilah had been snatched. If I hadn't won the money in the first place, she wouldn't have been a target.

Then again, if I hadn't won the money, Delilah wouldn't have found me.

I massaged my temples—my mind was doing nonsensical figure eights.

My phone rang, sending adrenaline spiking through my veins. When I saw Josh's name on the screen, my stomach did a funny little flip. I'd asked Ryan not to call in order to keep my phone free, but Josh... he didn't even know Delilah was missing.

I connected the call. "Hi, Josh."

"Hi, Mallory. Are you okay?"

"I'm fine," I said, forcing cheer into my voice.

"You and Nessie missed today's pet therapy session."

I winced—I'd forgotten all about meeting with one of Josh's patients. "I'm so sorry, Josh... something came up. I should've called."

"It's okay, we can do it another time. But this isn't like you— are you sure everything is okay?"

At his caring tone, tears filled my eyes. I bit down on my tongue to control my reaction. Emotion clogged the back of my aching throat. He deserved to know Delilah was missing... and might not come home.

"I need to tell you—" I broke off on a sob.

"What?" he said, his voice anxious. "You're scaring me."

The security system beeped. I looked at the monitor. *Car arriving.*

At the sight of the big black SUV I knew belonged to Detective Terry, my knees buckled.

"Mallory?" Josh's voice came to me, distantly.

The SUV came to a stop and the detective stepped out, looking weary. My breath stalled in my lungs.

Then the passenger side door opened, and out climbed Delilah, looking tired, but healthy and unharmed. My heart soared.

"Mallory?" Josh's voice sounded. "Are you there?"

"I'm here," I said in a rush of abject relief. "Everything is fine now. I'll call you. I mean... Delilah will call you." I disconnected the call, then set down my phone.

"Dad!" I yelled. Then I ran outside to greet my sister.

When she saw me, she gave me a tremulous smile, then held out her arms. We embraced, crying.

"I'm okay," she said. "I'm okay, Sis... I'm okay."

December 4, Friday

"ARE YOU sure you should do this?" I asked.

Delilah nodded, then slung her purse to her shoulder. "Mallory, I'm fine. I can't just hide out here, reliving the past few days in that hotel room. I need to work... and make some money."

"You don't have to worry about that right now," I soothed. "I told you I'd give you the money to pay off your dealer."

She nodded. "I know... and I appreciate it. But you spent half a million dollars to get me back. I'm not going to let you pay off my dealer." She lifted her chin. "The least I can do is earn the money myself."

I leaned on the kitchen counter and crossed my arms, surveying her spectacular outfit—a blue halter dress from my closet that I'd never worn... but it would never look that good on me. "Since the news is buzzing about the kidnapping, you're a bit of a local celebrity."

A small smile played on her mouth. "Which is why I need to make the most of it. I'll probably rake in the tips tonight." She came over and squeezed my hand. "Something good has to come from this."

I conceded with a nod that if she wasn't going to dwell on her time in captivity, the rest of us shouldn't either. "Okay... have fun."

She left with a twist. When the door closed behind her, I thought about what she'd said, then acknowledged that something good had come from all of this.

We were starting to feel like a family.

December 5, Saturday

"IT'S A little cold for fishing, isn't it?"

From the end of the dock, Gordon turned his head. "The fish have gone deeper and don't move as much. You have to use a longer line and flashy bait." He gestured to another rod and reel lying on the dock. "Want to try?"

"Sure." I raised the collar on my jacket against the nip in the air and observed while he adjusted the weight and the bobber. But he didn't make eye contact. I could tell he was still in a bad way, churning over the kidnapping incident. His hands shook. He was drying out, and suffering for it.

"Have you always enjoyed fishing?" I asked.

He nodded. "Too bad I can't make a living at it. But I did get a job at the marina."

"You did?"

"Yeah... not very impressive, I know, but they were willing to take a chance on an ex-con."

I was pleased—if he was going to stay sober, he needed to stay busy. "That's great, Dad."

"There you go," he said, handing me the fishing pole.

I cast the line and he grunted. "Not bad. Who taught you how to do that?"

"Danica Tumi. She took us kids camping a few times."

His expression went stony, then sad. "She's sounds like a good lady."

"Yes... I was lucky to wind up in her care."

After a few minutes of silence, he said, "I only talked to her a few times, but she seemed really nice. The way she spoke, she reminded me a little of your mother."

I seized the opening with a vengeance. "Tell me about her. I don't remember much."

He reeled in his line slowly, then recast. "Alice was wonderful," he said, his voice breaking. "She adored you, for sure. But it wasn't long after you were born that she started feeling sick. I tried to get her to go to the doctor, but she insisted she was just worn down." He sighed. "By the time I talked her into it, the cancer had spread. The doctors did everything they could, but it was awful—in and out of the hospital, rounds of chemo and radiation." He wet his lips. "It took its toll... on both of us."

At the emotion in his voice, my eyes watered.

"When she passed away, I was a mess, physically, mentally... and financially. The medical bills bankrupted us... I couldn't even afford to buy her a headstone." He cleared his throat. "I couldn't take care of you, and convinced myself you'd be better off in foster care. But the guilt ate at me. Your mother wouldn't have wanted that. I was... a coward."

I swallowed a throatful of tears. I was torn between relishing his torment and wanting to forgive him. I couldn't do either at the moment.

"I'm so sorry, Buggy. I will try to make it up to you, I promise."

"Where is she buried?"

"In Decatur, in her family plot. I'll take you there sometime."

My heart stuttered. I'd lived in Atlanta for years, and all this time my mother had been buried less than twenty miles away. "How about now?"

He stopped, then nodded. "That's a good idea."

We stowed the fishing gear, and I let Gordon drive my car. On the way, we stopped to buy a bouquet of flowers. Decatur was a picturesque older city outside of Atlanta with its own downtown area and historic buildings. After a few wrong turns, Gordon found the cemetery, a sprawling piece of grassy land dotted with a handful of trees and countless white and gray headstones. Once inside the gate, he stopped to get his bearings, then pointed. "I believe the plot is in that corner, near that big cedar tree."

"Is there a family headstone we can look for?" I asked.

"Yes… look for Mallory."

My head came around. "Mallory is Mom's maiden name?"

"You didn't know?"

I shook my head. "The records were piecemeal. Someone told me that Mallory means bad luck… I thought…"

"That we'd saddled you with a bad-luck name?" He gave a little laugh. "No… since her parents were gone, your mother wanted you to have her family name."

My chest felt warm with pride.

He pointed. "There it is."

A tall, simple gray granite headstone read "Mallory." Around it were a handful of graves and smaller headstones—my grandparents, and from the dates, what appeared to be aunts and uncles.

"Here it is," Gordon said, pointing to grave with a small footstone with the initials "A.M.M." "Here's where I buried Alice."

"Alice Mallory Miracle," I murmured, then lay the bouquet of flowers over the fading grass.

"Alice," Gordon murmured, "it's me and Buggy—you'd be so proud of how she turned out."

I blinked back tears. "Where did Buggy come from?"

"She started calling you that as soon as we brought you home from the hospital—she said you were as cute as a bug, and it just stuck. The two of you were inseparable."

I soaked in his words, trying to recall being hugged, being toted around, being doted on.

"Do you remember her at all?" he asked.

"I have a memory of being in a laundromat," I offered. "The scents and the warmth—the noise. I've always found it comforting. Did she take me there?"

His eyes filled. "No… that was me. When your mother was too sick to leave the house, I did all the laundry, and I always took you with me."

My heart softened toward him. "That was you?"

He smiled. "That was me."

We stayed a few minutes longer, clearing leaves from her grave. When we left to walk back to the cemetery entrance, I tucked my hand under his arm and absorbed his warmth.

December 6, Sunday

"I CAN'T imagine what you've been through," Ryan said.

He and I were sitting around the firepit on the rooftop deck, watching the sun set. My cheeks were cold, but we were warm under a soft blanket, holding mugs of coffee laced with bourbon.

"Delilah more so than me," I said.

"She seemed fine at dinner."

"She's resilient," I agreed. "And she's found a way to put a positive spin on things—you can't believe the amount of tips she brought home the past couple of nights." I gave a little laugh. "I wouldn't be surprised if she winds up selling the movie rights to her story."

"You have to admit it's pretty unbelievable."

I lifted my mug for a sip. "Ryan, I'm sorry I suspected you were involved. My head was spinning, I didn't know who to trust."

"No, it's fine." He leaned forward to set down his mug, then took mine and did the same. "You were right to be suspicious."

My heart pounded. "The other day on the phone, you said you had something to tell me, something you weren't proud of."

He nodded, his face creased with anguish. "I've been untruthful about something, and I need to get it off my chest."

He didn't care about me... he'd only been interested in my money... "What?"

"The woman in the photograph at the ATM... it's Maria, my ex-girlfriend."

I pulled back. "You and your ex stole from me?"

"No," he said, raising his hands. "I knew she was a little obsessed with you, but I didn't realize what she'd done until you showed me the picture. I was so shaken, I couldn't tell you the truth. I wanted to learn the extent of what she'd done."

"She followed me to Plaid," I said. "I saw her there and when she realized I noticed her, she ran. I thought she was a friend of my sister's, that Delilah had put her up to stealing the money."

He closed his eyes briefly. "I'm so sorry. I already put the money back into your account. I'll make sure she never bothers you again."

"It was her who called the night I was at your place? When you had to leave so suddenly?"

He nodded. "She's not well, was threatening to hurt herself. It's one reason our relationship ended—I care for her, but I couldn't take the stress anymore." He smiled. "And then I met you, and you were such a breath of fresh air."

I averted my gaze. "I thought now that my money is mostly gone, you'd change your mind about that."

He reached up to cup my chin. "You were wrong. I don't need your money, Mallory. I need your goodness."

Ryan leaned forward to kiss me—a slow, thorough, convincing kiss that put my head and body on tilt. This beautiful, successful, sensual man had feelings for me, mutually exclusive of my bank account.

It was exactly what I wanted… wasn't it?

December 7, Monday

"I DON'T know where to start," my therapist said with a laugh. Imogene Ramplett had sat with rounded eyes while I retold the events that had transpired since I'd abruptly left her office the week before.

"I saw the news story about the money floating through the air at the Marta station and people going crazy. That was you?"

"Well, that was my situation."

"And how have things changed between you and your father and your sister?"

"For the better, I think. Gordon has opened up a little, we're talking about my mother and his guilt for putting me in foster care."

"And have you told him how you felt about being abandoned?"

"Some… I'm not sure even I realize how much it's affected my life, who I trust and who I don't, the men I've chosen to attach myself to."

"That sounds like progress," she agreed. "And you and your sister?"

I shifted in my chair. "That relationship is harder to pin down. Delilah seems more aloof than before."

"More independent?"

I shrugged. "Maybe." Or maybe she was afraid of the DNA test results I would receive soon.

"Would it bother you if she didn't need you anymore? That she might not need your money?"

I hesitated. "No."

"You hesitated."

I shifted again.

"Mallory, it's okay to acknowledge the feeling of empowerment that having money gives you, and to admit you like it."

"*Liked* it," I murmured. "Past tense. My money is disappearing, it seems."

"The ransom money—did you get it back?"

I shook my head. "The police managed to recover a few thousand and they offered to appeal to people to turn in the money they found… but I decided it wasn't worth it. When I saw my money exploding and floating down into the hands of people who probably needed it more than I do, it felt right. After the past few months, I'm starting to realize the less money I have, the fewer worries I have."

She angled her head. "And how much money *do* you have left?"

It occurred to me the woman was probably wondering if her weekly invoices would be paid. "I'll find out later this week."

"Ah." She reached for her calendar. "So shall we make another appointment?"

I nodded. At least I hoped I was good for another week.

December 8, Tuesday

"IT'S UNBELIEVABLE," Josh said, his face animated. "Delilah told me everything—she's amazing."

I was holding Nessie, walking with Josh for a pet therapy session with one of his patients at the Shepherd Center. Not to diminish what she'd gone through, but I imagined Delilah had embellished her story of captivity a tad, had made being held in a hotel room sound slightly more harrowing that it had been. But she deserved the attention... and the admiration, I conceded.

"Yes, she's amazing."

"You must've been going out of your mind, Mallory."

"It was three days I'd rather not relive," I admitted. "It could've ended badly in so many ways."

"I'm just so relieved she's okay," Josh said, opening the door for the spine rehabilitation area.

Delilah hadn't come Friday night, had texted me she was spending the night "with a friend." I'd assumed she was with Josh, and it was obvious they were so much more than friends.

I gave him a big smile. "That makes two of us."

December 9, Wednesday

I WAS having lunch in the kitchen with Gordon when the security system beeped.

Car arriving.

I watched the monitor to see the United State postal truck making its way up the driveway.

"Here comes another batch of letters begging for money," Gordon said.

The truck lurched to a halt and when the postal carrier emerged, sure enough, she was carrying a bin that appeared to be overflowing.

"But," he added, pushing to his feet, "when people see a half million dollars scattered all over a train station for the taking, they probably figure you have lots to spare."

So true, I admitted, following him to the door. He took the bin of mail from the carrier and passed me. I stood on the stoop and thanked the woman for her trouble.

"Here's the rest of your mail," she said, handing me a small bundle.

I took the handful of envelopes, mostly junk mail and holiday flyers. But when I saw the return address on one envelope in particular, I froze.

The DNA results from the tests Delilah and I had taken to find out if we were truly sisters.

I walked into the house and carried the envelope to my bedroom, then closed the door. I put my thumb under the flap of the envelope and began to tear it open. Then I stopped.

I wasn't prepared to learn the truth... not yet.

I walked to a bureau, opened a drawer, and slipped the envelope under the clothes inside.

When I was ready, the results would be sitting there, waiting.

December 10, Thursday

I WAS sitting in a glass-walled conference room at Livingston Wealth Management waiting to find out if I had any wealth left to manage. Ryan had been scrupulously optimistic in our conversations, but I had a feeling the news wouldn't be rosy. The door opened and Anna, the associate Ryan had passed my account to, entered the room carrying a single legal-size folder, and wearing a tight expression.

"Hello, Ms. Green."

"Please, call me Mallory."

"Right... Mallory." She took a seat opposite mine. "Can I get you something to drink?"

I got the sense that she wanted one herself, something stronger than the bottle of mineral water in front of me. "I'm good, thank you. You can cut to the chase, Anna. How much of my lottery winnings do I have left?"

She gave a curt nod, then opened the folder and slid two documents across the table. "This is a line-item list of all the existing and anticipated payables on your accounts—the income taxes, property taxes, legal fees, fees to the publicist, your therapist, the cars and other assets you purchased for yourself and for others, the mortgage for Ms. Tumi, the medical bills for Mrs. Asfour and Mrs. Dell, the loan to your former boss at The Community Café, a headstone for your mother's grave, living expenses, as well as the cash loss in the recent, um, kidnapping."

I skimmed the enormous sums and swallowed hard. "What's the total damage?"

She pointed to a figure on the second document. "This is the amount you had after the two lawsuits."

I glanced at the figure—a fraction of the original fifty-two million printed on the over-sized cardboard check the lottery had awarded to me during the press conference back in August.

"And this," she continued, "is the total amount of outlay, to date."

I stared at the "outlay" number, which was larger than the amount above it. My mouth opened in stupefaction. "But… that means…"

She pointed to a third number, this one in red, with a negative sign next to it. "You're in a deficit."

Translation: I was broke, and in debt.

Again.

December 11, Friday

"I THOUGHT you might want to know," Delilah said casually, "that I paid off my dealer."

I looked up from my phone. "That's fantastic. And the Adderall?"

"I cut my use in half… and I made an appointment to get a prescription."

"That's such good news. You must be pulling down huge tips at the bar."

She nodded, then took a bite of French toast. Her tastes had morphed from the donut-eating, soda-swizzling young woman who'd first arrived. "But I'm looking for another job."

"You don't like working there?"

She shrugged. "It's okay... but I need to start thinking about the future. I mean, you probably don't want me to live here... forever."

She wasn't making eye contact. Was she fishing? Was she worried what I'd find if I opened the DNA test results hidden in my bedroom?

"It's good to think about your future," I agreed lightly. "The house is paid for, but I don't know if I can afford to maintain it."

She chewed slowly. "You probably wish you hadn't paid the ransom."

I frowned. "Of course not. I wasn't going to take any chances that you'd be hurt, Delilah."

She swallowed, then bit into her lip. "That means a lot to me."

I smiled. "Sisters look out for each other... right?"

But something had caught her attention on the TV. "Oh, my God—you're on the news."

I turned my head while she scrambled for the remote control. The picture on the screen was of me at the lottery press conference, looking like a deer in headlights in my gunnysack dress and flattened hair.

I looked even worse in high-definition.

An attractive news reporter was speaking to the camera. "You might remember the video that went viral earlier this year when Mallory Green won the Mega Dollars Lotto jackpot of fifty-two million dollars."

The video of me vomiting had been tastefully edited for family-time viewing.

"It makes you wonder if Green's reaction was because she'd heard stories of other lotto winners whose lives didn't turn out happily ever after. Since accepting her big check, Green has been sued three times—first by a customer where she worked as a cashier who claimed Green stole the winning ticket, then by her estranged husband who successfully claimed half her jackpot winnings as community property, then by a group of former coworkers with whom she participated in a lottery pool." A picture of The Community Café came on the screen.

"That's where you waitressed?" Delilah asked.

"Uh-huh."

"Cute place. Maybe I'll apply for a job there."

Doug would probably hire her since he'd lost his entire staff—now that they were all independently wealthy. I suspected he was going to default on the loan I'd given him.

Heck, I might apply there myself.

The reporter's eyes glittered. "And Atlanta residents will remember this astonishing video of money flying through the air at a Marta rail station after a recent foiled kidnapping plot of Green's sister."

"It has almost a million views on social media," Delilah supplied.

I distantly wondered if I could earn ad dollars on those views.

"Now comes word," the reporter continued, "that less than six months after winning big, the woman known as Lottery Girl is bankrupt, which has to be some sort of record for lotto winners going bust. But don't feel too sorry for the Atlanta woman—records show she still owns a mansion on Lake Lanier, and has been seen around town driving a pricey red convertible." The anchor angled her camera-pretty head. "For now anyway."

"What a witch." Delilah used the remote to turn off the device.

I sat stock still, raw with mortification. Now everyone knew I was broke.

But as the humiliation seeped in, miraculously, it began to fade. Now maybe my life would return to normal.

I turned back to my phone where I'd been perusing online help-wanted ads. As the reporter had implied, Lottery Girl needed a job.

December 12, Saturday

I WAS working on my resume, lamenting its lameness—an unfinished physical therapy degree, a string of unimpressive jobs, a questionable credit history, a failed marriage, a lost fortune—when my phone rang.

The name of Trent's friend Dale, who had helped him move furniture from our apartment, flashed on the screen. I'd once called Dale in a desperate attempt to touch base with Trent, only to find out my husband wasn't staying with him, but had instead moved in with his gorgeous girlfriend. My stomach clenched at the memory, and I was tempted to decline the call—both of Trent's closest friends had hit on me in the past.

But since I was in the market for a job, I decided I couldn't be too picky where my network was concerned. Dale had connections.

I swiped to accept the call. "Hello?"

"Mallory? It's Dale Hartwick."

"Hi, Dale." I forced civility into my voice—after all, Dale had been on Trent's big-ass boat when he'd driven a dangerous victory lap around my home on the lake, toppling me on a paddleboard. "Long time, no see. What's new with you?"

"I'm calling about Trent."

I rolled my eyes—Trent must've gotten his court settlement from the escrow account and was on a shopping bender. "If you're calling to rub it in—"

"He's gone, Mallory."

So Trent was traveling with my money. "Gone where? Australia? Hong Kong?"

"He's... dead."

I blinked... and blinked... and blinked.... *"What?"*

"This morning," Dale said, his voice breaking. "He took the boat out by himself. He must've slipped and fallen in. He drowned."

Shock and dismay washed over me. My mind spun, I couldn't think of the right words to say. "How... horrible..."

"We're all devastated," Dale said, sniffling. "Mal, I know the two of you ended on a bad note, but if it's any consolation, I think he still cared about you."

I closed my eyes. I was pretty sure that wasn't true, but I appreciated his attempt to soften the blow. "Thanks, Dale... for letting me know. I'll reach out to his parents." I ended the call and sat unmoving for a long while.

Six months ago my entire life had been wrapped up in Trent. Then he'd broken my heart and my trust. When I'd been in the depths of his rejection, secretly I'd hoped someday he'd get his comeuppance, but I didn't want... I never thought...

Then the palm-reader's warning came back to me.

You, or someone close to you, will die.
Her dire prediction had come to pass.

December 13, Sunday

"I'M SO sorry, Mallory." Ryan squeezed my hand. "I know there was no love loss between the two of you, but still, his death must be a shock."

"There *was* love loss between us," I corrected him gently. "It wasn't my idea to end our marriage. I was still in love with Trent when he walked out." At least I'd thought so.

"And that's to your credit," Ryan said.

"It's simply the truth. I'm not ashamed of my feelings... but they did change."

"I wasn't in the courtroom, but I know he said some hurtful things."

I nodded. "Although now I know how things can be magnified in a lawsuit, how people get pulled along by a tide of emotion. I'd like to think what I saw was an exaggerated worst version of Trent. He wasn't like that when I met him."

Ryan smiled. "You're so forgiving, Mallory. It's one thing I love about you—how you always see the best in people."

I froze. *Love?* I gave a little laugh. "I thought the worst of you."

"For ten minutes. Besides, I gave you reason." He trailed his finger down my arm. "I'm sorry your ex is gone... but I'm the benefactor of him being an idiot when he was alive, and for that I'm not sorry."

I smiled up at him. "Thank you for making me feel special."

His eyes darkened with desire. "Come home with me tonight?"

My body was willing, but my heart wasn't in it. "My divorce still isn't final," I murmured. "I know it's only a formality, especially now that Trent's gone... but when I took a vow to be faithful, it wasn't just to Trent, it was to myself."

Ryan sighed, then moved in for a kiss. "How did I get so lucky?"

I accepted his kiss, deepened it, relished it. Despite my dedication to my principles, it felt good to be wanted right now.

December 14, Monday

"SO HOW do you feel about the death of your estranged husband?"

Imogene was scribbling wildly in her notebook. I wondered if she was planning to write a book about me someday. Therapists did that now, confidentiality be damned. Change the patient's name and hair color and *voila!* They were covered.

"So many things," I murmured.

"Close your eyes and say the first word that comes to mind."

To humor her, I closed my eyes, and was shocked by the first word that occurred to me. "Guilt." My eyes popped open.

"Interesting," she said, setting down her pen. "Why do you feel guilty that Trent is dead?"

I let the feeling roll around in my chest for a few seconds. "Because if I hadn't won the lottery, he'd still be alive."

"Because he wouldn't have been able to buy the boat and subsequently drown."

"It's true," I insisted, blinking back sudden tears.

She angled her chin at me. "Is it? It appears to me that you're needlessly taking on responsibility for something you couldn't have caused... because you were no longer part of Trent's life."

I swallowed a sob.

She gave me a sad smile. "It's hurts, doesn't it? To be cast aside by someone you care about. I suspect that you feeling responsible for his death makes you feel closer to him. But don't take that on, Mallory. Your relationship was over. Trent alone made decisions that led to his accidental death. It's tragic. But it's not your fault."

I nodded, deeply breathing in and blowing out, over and over, willing away the pain.

It was a shame that soon I wouldn't be able to afford a therapist because it was clear I wasn't yet fixed.

December 15, Tuesday

IT WAS kind of Trent's parents to invite me to the memorial service, but I sensed it stemmed from their remorse for not reaching out during the divorce. In truth, though, I'd never been especially close to his long-distance parents, and I understood the certainty that they would side with their only son no matter the circumstances. Blood was blood, after all.

Which was why I hadn't yet opened the DNA results tucked inside my dresser drawer.

So when I slipped into the service, I slid into a back pew, far removed from the rest of the mourners, who were standing in prayer. From the back I recognized his parents, a few relatives, his girlfriend, various friends of his I'd met, and many people I didn't know. New acquaintances, I presumed, but then again, Trent had socialized a lot without me even when we were together.

When the crowd sat down, I saw the coffin that held his body, and it hit me hard. At that moment, he wasn't the hateful man who'd humiliated me in court—he was the flawed man who hadn't deserved to die so young. My tears flowed freely for the man who would never be what I knew he could be, and for the futility of his death.

An uncle read his eulogy. There was no mention of his former wife and our marriage—I had been redacted, a black blot in his life to be ignored. I couldn't blame his family—if Trent hadn't wanted me involved in his life, then it followed he wouldn't want me involved in his death.

At one point, though, his mother Alicia spotted me, and acknowledged me with a sad little smile before turning back.

I left before the closing prayer ended, wiped my eyes in my car, then drove away.

December 16, Wednesday

"DELILAH TOLD me about your ex," Josh said. His face was tense with concern. "I'm sorry, Mallory."

"Thank you," I murmured. "It was a shock."

"If you ever need to talk to someone—"

"I won't," I cut in. "But thanks." I gave Nessie's leash a little tug to rein her in. "She's eager to go."

He nodded, then morphed into all smiles. "Then let's go." He led the way through the halls of the clinic to the entrance of the brain rehabilitation area. "I think you're going to like my first patient."

The frosted double doors slid open to reveal an impressive array of machines partitioned off into different sections. Most were in use. I followed Josh, keeping an eye on Nessie to make sure she kept an eye on me. Fortunately, she seemed aware she was there for a reason, and remained focused even with all the distractions around us.

My chest swelled with pride. She was a different dog than the one I'd inherited, alert and energetic. I supposed everyone and everything needed a purpose.

When Josh rounded the corner and greeted the couple waiting, I broke into a smile. "Ramy... and Aisha."

Ramy's face lit up. "Mallory, what a nice surprise."

"For me as well. My dog Nessie is a therapy dog now."

Nessie had already made Aisha's acquaintance. Ramy's wife was patting the French bulldog's head. "So I see," Ramy said. "We miss you at the store."

"I owe Shawna a visit, I'll stop by soon." I turned to his wife. "How are you, Aisha?"

I noticed her smile was more even since the last time I'd seen her. "Ask my doctor here."

"She's doing great," Josh supplied. "Aisha is my star pupil. Let's get started so you two can get out of here before lunch."

I unhooked Nessie from her leash and stood by to instruct her if necessary. But Nessie seemed to sense when Aisha needed her encouragement to complete a task, like walking a straight line for balance or navigating a circuitous route for mobility. Aisha moved through the exercises slowly, but with good control.

"She seems much improved," I said to Ramy.

"She is," he agreed, his eyes shining with love. "This place has been good for her, thank you Mallory for making it possible."

"She's doing all the work," I demurred. "And Dr. English is good at his job."

"Yes, he's a good man, that one," Ramy said, arching his eyebrows my way.

"He's, um, taken," I said cheerfully. "He likes my sister."

"Too bad," he murmured. "The two of you would make a good couple."

I held up my wrist and pointed to the woven bracelet Josh had given me. "He and I are just friends."

"I married my best friend," Ramy said, then shrugged. "I'm just saying."

Exasperated, I didn't respond, but turned my attention back to Nessie... although strangely, my gaze kept straying to Josh.

December 17, Thursday

WHEN my attorney Lynette Shift's name came up on my phone, I groaned. If history was any indication of the present, she was not calling with happy news. I inhaled for strength, then connected the call. "Hi, Lynette."

"Hi, Ms. Green."

I winced at the grave tone of her voice. "I'm guessing this has something to do with Trent's passing?"

"Yes, I'm sorry to say."

I sighed. "I guess more delays in the divorce paperwork are unavoidable." Although I worried about how I would pay yet more legal fees... it seemed increasingly prudent to sell my flashy little red sportscar and buy something more... Mallory-like.

"Mallory," she said in an odd voice, "I assumed you knew. When a spouse dies before a divorce is final, the process is terminated."

I frowned. "Terminated?"

"Yes... legally, the divorce can't happen. You're considered a widow."

My jaw loosened as the news sank in. "A *widow*?"

"Yes... meaning the will the two of you made is still in effect."

My pulse picked up a notch.

"His share of your community property now belongs to you, including the money he was awarded in the settlement."

I gasped. "Are you sure? Won't his parents contest the will?"

"Mr. and Mrs. Green already waived their right to contest the will," she said. "They said the money was rightfully yours. I got the sense they didn't support their son's decision to sue you."

"I'm... speechless."

"I won't keep you," Lynette said. "I just wanted to give you the good news and to let you know it'll be a short delay while this is untangled, then the money will be yours."

"Thank you," I murmured, still reeling from the turn of events. Then an unresolved item popped into my mind. "Lynette... there's one more thing. I'd like to change my last name to my family name. Can you help me with the paperwork?"

"Sure. What's your family name?"

"Miracle."

"Mallory Miracle—that has a nice ring to it."

I thought so, too.

December 18, Friday

"GETTING KIDNAPPED was a good career move for Delilah," Wanda offered wryly.

We were watching my sister from across the bar. Tables had been pushed to the perimeter to make more standing room for patrons to watch Delilah perform.

"She could've been hurt," I chided. "Or worse."

Wanda harumphed. "For the money you paid to get her back, I would've found you another sister. More than one, in fact." She grinned. "You could've had me for half that price."

I laughed.

"Seriously, how can you be so calm about a half million dollars being sprayed all over the train station?"

I gave a little shrug. "It's only money."

Wanda cleared her throat. "I saw the news report that said you were bankrupt."

I sipped from my glass to avoid responding.

She cocked her head. "At least your asshole ex got himself drowned."

"I can't be happy about that," I murmured.

"I don't expect you to be. That's what friends are for—*I* can be happy he's dead."

I shook my head, knowing it was useless to chastise her. I understood what she meant and I appreciated the protective sentiment. And I'd decided to keep news of my "inheritance" to myself. No one needed to know I was rich again.

Not even my family.

I watched Delilah, struck anew with awe at her ability to entertain without being raunchy. That said, I was glad she was considering a career change. I nodded to Josh, who waved from the bar.

"Hm, that one," Wanda said.

I looked back to her. "What do you mean?"

"I mean I think your sister's boyfriend has a thing for his girlfriend's sister."

I squinted. "I've had too much alcohol to follow that."

"You know what I mean," Wanda said, wagging her finger at me in an exaggerated fashion. When I saw the ring on her third finger, I grabbed her hand. "Is that an engagement ring?"

She dimpled. "I wondered when you were going to notice. Rick proposed again and I said yes."

"Congratulations!" I raised my glass to hers. "I knew you still loved him."

"I do. And after seeing all the trouble your money caused you, I decided I don't want a rich man. Notorious B.I.G. said it best—mo money, mo problems." She hailed a passing waiter to bring us another round.

While I pondered her words of wisdom.

December 19, Saturday

I WAS sorting more letters that had arrived in the mail requesting donations. The stories tore at my heart. The dining room table was in danger of being obliterated by the stacks of paper. Gordon and Delilah had suggested I turn them all into compost since I no longer had the money to fulfill the requests. I played along, saying I might pass them to charitable foundations.

In truth, I wasn't sure what I would do with the money Trent had left me. After what I'd been through, having a nice, quiet nest egg sounded luxurious—and deserved. But it was more than I needed, and there were so many good causes that needed funding.

When my phone rang, I dug it out from under the papers, then smiled to see Danica Tumi's name on the screen. I connected the call. "Hi, Danica."

"Hi, Mallory. Is this a good time?"

"Absolutely. It's great to hear from you."

"I've been wanting to call to thank you for paying off the mortgage."

"I'm happy to do something for you and your kids."

"But, Mallory—I saw the news story that said you're bankrupt. I can't let you pay off my house if it leaves you with nothing."

My heart squeezed—the woman was decent to a fault. "I'm fine," I assured her. "In fact, I'm better than fine. I have my own house, and lots of resources."

"And a new family," she said.

"That's right. My dad is still here, and my half-sister."

"The one who was kidnapped?"

"You *have* been keeping up with the news."

"How's that going, your new family?"

"Better than when we last talked, but not perfect."

Gordon and Delilah bickered constantly and seemed directionless. We all moved within the confines of the palatial house in our own little orbits—it felt like a dysfunctional family reality show. I was starting to realize I'd be at loose ends until we were all on a path toward independence.

"Keep working at it," she said. "Family is worth the trouble, Mallory."

We chatted about her busy life for a while, but when I ended the call, Danica's words still rang in my head. I hoped she was right.

December 20, Sunday

"THIS IS a great house," Ryan said with a sigh. We were sitting around the firepit on the rooftop deck. It was a cold, clear evening with a thousand stars in the sky. Across the lake someone had erected holiday lights on a dock.

"I know," I said. "But it's too big for the three of us, and..."

"And?" he prompted.

"And I don't think it's healthy for us all to live together."

His dark eyebrows went up. "You're going to kick your father and sister to the curb?"

I laughed. "Not like that. But it feels as if we're all in limbo. We need to figure out the next steps in our lives."

"Sounds like you've been giving this a lot of thought." He put his arm around me and pulled me closer under the blanket. I didn't protest. "Are you worried about money?"

I was glad he couldn't see my face in the dark. I wasn't, but... "I do need to get a job."

"You could come to work in my office, but I can't promise not to be biased."

I gave a little laugh. "Thanks, but I'm pretty sure that's nepotism... and all the women in your office would turn on me."

"That's not true."

"It is true—they're all in love with you."

"Are you?"

I hiccupped. "Am I what?"

"In love with me."

"I... that's not..." I stumbled over my words. "Fair."

"You're right," he murmured. "I'm sorry to push, but you're not the only person who's been thinking about next steps." Under the covers, he clasped my hand. "I want you in my life, Mallory."

He kissed me and I kissed him back, hard and lingering, trying on the idea of what it would mean to be at Ryan's side. He'd proved himself—this amazing man thought I was broke and he still wanted me.

What else could I ask for?

December 21, Monday

"DOES YOUR family celebrate Christmas?" Imogene asked.

I balked. "I... assume so, but honestly, we've never discussed it, not in the religious sense."

"But in the secular sense?"

"Yes. Dad brought home a live tree, and Delilah bought lights and trimmings for it. We're going to decorate it this evening, in fact."

Imogene nodded. "So you're already establishing family traditions?"

"I... guess so."

"Holidays can be a source of stress for families," she offered. "Emotions run high, people are spending a lot of time together... it can bring issues to a head."

I nodded. "I can see why that would happen. Trent and I had usually bickered around the holidays, but it was always over money."

"That's not unusual. Are you and your father and sister exchanging gifts?"

"We haven't discussed it."

"Don't you think you should, considering you no longer have the resources you once had?"

I'd kept my unexpected windfall from my therapist, too, although I suspected that was against the rules, considering the reason I'd first come there was so she could coach me on the psychology of money. But she had a point.

"You're right," I said, nodding. "Christmas would be a perfect time for me to set some new boundaries—financial, and otherwise."

With that in mind, I had much to do, and a short time to make it all happen.

December 22, Tuesday

BANKER MALLORY extended a smile. "Good to see you again, Ms. Green. I'm, um, sorry that whole ransom situation went south."

"I got my sister back," I pointed out.

"Yes, but all that money," she began, then swallowed and manufactured a smile. "I mean... what can I do for you? If you're here to ask for an extension on the line of credit, I'm afraid that's not possible without the funds to guarantee it."

I smiled and lowered myself into her guest chair. "I don't need an extension... but I am here about funds." From my bag I withdrew a cashier's check for the amount I'd been bequeathed from Trent's assets. He'd bought a lot of nice things that were now mine, including the massive boat, but even he couldn't spend his half of the jackpot in such a short period of time.

The woman looked at the check and her eyebrows shot up. "Five million dollars?"

I smiled. "Yes. I'd like the money to be placed into two new accounts—one million in an investment account in my name, and the remaining amount in a charitable trust."

She was nodding exuberantly and taking notes. "With the investment account, you'll be placed with one of our top advisors."

"No, thank you—I'll be managing my own investments." I'd already signed up for an intensive online course on personal finance... it was past time that I developed a healthy relationship with my money.

"Duly noted. And do you want your name on the charitable trust?"

"No—I'd like for it to be generic... anonymous. But I'll be the sole executor." I withdrew Lynette Shift's business card. "Here's the contact information for my attorney, she's expecting your call."

"Yes, ma'am, right away."

"How soon can I write checks on the charitable trust account?"

She smiled. "I'll deposit this cashier's check now and I'll give you a booklet of checks for the trust account before you leave."

"Perfect."

December 23, Wednesday

IT TOOK hours of sifting and sorting through the mountain of letters to choose which requests to fulfill. I wished I could respond to each one, but in the end, I chose the ones I thought would make the biggest impact in the lives of the recipients. I wrote nearly two hundred checks to draw down half the amount in the charitable trust account. It took hours longer to pen a short response to include with each check explaining that since Mallory Green had been unable to fulfill the request due to a change in her financial status, she had passed the letters to the charitable trust and the trust alone was responsible for the good deed.

After I'd licked the stack of envelopes and stamped them, I was exhausted, but I wanted to get them out before the end of the year. And there was one more check I wanted to write.

When Josh had given me a tour of the Shepherd Spine Center, he'd mentioned the clinic was hoping to build a water training facility to extend its rehabilitation services to patients. I had pledged to myself if I had enough lottery money left after my accounts were settled, I'd donate to the project.

Hopefully a million would help to get them started.

December 24, Thursday

I'D ALWAYS wanted to go to the Atlanta Botanical Garden holiday lights event, but the last few years my weekend work hours and late shifts had conflicted with the times the attraction was open. As the Uber car climbed the hill to drop me, Ryan, Delilah and Josh at the garden entrance, I felt like a child. On both sides of the road, trees had been wrapped with millions—billions?—of colored lights, some flashing in time with others.

It was magical.

And a perfect night for strolling through the massive displays. The air was just cool enough for sweaters and scarves. Ryan bought a round of drinks to enjoy as we walked along trails, listening to Christmas music and stopping to enjoy spontaneous light shows. For the first time in a long time, my heart and feet felt less burdened.

The only nagging concern that still pinged my subconscious was the unopened letter of the DNA test results. But for tonight, I put it out of my mind.

Ryan and I walked behind Josh and Delilah. They often laughed and Delilah had tucked her hand under his arm.

"They make a nice couple, don't you think?" Ryan asked.

I nodded and smiled. "Yes."

He clasped my hand and intertwined our fingers. His comment that he wanted me in his life had been uppermost in my heart lately.

"Mallory?"

At the sound of a vaguely familiar voice, I turned to see a couple walking toward me. At first I didn't recognize them, but then I saw the woman's big pregnant belly. "Hannah... and Chance."

The tall brunette grinned. "I thought that was you."

"You look well," I said. "And happy."

"We are," Chance said, pulling her close to rub her belly. "Can't wait to see this little one."

"We miss seeing you at the restaurant," Hannah said. "The food is still great, but business seems to be falling off. It needs a good manager, I think."

"I'll talk to the owner," I murmured.

"I've seen the news," Hannah offered with a sympathetic smile. "I'm not so sure I did you a favor by giving you that wishbone."

"Don't think that," I replied. "Much more good came from the lottery win than bad."

She nodded. "If you say so. Merry Christmas."

"Merry Christmas," I said as they moved on.

"Who was that?" Delilah asked, falling back from walking with Josh.

"Customers from the restaurant where I used to work." I smiled. "Are you enjoying the show?"

She grinned. "It's terrific, Sis, really. I can't remember when I've had such a nice Christmas."

I looked ahead to where Ryan had joined Josh.

"I'm sure Josh feels the same."

She squinted at me and gave a little laugh. "Not because of me... his heart is somewhere else."

I opened my mouth to ask her where, but we were interrupted by strolling carolers who stopped in front of us to sing.

Have yourself a merry little Christmas… let your heart be light…

December 25, Friday

WE ENJOYED a feast for Christmas brunch. Gordon and Delilah cooked—she was beginning to shine in the kitchen. Ryan made mimosas, and Josh lit candles for the table. When we were finished eating, I asked for everyone's attention.

"I have a few announcements to make."

They all quieted and looked my way.

"Most of you know what a soft spot I have for the foster care system. For a while now I've been thinking this house is too big for the three of us, and too far from the city. With that in mind, I've decided to give the house to the foster care program to use as a year-round camp."

Josh began to clap, and Ryan joined in. Delilah and my dad were a little late to jump in.

Delilah's smile was watery. "But… where will we all live?"

"I'm glad you asked." I handed a red envelope to Gordon, and one to her. "Merry Christmas."

"What's this?" Gordon asked.

"Open it."

He looked dubious, but slid his finger under the flap and pulled out a photo of a boat—Trent's boat, but he didn't have to know that. "What is it?"

"It's yours," I said. "A boat to live on and maybe run a charter fishing business."

His mouth erupted into a grin. "I can handle that." He stood and clasped me in a bear hug. "Thank you, Buggy, for… well, for everything. I love you." When he pulled back, his eyes were wet, and so were mine.

"You're welcome. I love you, too."

Delilah was eyeing her envelope with trepidation. She leaned in to whisper, "Are these the results of the… you know?"

So she *had* been worried, I realized. "Open it," I urged.

She swallowed hard, then loosened the flap. She pulled out a menu and squinted. "The Community Café."

"Your new restaurant," I said. "If you want it."

She blinked, then covered her mouth. "You bought me a restaurant?"

I nodded.

She jumped to her feet to hug me, rocking me back and forth. "You're the best sister ever," she said close to my ear. "I love you."

I was caught off guard, but I didn't hesitate to respond. "I love you, too. And I expect free food."

She laughed. "You got it."

After the meal was cleared and everyone had left—Josh to go home, Dad to the marina where his boat was moored, and Delilah to check out her restaurant, Ryan and I were alone on the rooftop deck, soaking up the fire in the afternoon chill, drinking mulled wine.

"I have something for you," I said, reaching for a box.

He frowned. "We agreed—no gifts."

"I know. But I had to do this."

He opened the box to reveal the diamond tennis bracelet he'd given me. "I don't understand."

I wet my lips, searching for the right words. "I can't keep it, Ryan. I don't... love you. You're a wonderful man and any girl would be lucky to have you, but I don't see a future for us. I'm sorry."

His shoulders sagged and he heaved a heavy sigh. "So am I, more than you know." Then his mouth quirked. "I've enjoyed getting to know you, watching you bloom.... Lottery Girl."

I was glad we could end things on a smile.

December 26, Saturday

THE NEXT day was one of those freakishly warm days Atlanta sometimes gets in December. I decided to take advantage of the sunny warmth and take Nessie to the park for a treat. At the last minute, I donned my old running shoes to see how out of shape I truly was.

By the second time around the crushed rock running track, I was panting for breath and nursing a stitch in my side.

"You're probably dehydrated," said a voice behind me.

I stopped and turned to see Josh jogging up. He removed a water bottle from his belt and extended it. "Have some."

I took the bottle gratefully. "I thought you were done with running after the 10K."

He grinned. "I started liking it, I think I'll sign up for another race. Delilah said she'd train with me."

I swallowed a mouthful. "Good."

"By the way, that was really nice what you did for her and your dad."

I shrugged. "I wanted to give them both a fresh start."

"Goodwill abounds during the holidays," he mused, scratching his temple. "I got word today that someone made an anonymous donation of a million dollars to the Shepherd Center to break ground on the water training facility."

"That's great news," I offered.

"Isn't it? Except the director wanted to know which one of us had let the cat out of the bag because only a handful of people knew the project was being considered."

I pressed my lips together. "Hm. Sounds like the Center has a friend somewhere."

He reached forward to clasp my wrist and examine the woven bracelet he'd given me. "I thought the same thing."

I gently pulled away and handed back the water bottle. "Thanks for the drink."

"You bet."

I tugged on Nessie's leash and took off running in the opposite direction.

"See you around?" he called behind me.

"Probably," I answered over my shoulder.

December 27, Sunday

WHEN THE next day dawned just as warm, I decided it was time to take care of a chore I'd been putting off.

From the garage I retrieved a wetsuit, life jacket, and paddleboard, then braved the chilled water to do a slow tour of the cove. The water was glassy and sparkled like diamonds under the low winter sun. It was a glorious day to say goodbye to my little corner of the lake before the house would transfer to the state organization.

I lifted my face to the sun and inhaled fresh air scented with pine and fir that dotted the rocky shore. With easy strokes, I paddled out to the deepest part of the lake to sit down on my board and enjoy the quiet. I closed my eyes and imagined the laughter of the children who would enjoy the house and the water for decades to come. Maybe it would be a bright spot in the lives of kids who were accustomed to being overlooked.

After a while, I stood and reached into the bulky vest to withdraw my gun case. The revolver had caused too much grief to keep around—the vision of my paroled father packing it in his belt still kept me up at night. I opened the case, removed the unloaded gun, then dropped it into the water with a heavy *plunk*. It disappeared, sinking to depths that would keep it out of circulation.

From the case I removed an envelope—the DNA results that would tell me if Delilah and I were blood sisters. It was time to put the question to rest.

From another pocket I pulled a book of matches, struck one, then set fire to the end of the envelope. I held it until it had dissolved into a charred corner that I dropped into the water where it sizzled out, then disintegrated.

Then I turned to paddle back to the house.

December 28, Monday

"THIS IS our last scheduled appointment," Imogene said.

"I know." I made a rueful noise. "I doubt whatever job I land will pay me enough to cover therapy." Not a lie.

She smiled. "I hope you think it's been worth your time—and money."

"I do," I assured her. "I've learned it's wrong to expect someone else to take care of me and my money—I alone am in charge of my life."

She angled her head. "I just wish it hadn't been such an expensive lesson for you."

I shrugged. "Not everyone can say they won the lottery, and survived. I think that's a win."

Imogene laughed. "I've heard of lottery winners getting lucky again and hitting another jackpot."

I shook my head. "Not me."

As I left the building, I glanced down to see a shiny new penny on the sidewalk. A childhood rhyme floated through my mind.

See a penny, pick it up, and all the day you'll have good luck.

I kept walking.

December 29, Tuesday

AS MUCH as I'd been dreading to see my final divorce decree, I realized the absence of it left a gaping hole in my sense of closure.

So I bundled up Nessie for an outing—the December chill was back—and drove to a cemetery in Buckhead.

With no family burial lot, Trent's parents had purchased him a plot in a toney cemetery with nice views and impressive family names on the grave markers. His headstone was heartbreakingly new, and the grass on his grave was still covered with straw to protect it from the cold. Nessie sprawled on it as if she knew where we were. A pretty, but faded bouquet of silk flowers were tucked into a metal vase. Trent would hate them, I thought with a sad pang.

From my pocket I removed the box containing the mechanical pencil I'd bought him for our ill-fated anniversary. I'd been so sure he would love it... and I remained certain he would've on another day, maybe even a day in the near future if he'd lived.

I opened the box and set it on the bottom of his tombstone. Above me, a bird soared overhead, singing. I was thinking how poignant, then the bird dived and pooped on the corner of the headstone.

I decided to let the universe have the last word.

I picked up Nessie's leash, then turned around, and closed that chapter of my life.

December 30, Wednesday

WHEN I pushed open the door to the GiddyUp GoMart, the chime sounded.

Link and Shawna were behind the counter, arguing good-naturedly as they waited on customers. Shawna lit up like a bulb when she saw me and came running for a hug.

"Did you have a good Christmas?" I asked.

"The best," she said. "Bob is doing great. The man he used to work for asked him to come back after the first of the year." She grinned. "I might be able to drop back to part-time, wouldn't that be something?"

I nodded. "You deserve a break."

"Then maybe I can pick up some more hours," Link said, working the cash register. When the customer left, Link leaned across the counter and grinned at me. "I need the money since I'm dating your sister."

I squinted. "Since when?"

"Since two days ago. I asked her out a hundred times, but she kept turning me down." He shrugged. "Guess something changed."

Hm. Then I glared at him. "Be good to her."

He straightened. "I will."

"No pills."

He lifted his hand. "Scout's honor."

Another clump of customers came in. I looked around, glad to see some improvements had been made. "Business must be good," I said to Shawna.

She nodded. "Getting better every day, thank goodness."

"I'll let you go, just wanted to say hi. I'm happy for you, Shawna."

She blew me a kiss and waved. "Don't be a stranger."

As I left the store, I noticed a garbage can on the sidewalk. Stuffed down in the top was the crushed, soiled hand-lettered sign reading "The $52M winning ticket for the Mega Dollars Lottery was sold here!!!"

A fitting end.

December 31, Thursday

WHEN I pulled into the parking lot of the Noble Plaza building, a smile tugged at my mouth. It seemed impossible that a mere six months had passed since I'd worked there in a constant state of low-grade panic I'd do something to draw undue attention to myself. It was difficult to remember the person I'd been then—moving through life like an automaton, mired in debt, deteriorating in a dysfunctional marriage, letting life happen to me.

Pure, unadulterated gratitude pulsed through my veins to know regardless of what obstacles lay ahead for me, I could rebound... and thrive.

I wheeled into a visitor parking spot and put the little red sportscar into Park. I'd just had it detailed—it looked as new as the day I'd driven it off the lot when I'd gone on a car-buying spree.

I would miss it some.

The doors to the office building slid open to reveal a handful of employees who were getting a head start on the holiday weekend, including Wanda Sandoval. Her head swung, looking for me. I flashed the lights of the car and she grinned, then waved as she hurried toward the parking area. When she opened the door and swung inside, she squealed.

"I love this car! I'm so bummed you have to get rid of it."

"My old car is fine—and it's fixed."

She caressed the beautiful tooled-leather interior and gave me a sad smile. "Being rich was good while it lasted, though, wasn't it?"

"Some good things came of it, for sure. Thanks for helping me swap out the cars, by the way."

"Are you kidding? I'm happy to have the chance to drive this beauty, even if it's only back to the dealership."

When I turned the car around and drove past the building, I spotted Ryan walking out, looking as handsome as ever. He didn't see us. His head was bowed and he seemed deep in thought.

Wanda made a rueful noise. "Too bad that didn't work out."

"It's for the best," I assured her. "We were too different, and the next time I want to get it right."

"You will," she said, angling her head. "You seem... older."

I laughed. "Thanks a lot."

"I mean it... wiser, maybe, than when I first met you."

God, I hoped so. "How are you and Rick?"

She beamed. "So happy." Then she sobered. "Mallory... every time I think about what a snob I was when he proposed, I cringe. I really believed only a rich man would make me happy. I feel so lucky that he gave us another chance."

"I'm sure he feels lucky, too." I smiled. "Maybe we've both gotten a little wiser."

As I steered toward midtown, we chatted about her and Rick's plans to ring in the New Year at a local restaurant.

"Nothing too elaborate," she said, "since we're saving for our wedding. What are you doing to celebrate?"

"No big plans," I said. "Delilah is getting the restaurant ready for a grand re-opening, and Dad is going to an AA meeting." I nodded to Nessie's carrier in the back seat. "Nessie and I will probably stay in, maybe do some laundry."

Nessie yipped her agreement.

Wanda scoffed. "Laundry on New Year's Eve?"

I shrugged. "Start off the new year clean."

She shook her head. "Okay, I'm not going to argue—you've had enough excitement to last a while."

A few minutes later I put on my turn signal for the shop that had repaired my car. In truth, when I saw it sitting there, I felt bad that I'd let it languish for so long. I parked the sportscar next to it, then went in to collect my key and pay the remaining balance.

When I came back out, Wanda was already seated behind the wheel of the red convertible. Laughing at her eagerness, I retrieved Nessie's carrier and removed a suitcase from the trunk, then transferred them to my old car.

When I walked back to Wanda, she grinned. "Can we take the long way?"

"Absolutely," I said. "In fact, when we leave here, head for the interstate, then keep driving until you get home."

She squinted. "Home?"

"It's yours."

"What's mine?"

I laughed. "The car."

Her eyes rounded. "What? No!"

"Yes," I insisted. "I want you to have it. It's not my style. You look better in it than I ever could."

Her jaw dropped. "Mallory, I don't know what to say."

"Say you'll invite me to the wedding."

She grinned. "Of course I will! And thank you so much!"

"Go," I said, gesturing to the road. "Have fun."

I watched as she turned the flashy car around, then peeled away, already more attached to it than I'd been.

I was still laughing when I climbed behind the wheel of my old car. "Hi, old friend," I murmured. It must've missed me, too, because when the engine started, it fairly hummed.

Dusk was falling when I made the familiar turn into a familiar parking lot. As luck would have it, my old apartment had been available, newly painted and carpeted. As Josh had once pointed out, it was a great location, close to the park, and close to the Shepherd Center, where I hoped to keep volunteering while I forged a new career path. I spotted his sporty hatchback and parked nearby.

"We're home," I said to Nessie as I lifted her carrier.

With my other hand, I claimed my suitcase, then walked to the building entrance. A crisp breeze had kicked up, and the night was clear. I passed a clump of people dressed in party clothes, already raucous and laughing, hours before midnight.

In the hallway I glanced at the door of Josh's apartment, wondering if he was staying in tonight, or going out to celebrate the new year. I almost knocked, then chickened out. Just because my feelings toward him had changed didn't mean he still felt the same. I wouldn't blame him if he'd decided we should just be friends, as the bracelet he'd given me signified.

I unlocked the door to my apartment and walked inside, holding my breath, hoping I wouldn't be besieged with regret and bad memories. I turned on lights, gratified that the paint and carpet had transformed the interior. Gone were holes in the walls where pictures had once hung. The kitchen had a new stove and countertops, and the bathroom fixtures had been upgraded. It was as if my previous life had been filled in and spackled over... restored.

I let Nessie out of her carrier and turned on the heat. I'd packed a sleep sack in my suitcase—tomorrow was soon enough to begin collecting furnishings as I needed them. For now, the emptiness felt freeing. I wasn't in a hurry to once again own things that would own me.

When I heard a noise in the hallway, I looked out the peephole to see Josh emerge from his apartment with a laundry basket. He was whistling under his breath. And was it my imagination, or did he glance toward my door?

I took it as a hopeful sign. I opened my suitcase and hastily gathered an armful of clothing, then fished dollar bills out of my wallet. After a quick check on Nessie, I left the apartment and made my way to the laundry room.

The soft, warm scent of fabric softener reached me, evoking feelings of protectiveness and love. Josh was the only person standing among the machines, feeding clothes into a top-loading washer. He was wearing worn jeans and a faded T-shirt... and he looked so good to me.

I made my way to the machine next to him. When he saw me, his eyebrows dove into a little frown—not a good sign. "Mallory?"

"Hi," I said with a shaky smile.

"What are you doing here?"

"My laundry," I said, lifting the lid to the washer and dumping in my already clean clothes. "I, um, moved back into my old apartment."

He was quiet for so long, I started to think I'd made a big mistake. Then like ice melting, his mouth cracked into a smile. "You did?"

My heart fluttered. "I did."

"So... we're neighbors again."

I smiled. "Looks like it."

His Adam's apple bobbed. "Is there anything... *neighborly* I could do for you?"

I lowered the lid on the machine. "Actually, there is one thing."

A fire lit his eyes. "Name it."

"I was hoping to borrow those textbooks you offered."

The fire banked. "Oh. You're going to finish your degree? That's... great." He turned back to the washer and punched buttons. "Of course you can borrow the books."

"Thank you." I fed a dollar into the machine, then adjusted the settings for a quick wash. "Oh... there is one more thing."

Josh's head came up. "What?"

I held up my wrist, then with a tug, I removed the woven friendship bracelet he'd given me. "I'm giving this back."

He looked pained, but nodded and reached for it. "Okay."

"Because," I said, capturing his hand. "I don't want to be friends, Josh. I want... more."

His eyes were wary. "You do?"

"Am I too late?" I asked, holding my breath.

He squeezed my hand, intertwining our fingers. "No, Lottery Girl... you're not too late."

"I'm not Lottery Girl anymore," I murmured. "My winnings are gone."

"Good," he said, pulling me close. "We'll build our own fortune, even if we're never rich."

He lowered his mouth to mine, testing me, tasting me. I opened to him, breathing him in. As our kiss ignited our bodies, I was shot through with wonder and a sense of utter rightness.

I finally felt like I'd won the jackpot.

- The End -

About the Author

STEPHANIE BOND was seven years deep into a corporate career in computer programming and pursuing an MBA at night when an instructor remarked she had a flair for writing and suggested she submit material to academic journals. But Stephanie was more interested in writing fiction—more specifically, romance and mystery novels. To-date, Stephanie has more than one hundred published novels to her name, including the popular BODY MOVERS humorous mystery series. Her self-published romantic comedy STOP THE WEDDING! is now a Hallmark Channel movie, and her self-published serial COMA GIRL is now available as a podcast. Stephanie lives in midtown Atlanta, where she is probably working on a new story at this very moment. For more information on Stephanie and her books, visit **www.stephaniebond.com.**

Other works by Stephanie Bond

In the Body Movers humorous mystery series, an Atlanta woman works for Neiman Marcus by day and helps her younger brother move bodies from crime scenes by night!

PARTY CRASHERS (prequel)
BODY MOVERS
2 BODIES FOR THE PRICE OF 1
3 MEN AND A BODY
4 BODIES AND A FUNERAL
5 BODIES TO DIE FOR
6 KILLER BODIES
6 ½ BODY PARTS (novella)
7 BRIDES FOR SEVEN BODIES
8 BODIES IS ENOUGH
9 BODIES ROLLING
10 BODIES LYING
11 BODIES MOVING ON
12 BODIES AND A WEDDING

Other humorous romantic mysteries:

COMEBACK GIRL—*Home is where the hurt is.*
TEMP GIRL—*Change is good... but not great.*
COMA GIRL—*You can learn a lot when people think you aren't listening...*
TWO GUYS DETECTIVE AGENCY—*Even Victoria can't keep a secret from us...*
OUR HUSBAND—*Hell hath no fury like three women scorned!*
KILL THE COMPETITION—*There's only one sure way to the top.*
I THINK I LOVE YOU—*Sisters share everything in their closets...including the skeletons.*
GOT YOUR NUMBER—*You can run, but your past will eventually catch up with you.*
WHOLE LOTTA TROUBLE—*They didn't plan on getting caught...*
IN DEEP VOODOO—*A woman stabs a voodoo doll of her ex, and then he's found murdered!*
VOODOO OR DIE—*Another voodoo doll, another untimely demise...*
BUMP IN THE NIGHT—*a short mystery*

Romances:

FACTORY GIRL—*Long hours, low pay, big dreams...*
COVER ME—*A city girl goes country to man-sit a hunky veterinarian who's the victim of a "cover curse"!*
DIAMOND MINE—*A woman helps the one who got away choose a ring—for another woman!*
SEEKING SINGLE MALE (for the holidays)—*A roommate mixup leads to mistletoe mayhem!*
MANHUNTING IN MISSISSIPPI—*She's got a plan to find herself a man!*
TAKING CARE OF BUSINESS—*An FBI agent goes undercover at a Vegas wedding chapel as the Elvis impersonator!*
IT TAKES A REBEL—*A former hotshot athlete is determined to win over the heiress to a department store empire who clashes with the new spokesman—him!*
WIFE IS A 4-LETTER WORD—*A honeymoon for one... plus one.*
ALMOST A FAMILY—*Fate gave them a second chance at love...*
LICENSE TO THRILL—*She's between a rock and a hard body...*
STOP THE WEDDING!—*If anyone objects to this wedding, speak now...*
THREE WISHES—*Be careful what you wish for!*

In the Southern Roads romance series, three brothers reunite to rebuild their hometown swept away ten years ago by a tornado...and advertise for 100 women with a "pioneering spirit" to move there!

BABY, I'M YOURS (prequel novella)
BABY, DRIVE SOUTH
BABY, COME HOME
BABY, DON'T GO
BABY, I'M BACK (novella)
BABY, HOLD ON (novella)
BABY, IT'S YOU (novella)

Nonfiction:

GET A LIFE! 8 STEPS TO CREATE YOUR OWN LIFE LIST—*a short how-to for mapping out your personal life list!*
YOUR PERSONAL FICTION-WRITING COACH: *365 Days of Motivation & Tips to Write a Great Book!*

Copyright information

All rights reserved. No part of this publication may be reproduced, stored in or introduced into a retrieval system, or transmitted, in any form, or by any means (electronic, mechanical, photocopying, recording, or otherwise) without the prior permission of the copyright owner.

This is a work of fiction. Names, characters, places, and incidents either are the product of the author's imagination or are used fictitiously, and any resemblance to actual persons, living or dead, business establishments, events or locales is coincidental and/or embellished for literary license.

The scanning, uploading, and distributing of this book via the internet or via any other means without the permission of the copyright owner is illegal and punishable by law. Your support of the author's rights is much appreciated, and makes it possible for the author to continue writing. *Thank you so much.*

Copyright 2020 by Stephanie Bond

Cover by Andrew Brown at clicktwicedesign.com

Printed in Great Britain
by Amazon

67344222R00189